WOLVES
OF
WINTER

DAN JONES

WOLVES

OF

WINTER

An Aries Book

9 7 5 3 1 2 4 6 8

A catalogue record for this book is available from the British Library.

ISBN (HB): 9781838937942
ISBN (XTPB): 9781838937959
ISBN (E): 9781838937898

Lyrics from "I Am the Wolf" by Mark Lanegan, copyright © 2014.
Printed with permission of the Mark Lanegan Estate.

Cover by Ben Prior
Map design by Jamie Whyte

Printed and bound in Great Britain by
CPI Group (UK) Ltd, Croydon CR0 4YY

MIX
Paper | Supporting
responsible forestry
FSC
www.fsc.org
FSC® C171272

Head of Zeus
First Floor East
5–8 Hardwick Street
London EC1R 4RG

WWW.HEADOFZEUS.COM

For Ivy

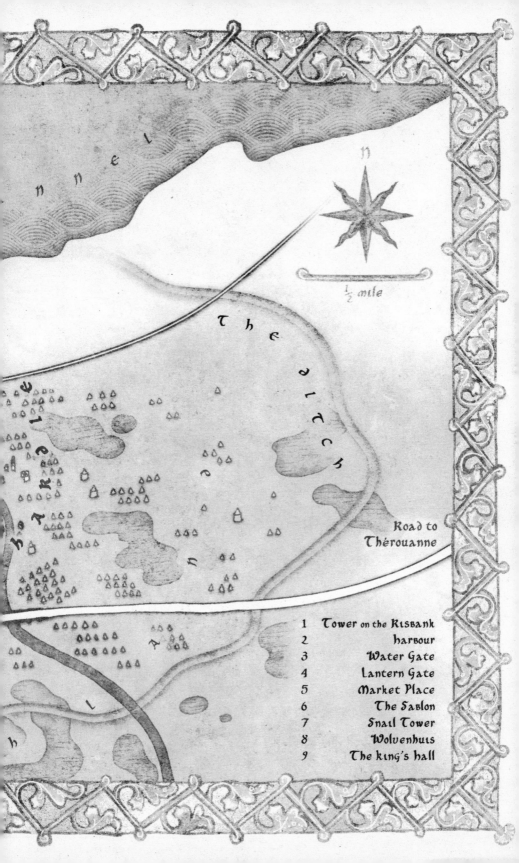

N

½ mile

The ditch

Road to
Thérouanne

1   Tower on the Risbank
2   harbour
3   Water Gate
4   Lantern Gate
5   Market Place
6   The Sablon
7   Snail Tower
8   Wolvenhuis
9   The king's hall

'Our expedition has been very long and continuous. But we do not expect to depart the kingdom of France until we have made an end of our war...'

Edward III, Calais, 1346

'There is nothing left here which has not been eaten, unless we eat the flesh of men.'

Jean de Vienne, Calais, 1347

Prologue

JULY 1345

Dusk was falling as the Captain peeled away from the thinning crowds on the Pont au Change and slipped between two wooden shop fronts, down a narrow alley that led to the barrier at the bridge's edge.

He leaned on the rail and looked out. *Paris*. On his left, the dying sun's last light bathed the Île de la Cité, on which stood the royal palace, Sainte-Chapelle and the cathedral of Notre-Dame. To his right, it lit up the sprawl of the city proper: a vast, seething metropolis of thousands of houses, shops and churches, all crammed within the old defensive walls.

Below flowed the Seine. The river quickened and eddied where its waters rushed through the bridge's narrow arches. Thick brown foam bubbled on top. The Captain caught the stink of the public jakes, which emptied a short way upriver. Ripe on a summer's night. He covered his nose and inhaled through his sleeve. He counted breaths like paternosters. All around the city, he heard vespers bells tolling.

'So he's dead.'

He knew the voice so well that he did not bother turning. And when he pulled his sleeve down from his face he knew the breath, too. Meat rotting between yellow teeth.

'He seemed so when I left him,' said the Captain. 'I've never known a man have his brains trampled out of his ears and live to hear another Mass.'

He was still staring downriver. A week ago, on another night and in another city, he had watched a mob stab and stamp to death Jacob van Artevelde: Flemish autocrat, political firebrand, friend of kings and double-dealing charlatan known as the Brewer of Ghent.

'How did you get out?'

The Captain turned at last to look up at the speaker. The man stood a clear head taller than him. A thick brown beard, flecked here and there with grey, covered his face so fully it almost skirted his eyeballs. He was missing a portion of one eyebrow, and his nose had been broken many times. His moustache drooped long at the corners of his mouth, like a carp's barbels.

'Getting out is never hard,' the Captain said. 'If you work alone. And if you do not tarry to admire what you've done.'

'Of course. You work alone now.' The man smiled wryly. 'Our king will not thank you.'

'Nor was he meant to,' said the Captain. 'Artevelde was the last man who believed King Edward could force his son the prince on Ghent as Count of Flanders. Now that's over. The Italians will take control. For a time.'

'Indeed.'

The two men said nothing for a moment. The Captain broke the silence.

'Are *you* here to thank me?'

The bearded man broke into a short laugh. 'No,' he said. 'I am here to pay you.'

He handed the Captain a purse made of fine calfskin. The Captain weighed it in his hand. When he opened it, gold coins caught the fading light. English nobles, minted very recently. The Captain held one up. It was stamped with an image of a galley at sea, and, on the reverse, King Edward's bold new coat of arms: English lions quartered with French fleurs-de-lis. His heart fluttered at the sight. He put it back in the purse and kept his face set cold.

'War gold,' he said. 'Not popular here.'

'Do you mean to stay in Paris?'

'Perhaps.'

'Gold is gold. Either keep it or come back tomorrow and exchange it for something you like better.' The big man gestured with his head back towards the alley. The bridge was lined with money-changing houses, now shuttered for the night.

'Changers have no stake in the squabbles of kings. Except as it touches their own profit. Any one of them will give you deniers or pennies. They will give you Saracen bezants if that is what you want. Of course, they will punish you with their rate of exchange, but…'

The Captain shook the calfskin purse gently and finished the man's sentence for him: '…it is as it is.' He shook the purse again, then put it in the leather bag at his side. 'Tell Pulteney—'

The bearded man cut him off. 'Sir John sends his greetings. Naturally, *he* thanks you – and God – for this… fruitful development.'

'He has more work for me?'

'Not now. But you know how things are. We are at war. In war there is always work. And this war will last a long time. Don't worry. By the end of it, you'll be the rich man you've always wanted to be.' He paused. 'When we need you, we will find you.'

'So be it.' The Captain did not ask how they would find him. They always did.

He made to leave, but the bearded man put a hand firmly on his shoulder. Something shifted in the man's eyes. He flashed a glance behind him.

'Don't—'

The Captain shoved the bearded man hard in the chest. He stumbled two paces backwards, but he regained his balance and managed to block the alley. He grabbed the Captain's wrist and, surprisingly deftly, spun the Captain around and held him with his arm pinned tightly behind his back. Twisted him so he was once again facing the river. He whispered into his ear, 'Don't look.' Then he pulled hard on the Captain's arm, forcing his hand up towards the nape of his neck.

The Captain's shoulder burned. His eyes stung. He tried to keep his voice level and spoke through his teeth. 'What is this?'

The bearded man moved even closer. 'We've been followed. Head for the island. Someone will open the gate. You understand?'

The Captain nodded. 'What— Who—'

'Just do it.' The man jerked his arm again. 'Now tread on my foot.'

The Captain lifted his right boot and drove it down behind him.

The bearded man gave a yelp, let go of the Captain's arm and hopped about theatrically. At the same time, he turned the Captain roughly around and shoved him down the alley. 'Go,' he whispered. 'And Godspeed.'

The Captain did not stop to argue. He sprinted, running lopsided as he held his aching shoulder, back along the alley towards the main thoroughfare of the bridge.

When he got there, he knew something was wrong.

The Pont au Change was lit by the bone-yellow light of a rising moon. It was completely deserted. At dusk it had been bustling. Now it was silent.

The Captain felt blood pumping in his ears. He reached for

his bag and the purse. It was still there. He pulled out a handful of the coins and stuffed them into his breeches.

He reached for the short-bladed dagger he wore in his belt. That was gone.

Of course.

He edged out of the alley and pressed himself into a doorway. He pulled up his hood and peered cautiously from under it, towards the palace complex on the royal island. The grand buildings there now loomed huge and grey in the moonlight. The gates to the island flickered with the sickly orange glow of torches.

The Captain rubbed his shoulder, trying to restore some life to it. He reckoned the torchlit gates to be about a hundred paces away. It would not take him long to cover the ground. The bearded man had told him one of them would be opened.

Yet he also took my knife.

The Captain cursed. Time was against him. He had to choose. He decided to trust his instinct.

He buried his chin into his chest, pulled his hood even tighter around his face and set off back towards the city, sliding stealthily from doorway to doorway.

Straight away he heard the echo of footsteps. Several sets, coming towards him. Moving fast. Cutting him off.

Again he cursed and switched direction, now heading back towards the palace.

The footsteps behind him quickened.

The Captain did not bother looking back. He just ran, as fast as he could. His feet pounded the boards of the bridge, the clatter of his boot soles bouncing crazily off the deserted shop fronts.

His palms were slippery with sweat. His lungs burned. But

he kept running. And he kept his eyes fixed on the palace ahead of him. With every pace, the lights were getting closer. Seventy paces. Fifty. Forty. He was almost there.

Twenty.

A guard in plate armour, wearing King Philippe's royal livery, stepped out of the porterhouse beside the gate. He bellowed something, calling to some other guard. It did not sound like an order to unbar any gate.

The guard drew a sword. And the Captain knew for certain. *He had been set up.*

Out of the corner of his eye, he saw another alley leading between the bridge's shuttered buildings. He hurled himself into it and crouched for a moment, breathing as silently as he could through his nose. His chest felt as though it was about to burst.

He strained his ears to listen over his heartbeat. He could no longer hear any footsteps. He edged deeper down the alley, hoping that it might cut behind the shops. Hoping it might lead anywhere. He moved by touch alone, allowing the wall's rough timber to scratch his back through his shirt. The alley was so dark that the void danced with bright colours he knew were not there. Green and red. Sparks of yellow.

He heard the footsteps once more. They passed the entrance to the alley. He heard the guard call again. Then a rapid conversation. After that, the footsteps retreated, getting quieter as they headed back towards the city.

The Captain puffed out his cheeks in relief.

And felt the point of a dagger at his throat.

The putrid breath told him who was holding it. The Captain froze.

'Sorry, my friend,' said the bearded man's voice. Then he

lifted his foot in the blackness and slammed his heel into the side of the Captain's right knee.

White pain shot through the Captain's leg. He tried to keep silent. He bit through the tip of his tongue. Blood flooded his mouth. In the blackness he saw the Brewer of Ghent, his head cracked open like a marrow. Eyes bulging impossibly out of the skull like the slick orbs of a skinned rabbit.

The Captain collapsed sideways over his broken leg. Two pairs of hands grasped him roughly below the armpits. One of the hands reached inside his bag and removed the calfskin purse. Blood was leaking from his mouth. Green stars danced around his eyes.

In the blackness, he heard another voice. A woman's.

'*Dépêchez-vous!*' she said. '*J'ai froid.*'

Hurry up. I'm cold.

The Captain coughed and drooled more blood. He felt the arms beneath his shoulders heave him upright. Each rough jolt sent pain coursing down through his knee. The arms dragged him fifteen paces backwards, until he felt his back pressed against the rail at the bridge-side.

Then he felt a face beside his, and smelled a new mouth. The woman's. Fragrant with good wine. She whispered in his ear, '*C'est vrai. Le roi ne vous remercie pas.*'

It's true. The king does not thank you.

She kissed him on his cheek. '*Mais je vous remercie.*'

But I do.

Then she was gone, and the rougher arms heaved the Captain upwards and backwards once more, hauling him so his upper body was now all the way over the rail. He dangled there a moment, half on the bridge and half off.

The hands let him go.

For an instant, the Captain felt weightless. As though he were an angel in flight. As though he might rise, high above the bridge. Above Paris. Above it all. He flapped his arms frantically, trying to grab something. Anything. His fingers gripped only cold air. And suddenly he was no longer weightless. His stomach churned. His bladder gushed empty.

He was falling, fast, hurtling towards the reeking Seine.

As he somersaulted through the blackness, the Captain saw the lick of a single lantern above him, dancing wild circles. Flame-lit faces swirled together, stretching and collapsing into one. The fire of the torch between them turned around and around, switching places with the frozen blaze of the night's first stars. Each one winking like a tiny, polished coin.

The Captain thought once more of the Brewer of Ghent. He thought of the life he had chosen. Of the men he had left behind.

As the water rushed towards him, he could hear somebody screaming.

As he slammed through the surface, he realized it was him.

PART 1

FLEMINGS

I

They took much pains to examine all the dead, and were the whole day in the field of battle... [finding] the bodies of eleven princes, twelve hundred knights and thirty thousand common men.

Chronicles of Jean Froissart

'Let's get him up.'

'Loveday' FitzTalbot stood, holding his aching lower back, and watched Tebbe and Thorp take hold of the knight's limbs and yank. He clapped his hands to encourage his men. 'Come on, boys, it might be someone who matters.'

The knight was lying face down, trampled so heavily he was half-buried in the earth. Dead. He had been a big, barrel-chested man. Now he was a sprawled, broken mess, his body mangled by feet and hooves and pressed deep into the churned mud of the field. The plate armour on his back was crushed and in places it had split. The surcoat bearing his insignia of arms, which in life had identified him, was tattered and bloodied beyond recognition.

The archers heaved.

'He's stuck,' complained Tebbe. 'We'd be better off digging the bastard out.'

Thorp let go of the knight's leg for a moment and gave the dead man an angry kick. 'Tebbe's right. We'll never move him,' he said. He puffed out his cheeks. 'Let's just cut that rag off him and send it to the king's men so *they* can work out who he was. Then we can move on.'

Loveday said nothing. He understood his men's frustration. They were all sore, hungry, dirty, bloody, thirsty and worn out. He handed Thorp his flask. The dark-haired bowman grunted thanks then drank deeply. He swallowed a couple of times, spat out half a mouthful of the murky liquid and scrunched up his face. 'Water?'

'Aye,' said Loveday. 'That's all they're giving out for now. Ale's gone.'

Thorp shrugged, resigned. 'We'll be back in England soon enough. Thank fuck. Plenty of ale there.' He shielded his eyes from the late summer sun and glared around the field. Everywhere, groups of men just like them were picking over corpses, removing anything valuable before the bodies were dragged away feet first for burial in long pits. There were thousands of them. All had fallen in a battle that took place there two days earlier, beside a vast, dense, dark green forest called Crécy. The six Essex Dogs had fought in the thick of that battle. Now they sorted and pilfered its dead.

Thorp turned back to the knight and booted him again, though with less force than before. Tebbe put his hand on his friend's shoulder. 'Come on,' he said. 'One more go. No point giving up. He could have something good on him.'

Tebbe flicked his long, grey plait of hair over his shoulder. It was stiff with dried sweat and blood. He re-gripped the knight's right arm. Thorp sighed and grabbed the right leg. Then the two men heaved again, bending their knees, digging their heels into the uneven ground and straining until the veins sprang on their foreheads.

With a sucking noise, the knight began to lift. But his left arm was thrown out awkwardly behind him, and once the archers had him half-turned, Tebbe slipped, and the knight flopped back down on to his front.

Loveday felt a heavy trudge behind him and turned to see Scotsman arrive. The gruff-tempered giant was one of Loveday's oldest comrades and friends, although in size and temper the two men were very different. Today, despite the chill in the air, Scotsman stood stripped to the waist, showing off a broad torso that was badged with bruises. He grinned as he considered the knight on the ground and the archers panting beside him. Then he picked a few scabs of grime from the rancid, greasy ropes of his ginger beard. 'Christ's stinking loincloth,' he said. 'You fuckers are making hard work of this.'

As Scotsman groomed his beard, Loveday noticed the big man's fingers, which sprouted with orange hair and were as thick as most men's thumbs. Each bore several glinting gold or silver rings. The Scot had been scouring the battlefield for trinkets.

Scotsman saw Loveday looking. He turned his hands to show off his haul.

'Plenty worth selling, next town we visit,' Loveday said. 'God knows we need something to take home with us.'

'Aye. That we do. I've got nearly two dozen here. We're going to be rich enough to spend the whole winter in a whorehouse.' The Scot chuckled and turned his attention to Tebbe and Thorp, who were still struggling with the half-buried knight. 'Move over, you flea-bitten English bastards,' he said. The archers stepped back, exhausted. Scotsman took hold of the dead man with one hand and heaved. Within seconds, he had flipped the corpse and dropped it on its back. 'Easy,' he laughed.

Behind him, Thorp threw his hands up in exasperation. 'Baptist's bollocks, Scotsman. We did all the hard work, and you just stroll in and...'

But as he looked down at the knight, he tailed off.

The visor of the knight's helm was missing. That, Loveday supposed, was what had got him killed. The left eye socket had been hit with something heavy, swung very hard. Where it had landed, the knight's skull had collapsed, caving inwards. Around the wound, the flesh was blackened and broken. The forehead above it was grotesquely swollen with blood.

But the right half of the face was unmistakeable, and each of the Dogs knew it. It was even uglier in death than it had been in life, but the piggish right eye and the lips, squeezed in a tight pompous pout, could only have belonged to one man.

'Sir Robert le Straunge,' chuckled Scotsman. 'You fat, dead cunt.' He knelt and wiggled the knight's metal gauntlet until it came off. He untied the soft leather glove beneath. On his rigid third finger Sir Robert wore a thin band of gold, which flared into a lozenge etched with the head of some fantastical beast.

Scotsman worked the ring free and slipped it on to his own left hand, where it sat just below the knuckle of his little finger. He looked up at the Dogs. 'What? He can't use it now. In any case, the fucker owed us all forty days' pay.'

Loveday sighed. It was true. Each of them bore the scars of seven hard weeks in the field, marching through the hot French countryside, joining the king's assaults on cities and villages, risking their lives and losing their friends. They had done it for the same reason they did anything. So that a richer man would pay them for their service and they could go back to their ordinary lives with their pockets full of coin. Now that richer man, Sir Robert le Straunge, who had first recruited them to join the king's army, lay dead at their feet.

Loveday scratched his chin. 'We haven't lost that much,' he said, trying to sound more cheerful than he felt. 'Sir Robert was ill-disposed to us. In any case, the obligation to pay our forty had been transferred to...'

Thorp cut in and finished the sentence for him. 'Sir Godefroi d'Harcourt?'

Loveday nodded. 'Aye, Sir Godefroi.'

There was an awkward silence around the group. Millstone had wandered over to join them, and he too was now examining Sir Robert's remains with detached interest. After a moment, he spoke. His voice, with its soft Kentish burr, was calm. 'Sir Godefroi has abandoned the king's cause. He's gone back to Philippe. He saw his brother killed among the French ranks, and it broke his heart. I've heard the story told many times today.'

Tebbe snorted. 'Once a traitor, always a traitor. He fucked the French king over, now he's fucked the English. One day he'll get his reward.'

'Which is more than we will.' Thorp spat on the ground. 'Christ's teeth and claws, that's our pay for the whole campaign gone. The rich bastards have got richer taking each other alive for ransom. And here we are, with no wages, wrestling with dead men for their clothes.'

He was right and Loveday knew it. With Sir Robert dead and Sir Godefroi having vanished, the Dogs now had little hope of claiming the wages they were due for their weeks of fighting. All they could take home would be a diminished pile of coins they'd earned selling plunder to a sailor called

Gombert in a city called Caen, and whatever they could strip from the fallen in the short time before the army broke camp to march for the coast.

Loveday stared around the battlefield, littered with arrows and broken shields and corpses. Black, sharp-beaked birds were hopping hungrily around. Twenty paces from where the Dogs stood, a sleek she-crow was digging at a dead crossbowman's eyeball.

Loveday felt his men's disappointment bore into him. He cleared his throat to address them. But Millstone spoke for him. 'Never mind. Let's get back to work. We're here. We should gather anything we can, no matter how worthless it looks, and load it on the cart. The loot-brokers will be here soon.'

Scotsman grunted. 'Where is the fucking cart, anyway?'

Millstone pointed towards the road, where, during the battle, wooden wagons of all types and sizes had been turned on their sides to form a wall against the French assault. Most had now been righted and claimed by English companies. Loveday spotted Romford, the Dogs' youngest member, perched on one.

The boy looked thin and frail. His cheekbones stood out and his eyes were surrounded by dark patches. He wore the livery of the Prince of Wales, which he had been given during his short time as a squire to the sixteen-year-old lord. But the green-and-white jacket was torn and ragged, caked in mud and barely recognisable. Romford was swinging his legs back and forth and staring at the ground, as though he were searching for something. His top lip had been split and was crusted with blood. But his loose curls of hair glowed golden in the afternoon sun. Sensing the Dogs talking about him, Romford looked up and waved a shy hand.

Loveday waved back. Scotsman shook his head. 'That one's not right,' he said.

Loveday ignored him. He turned back to the dead knight. 'Should we bury Sir Robert?'

Scotsman glared at him as though he were a madman. 'Are you fucking joking? Leave him for the crows.'

By sundown the Dogs had piled their cart high, and the loot traders had begun to arrive. Some were mere opportunists – peasants who had wandered along the roads beside the forest to bargain with the triumphant English. Others were artisans from nearby towns. Blacksmiths' boys paid tiny silver coins for sacks of arrowheads and horseshoes. Skinners haggled for dead horses and donkeys, flaying the carcasses quickly before trudging away with the wet and bloody hides draped over their shoulders, as though they were the actors in a nativity play.

The more enterprising traders worked in twos and threes, setting up makeshift stalls, calling across the field to advertise their particular interest and sending out apprentices to drum up business. Some bought saddles and bridles, others maces and swords. Lines formed around several of the stalls – particularly those where the traders were handing out free mugs of wine.

'They have accents,' Romford said to Loveday. 'Where are they from?'

Millstone, standing on the far side of the loaded cart, cut in and answered.

'Flemings.' He wrinkled his nose.

'What's wrong with Flemings?' asked Romford.

The stonemason just grunted.

'Lying, cheating, swindling, godless, pox-pintled sons of whores,' said Tebbe. 'And that's the nice ones.'

Romford seemed satisfied with the answer. He stood up and stretched his legs. 'Flemings,' he repeated, as though he had never heard the word before. Then he said, 'I'll get wood for the night-fire.' He slid off in the direction of the forest's edge.

Loveday watched him go. The campaign had changed Romford, Loveday thought. The boy had seen things that could not be unseen. The Dogs' round-bellied, thin-haired leader felt a pang of guilt, as he often did when he thought of Romford. As usual, he tried to reason it away.

He came here because he wanted to. Same as we all did.

After Romford left, a young Fleming not much older than him approached the Dogs' cart. By now, the sun was very low. Salty wood smoke was drifting across the field. Loveday felt his arm-hairs rise. For the first time that summer, the air had a bite to it.

The boy strolled up to the Dogs without fear and spoke to them in English, though with a thick accent. 'What have you to sell?' he asked. *Wot hiv. Shell.*

Loveday looked at the jumble on the cart. 'Armour,' he replied, 'mostly. Breastplates, some of them are in good condition. Two or three mail coats that could be easily repaired. A few crossbows, still strung. Genoese, I think. A pike. Needs a bit of—'

The boy laughed scornfully. Loveday felt Scotsman and the archers stiffen.

'What's funny?' demanded the Scot. 'Mother of God bent over the fucking bramble bush, our stuff's as good as any other bastard here will sell you.'

The boy raised his hands in apology. 'I'm sure your things is good, by God. But we cannot pay for this. You have heard the king's edict.'

He looked around them, still smiling, enjoying the fact that he knew something they did not. 'You didn't hear? Your king has said enough armour is taken. He has forbidden to sell any more of it. He thinks we will sell it back to the French. Which we do.' He laughed. 'Your king's men are burning and melting it. You smell, I think, the fires.'

Tebbe shook his head. 'God's guts, I don't believe you. My old woman's at home expecting me to come back with a few bloody shillings at least. Now name us a price or get out of here.' Loveday admired the archer's spirit. But all the Dogs could now smell smoking charcoal and the tang of molten metal.

The boy was about to retort, when out of the gloom of the field appeared a tall, square-jawed knight with huge shoulders and long brown hair. He wore the livery of William de Bohun, Earl of Northampton and Constable of the English Army. At the sight of the knight, the boy's cocksure manner evaporated. He glanced shiftily around him, weighing the possibility of running away.

The knight took the decision away from him. In two long strides he reached the Dogs, and in the same easy motion he shot out an arm and seized the boy by the nape of his neck. The boy squirmed and yelped.

'Sir Denis,' said Loveday, nodding in greeting.

Sir Denis of Moreton-on-the-Weald smiled. Laughter lines bunched at the corners of his eyes. Yet there was something hard and unwavering in the eyes themselves. He shook his long hair, still oddly clean and glossy. 'Essex Dogs,' he said, half bowing. 'Is this young rogue troubling you?'

Loveday pressed his shoulders back and tried to mirror Sir Denis's straight-backed stance. 'No, Sir Denis. He was... we were hoping to make a small gain on the spoils of the battle.'

The boy wriggled again. Sir Denis shook him like a puppy. He smiled politely at Loveday, inviting him to continue.

'We were... We have had some misfortune,' Loveday said. He was babbling. 'Sir Robert... Sir Godefroi... we are hoping before we go back to England...'

Sir Denis nodded. 'We are destroying armour now. Not selling it.'

'And what if we do sell it?' Scotsman growled.

'I think you know what.'

Sir Denis let go of the boy, who stood rubbing his neck angrily, though he did not yet dare to move away.

'You can take your gatherings to the blacksmiths in the morning,' said the knight. 'The king will pay you a penny per piece.' He paused. 'But I would not waste your time. If you want real pay, you should seek out my lord, Northampton. I think he will remember you.' He laughed once more. 'Not all of us are going back to England,' he said. He winked. 'But I didn't tell you that.'

'Not going—?' Thorp began to protest. But as he did, Romford returned, dragging two large branches behind him and softly whistling to himself. 'Firewood,' he said, as though it needed explaining.

Sir Denis regarded Romford as though he were trying to place him. 'I know you,' he said thoughtfully. But he said no more. Instead, he turned back to Loveday. 'Think about it,' he said.

'And you,' he said, reaching out his finger and thumb and flicking the Flemish boy hard on the ear, 'fuck off.' He clasped his hands as if in prayer and pointed them at the Dogs, then strode away.

The young Fleming glowered at the knight's back, then started walking off as well.

Scotsman called him back. 'Hey boy. You buy rings?' He raised his right hand and flexed his jewelled fingers.

The boy turned. He moved his hand inside his loose linen shirt and pulled out a thick piece of cord, tied necklace-wise around his neck. On it hung at least forty rings, set with onyx and crystals, precious stones of green and ruby. He took it off his neck and whirled the string around his index finger, making the rings clatter together.

'You know how many lords died here?' he called. *Lorts dite.*

He caught the necklace, put it back over his head and tucked it once more inside his shirt. 'Everyone has a *rink* today.'

Scotsman's shoulders fell. He said no more. Loveday patted him on the back, as consolingly as he could, and all the Dogs stared around the field, piled everywhere with dead men and abandoned possessions. Thick smoke from the royal furnaces was billowing in gusts and the dusk was turning to night. The Flemish boy skipped away from them, poking his tongue out as he went. Before he had gone more than twenty paces, he had vanished into the shadows.

2

We have lived off the countryside with great difficulty and
with much harm to our men... we are now in such a sore
plight that the refreshing of our supplies must be met...
Letter to England from a royal clerk, September 1346

Romford helped Millstone build a night-fire from the wood
he had scavenged in the forest, and the Dogs sat around
it watching darkness fall. They ate a meagre supper of gritty,
yeastless bread and Scotsman's familiar bland gruel. They were
all very tired. Scotsman and the archers Tebbe and Thorp kept
up their complaining about the lack of ale provided by the
king's men. 'Fucking torturing us,' moaned the Scot. 'After
everything we've done.' Loveday tried to pacify them, but they
would hear none of it.

So as the fire crackled and the clouds and stars drifted, the
Dogs either grumbled or spoke of small things: the chill of
the night, the chance of rain or sunshine the next day, and the
time at which they might break camp. Occasionally they spoke
of their homes, which until now Romford had never heard
them mention. Tebbe and Millstone talked of wives and other
women awaiting them. Scotsman of taverns he missed.

None of them talked of their deeds in the battle. The
exhilaration of the fight had long passed. What was done was

hard even to remember. Romford tried to recall what he had felt and seen, but his thoughts came only in scraps. He knew there had been a time when he was scrambling on the ground among feet and hooves. Another when he had been deafened by some weapon that gave out a great roar and belched billows of smoke that stank like rotting eggs. He remembered shooting an arrow through that rank smoke. He remembered the smell of piss and horse dung. The scratch of dust and grit in his throat and nose. His lip split by a stray boot. His smarting eyes meeting those of the dying and dead.

But he could not put it all together in a story that made sense. And he could not connect the excitement and terror of that recent time with what he now felt, even though he lay on the land where it had all taken place. He did not know if this was normal. Unlike the other Dogs, Romford had never been to war before. Did all campaigns end this way? In such sadness and squalor? Back when his father and brother had dragged him around London's taverns, he had heard old soldiers talk about war as though it were a heroic game, full of adventures that ended in glory or the awesome mystery of death. But his father was gone, hanged. His brother vanished and spoken of as though he were in his grave too. And here he, Romford, sat with his comrades, stealing from the dead and speaking of the weather.

Romford felt inside his arrow bag.

When he had been in the forest foraging the firewood, he had found something interesting nestled in a pile of decaying oak bark. It was a sort of mould – a fungus that rose on thick brown stems carrying flat, pale hats the colour of dry bone. He recognised it from the same rank London taverns of his youth. He had heard men call it various things. Some called it bog moss, and others madman's mould. The godless called it Christ's Body or Host. All reported that it melted the line between waking and dreams. Romford had never tried it, but one shifty-eyed friend of his father's, a man whose face and bristling whiskers made him resemble a Thames rat, said it revealed where the saints and angels walked among us.

Romford considered all this. It had been a long time since he had tasted any of the mind-dulling powder he was used to stealing from apothecaries' shops. He did not know when he might find any again. And this Host had grown so thickly on the oak bark that it seemed too good an opportunity to miss. So he had packed his arrow bag half-full. He slipped a few pieces of the soft flesh into his mouth and chewed. It tasted of nothing very much.

Disappointingly, it did nothing very much either. Romford was used to apothecaries' powder taking effect in moments, numbing his mouth and cuddling his brain. The Host did no such thing. Romford fancied he could see a certain new brightness dance in the fire's flames as he sat and listened to the Dogs slurp their gruel. But that was all.

He worried briefly that he had picked something that was not Host. That it would make him very sick. But he felt no nausea. So after a while he wrapped his thin woollen blanket tight about his back and shoulders, lay down close to the fire and went to sleep.

He awoke in the dead of night. Soft voices around the embers of the fire had stirred him. He tried not to move under his blanket, so that no one would know he had woken. He just lay still and listened.

'Tell us again what you saw.'

Loveday was speaking softly, as though he feared being overheard.

Romford heard Scotsman snort. 'Christ on the tree, Loveday, how many times are you going to make him turn it over? He was on his way to find Hugh Hastings' mob, he got as far as some shite-hole of a port near Flanders, he saw...'

'It wasn't quite like that.' That was Millstone's soft voice.

'Aye, well. Whatever the fuck it was *quite like*. Loveday, come on. You've heard all this already. Maybe he saw the Captain. More likely it was someone who looked like him. He doesn't know for sure. As far as we knew, three days ago that false fucker was dead and with the devil, getting what he deserved. There's no reason to think anything else now.'

'It was him,' said Millstone calmly. 'I know it was.'

Scotsman let out another snort. 'And what if it was? He fucked us all off. Why would we even care if he's alive or dead?' He spat. 'If I see him again, he'll wish he was dead. Christ, have we really nothing at all to fucking drink?'

Tebbe farted in his sleep. He groaned in relief, turned over and began snoring.

'There'll be drink once we move,' said Loveday. 'We'll be heading for the coast tomorrow. There'll be ships and sailors. And if there are sailors...' He tailed off. And he left Scotsman's question unanswered. 'Please. Millstone. Just tell me one more time.'

With an exasperated sigh, Scotsman took himself away from the conversation and lay down. Moments later, he too was snoring.

Millstone sighed. 'It wasn't quite like that. It was after Saint-Lô, and... everything that happened there.'

Beneath his blanket, Romford shivered. He remembered Saint-Lô only too well. Millstone had saved his life in an apothecary's shop there, rescuing him from Shaw, monstrous leader of the East Anglian crew who had tormented the Dogs on the first part of their march. Millstone had smashed Shaw's skull with his hammer. Spilled his evil brains on the floor. Romford owed his life to the quiet, sturdy stonemason. But he also knew the whole crew had suffered because of it. He by being sent away to the prince, who had treated him kindly, then cruelly, and had broken his heart. Millstone by being forced to flee Sir Robert's vengeance. And Father…

Father was dead. Thrown from the top of a tower by a mad bishop. But in his mind's eye, Romford now saw the old priest crouching like a maddened ape on the apothecary's floor. The vividness of the image shocked Romford. It was as though Father were really there again. His face wild, blood dripping from his brown and broken teeth. Father looked him in the eye and snarled. Romford shook his head and Father went away. He kept listening.

'After Saint-Lô…' Loveday was saying.

Millstone cleared his throat. 'I went back to the coast. I kept away from the roads and went north. When I went to towns I stuck to ports where there were all manner of people – French, Italian… and a lot of Flemings. Mostly merchants and traders looking to make money from the war. There was a lot of talk of another army coming. One of ours. From the north. And of ships bringing new troops. The trouble was, no one knew where the ships were landing.

'I just wanted to get home. So I asked in the usual places if there was anyone who fixed that sort of thing. People kept saying the English ports were all closed except to military traffic. But that there was one man who could arrange it. They called him all sorts of things. The Burned Man. The Broken Man. The Cripple.

'I heard he was in a town called Calais. Or that he was somewhere called Crotoy. Or that he had gone to Ghent to take revenge on whoever had broken him. I heard so many things about him that didn't agree. It felt dangerous to ask too much. So I gave up looking for him. I decided to look for the other army.'

Loveday was silent, listening intently. Romford shifted on the ground, trying to make it sound as though he were just turning in his sleep. He opened his right eye slightly, and he could see Loveday's face, lit a ghastly orange by the fire's embers. Romford shut his eye tight again.

Millstone continued. 'I was on the road back here from the coast when I saw him. There was a group of merchants, three or four. They'd stopped to graze their horses by the roadside. They had a couple of carts with cages on the back – the sort they put prisoners in when they're off for hanging. You know what I mean?'

'I know.'

'Aye. Well. I wouldn't have paid them any mind, but as they stood there, there was a cripple among them. He seemed to be following them. Trying to get something from them. Or learn something. He walked in this strange way. You know how it is on the ships?'

Romford understood what Millstone meant. Though he was lying on the ground, he felt as though he were back on the cog *Saintmarie* that had brought them to the beach weeks ago. Lurching from side to side. So that men walked with stiff legs. He felt sick, just as he had at sea.

Millstone carried on. 'Anyway. I was keeping to the hedgerow, and taking no chances with anyone. I kept to the other side of the road from them. But I saw him. There was something in his face. A look. You know how we used to say he was always a handsome bastard? How he was proud of it?'

'Aye.'

'He had this hat pulled down, but he looked right at me and I knew. It was his eyes. He was older, for sure...'

'It's been two years and more.'

'Aye, but a lot older. Like someone from another time. All grey... but his skin was red and blistered. And his leg... I couldn't tell, but I think it wasn't his own. It was made of some animal bone or wood. He must have fallen on bad times. But his eyes...'

'Did he recognise you?'

'I don't think so. I don't know.'

As Romford lay in the dark, the man Millstone was describing to Loveday formed out of the blackness. The face was more disturbing even than Father's, though he had never seen it. It scared him. Romford gasped and opened his eyes. The face melted into the fire's dying coals.

He sat up.

Loveday and Millstone stared at him.

'Bad dream, lad?' asked Millstone.

Romford didn't know what to say. He shook his head. Behind the two Dogs, he saw the stars were still out. Each star burning with a light impossibly bright. As though they were not stars but each an angel holding a flaming sword, pointed towards him alone. He tried to block them out with his hand.

'Are you sick?' Loveday asked him.

'No... I mean... I ate something,' said Romford. His voice

stretched like a bowstring, went taut then loosened. He hiccupped. The cut in his lip stung.

From around the fire, Thorp hissed. 'Saints' bones, will the lot of you hold your fucking peace? You're worse than my old woman at home. I'm trying to sleep.'

'Get some more rest,' Millstone said to Romford. Then to Loveday he said, 'I'm telling you. That's what I saw. I know it's not much. But it was enough.'

'What did he tell us when he left us?'

Loveday took a deep breath and exhaled slowly.

'He said we were looking at war the wrong way. That a new world was coming and the way we did things was ending. That it was time to seek our fortunes in new places, on our own terms. He meant by himself.'

'Aye,' said Millstone. 'What else?'

'He said we would have to change. Or the world would come along and change us.'

Millstone nodded. 'Well, he's changed. Have we?'

Romford held on to the ground around him, feeling that the Earth was tilting. That he might fall off it. Millstone sensed he was still awake. 'Go to sleep, boy,' he said. 'You don't need to worry about any of this. We're just talking about an old friend.'

'An old friend,' Romford said, trying to match his words to the echo of Millstone's. 'Talking about an old friend.' He looked beside him. Father was sitting there.

'Rub my gums, boy,' said Father, his mouth hanging open. A part of his jaw dangled free and fell off. It rolled forward into the fire, as if it were pulled there by the hunger of the flames. It touched them and burned up in an instant.

Father disappeared.

Millstone's voice was harder now, and it echoed around the field, booming like the strange weapon of the battle.

'Sleep boy, boy, sleep boy sleep boy sleep,' he said.

Suddenly terrified, Romford squealed and wriggled inside his blanket, pulling it tight over his head and curling up in a ball.

'Leave him be,' he heard Loveday say. Romford squeezed his eyes as tightly shut as he could and held his breath. Soon everything was black and quiet. Dreams began to come. He felt himself pressed into the prince's back in a warm tent, where a bird flapped its wings in the canvas high above. He saw Father and Pismire, alive once more and laughing at some old joke. Saw a woman they had met once in a town called Valognes, her quick eyes darting around as she sharpened a knife. Heard the smoking weapons roar.

He saw hanged men with their eyes popping out of the sockets, and rich men at a banqueting table, stuffing food into their mouths and counting out piles of coins. He saw his father dying on the gallows, and his brother drunk in a Southwark gutter, having his guts kicked and his fingers stamped for another gambling debt gone unpaid. He saw a woman he thought may have been the mother he had never known.

And he saw again the face of the man called the Captain, a cripple whose memory haunted Loveday and Millstone so much. They all seemed to be trying to speak to him, but from their mouths spilled a language Romford did not understand. That he had not yet learned.

Trying to listen wore him out. And when he woke in the morning, he was as tired as before he slept, and cold to his bones. The ground was chilly. A light rain was falling from a flat grey sky.

The Earl of Northampton was standing over him.

3

The King of England wished to hold the love of the Flemings
because they had come to his side... and they could prove
to be of very great value...

Chronicles of Jean Froissart

'**C**hrist on a three-legged donkey. The saints must have
mixed you fuckers up with six mouth-breathers worth
saving.'

The Earl of Northampton was in a good mood. He clapped
his gloveless hands and warmed them on the Dogs' rekindled
fire. The drizzle that had been falling all morning formed small
droplets on the fur-trimmed shoulders of his cloak. Loveday
had intended to seek him out, but the impatient earl had found
him first.

'God saw fit to save us for another day, my lord,' said
Loveday. The back of his throat tasted of fire-smoke. He
coughed and brought up ashy phlegm.

'Aye, well, the kingdom of heaven is full of fucking
mysteries.' Northampton glanced at his bodyguards, Sir Denis
of Moreton-on-the-Weald and Sir Adrian, a lean, intense figure
with dark skin and greying short-cropped hair. The two knights
hung back, affecting not to listen to their lord. 'Isn't that what
the Bible tells us, boys?'

'Said like a preacher, my lord,' replied Sir Denis.

Northampton grunted, something less than a laugh. He regarded the Dogs and narrowed his eyes. 'There used to be more of you.'

Loveday nodded solemnly. It was not only Pismire and Father whom they had lost. They had begun the campaign with a pair of Welsh archers in their crew – brothers called Darys and Lyntyn. But they had abandoned the Dogs many weeks ago, stolen several fine horses from a pair of cardinals and disappeared into the French countryside. He coughed as he addressed Northampton. 'Aye, sir. If you recall—'

'FitzTalbot, I don't *recall* the last time I shat indoors. But I'm not fucking blind. I can see you're down on men. Did you lose them in the battle or before?'

'Before, my lord.'

'Right.' The earl scratched his chin, the thick bristles recently clipped. He noticed Romford, just awaking on the ground, and prodded the lad with the toe of his leather boot. 'Get up, son.'

Romford scrambled to his feet, blinking in confusion. He skittered out of the earl's range and stood beside the other Dogs, drawing his ragged blanket around his shoulders to keep off the drizzling rain. Loveday winced. The lad had been babbling all night in his sleep. Some queer language of his dreams.

Northampton let him be. 'You take any prisoners in the battle?'

Loveday looked blankly at him. 'No, my lord. We...'

'You wouldn't be here if you had, right? You'd be off selling them to the fucking ransom boys.' The earl paused and considered matters. 'Well, we need to fix you up with another crew,' he said after a few moments. 'You're no good as six.'

Loveday felt his stomach tighten. 'Another crew? My lord, we thought we were going home—'

'Home?' The earl barked a laugh. 'Yes, that would be nice, wouldn't it, FitzTalbot? I'd like to go home. Kiss my wife, fuck my girlfriend. But in case you hadn't noticed, we just won the most famous victory over the French since the high sultan of the camel-drivers pulled Saint Louis' breeches down and sent him scuttling back to his mother with dysentery and pubic lice.'

Loveday had only the dimmest idea what the earl was referring to. But the earl did not notice or care. He ran his thumbs along his thick grey eyebrows to press rainwater from them, and flicked it behind him. 'The good tidings, if you care to hear them, are that we're heading to the coast. That's almost home, I suppose. I gather we'll be close enough to England that when the wind is right you can hear the nightwatchman at Dover Castle beating his pintle.

'And if we get really lucky, we'll get some fucking fresh supplies. So you'll have something other than this muck to eat and drink.' The earl kicked over one of the Dogs' wooden bowls containing the remnants of the previous night's meal. Nothing came out. The slop stuck to the sides.

'But unless you're missing your feet or carrying your guts around in a leather satchel, the king is courteously *demanding* that you stick around.

'He wants to finish what we've begun. Which means taking a properly fortified port along the coast and turning it into a little bit of England. So there's work to do.' The earl put his hands on his hips. 'Any questions?'

'Why?' said Millstone.

Northampton frowned. 'Why what?'

Millstone's expression did not change. 'We've won. Why are we now doing this?'

'Why? You want the real answer? Because my lord the king is holed up in a manor house about half a day's ride from here with a lot of bankers and merchants in his ear. They like the idea of having a secure English port on this side of the Channel. And frankly he's in no position to argue with them. We're up to our tits in debt to virtually every fucker who lends money between here and Tartary.'

'Where's Tartary?' asked Scotsman.

'It's where tarts come from,' snapped Northampton. 'Any *more* questions?'

The Dogs said nothing.

'Good. So here's what I want from you. While the army marches to the port in question, I need to soften up a few places that might serve as boltholes for our enemies. I want you lot to help me and a few other friends do what needs to be done. If you serve me well, I'll cover the forty days' pay you're already owed for coming over here, and a little extra, which I know you need because I can see for myself that you've ended up with nothing to show for the last six weeks but boils on your arses.

'How does that sound?' He paused. 'Actually, don't tell me. Just say "thank you, Lord Northampton".'

'My lord,' Loveday began. 'I wonder...'

Northampton grimaced. 'Holy Christ, FitzTalbot, am I giving you orders in fucking Turkish? Should I send for the king's jester and have him stick a sackbut up his arse and fart it out in song? I said: "just say 'thank you, Lord Northampton'".'

'Thank you, Lord Northampton,' said Loveday.

Northampton looked around the rest of the Dogs. 'Thank

you, Lord Northampton,' chorused Tebbe, Thorp and Romford. The earl locked eyes with Scotsman, challenging him. 'Aye, fucking right,' muttered the Scot.

Northampton didn't look at Millstone.

'Grand,' he exclaimed. 'March with the rest of the army to our next stop. It's a place called Wissant. We'll kick out anyone who's stupid enough to have stayed there, rest up a few days, burn it down, then ride out to start the party. If you can find another crew to join with, do it. If not, I'll find one for you.' He winked. 'I do *recall* you liking East Anglians.'

Loveday shuddered.

'And one more thing.' Northampton motioned to his knights. From somewhere about his person Sir Adrian produced a wineskin and threw it to Scotsman, who pulled out the stopper with his teeth and drank until his eyes watered.

'We're alive. We're winning. Don't look so fucking serious.'

They reached Wissant around mid-afternoon on Saturday. They marched at an easy pace. It took three days to cover a distance that earlier in the campaign the army might have crossed in less than two. But the lords leading the men recognised they were all hungry and weary, and did not push them. They seemed unconcerned about the prospect of ambush. Loveday heard it said many times that the French king had disbanded what remained of his army in shock and retreated to Paris, where he wandered around deserted cathedrals, railing against traitors, tearing his clothes and beard and mourning his dead. English outriders went around setting fire to undefended villages and the suburbs of the few towns with gates and walls. They met no resistance.

'Fucking French. Soft fuckers don't deserve their own country,' growled the Scot more than once. But beneath his gruff jokes, the big man was lost. Loveday knew he missed Pismire. The two of them had always been able to while away long marches by bickering. Now Scotsman traded barbs with himself.

Wissant was a city of moderate size, spread out from a harbour in which stood an ancient and half-ruined lighthouse built from brown brick, grey stone and powdery mortar. Seabirds circled its top, perching in their dozens on the iron basin where the signal-fire was lit, screaming and swooping, and plastering the ground with their sloppy, purple-flecked shit. The gulls and a few listless whores were the only inhabitants of the city who had remained to greet the English. The king, his earls and bannerets, and the countless officials of his travelling court took over the tall merchants' houses in the quarter nearest the harbour: timber-framed buildings that soared three storeys high, many of them lit by glazed windows. The Dogs camped in the suburbs, in an abandoned baker's premises with two large rooms, fixed shutters on the windows and a stone oven in the yard at the back.

Once they had unloaded their meagre possessions and weapons inside the building and lit a fire in the oven to dry their damp blankets and clothes, Scotsman called the men together.

Loveday was all too happy to let the big man take the lead. He also knew what the Scot would be thinking.

'There were ships in the harbour,' Scotsman said, flexing his huge hands so that his knuckles popped and the rings on his fingers clinked. He pulled one off. It flashed darkly. A sapphire set in gold seemed to glow with a light of its own.

'Let's see if we can't trade this in for a proper drink.'

* * *

For the first time in many weeks, the army was in carnival mood. Most of the ships at the docks were Flemish-owned, their long, curved hulls emblazoned with names in the northern tongue. Millstone knew his letters and read the names. *Santalbrecht* and *Chrodogang*. *Margharite* and *Tatterschallcastell*. Several had been on wine-trading runs, Loveday guessed to the French south, and their enterprising sailors had sprung open the great wooden wine casks and run timber gangplanks from the dockside to the ships' decks. They filled jugs and wineskins and bantered with the thirsty soldiers who swarmed aboard. A few liveried royal men-at-arms idled dockside, watching for trouble. Others, off duty, joined the revelry.

Scotsman, flanked by Tebbe and Thorp, led the Dogs towards a vessel of dark painted oak.

Millstone read the name. '*Homobonus*. This one do us?' he asked.

Loveday looked it over. Barnacles and weed clung to the long, wet timbers of its hull. Flags bearing bright golden, winged horses flew from its stern. And the decks heaved with drinkers, most clustered around a tavern-style bar set up on the raised aft-castle. The crowd was mostly footsoldiers and archers, some English and others Flemish. Amid the throng, lusty voices were singing a song Loveday recognised from his youth.

I am the wolf
Without a pack
Banished long ago

'Aye,' he said, 'this'll do well.'

The Scot bounded up the plank-bridge, the wood bouncing under his weight. Tebbe and Thorp were close on his heels.

'Who's Homobonus?' asked Romford, as he put a foot gingerly on the gangway.

'An old merchant, lad,' came a voice from behind them. Loveday swivelled and found Sir Denis smiling down at him. 'Famous for his generosity.'

Seeing the burly knight, Loveday hesitated, wondering if the Dogs ought to have reported for duty with Northampton instead of stepping out in search of wine. Sir Denis sensed his awkwardness and laughed. He wound his long hair into a knot at the back of his head, stuck a thin stick through it to keep the knot in place, then clapped Loveday on the shoulder. 'Go,' he said. 'Enjoy yourselves. You've a few days before we head out. Be sure to save one of them to sleep it all off.' Then the big knight sauntered away towards the next ship.

Millstone and Romford went up the plank to join the other Dogs. Loveday, slower and less nimble, followed them, feeling his belly wobble as he jumped down on to the ship's lower deck, then holding it in as he squeezed his way up to the aft. The Dogs had made themselves a space in the corner, where the bar butted up against the deck's wooden rail. The air around them smelled of salt and sweat. They all wore wide grins.

Scotsman had evidently made a deal. He waggled his fingers. 'Nineteen left now,' he said. 'But it's fucking worth it.' Tebbe handed Loveday a beaker of wine. It was dark and glossy, the colour of oxblood, and it looked as good as anything Loveday had drunk in his life. 'Best stuff in France,' Tebbe said. He raised his mug and knocked it against Tebbe's. He thought of toasting to Pismire and Father. But he decided not to dampen the mood.

'Like angels dancing on your tongue,' said Scotsman, draining his mug in one draught. He belched enormously and wiped the back of his mouth with his hand. 'Thorp, get the next jug.'

As he spoke, the ship rocked gently on the water, and the Scot stepped backwards to steady himself. In doing so, he backed into a drinker from the group pressed next to the Dogs. A burly, square-jawed figure, with a chest as broad as the Scot's, turned around in annoyance.

'Sorry, pal,' the Scot muttered.

As the drinker turned, Loveday saw to his surprise that it was a woman – a huge woman, with a deep voice and wisps of wiry black hair curling here and there from her jawline. She glared at the Scot but did not answer him. Instead, she turned back to her three friends, saying something in Flemish. The group sniggered.

Loveday let it go. Somewhere on the boat the old song was still being sung. He hummed along quietly.

All I've learned is poison stings
No one remembers martyrs and kings

Within the hour, the Dogs were all very drunk.

The second time Scotsman bumped into the thickset woman behind him, she let it pass. But the third time, when he swung an arm around, acting out some escapade from long ago in the Dogs' history, he caught her elbow and sent her wine mug clattering to the floor.

As long as Loveday had known the Scot, he had always been a lively drinker. Drink seldom made him seek out trouble. If anything, it curbed his normal wrath. Yet when he was excited, he was prone to let his giant limbs flail and windmill.

The woman stood a head shorter than the Scot – only a little taller than Loveday and Millstone. But she was as burly as a fairground wrestler. And as she whipped round once more and took a great handful of the Scot's grease- and sweat-stained shirt, Loveday saw she had not a scrap of fear in her. She tugged the surprised Scotsman's shirt so hard that his face came down to hers. She pressed her nose hard against his.

'You can't keep control of your fucking arm, I'll cut it off,' she growled. Her deep voice, harsh Flemish accent and the flash of her grey eyes gave the words great menace.

As startled as he was drink-addled, Scotsman put his hands up, wide and apologetic. 'Christ, pal,' he slurred, 'I didn't fucking mean it.'

'Didn't mean it three times? If you can't handle your wine, stick to fucking ale,' she said. 'And I'm not your fucking pal.'

Loveday instinctively balled his fists. Millstone, standing beside him, placed a firm hand on his wrist.

The Scot was trying to calm the situation. But the wine was tying his tongue in knots. 'Listen, mate, I'm fucking, I didn't... I'm just with my fucking pals, mate.'

The woman let go of his shirt, but she didn't turn around. Nor did she back down. She prodded Scotsman in the chest. 'Touch me again, and you're dead,' she said. 'Got it?'

Hands still up, Scotsman nodded. 'Aye,' he said. 'Aye. Got it. We're just having a fucking drink.'

The woman stared at him with her angry grey eyes for a few moments, then turned back to her group, who were no longer whispering or sniggering. The Dogs looked at one another in surprise. Scotsman was flushed. Loveday could tell humiliation and anger were rising in his chest.

His face hardened.

Loveday shook his head. 'Don't,' he said. But he was too slow. Scotsman went back to the woman. He tapped her on the shoulder. 'Hey, pal,' he began.

With extraordinary speed, the woman pivoted on the balls of her feet, swung around and punched the Scot in the face.

The Scot staggered backwards. Then he let out a roar and threw himself at the woman, launching himself at her stout midriff, wrapping his arms around her and attempting to drive her to the floor. But the woman was astonishingly strong. She absorbed the force of the Scot's tackle, crashing backwards and sending nearby drinkers on the boat flying. She started beating Scotsman's back with her fists, raining down blows on his shoulder blades and ribs.

After several hard punches she managed to land her fist above the Scot's left kidney and, stung by the pain, he released his arms. The woman slipped from his grasp and the Scot slipped so he was momentarily on all fours on the deck. Revellers hooted. The woman's companions cheered her on as she drew back her foot and aimed a huge kick at Scotsman's guts. It landed clean. Scotsman vomited wine on the deck. He lay and gasped for a moment, then staggered to his feet.

Again Loveday moved towards his friend, but once more Millstone held him back. Tebbe, Thorp and Romford stood rooted in confusion. Millstone pointed dockside, where two royal men-at-arms were making their way towards the gangplank. He shook his head. Loveday's brain was swirling. He dragged Millstone's hand from his arm and started to push his way through the crowd who had formed in a ring around the fighters.

They were stalking each other, fists up. The Scot had chunks of purple vomit in his beard. He lurched. The woman was grinning, but she was breathing hard, and Loveday could see her smile masked a grimace. His guessed the Scot had bruised or broken one of her ribs.

Laughter and catcalls rang around the deck, and the press of bodies around Scotsman and the woman made it impossible for Loveday to get any closer. He could only watch helplessly as the Scot threw a huge, looping punch towards the woman. She ducked it, slipped to her left and pushed the Scot hard. The heavy swing of his arm, combined with the force of her shove, carried him two paces forward towards the ship's side. The crowd heaved apart. Scotsman hit the rail at the side of the aft deck. The woman pursued him like a hound sniffing a kill. With all her might, she kicked Scotsman in the arse.

He crashed straight through the rail, the wood bursting under the impact of his huge bulk. For an instant, he tottered. Then he was gone.

A huge splash told Loveday where.

Using every ounce of his strength, Loveday hauled his way through the baying crowd and looked over the broken rail. The packed cog sat low in the water of the harbour. Scotsman had not fallen far.

But there was no sign of him.

'Shit,' Loveday said.

The woman had her arms raised above her head and was

being slapped on the back by her small gang of friends. She was laughing and coughing, and wincing where they hit her battered ribs.

She lowered her arms and went to peer over the rail. 'Can he swim?' she asked.

Loveday was scanning the water, panic creeping up his spine. 'Not well.'

The Dogs, along with all the other revellers, piled to the edge of the deck and peered down into the harbour, where huge ripples were now disappearing.

Loveday began to strip off his shirt, ready to jump in. He got his arms tangled and tied up in his sleeves.

Before he could free himself, a huge head and shoulders appeared on the water's surface, and Scotsman appeared. He was beating his hands hard to keep afloat, sending spray all around him. He shook the soaked and jumbled ropes of his hair and spat blood and water in a short arc in front of him. 'Fucking Christ,' he was spluttering to no one in particular. 'Fucking Christ!'

Then, as he looked back up towards the deck where the Dogs and dozens of other drinkers – now including the two royal men-at-arms – looked down, he saw the absurdity of the situation. He threw his head back in the water and howled.

The woman turned to Loveday. 'See, he can swim,' she said. 'A little. What is his name?'

Loveday told her. Then he added: 'But everyone calls him Scotsman.'

She nodded. 'He fights pretty good for a man,' she said. 'But I could teach him some tricks.' She clapped Loveday hard on the shoulder. 'You can call me Fleming if you like,' she said. Then she pointed to her friends, who were standing with Tebbe and

Thorp, all shouting friendly insults down to Scotsman while lowering a rope for him to heave himself back aboard the boat. 'But these soft-cock fuckers call me Hircent.'

4

A large division left the King of England's army under the command of the Earl of Northampton (though some claim the Prince of Wales took part in the operation)... and they travelled until they came before the city of Thérouanne...

St Omer Chronicle

The Dogs stayed in Wissant for nearly a week until Sir Denis came to find them in their smoky bakery.

In those days, life fell into a rhythm Romford felt was almost like being among a family again, something he had not known since he was a child. His lip began to heal. In an abandoned shop in the tailors' quarter he found new clothes, cleaner and more comfortable than the tight outfit he had been put in by the prince's men, which had hung shredded from his body after the battle. In place of his stripy hose he now wore a pair of loose raw linen trousers, cinched at the waist with a simple rope belt, and a comfortable thigh-length woollen shirt.

He began to fill his clothes once more, too. The Dogs ate regular meals, supplied from stalls around the docks by cooks and servants of the royal household. Scotsman traded another two rings for several large barrels of wine. So as the men ate and drank and slept well for the first time in two months, their bruises faded and the bags under their eyes shrank. And as their strength returned, their mood lightened. Although they still spoke of their homes, they accepted that for a few weeks more they were at the mercy of the king and his orders. They speculated about how much the Earl of Northampton might pay them for their service, if they did it well. From time to time they fantasised about capturing some valuable prisoner and exchanging him for a great fortune. Even Loveday seemed less anxious than normal, and Romford sensed that for once the kind, round-bellied leader was not worried for the safety of his men.

So for a few days, Romford was happy. He was busy too. Each morning Tebbe and Thorp took him down to the harbour's great lighthouse, to the range where the king's officers had set up butts for the archers to keep their eyes sharp and arms strong. All three were excellent shots, and with several hours of daily practice they all saw their aim improve to somewhere near their best. Romford could hit the small circles painted in the centre of the fat straw targets with around nine arrows in ten. At first, he was accurate from one hundred paces. As the days went by and his drawing arm strengthened and steadied, he was proficient from two hundred, and finally nearer two hundred and fifty. Other archers would stop and watch when he took his longest shots, whispering intensely about the way he drew his right arm to the point of his shoulder, and laying wagers on his accuracy.

One afternoon, when he played a game of six-arrows with Tebbe and Thorp, the Dogs drew a crowd of several dozen onlookers. There were gasps and cheers when Romford hit all six of his shots clean in the small circle from three hundred paces – the furthest distance the range allowed. After Romford landed his arrows and they inspected their targets, the other two archers pounded him on the back while the crowd whooped. 'Show him which way Paris is and the little bastard could put one clean through King Philippe's eye,' said Thorp, shaking his head. 'War'd be over in one shot.' Romford felt such a rush of pride that he was lost for words. His face reddened as he smiled shyly at the handsome Thorp.

After archery practice each day, the three archers would rejoin the rest of the Dogs to get drunk. Romford did not drink nearly as much as his older companions. Neither did he discover in any of Wissant's apothecaries the soothing, mind-dulling powder he had sought out in other towns they had visited. But he did not mind, and he did not itch for the powder as he had done in the worst moments of the march before the battle. He was content sipping his wine, and occasionally nibbling a tiny piece of the Host he kept packed in his arrow bag; just enough to make the colours brighter and the jokes the men told funnier. The combination allowed him to enjoy the other men's company as they drained their mugs, and became loose and red-faced and jovial. It was like the first days he had ever been with the Dogs, when he met them in the Portsmouth tavern and begged them to take him away with them. He joined their games of cross-and-pile and arm wrestling, and watched the cockfights held in the streets in the hour before dark each night. He was glad things never again grew as riotous as on the day when Scotsman had fought the big Flemish woman called Hircent.

In fact, Hircent and her own small company became regular companions of the Dogs. From their talk, Romford understood that they vaguely hoped for the king's army to swing north and capture various towns of Flanders that were held by the

French. But it seemed to him they were mostly interested in finding, or causing, mischief.

After the fight on the boat, the strong, broad-shouldered woman and Scotsman struck up a curious relationship, like a pair of competitive siblings. They jostled and joshed one another, bickering theatrically for the amusement of the rest of the group and trying to best one another in every game, trial of strength or conversation. The fact that Hircent was a woman passed unremarked by any of the men, either among the Dogs or her own crew, which was made up of three pikemen called Heyman, Jakke and Nicclaes. They treated her as though she were a man, never addressing her as 'she' or 'her'. When there was bawdy talk of women the others claimed they had fucked, or intended to, Hircent roared along with it as though she too were a man, with a man's lusts and urges.

Romford had known women like this before in his London life. They almost always ran brothels. But he had never seen a woman so proficient at handling weapons. The men in her crew had no experience with the longbows that Tebbe, Thorp and Romford had mastered. Nor did they show any interest. Hircent was different. She was intrigued by the Dogs' weapons, and would spend long hours watching Scotsman put a new edge on the blade of his axe or Tebbe obsessing over the cut and fit of his arrow feathers.

One day, Romford listened while Hircent quizzed Loveday in detail about his preferred tactics for fighting with a short sword.

'You can't lift anything bigger?' she asked Loveday, part jokingly, but with an edge of scorn in her voice.

'I'm no knight,' Loveday replied. 'Shorter blades are easier on the purse. And they're better when the fighting is thick and close...'

Hircent smirked. 'One day you will come to your senses,' she said, 'and use a real man's weapon.'

With this, she hoisted and swung her own favourite war tool: a stout club called a *goedendag*, tipped with a heavy metal spike driven into its head. The spike whistled close to Loveday's nose, and the Dogs' grizzled leader pulled his head back out of its way and frowned. Hircent laughed, and stuck the spike in the ground at her feet. She tapped the *goedendag*'s heavy shaft. 'I call this one *Heartbreaker*.'

The Dogs and Flemings were warming themselves around the bread oven in the yard behind the bakery one grey morning, when Sir Denis pushed open the small store's creaking wooden door, stepped through its stuffy rooms and called them to order. He looked over the group approvingly. 'I see life in Wissant agrees with you,' he said. He pointed at Romford and mimed shooting an arrow into an imaginary target, far away. Then the big knight looked at the Flemings. 'And you have made some friends among our *northern allies*.'

'We have,' said Loveday, looking awkwardly at Hircent. 'We met in—'

Sir Denis cut him off with a laugh. 'I watched your introduction,' he said. 'An entertaining bout. Lord Warwick himself paid to repair the damage.' He waved a hand to dismiss any further talk. 'I will be brief. Tomorrow our army moves to Calais: a city much like this one, except with high walls, two moats, marshland all around it and gates barred against us. Yet we will not all go together. Lord Northampton has asked me to remind you of your undertaking to ride with him to a different town, which must be made secure. I trust you have not forgotten.'

'No, sir,' said Loveday.

'Good.' Sir Denis raised an enquiring eyebrow. 'And your friends? It would spare me the task of finding another crew to join you with. And since King Edward is paying our allies' wages at lavish expense to his treasury...'

The Dogs and Flemings exchanged glances. '*They* can ride with *us*,' said Hircent. 'If they can keep up.'

'Good,' said Sir Denis again.

'So where are we going?' grunted Scotsman.

'Thérouanne,' replied the knight. 'You know it?'

Hircent cut in and replied contemptuously, 'Of course. *Verdomt honden hol.*'

Sir Denis translated for the benefit of the English-speakers. 'A goddamned doghole,' he smiled. 'But it looks to me as though you are at home in *dogholes*? Or maybe just among Dogs.' He took a moment to enjoy his own pun, then grew serious. 'Make whatever last preparations you require, and meet us at dawn tomorrow by the lighthouse,' he said.

Sir Denis made as if to leave, then turned back. 'One more thing,' he said. 'You should know that our expedition will be formally under the command of the Prince of Wales. My lord Northampton will of course be assisting him in every way His Grace requires. But...'

For just a heartbeat, he glanced at Romford. '...well. It is as it is.'

The knight ducked through the small door back into the baker's house and returned to the street. Behind him, the group buzzed with excitement. But at the mention of the prince's name, Romford's heart beat hard and his stomach gave an ugly somersault.

There was a brief time when he had been the prince's squire and companion. When they had eaten powder together and passed out next to one another, their limbs entwined. Yet as Romford had learned painfully, the prince was a man of fleeting tastes, and his concerns were those of another world to Romford's. He had rejected him, and scorned him.

Romford hated the prince. But he also loved him. He had hoped never to see him again. Yet he also burned with a desperate urge to be touched by him just one more time.

In the bakery, the Dogs and Flemings were bustling around, starting to pack up and check their weapons and armour in readiness for what lay ahead in Thérouanne. Romford let them work, and though he did his own duties it felt like his body was controlled by someone else. His throat stung and from time to time hot tears pricked his eyes. When they came, he blinked them away. But as it neared the hour for sleeping, he reached inside his arrow bag and ate a large piece of the Host.

They left Wissant at dawn the next morning, riding horses from the pool of animals looted on campaign. Romford had not ridden for some weeks, so his legs and lower back were numb from the saddle by the time they arrived in the evening at a large and ancient abbey set in rich farmland. But when dusk fell, and the Dogs assembled with the rest of the company in the abbey's refectory for a briefing from the Earl of Northampton, he was feeling less troubled than he had before. The mood of the men on the ride had been cheerful and excited, and Romford found that if he ate just enough Host, he could tap into their optimism and keep his dark feelings about the prince at bay.

The refectory was a long, high-ceilinged room, lit by tall, thin windows spaced evenly along its bare stone walls. At the head of it, above the abbot's table, a huge painted wooden crucifix hung from the roof beams, suspended by invisible wire. Christ's suffering was skilfully carved, his face gaunt and mournful as he examined the bloody gash in his ribs. Beneath him, Northampton was pacing impatiently.

As soon as the doors were closed and the men came to order, Northampton clambered on to the abbot's table. He had a broad grin on his face.

'Thank you, brothers,' he said, clasping his hands in mock prayer towards the monks who closed the refectory's great doors, and giving them permission to retreat. He waved an apologetic hand at the crucified Christ above him. 'And sorry, Lord,' he said, 'for what you're about to hear.'

Laughter carried around the heaving refectory. Romford popped a little piece of Host in his mouth. The whole company was assembled, with most of the men packed together on long benches set along three huge wooden dining tables that ran the length of the room. The Dogs and Flemings had found a space at the end of the middle table, their packs and weapons jammed at their feet. Other crews had not been so lucky. Some of the last crews to arrive were sitting cramped together on the floor and in the window bays.

Romford listened with interest as Northampton addressed them all. 'First of all, well done. I mean that.' The earl's rasping voice echoed into the roof beams, where a couple of bats flitted. 'It's been a long road that brought us here. And God's a fickle fucker. I know a lot of you buried your friends at Crécy. That's hard. But it's better than them burying you.'

He paced a couple of steps along the tabletop. 'Now, Sir Denis and Sir Adrian have spoken to most of you, and we all know why we're here. But for anyone who's spent the last week pissed or asleep, let me spell it out.

'Right now, King Edward is leading the rest of our army to Calais. If Christ and the saints are on our side, that lot are going to kick the fucking gates in, turn out everyone who's not agreeable to being an English subject, raise the king's banners over the walls and fuck off home in time to eat our Michaelmas goose and blackberries off tavern wenches' naked bellies.'

The men gave an enthusiastic cheer. Fists drummed the wooden tables. Scotsman and Hircent competed to thump their fists the hardest.

Northampton waited for the noise to subside. 'But before we get to the wenches and the blackberries, we've got to do our bit. A mile from here there's a town called Thérouanne. Tomorrow it's market day. We're going to go down there and do some shopping.'

The cheers went round again, louder still.

'But we're doing it properly. There's a bishop in charge of the defences.'

Now Northampton looked serious. 'Laugh all you like. But we've seen what happens when you give a bishop a garrison. He gets a hard-on and imagines he's El fucking Cid. Who here was at Caen?'

Hands went up. Romford felt the mood among the Dogs dip. He knew why. Caen was where Pismire and Father were now buried. Loveday and Scotsman had only just come away from the place with their own lives. The mention of it etched lines on the faces of the older men, and as their brows furrowed, Romford felt his own mood shift too. He ate another piece of Host to try and hang on to his good cheer.

Feeling the room grow sombre, Northampton changed tack. 'So here's what we're going to do. I'll keep it brief because I know you've been riding all day and most of you must be hungrier than Christ in the fucking desert. At daybreak tomorrow, we assemble in the courtyard and head out south-east...'

Speaking rapidly and clearly, the earl began to set out an order of attack on the nearby town, involving a cautious frontal assault of men-at-arms and footsoldiers, supported by archers. Yet as he spoke, there came the sound of voices outside the refectory. Quiet at first, they gradually rose in volume until they were impossible to ignore. Through the thick studded doors, it was hard to work out what was being said. But it sounded like an argument, with three or more voices raised at once.

Northampton felt himself losing the room. He broke off his speech. 'Saint Lawrence's arse roasting on the fucking griddle.' He jumped off the table and started down the hall, exasperation scored on his face. But before he could make it to the end of the hall, the doors swung open.

Around the Dogs, men stood to gawp. Romford craned his neck. But in his heart he knew exactly who was coming.

At the head of the group walked the Earl of Warwick: tall and elegantly dressed, with a mane of glossy hair, smooth skin and gleaming eyes, but his face set tense. Behind him sauntered a tall nobleman with a crooked nose. He wore a thigh-length leather coat, and boots printed with the skeletons of beech leaves, their toes tapered into long points. On his head he wore a bright-orange wig, made from the hide of some rare breed of cow.

Between these two came the prince. The sixteen-year-old heir to the English crown wore a doublet of exquisite dark green velvet, trimmed in gold cord, matched with a pointed cap of the same design. His knee-length riding boots were adorned with gleaming golden spurs. By his side he wore a heavy sword with a jewelled hilt.

'Fuck does that cunt look like?' breathed Scotsman. Romford felt a pang of defensive anger. But the prince swept along the tables and past Northampton, ignoring the earl completely and marching to the lectern. As he passed the Dogs, Romford tried as subtly as he could to catch his eye, hoping for a glance or a word: anything that might hint that the prince still remembered him. But all he caught was a waft of the sweet perfume he knew so well. Lavender and sandalwood. The scent drifted into his nose, filled his head and seeped into his soul. It made him feel half-mad with a combination of desire, revulsion and longing.

Romford reached into his arrow bag and pulled out two more pieces of the Host. He ate them and slumped at the table, staring straight down.

All around the room, the men were muttering about the prince's arrival. The Fleming Heyman nudged Loveday. 'Your prince is a great battle hero, I think?'

Loveday mumbled, trying to give nothing away. Heyman persisted. 'He escapes from capture? Holds the great blind king Johann's head as he dies?'

Scotsman leaned across the table. 'Where'd you hear that shite? He's a little fucking whelp who needs some sense whipped into him.'

Again Romford bridled. He wanted to stand up and shout –
to tell them all how little they knew of anything. But shouting
was quickly becoming beyond him. His belly was now full
of Host, and he found it was becoming harder and harder to
understand what people were saying.

To try and stop himself from slithering off his bench,
Romford spread his fingers wide on the table and stared very
hard at them.

He heard a dripping sound coming from the front of the
hall. He snapped his head upright and saw what it was. On
the cross above Northampton's head, Christ was writhing in
agony, trying desperately to close the wound in his side by
curling his dying body around it.

'Help him,' Romford whispered.

Loveday heard him. 'What?' he said.

'Help him.'

Loveday seemed to think Romford meant the prince, who
had now clambered on to the abbot's table, where Northampton
had been standing.

Romford pointed fearfully at the crucifix above his head.
Loveday looked in bafflement at Millstone, who put his arm
on the boy's shoulders.

'Maybe the heat?' he heard Millstone say.

Romford looked sideways through his fingers at the prince.

'Men!' the prince began. He had his hands on his hips. His
voice was thick and slow. 'I have something to ask of you all.'
He paused theatrically, nodding around the room.

'I need you...' He coughed a few times.

'...I need you to bring me a drink!' He cackled and slapped
his velvet-clad thigh.

The knights and lords standing around the table looked at

one another in embarrassment. Northampton, grinding his teeth, motioned to Sir Denis, who produced a silver cup and passed it to the prince.

Romford ground his own teeth too. He hated it when the prince was drunk.

The prince raised his cup, then squawked 'King Edward! Chivalry! Virtue! And wine!'

He drained the cup, tapped it upside down on top of his head, then tossed it sloppily in Sir Denis's direction. The knight shot out a hand and caught it.

The prince laughed his high-pitched laugh, then wandered out of the refectory, leaving the other lords staring after him. Northampton was white with fury. Warwick also looked grim. But the third nobleman, with the wig and the bent nose, wore an amused smirk. He clapped his hands approvingly.

'Who the fuck is that?' growled Scotsman.

Millstone answered Scotsman. 'Sir Hugh Hastings.'

Romford ground his teeth some more. Drool dribbled down his chin. He wiped it with his sleeve, then rested his head on his hands and tried to concentrate on his breathing.

He sat there like that for some time, as the nobleman called Hastings launched into a lengthy speech explaining how, while the king's huge army had been burning a swathe through Normandy, he had led a smaller war band made up of Flemings and English, attacking French-held towns in the area where they now stood. He seemed at pains to point out that his mission had been the more difficult, and that he alone understood how to fight in the region where they now found themselves. He slyly disparaged the other lords around him.

The speech went on for a very long time, and as it did, the room grew restless. A pair of archers picked their noses and flicked sticky balls of snot at one another. At the back of the hall, men got up from their seats and formed a line to piss in the corner. Yawns and even snores could be heard.

Yet Romford did not mind the length of the speech, for as it went on, he felt the worst of the Host's effects pass. By the time food was served, cold and gluey, he was well enough to put some of it in his mouth, and even engage in the small conversation around the table. The other Dogs seemed to assume that it was hunger and tiredness that had caused him to act strangely, and he felt relieved that no one seemed to understand what he was doing.

'Got too used to the easy life, did you, lad?' said Thorp, chewing a piece of cold yellow gristle and licking his fingers. 'Long day's ride took it out of you?'

Romford smiled and nodded.

Thorp gave him a friendly punch on the arm and poured him some ale. Before long, Romford was feeling his mood improve once more. The prince was out of sight, and although it had been painful to see him, and the Host had gripped his mind in powerful fashion, Romford felt pleased at having survived. What was more, though he had been scared at first to see Christ writhing on his cross, and though the confusion the Host produced had been difficult to manage at times, he could not deny that he also enjoyed the thrill of having his senses so wildly rearranged. The experience was very different to eating powder. But his compulsion to repeat it was just as strong.

So by the time the Dogs turned in to sleep in a stable loft, bedded down in scratchy straw above the shifting, farting horses, Romford had even started to tell himself that the tactic of eating Host to dull the pain he felt when he saw the prince might be a good one.

That seemed just as well. Hastings in his address had said that the next day the archers in the company would accompany him and 'Prince Edward of Wales, heir to our mighty sovereign king', while the rest of the men would go with Northampton and Warwick.

Romford believed he had found a way to cope.

5

The Earl of Warwick with many others rode to the market at Thérouanne, and they came upon many men-at-arms stationed there to protect the market, namely the bishop of Thérouanne with his retainers...

Chronicle of Henry Knighton

The company set out from the abbey towards Thérouanne divided into two groups, as Hugh Hastings had demanded in his speech at the refectory. The three archers went with Hastings and the prince. Loveday, Millstone and the Flemings joined a column led by the Earls of Northampton and Warwick. The archers set off on a looping march behind a set of small hills, to bring them out at the city from high ground. Everyone else marched cautiously in double file along the track that led down to the city's suburbs. The earls and their knights led the way, their flags dancing in the light breeze and their horses dropping shit the men behind had to step over.

Loveday and Millstone tucked into the middle of the earls' column, with Scotsman and the Flemings behind them. The three Dogs all wore old-fashioned kettle hats and heavy, tightly padded overshirts. Loveday had slung a sleeveless coat of mail over his. It was hot and heavy, but he was glad to have it. They were in unknown, hostile territory, with little patches of woodland on either side of the road. 'Perfect cover for an ambush,' muttered Millstone, and Loveday could not disagree.

The earls clearly felt likewise, as from time to time Northampton's knights dropped back along the column, barking instructions for the group to watch their flanks. Loveday and Millstone nodded respectfully as they received their orders.

But when the knights passed the same word to the Flemings, Loveday heard them snigger and call jokes to one another in their own language. He heard Scotsman's booming laugh too. The Scot was swigging from a wineskin, with Hircent patting him on the back and egging him on.

Loveday frowned at the Scot, who blinked guiltily, half looked at Hircent, and then back to Loveday. 'Sorry, mate,' he said, his voice slurring, and handed the wineskin to the big woman. Loveday shook his head and turned back to the road. Behind him he could hear Jakke and Nicclaes laughing. He assumed they were making fun of him. But there was no time to take the matter up, for about half a mile ahead, Thérouanne was now coming into view.

It was a small city, run round with poorly maintained walls, missing whole sections of masonry in places. There were one or two guard towers with arrow slits in their sides. Outside the walls stood a few shabby suburbs – little more than thatched shacks and uneven outbuildings. There was no sign yet of the market. But within the walls soared a vast cathedral, built in the modern style, with several spires, a large central tower, buttresses supporting the walls from the outside and sweeping sheets of brightly coloured glass. 'It really is a bishop's city,' said Millstone.

Loveday agreed. 'And there's the bishop.' Ranked in two

lines outside the main gates of the city was a force of men roughly the size of their own. At their head was a figure dressed in crimson. The Bishop of Thérouanne was passing a crozier to an attendant and being helped on to a large black horse by a pair of servants.

They had come to a place where the land opened out on either side of the track. Pasture rolled down towards where the bishop had mustered his force to defend the city. Northampton's rough voice rang out along the line. 'Form up and hold our position here.' He sounded clipped and irritable.

The earl's knights went around organising the men into ranks – the riders on the flanks, and those on foot, including the three Dogs and the Flemings, in lines between them. As the reality of battle crept closer, Loveday found his breath was coming quickly, and despite the cool of the morning, his back was damp.

'Doesn't matter how many times...' he started to say to Millstone. But before he could finish his thought, Hircent blundered into him, throwing one of her heavy, fleshy arms around his shoulders. She stank of sweat. Hircent put a flask of wine under Loveday's nose. 'Never charged a city before?' she asked.

Loveday gave a thin smile, accepted the flask, took a small swig of the wine and handed it back. 'Once or twice,' he said. In truth, it was more times than he could remember.

'Loosen up, then,' boomed Hircent. She released her bind on his shoulder, but then wrapped her arm around Millstone instead. 'What about you, Curly?' And she ruffled Millstone's tightly sprung hair. 'You know how to handle yourself? Or you want me and my boys to show you how it's done?'

Millstone stiffened slightly, but stared straight ahead,

ignoring Hircent and fixing his gaze on the tower of the cathedral in the city ahead. Scotsman reached over and dragged a laughing Hircent away.

Ahead, the Earls of Warwick and Northampton had been conversing intensely with an envoy sent from the bishop's men at the city gates. Their conversation came to an abrupt end. Loveday saw the envoy bow in the saddle and wheel his horse back towards Thérouanne. As he rode off, Northampton called after him, '…and he can put that crozier away, by Christ, or I'll stick it up his arse and snap it off!'

He turned towards the men ranked behind him, at last with a grin on his face. 'Men! Who's ready to raise hell again?'

A roar went up. Somewhere a trumpet blasted and drums began to beat. Northampton called over the din, 'We go as one! On my call! Riders charge, the rest of you fuckers catch us up or go to hell!'

Loveday had seen the earl in this mood before, and felt a familiar shudder as the grey-haired nobleman stirred dozens of men by the sheer force of his voice.

He turned to Millstone. 'How many towns *is* it now?' he said softly.

Millstone shook his head very slightly. His face was set as hard as granite. 'Too many,' he said. 'But still we keep coming back for more.'

The first time Loveday ever charged a city had been nearly twenty summers ago. A little before he met the Captain. He was fighting one of his first campaigns during the early years of King Edward's reign: part of the chaotic border skirmishing in the last days of the war with the bloody-minded rebel-king

Robert the Bruce. It had been thrilling. Loveday remembered the sense of being part of a great war beast with thousands of legs, and many sharp spines, rumbling and roaring towards its prey.

He remembered feeling then as though his body were made of iron, that no sword or lance or axe could pierce him. That he was the fastest, fittest and fleetest man alive. With that confidence surging in him, he had fought well, hacking and slashing and dodging blows. The English had been held at bay that day, and retreated without taking the town; the war was turning the way of Bruce and the Scots. But it had seemed to Loveday for a time afterwards that he had found what it was God had put him on Earth to do, which was to bear down on towns with other groups of hard young men, screaming bloody threats and brandishing his short sword above his head, sincerely ready to carry them out.

Now as he set out at a run with the rest of the footsoldiers, he felt that same flush of excitement: a fluttering in his stomach, and sharp prickling in his fingers as his feet pounded across the greasy grassland.

Yet as he tried to keep pace with the rest of the group, he also realised that his legs were no longer as strong and fast as they had been twenty years ago. Or even two years ago. The men had barely run fifty paces before his lungs were heaving and he felt bile rising in his throat. The blood pounded in the veins at his temples and his belly flopped around. His kettle hat fell over his eyes and he had to keep pushing it back. On either side, men were passing him, some elbowing him in their eagerness to get by. Scotsman and Hircent went past him, then the rest of the Flemings, hooting and waving their spiked *goedendags* above their heads. Millstone gestured back at him, urging him to keep up. But the harder Loveday pushed himself, the heavier his coat and his weapon seemed to weigh. The older and bulkier he felt.

Ahead came a great crash as the knights and men-at-arms who had kicked their horses the hardest clattered into the first ranks of the bishop's defenders. Loveday heard whinnying and men's yells of effort and pain. Still he ran, but he was now slowing, and stumbling on the grass. He tried to let out his old war cry,

'*Desperta ferro!*'

Awake, iron!

But he could barely get the words out over his panting. He was among the last of the group to reach the melee – and when he arrived, he was at the back of a crowd of bodies heaving and swaying together.

He stood there for a moment, braced and holding his sword up before him, but saw no one to fight. Before him were only men of his own company. He felt as awkward as he had at village dances when he was a boy, looking for a partner and finding no one to take his hand.

Then he spotted Millstone. The stonemason was to the right of the press of men, barging his way through the melee. He was already well stuck into the fight, as unyielding as he had been throughout the eight years Loveday had known him. Millstone moved with brutal force and speed. He seemed to have an uncanny sense for where the next attack was coming from. As Loveday stood casting around for anyone to fight, Millstone was slamming his elbow into the nose of an armoured man who made a lunge for him with his visor raised. Next he whirled around and crunched his hammer into the chest of a young Frenchman who stood holding a spear as if he had only picked it up for the first time that morning. The hammer shattered the young man's ribcage. He crumpled to the grass.

Millstone wiped his brow and waved Loveday over. Exhilarated and relieved to see his friend fighting so fiercely, and relishing the chance to work together, Loveday started towards him.

As he did, a short man-at-arms came striding out of the press, with a long sword raised high. The man was protected from his head to his feet with plates of metal armour and sheets of mail links. From within the pointed, visored bascinet covering his head, the man-at-arms shouted something. What emerged was a metallic jumble of words Loveday could not make out. But it was clear what they meant. He had spotted Loveday and was intent on doing him harm.

He had been looking for someone to fight. Now someone had stepped up.

Loveday swallowed hard. Fear suddenly coursed through him. He let it. Long experience told him that fear was no bad thing.

It's a sign of your body trying to stay alive.

Readying himself for the attack, Loveday set up in the stance he had adopted so many times before. Left foot forward, his right planted with knee bent, and his weight loaded over his right knee. He gripped his short sword tight in both hands, his fists tight around the hilt, knuckle of his right thumb brushing his cheek, and the blade levelled straight out in front of him.

Sweat rolled into his eyes. He blinked it out. As he did, the weak sunlight of the grey early morning caught the burnished cuirass that covered the man-at-arms' chest. And Loveday saw what he needed to see.

Protecting the man-at-arms' neck at the top of his breastplate was a wide mail collar of tiny round links.

Perhaps it was borrowed. Perhaps he had won it in a tournament. Perhaps it was an heirloom from some grandfather who had fought one of Loveday's ancestors in another age of endless war.

Loveday did not know. Nor did he care. What he did know was that the mail was much too large. As the man-at-arms brandished his sword, twisting and setting it towards Loveday, small gaps opened at the neckline, exposing skin that was covered only by cloth to stop the armour chafing.

Hit him there, and he's dead.

The fear that washed Loveday's body changed to something just as familiar. It was a sense of awful certainty. The clear understanding that if he did what he knew he could do, he could take another man's life. And save his own.

The man-at-arms shouted something else. Again, Loveday did not understand it. But he nodded grimly. Then he stood up straight and made a prod with his short sword towards the knight's bascinet.

It was a weak, inexpert, pointless prod made from a deliberately vulnerable stance. No skilled fighter should ever have made such a useless thrust. But Loveday did not want to look like a skilled fighter. He wanted to look like a peasant. A yokel. A bumpkin. He wanted to goad the man-at-arms into doing something stupid.

And he did. Through the tiny eye slits in the bascinet, the man-at-arms looked at Loveday. Though he could make out nothing of the man's face, Loveday knew what the man thought *he* saw: an out-of-shape, panting, ground-down, older opponent, whose skill in combat had long since deserted him. A beaten-up veteran. An easy kill.

He was almost right.

But not quite.

Sniffing easy prey, the man-at-arms swung his sword as hard as he could in a flashing arc aimed at Loveday's upright chest. It was a lazy stroke. Too hard, too eager. Too certain of success.

Loveday was certainly old and fat and out of breath. But he had been in many more battles than this man-at-arms. He had invited the sword stroke. He saw it coming even before the man-at-arms knew he was going to deliver it. And in the time it took the man to wind up his wild slash, Loveday was able to duck, crouch, then dive forward, throwing all his weight into the man's metal-plated legs.

There was nothing elegant in the way he hurled himself. In truth, Loveday knew he must look like he was flopping belly first into a fish pond on a hot day. But Loveday had never cared how he looked when he fought. And he knew one thing for certain. Whatever he looked like, the bundling forward of his considerable weight, combined with the momentum of the man-at-arms' sword stroke, was all it took to knock him clean off his feet.

Now Loveday worked on pure instinct.

The man-at-arms hit the ground on his side. Loveday scrambled to his hands and knees. He clambered so he was sitting on the man-at-arms' chest. One of the man's arms was pinned to the ground by his own body. Loveday had the other arm squeezed between his legs.

From inside the bascinet, the man's muffled shouts became frightened, disoriented squeals. Loveday knew he had him.

But then the man-at-arms gave a huge thrash of his legs and bucked Loveday off.

Suddenly, Loveday felt fear shoot through him. He thought he had pinned the man. Now he had lost him.

They both scrambled to their knees. Loveday still had his short sword. He brought the hilt of it down as hard as he could on the man-at-arms' helmet. The man yelped inside. He flailed at Loveday with a gauntleted hand and managed to hit him in the throat. Loveday retched, slipped on his side and rolled away. Then he pushed himself to his feet.

The man-at-arms had done the same. They were back to where they started.

Loveday was breathing hard. The man-at-arms' mail collar was now hanging at an even worse angle than before. His weak spot was wide open. But Loveday had missed it, and now he would have to work his way towards it all over again. He cursed and set himself, trying to summon energy from somewhere within him.

As he and the man-at-arms circled one another, each preparing to lunge, Loveday tried to cast desperately for anyone he knew who might come and help him.

Then he almost yelled in happiness. Over the man's shoulder he saw Millstone striding towards them, hammer raised, and eyes fixed on the man-at-arms' unsuspecting back.

He nodded at Millstone – old code between them.

I'll keep him busy. You hit him.

But as he did, he saw something that made his blood freeze.

For an instant the crowd behind the marching Millstone seemed to part, and through the clear air, away in the distance, Loveday caught a glimpse of something strange.

Something he knew.

A face.

The sight knocked all the air from his lungs. It made him gasp and loosen his grip on the sword.

The gap in the crowd behind Millstone closed up as quickly as it had opened, so that all Loveday could see now was the swaying press of fighting bodies.

The face was gone. Yet he knew he had seen it.

Millstone was no more than ten paces away. But Loveday couldn't wait for him. In the space of a heartbeat, Loveday made a decision. It was the easiest decision he had made since they arrived in France.

He looked at the circling man-at-arms, whose confidence was returning. Heard him muttering threats once more, instead of scared squeals. He looked at Millstone preparing to deliver a death blow to his back.

He looked at the rest of the melee around him.

Then he broke and ran.

Loveday ran past Millstone. He dodged knights lashing at one another from their saddles, axes and maces and swords splintering shields and crushing armour. He passed footsoldiers grappling – some swiping with clubs or blades, others rolling on the damp turf, growling and cursing as they tried to beat each other into submission. He ran past loose horses snapping and rearing and whinnying, their eyes wide in panic as they struggled between their instinct to flee and a lifetime of training in which treats and beatings had created in them a duty to fight.

Though he was still out of breath, and his legs were agonisingly stiff from gripping the man-at-arms, the bright urgency of what he had seen gave him a new burst of energy.

And with every heavy thud of his feet, he became more certain of what he had seen.

Who he had seen.

It had been the face of the man who had taught him everything he knew. Who had been a friend and guide, leader and teacher. Who had saved his life on more than one occasion. Who had led him and the Dogs into many dark and dangerous spots, telling them always that they should leave no man behind.

The man who had one day in the winter of 1344 announced to them that everything they thought about war was wrong, that a new world was coming in, and that he was leaving *them* behind to find it on his own.

The Captain.

When Loveday finally stopped running, he was more than two hundred paces from the battle outside the city, standing by the side of what seemed to be a small granary, propped on low wooden stilts, not far from the main gatehouse in Thérouanne's walls.

This was where he was sure he had seen him: leaning against the granary wall, his piercing eyes scanning the action from the half-shadows. Doing what he always did best.

Watching. Thinking. Calculating.

Now, though, there was no one there. The granary was deserted. Loveday turned around in a full circle. He walked the length of the building and back. He dropped to his knees and peered under it. There was no sign of anyone at all.

Suddenly feeling frustrated and exhausted, Loveday leaned against the long wooden planks of the granary's side wall. His chest was still heaving from running, and sweat was dripping down his face like tears, pooling in his whiskers and dripping from his chin. He was bleeding from somewhere, though he did not know where.

Loveday sank for a moment to his knees, threw down his kettle hat and wrestled his way out of the heavy mail vest. Once he had it off, he pushed his kettle hat back on his head and rested the point of his short sword on the ground. He unstoppered his flask and took a huge gulp of the thin ale inside, then he looked back towards the battle, which seemed to be reaching its fiercest point.

He wondered if this was what the Captain had seen. Wondered what he had been looking for. What he had made of it all.

He found himself hoping, pathetically, that the Captain had seen him overpower the man-at-arms. Had been urging him to plunge his short sword into the man's neck. He hoped he had been proud to see him, still fighting, despite the heaviness of age and time that rested on his back.

He hoped. He could not know.

For a few seconds, Loveday closed his eyes and leaned against the granary. He let his breath slow. He let his pulse calm. He tried to think.

A hand clapped him on the shoulder.

A voice said: 'You're dead.'

When Loveday opened his eyes in fright, Sir Denis was standing in front of him, the visor of his helmet pushed up. He looked clean and relaxed. His sword was sheathed at his side.

'Didn't fancy it, did you?' said the big knight.

Loveday's shock was replaced by confusion. 'Fancy it?'

Sir Denis' eyes flashed dangerously. 'Nerve failed you,' he said. 'I know. It happens. One day you've just had enough. You can't take another moment of it. So you run. Or was it pride? Come all this way, you think. See everything we've seen, and end up run through the guts here, outside the gates of some nothing town in the middle of nowhere?'

Loveday shook his head as he realised what the knight was suggesting. 'No, Sir Denis. I wasn't – I didn't run—'

'Didn't run? So what was it? Angels pick you up and drop you here to pray for salvation?'

As usual, it was hard to tell whether Sir Denis was being quite serious. Loveday could feel his own face reddening. 'I saw someone,' he said lamely.

'Good for you. Nice girl? Big tits?'

Loveday frowned. 'It was an old friend. Well. Someone I used to know. I was fighting a man-at-arms. He had a hole in his armour. And then—'

Sir Denis raised a finger and put it to Loveday's lips, as though he were a babbling child. 'You don't need to make excuses,' he said. 'I've seen it happen more times than you could imagine. How old are you now?'

Loveday bridled at the knight's patronising tone. 'Old enough to know I'm no coward.' He puffed out his cheeks. 'Sir Denis – have you seen a man here? With one leg, maybe? Watching the battle. Observing, I mean...'

'Have I seen a man with one leg... maybe?'

'Aye.'

'I have not. But you have?'

'Aye. No. Well, I did – and now...'

Loveday tailed off. Embarrassment and hopelessness now

vied for position in his heart. Sir Denis held his gaze, smiling his usual inscrutable smile. By the city gates, screeches and war cries mingled with the clang of metal.

A squire of no more than twelve summers ran up to Sir Denis with a bundle of straw pulled from a thatched roof in his arms. He stared impudently at Loveday.

'Where now, sir?' the squire asked Sir Denis, still eyeing Loveday.

'Here seems as fine a place as any,' Sir Denis answered. The squire nodded. Sir Denis introduced Loveday. 'This is FitzTalbot. He ran from the battle, but not *away*. He's looking for a man with one leg. Have you seen any?'

The squire smirked. 'There'll be one or two with legs missing over there by the time the day's out,' he said, pointing back towards the fighting.

Sir Denis laughed. The squire grinned and set to work packing the dry tinder under the floor of the granary. Several more boys around his own age came and joined in.

Satisfied that they were well occupied, Sir Denis folded his arms and looked back towards Thérouanne's gates. The fighting appeared to be coming to its end. 'Bishop's off,' Sir Denis said. He pointed and Loveday saw the crimson robes of the prelate billowing behind him as he and a few attendants galloped away from the melee and over the open countryside. 'Perhaps he saw a one-legged man too.'

From under the granary, one of the squires sniggered. Loveday felt suddenly annoyed. Sir Denis caught him before he snapped. 'I'm jesting you, FitzTalbot,' he said. 'I don't know what you're really doing here, and I won't ask any more. But I'll tell you two things I do know.

'First, my men are about to burn these suburbs to the ground, so unless you want to be roasted like a hog, you should find somewhere else to be.

'Second, I think I *observe* your mate with the hammer coming looking for you. So you'd better get your story straight for him.'

Just as the knight said, Millstone was approaching the granary. There was a fresh graze on his face. A clump of skin and blond hair clung to the head of his hammer.

'Loveday,' he said. 'What—?'

Sir Denis raised a hand to both greet and quiet Millstone. 'FitzTalbot here has seen an old friend of yours – or so he says.'

'What happened?' said Millstone.

'The Captain,' said Loveday. 'I saw him.'

Millstone pursed his lips. Several times he looked from the gates of Thérouanne to Loveday's imploring face and back again.

'Here?'

'Aye.'

Sir Denis drummed his fingers on his thigh. 'I hesitate to be discourteous,' he said. 'But I truly do need you both to fuck off.'

'You really want to find him?' asked Millstone.

Loveday nodded.

Sir Denis sighed. 'Look. I don't know what or who you're looking for, but my bet is that if he's not here, he's gone over there.' He pointed out one of the patches of woodland the Dogs had marched past earlier that day. 'Clear of danger. Lots of cover. Nice and private. There's a fine beech tree in there that I've been pissing against all morning.'

'Let's go,' said Loveday.

'I don't know,' said Millstone.

'Go on, get out of here,' said Sir Denis. 'Before I tire of this.'

The two Dogs set out walking towards the woods, an awkward silence hanging between them. Behind them, dry timber crackled, then roared, as Sir Denis's boys put the suburbs of Thérouanne to the flame.

6

They went through the country burning and laying everything waste, until they came to Thérouanne... they entered the church of Our Lady and smashed the images; and then they did worse...

St Omer Chronicle

A s the Earls of Warwick and Northampton marched their men out from the monastery towards Thérouanne that morning, Hugh Hastings and the prince had taken their band of archers in another direction, along a path that wound up and down a small cluster of hills. Tebbe, Thorp and Romford were in this half of the company.

Tebbe and Thorp walked along at an easy pace, swapping occasional comments about the countryside around them, and trying to shake the weariness of the last day's march and a poor night's sleep from their eyes.

Romford walked behind them. From time to time, he took little sips from his flask and winced at the foul taste. Determined to eat Host during the march, but worried he would be caught doing so, he had shoved all his remaining pieces of the fungus inside the flask and steeped them in ale. They had combined to produce a tincture. The brew tasted horrible, like mud and a man's seed. But a few drops on the tongue had a powerful effect.

Unfortunately, at that moment their most alarming effect was to have conjured up Father.

The old priest clung to Romford's shoulders as they followed the winding track that ran around the hillsides. He wrapped his broken legs around Romford's waist, hanging on his back like a pack of jagged, splintered bones. He rested his head on Romford's shoulder, his rank tongue lolling from the missing section of his jaw. He ground his bony hips into the middle of Romford's back. His poisonous breath curled like smoke from his nostrils. It made Romford feel sick.

Father watched Romford drink and started thrashing. 'Wet my mouth, boy,' he snarled. 'Warm your old friend's throat.'

'No,' whispered Romford. He spoke as softly as he could, hoping no one would hear him. 'It's not good for you.'

Father flew into a rage. He jerked and slammed his groin angrily into Romford's back, thrusting at him like a rutting boar. Romford tried to ignore his tantrum, but Father's writhing was making his own body jerk as he walked along.

Thorp turned around. 'What you doing, lad?' he hissed.

With some effort, Romford held his body still. He gritted his teeth and held his breath and managed to get a few words out. 'Nothing,' he said. 'I'm just... I'm... cold.'

Tebbe also turned and stared at Romford. Romford was not sure if he could see Father or not.

'Cold? Try being dead,' said Father bitterly. 'And tell those two to turn their ugly nebs around, or I'll have their guts for my sausages.'

Brown spittle frothed out of the smashed holes in the priest's face. It leaked down Romford's shoulders. It chilled his flesh where it touched.

Romford forced a smile he hoped would convince Tebbe and Thorp to pay him no more mind. They looked suspicious, but eventually turned away. Relieved, Romford took another sip of the tincture. It made the sky flash orange and purple, like evil lightning. This seemed to scare Father. He dug his icy claws into Romford so hard they felt like knife points. But for a moment he was still.

At last, Thérouanne came into view. Hugh Hastings called the archers to a halt. From the hillside where they now stood, they could see the small city – a warren of tiny streets amid rooftops and spires, all crammed around the huge edifice of the cathedral. They could hear a commotion coming from somewhere beyond the curve of the crumbling stone walls. Smoke was rising from roughly the same area. A buzz, half excitement and half confusion, ran around the archers.

Hastings held his helm under his arm. With his other hand, he adjusted the orange cow-hair wig on top of his head. 'Archers,' he said, 'this is our target. Thérouanne. As I explained to you last night...'

A voice called out from among the archers. 'It's already burning! We've missed the fight, sir!'

Another, less respectfully, shouted: 'Shame!'

The prince, standing apart from the group gazing quietly at the city, now strode towards them and spoke over Hastings. The visor of his great helm was raised. The top was adorned with three exotic bird feathers. Romford noticed the prince's helm was burnished black – just like the small helmet he himself had worn at Crécy, which he had offered the prince after the battle. The prince had snubbed him then, and mocked him. *No prince wears black armour.* Clearly, he had changed his mind. Yet at the same time he no longer seemed to recognise Romford, or if he did, he paid him no attention whatever. Romford felt his heart stab with a strange mixture of anger and longing. He took a sip of the tincture and it went away. He watched the feathers on the prince's helmet flutter.

'We have missed nothing,' the prince cried, his voice high and cracking. 'Quite the opposite. Thanks to the excellent order of battle devised by myself and Sir Hugh, we have allowed the advance party to prepare the way for our chastisement of the city proper.

'Now it is our time to advance. We will march as one. In the city yonder you will find a market. We will requisition the supplies there for the good of my father's army in their advance on Calais. We will take whatever action I deem necessary to take possession of those supplies. And by Christ's arms, we will suffer no resistance.'

Father opened one eye and looked at the prince suspiciously. 'Nasty little worm,' he leered. 'Coward. Suckspittle. Pintle-licker. Slug.'

'Shut up,' Romford hissed. 'He's doing his best.'

Thorp, standing next to him, elbowed Romford hard. 'Stop that groaning,' he muttered. 'Christ, boy, try and keep it together. We're moving out. Just stick with me and Tebbe and don't shoot anyone unless we tell you to.'

Father laughed bitterly. '*Listen to me,*' he mimicked. '*Stick with me. Shoot what I shoot.* What do they know? You shoot what you want to shoot.'

He pulled the shaft of Romford's bow, which was slung across his shoulder, and let it go. The bowstring twanged and the strong, slender length of yew slapped into Romford's back.

'Shut up,' said Romford again. But he could say no more, because at that moment, Hastings adjusted his wig one more time and waved the company of archers down to Thérouanne, around the walls towards the gatehouse.

They went down at a jog, keeping pace with Hastings and the prince on horseback. When they reached the gatehouse, they found the rest of the company – the men-at-arms and footsoldiers – in complete control. Half a dozen or so men lay dead on the churned ground. Their sightless eyes seemed to stare at Romford in disbelief. The rest of the defenders had fled and Warwick was directing the opening of the gates. Smoke from fires lit in the suburbs was gusting around, uneven clouds blowing on a limp breeze.

The earl broke off his work to greet the prince and Hastings, but he did not look happy to see them.

'Thank you for joining us, Your Grace,' he said, nodding around the prince's company. The muscles in the corner of his large square jaw were tight. 'And with so many archers, who might have helped us had you been here earlier.'

The prince had removed his black helm. He tossed his shiny hair. 'Quite so, cousin. We can never have too many archers. Indeed, I have sent to my estates in England and Wales for more,' he said. 'Perhaps you should do the same. If your finances so allow.'

The earl stiffened at the prince's sneering tone and his familiar use of the name 'cousin'. He turned back to the gates. His team of men-at-arms had hacked through the simple bar that was holding them closed. Warwick called on the assembled men to ready themselves to enter the city. But the prince interrupted.

'Seize everything and give no quarter!' he cried. 'Let the fate of these rebels be a warning to all who would defy my father!'

Warwick looked exasperated. Romford saw the Earl of Northampton shaking his head. But from the archers around him and a good many of the others in the company, there came whoops and war cries. The men-at-arms by the gates looked uncertainly from the earls to the prince. Warwick shook his head wearily then gave them a signal to proceed. The gates slowly swung open.

Father, still clinging to Romford's back, started yelping and baying. Romford tried to ignore him. He looked around for the rest of the Dogs. Tebbe and Thorp were still close by, but among the crowd he could not see Loveday, Millstone or Scotsman, nor any of the Flemings. He felt very uneasy.

Romford took a sip of his tincture.

One of the dead men on the ground blew him a kiss.

The street from the gatehouse led straight through the city to a square beside the cathedral precincts. The company jogged along it, watched sullenly from doorways by the townsfolk who had remained inside while the bishop went out to defend their homes. Few dared say anything. Once or twice, stones were hurled from alleyways. But the throwers quickly vanished and no one bothered to pursue them.

Romford went with Tebbe and Thorp. Hastings had ordered all the archers to proceed with bows nocked, watching for ambush. Like the older men, Romford had obeyed the instruction. But with Father on his back and the shape of the world shifting in unpredictable ways, he found it hard to concentrate.

They arrived at the market to find wooden stalls stacked high with goods of all sorts. Some of the stallholders had stayed to try and bargain with the English. Others had fled. The company began to help themselves. Greedy hands seized woven baskets full of the harvest's first ripe apples and pears, along with sacks of flour and dried beans. Others carried off large smelly round cheeses, bristly pig carcasses, and cages containing scolding hens and honking geese. One group of archers raided a table stacked with dripping honeycombs, holding them over their open mouths and letting the sweet sticky liquid dribble all over their chins.

With the tincture pinching his guts, the sight of all this fine food made Romford queasy. To make it worse, Father began whispering into his ear. 'Not fair, boy, is it?' he purred. 'Never had this when you were a lad. Water full of bugs and whatever dry crusts you could scavenge, wasn't it?'

Romford tried to swallow down bile. 'Beatings if you didn't eat whatever slop the old man served up,' breathed Father. 'While this lot ate like kings. What did you do to deserve that? Does God not like the look of you?' He prodded Romford above the kidneys with his cold, sharp claw.

Although he knew it was a bad idea, Romford pulled out his flask and sipped more tincture. White and brown piglets in a makeshift wooden pen swapped faces with the men guarding them. The men grew snouts and squealed. Romford started sweating. From somewhere on the other side of the market there came a loud crash. It startled him, and he spun around to see Scotsman and Hircent competing to lift stalls and turn them over. Romford turned away. High above the city, the cathedral's spires stretched and twisted like fingers on a vast stone hand.

Another dig in the kidneys from Father turned Romford's attention back to the market. The dead priest was now cursing a merchant selling expensive spices on the far side of the market. 'Hark at that rich cunt,' said Father. 'Probably doesn't even speak English. What's that muck he's selling? Places they grow that shit the heathens fuck their sisters and worship the sun.' He hawked. Phlegm and spit drooled out of his flapping jaw. 'Why should he be rich and you and me have starved our whole lives? Where were the merchants in Paradise? You know what they say: "When Adam delved—"'

Romford tried to block out Father's ranting. He looked around desperately for Tebbe and Thorp. But suddenly everyone in the company had their faces. He gasped and Father reached around and rubbed his eyes for him. When he opened them, he saw the real Tebbe and Thorp. They were arguing with the Flemings Jakke and Nicclaes, who were also tipping stalls over. Scotsman had given up, and was sitting on the floor in the middle of the crowd, laughing so hard that tears were running down his face.

'Never mind them,' said Father. He tugged at Romford's bow. 'Get that rich cunt,' he said. 'Get him good.'

Somewhere, a piglet was squealing. Romford wanted to ignore Father, but the priest would not let up his nagging. So eventually he did as Father said, and took his bow from his back. 'Good boy,' said Father. 'You get him.'

The merchant's stall was a hundred paces away across the crowded market. Romford drew his bowstring and sighted, looking with his right eye along the arrow shaft. As he steadied his arm, he saw the arrow's path light up as a thin golden beam.

Heads and bodies kept tumbling through the arrow's path.

Father was now gripping him tight around the back. Romford felt a hard bulge press into him from Father's hips. The priest was making a peculiar noise, halfway between moaning and humming. When Romford listened carefully, he realised it was a song. A tune he had heard before.

I am the wolf
without a pack

For an instant, the crowd cleared and the arrow's light shaft shone straight at the merchant's chest. He wore a doublet of soft black velvet. Using the light of the golden beam, Romford could see through the cloth. He could see the iron links of the thin mail vest the merchant wore for protection in the streets. He watched the currents of the air through which the arrow's light shaft passed. Allowed for the cross-breeze and adjusted his aim by a hair's breadth. He knew that at this range and with his draw strength, the light gauge of mail would not stop the arrow from sinking into the merchant's chest. The arrow would pass between the sixth and seventh ribs on the left side. It would bury itself a handspan inside him. If he did not die when it went in, he would die when it was pulled out.

Father grew tense with pleasure on Romford's back. His bulge throbbed. The priest kept humming, but the tune slowed, until its rhythm merged with Romford's heartbeat.

I am
The wolf
I am

Out of the corner of his eye, Romford saw the prince

ordering men to set loose a pen of sheep. Hircent tipped over a fruit stand. Apples rolled and bounced around the marketplace. They moved impossibly slowly. As though God had ground time almost to a halt.

He heard only the beat of his heart.

The wolf
I am

He took one last deep breath. Relaxed his thoughts. His eyes. His lungs.

He let the arrow go.

As the bowstring sprang smoothly forward, it gave a sweet chime like the ring of a bell. The arrow slid from its caress with almost heavenly grace. Romford moved no muscle save those in his fingers. He just watched the arrow glide along its golden path.

The sky flashed orange and purple again, but gently now, like the flickering of a church candle.

Father sucked air. It rattled through the holes in his face. Romford felt a warm wet patch spread on his lower back.

He kept watching the arrow. Ahead of it, he saw the merchant's eyes open wide. Saw him turned sideways, pulled by his arm. Saw him yanked hard out of the path of the arrow.

Romford was confused. This made no sense. He knew the shot had been perfect. He had measured the wind, the line, the gap in the crowd. He knew the arrow travelled too fast for the merchant to have seen it.

He thought about it for what felt like many hours. But he could not fathom it. So there was nothing to do but turn his attention back to the arrow, and watch it complete its markless path, through the place where the merchant had stood.

The arrow slammed into a great earthenware pot.

The pot vanished. In its place erupted a vast cloud of yellow dust the colour of meadow buttercups. It was a spice, thought Romford, as he watched it billow. A spice that formed a cloud and settled its colours on the faces and clothes of everyone for yards around.

It was beautiful.

For a second, Romford stood transfixed by the dust. He felt the first grains of spice dust begin to tickle his nose. He smelled sunshine and young men's hot necks and backs. In that moment he did not mind that he had missed the merchant.

He did not mind anything at all.

But then time started moving quickly again. And Romford realised that Father minded. That the bodyguards attending the merchant minded.

Father started screaming and beating Romford with his horrible fists, clawing at his back with his nails. The wet patch he had made was cold and nasty on Romford's spine.

The men ran towards Romford, pushing through the chaotic marketplace. Coming right for him.

The bliss Romford had felt at the sight of the yellow spice now gave way to panic. He slung his bow on his back and scampered away through the market with Father on his back, beating him like a rider in a horse race.

Keeping his head low, Romford slipped under stalls and past grabbing hands. He scrambled under a low fence and found himself on a cobbled street. He bolted along it, trying to keep his footsteps light. He went through an open set of ornate wooden gates and across a wide courtyard. Then he scuttled towards a vast stone edifice, at least a hundred feet high, decorated with thousands of carved stone figures and faces, some of them solemn and others grotesque. Saints and bishops and demons and imps. Above the door itself was Christ's face: solemn and sorrowful, his hair curling to his shoulders and the tip of his nose missing. The saints and imps grinned as they saw him arrive. Christ just looked sad.

Romford went towards the huge wooden door beneath the faces. The stone men hallooed and jeered as he went in.

'Stop it,' Romford said aloud. 'Leave me alone!'

Now he was through the door, his words echoed massively, twisting and turning and booming back at him. For a moment, Romford assumed this was another odd effect of the Host. But then he realised that his voice was echoing because he was inside a cathedral. Its cavernous belly was lined with soaring stone pillars and its walls were painted with biblical scenes. The chapels lining each wall were stacked with gold and silver trinkets: candlesticks, jewelled chalices and statues.

Romford could hear other voices somewhere in the middle of the cathedral, behind a painted wooden screen. He paid them no mind. He was more worried about the merchants' thugs, whom he feared might be tracking him, and might not respect the sanctity of his hiding place. He skipped behind a pillar and kept very still. He tried to wait for a long time, though he knew he had lost the ability to know what was a long time and what was a short one.

'Maggot,' Father was muttering sullenly, on his back. 'Toad. Can't even shoot straight.'

Romford felt a surge of anger. From the chapel nearest to him, a life-size statue of a doleful-looking woman in a blue headdress raised her eyes and glared at him. She snarled in Father's voice. 'No good for anything but fucking,' she said.

Suddenly furious, in one swift action, Romford pulled his bow from his back again, nocked an arrow, drew and shot. The statue was so close he barely needed to pull the bowstring. The arrow laid no gold path before it now. It simply flew into the woman's head. There was a spray of stone and plaster as the head shot off the woman's shoulders and clattered on the floor.

Father screamed with evil laughter. 'You just killed the Virgin,' he howled. 'Knocked the bitch's head off.' He started lurching around again, chattering like an ape.

Still angry, Romford dropped his bow, reached around over his own shoulder and grabbed Father by his thin arm. He pulled as hard as he could. With a ripping sound, he yanked Father off his back and hurled him to the stone floor of the cathedral, where he lay, helpless, a tangle of shattered bones and mottled, bruised skin. Father's laughter turned into shrieks of fury.

Romford covered his ears. 'Leave me in peace!' he shouted. 'Go back to being dead!'

Then he ran away from his tormentor, heading deeper into the cathedral. And as Father's shrieks receded, Romford felt the effects of the Host finally starting to taper off. He shook his head violently, trying to hurry his senses back.

As his head cleared, he realised he knew the raised voices coming from the middle of the cathedral. Guttural Flemish echoed off the high wooden roof beams, tangling with the raucous, drink-soaked bellow of a Scot. Romford was exhausted, but elated to hear these familiar tones. He set off towards them. His boots clattered on the stone pavement. His heart skittered.

He rounded the wooden screen and came to a vast stone altar hung with a cream cloth trimmed with rich crimson.

He saw the faces of his friends.

Tebbe and Thorp were there. They both had their arms folded and looked tense.

Scotsman was there too, but he was in a very different mood. In one ring-covered hand he held a silver chalice filled with priests' wine. He was swaying and laughing as he swigged from it, the glossy liquid dripping from the tips of his beard. He raised his chalice in recognition as Romford arrived, laughing even more uproariously as he boomed: 'Youngster! All the merry saints in Edinburgh's finest fuck-den, where've you been?'

Jakke, Nicclaes and Heyman were also drinking from holy cups. Nicclaes looked sheepish. Jakke had the same dumb, vicious look in his eyes as ever.

Romford saw what they were laughing about.

On top of the altar was Hircent. The enormous woman was squatted with her legs wide, her elbows pressed into her knees and her archer's trousers around her ankles. She was grinning.

Romford met her eye, then dropped his gaze to the black, matted tangle of her cunt. He tried to understand what he was seeing.

Beneath Hircent's naked arse, something round and flat glinted silver. Hircent reached down below her and adjusted it, then returned both her elbows to her knees.

She grunted.

'Get it out, for the love of Christ,' Scotsman cheered.

'Stop distracting me,' said Hircent. She heaved and grunted once more.

'God have fucking mercy,' growled Thorp. He turned away.

Still squatting on the altar, Hircent let out a noisy stream of piss, which spattered the platter and the cream cloth and splashed up into the air around her. 'Ahhhh,' she groaned. Then the piss stopped, and Hircent took a sharp breath. She held it in and strained. Her cunt twitched and her face went the colour of a plum.

She laid a thick turd on the cathedral's Eucharist platter.

A few small wisps of steam rose from the huge shit, and Hircent stood up in triumph. Her legs briefly framed a golden crucifix behind her. The last of her piss dripped on it. Then she leapt down from the altar and wiped her arse on her sleeve.

Scotsman, Hircent and the Flemings roared with drunken laughter.

Romford turned. All the bile the tincture had produced in his stomach suddenly rose at once. He bent double and vomited between his feet.

When he lifted his head, he saw that Hircent had pulled her trousers back up. She and Scotsman were clapping one another on the shoulders and howling with mirth.

'The body of Christ,' roared Hircent. She crossed herself.

Scotsman wiped tears of laughter from his eyes. He pointed to Romford. 'He's been sick,' Scotsman said.

Hircent turned her bloodshot eyes on Romford. 'Dirty bastard.'

Tebbe and Thorp were shaking their heads in disbelief. Tebbe took Romford's arm. 'We're going,' he said.

The smell of the shit on the altar was wretched. Romford

thought he was going to vomit again. Tebbe pulled him away, back towards the door to the marketplace.

They had barely gone ten paces before they ran into a large knight. He rounded the pillar by the wooden screen, stopped and surveyed the party around the altar.

'Christ on the fucking tree.'

Sir Hugh Hastings saw the shit and the puddle of vomit, the drunken Flemings, the near-legless Scotsman and the archers making to flee. He exhaled hard through his nose. 'There's always one mob who goes too far.'

The knight removed his orange wig from his head for a second, turned it around on his hand, brushed dust and spice out of it and replaced it over his shiny bald pate. 'What in the fuck are you lot doing?' he asked. All the smoothness of the voice he used in the prince's company had vanished. A rasping East Anglian accent came through.

'Actually,' he said, 'I don't give a fuck. Just get out of here now, and go and find the constable.'

'Northampton?' said Thorp.

'The very same,' snapped Hastings. 'Big Bollocks Willikin wants all his men back. Right now. He isn't happy.'

The Dogs and Flemings looked at Hastings blankly. He sighed again, as though he were telling village dolts how to build a hayrick.

'You don't know? Some sneaky bastard has murdered his favourite knight. The big one. You know: square jaw, long hair. Always got something smooth to say.'

Thorp gasped. 'Sir Denis?'

'Aye, that's the one,' said Hastings. He stared aggressively at Thorp. 'What? Was he your boyfriend?'

Thorp glowered insolently, but eventually lowered his eyes.

'Exactly,' said Hastings nastily. 'Good decision. Now get out of here, all of you.'

As the Dogs and Flemings shuffled past him, Hastings looked at the filthy altar.

'Fucking disgusting,' he said, to no one in particular. 'Pack of fucking animals.'

7

Milord Arnoul d'Audrehem... was dismounted and broke his leg and was captured...

St Omer Chronicle

It was almost too easy.

The young woman from Valognes had spotted the small wood by the road the previous night.

It offered perfect cover. Beech and ash, the trees grown tight around a small water pool, still holding their leaves. She camped overnight beneath the canopy and dreamed strange dreams.

In one she was back at home, sitting by the fire and laughing as her father played a conjuring trick, hiding a coin and pulling it out from behind her ear. In another she was a wolf, padding on sand. Licking saltwater and recoiling from the taste.

In a third she saw a prince. The prince. The one who had treated her so badly in the time that marked the end of her old life and the start of this, her new one. He was standing beside a river, looking at her with contempt. 'Catch me if you can,' he kept saying.

'Catch me if you can.'

She woke at dawn, and watched the men tramp past her on their way down to Thérouanne.

As they moved, she tracked them with her crossbow sights. Thought about picking one or two of them off as they went by. She judged against it. Better to let them fight first. Let them wear themselves out before she took her pick of what was left.

There was no need to rush anything. After all, she had been tracking them long enough. Three months ago, the English had come into the town she grew up in, killed her family, driven her friends away and burned all the houses. They had captured her. The prince had abused her. She had escaped.

Now she was taking her revenge.

Revenge on the English devils who had destroyed everything she loved. Revenge on the French devils who had done nothing to protect her.

While the devils did battle in front of the city gates, she passed the time studying her reflection in the polished steel blade of her knife. Or rather, the knife she had taken from the round-bellied Englishman. One of the few who had helped her.

She stared at her own face, warped and misshapen by the blade's curve. She barely recognised it. Her hair, once so long and fair, was now filthy and cropped boyish-short. Her dark eyes sunk deep. She had never carried much weight – growing up in Valognes, her sweet, gentle mother teased her for looking like a skeleton, and gave her the pet name Squelette. Her weeks on the road had drawn the skin of her face even tighter across her cheekbones. Her nose protruding like a snout.

Squelette.

Her mother was dead now. They were all dead. And she would avenge them.

Squelette sat on her haunches and peered around a tree trunk, watching the knight she had shot a little while earlier writhe on the ground.

He was in a lot of pain. Sweat plastered his shoulder-length blond hair across his face. Dried blood and leaf mould and woodland soil dirtied the blue-and-white diagonal stripes of his tabard. He was moaning in French, with a hard northern accent. She guessed he must be from somewhere near here.

Not that it mattered. They were all the same.

She assessed her work. She had done well. One bolt in the back of his left knee, in the tiny gap between armour plates. That had brought him down. Then, when he had ripped off his gauntlets and cuisse to examine the wound, she had shifted angles, and shot him again through the right hand, pinning it to the ground. Squelette smiled. That was hard to do.

Over the knight's moans, she heard something else.

Feet crunching in the dirt. Two sets. They had entered the wood from the way of the city. Now they were moving cautiously, as though they expected others.

She kept low, loading her crossbow as she went. She crept from tree to tree until she came to the stricken trunk of an old felled beech. Pressed herself behind it and watched.

It was him.

The round, sad, kind man whose knife she had. He was with one of his friends. The one with the brown face and curly hair.

She eased the crossbow down and watched.

The men were talking. They spoke tersely, as though some quarrel hung between them. They seemed to be looking for something. They were so focused on their work that they almost fell over the knight she had shot.

The knight groaned. He looked up at them. He realised they were English.

'Help me,' he said, speaking to them in their own tongue, although not very well. 'Make me your prison.'

The kind man and his friend talked among themselves quietly so she could not hear them. She already knew what they would do. It was not the same as what she would do. But they were not her.

'Make me your prison,' said the knight again.

Squelette left them to it and crept off through the woods. By the time they had the knight up, his arms slung across their shoulders, eyes rolling back with the agony of moving, she had gone.

But she had not gone far before she found another knight.

This one had his helmet off and his back turned to her. He was pissing against a beech tree.

She shot him in the back of the neck and he went down without a word. She leapt on him as he fell and cut his throat from ear to ear.

When she yanked his head back to let his hot blood splash into the woodland floor, she smelled his long brown glossy hair. The scent took her somewhere she had been just weeks before. A camp. A tent. A darkness. Her inside the tent with the English prince. Him outside standing guard.

She knew him.

Squelette licked his blood from her fingers and felt a thrill at its metal tang. Not so different from the blade that had freed it. She left him face down and slipped off into the trees.

As she went, she took a moment to congratulate herself, and to thank God for giving her this mission. Vengeance was underway. There was one less knight in the world.

It was a start.

PART 2

PIRATES

October—December 1346

8

The ships guarding the port of Calais captured about twenty-five [English supply] ships...

Chronicle and Annals of Gilles li Muisit

'Fuck off, cripple.'

The tavern on the edge of the village was loud and rough. The green thatch of the roof was slimy with damp. Wood smoke and dirty laughter drifted from deep within, through window shutters hanging loose on their hinges. There was music, too. The sharp whine of a shawm. Voices singing out of tune and time. Some fool sea dog piping up a shanty.

A crooked sign suspended on chains above the door creaked in the stiff sea breeze and advertised the tavern's name.

Le Pot d'Étain.

The Tin Jar.

It was just as the Captain remembered it.

But he did not recognise the sailors who sat around the table outside the tumbledown building, and who had watched him hobble along the sand track that led to its door.

The Captain eyed them cautiously. He stopped before he reached them, and leaned on his stick. It was a relief to stand still. He had slept that night beneath a hedgerow, waking damp and cold with thorns in his skin and spiders in his boots.

Since watching the battle at Crécy, he had been walking for many days.

He had taken a long route, keeping well away from the English army as it moved through the countryside. Detours had added many miles to his journey. His belly gnawed. The wooden cup of his false leg had chafed the skin on his stump raw. Its leather straps bruised and pinched his hips.

The ravaged skin of his face, half-eaten by the plague he had caught from his bellyful of river water, burned even more than usual.

He nodded his head in greeting and spoke French, trying to match their dialect. 'God bless you, brothers,' he said. 'I've come here for a drink. A meal if there is one. Nothing more.'

The smallest of the sailors leered at him, a cruel smile playing at the corners of his mouth. 'No drinks for cripples.'

'A meal, then. I've been walking all morning. I have a few coins. I'll pay.'

'No meals for cripples.'

The Captain nodded slowly. 'Then all I'll trouble you for is a seat by the fire inside, to rest before I travel on.'

The small sailor rose from the creaking bench. He took a couple of paces towards the Captain and blinked wet, red-flecked eyes as he spoke. 'There's nothing here for cripples. We don't want no bad luck. Turn around and limp away, or by St Andrew's bloody fishhooks, you'll be hurt even worse than you are already.'

The Captain shifted his weight and leaned again on his stick. 'I'm not sure about that,' he said. 'Where is your master?'

'Not sure? Fucking hear this, boys!' The small man sneered at the Captain. 'We have no master.'

'I think you have.'

'You deaf as well as lame and ugly? We have no master,' said the mean-faced sailor again, and he took a few more paces towards the Captain, coming close enough that the Captain could smell mackerel and strong drink on his breath. 'Now fuck off before I—'

Before he could finish his sentence, the Captain put all his weight into his left foot, raised his stick, threw it up, caught it by its base, and whipped it through the air. He hit the sailor with the stick's heavy, curved handle.

The connection was perfect. The stick was stout, its shaft cut from seasoned blackthorn. The Captain had chosen it carefully. He had commissioned it from the finest craftsman in Paris. The same man who had made his leg.

The same man who had sawn his old leg off.

At the top of the stick, a handle was carved from a separate piece of wood, spliced expertly into the shaft. This handle was smoothed and fitted comfortably to his right armpit. It was half as heavy as the shaft, so that when the Captain swung it, the stick cut through the air with the balance and weight of a knight's mace.

The handle hit the small sailor's left temple. The sailor gasped as though he had been plunged into icy water. Then he went down, silent and hard. The Captain knew he had judged the swing well. He had felt the skull crack. It was not enough to kill the man, but he would have a headache every day for the rest of his life.

The sailor's friends stood up from the table. They seemed uncertain what to do next.

The Captain flicked his stick up, caught it, and rested on it once again. He inspected his work. The sailor lay face down on the damp, gritty sand of the path, his legs twitching. He was slowly pissing himself.

'A drink. A meal. A seat by the fire,' said the Captain. 'Would you deny a poor cripple that?'

The reply came from a thickset man who had watched everything from the door of the tavern. Even as a silhouette in the gloom, the Captain knew who it was. The man wore his shoulder-length greasy black hair tied in a knot at the back of his head. His sun-wrecked face was crossed by scars. He carried a curved knife with a jewelled handle in his belt. A beautiful piece, prised from the dead hand of a Saracen many years ago, kept sharp enough to slice falling silk.

The pirate Jean Marant stepped outside the doorway of the tavern and grinned at the Captain. His gold-studded teeth caught the thin light of the overcast morning. 'Beating up my men, Captain? That's a way to announce yourself.'

The Captain looked long and hard at Marant. 'They told me they didn't know you. So I didn't think they were your men.'

'New recruits,' said the pirate. 'Still breaking them in.' He motioned his men to sit once more. Marant looked the Captain up and down. Then he stepped forward and embraced him hard, pulled back and kissed him on the forehead. 'I heard you were dead, but I didn't believe it.'

'When I heard I was alive, I felt the same way,' said the Captain. He steadied himself after Marant's forceful hug.

Marant nodded. 'Your face looks worse than mine. But here it is. And just in time. You heard your countrymen are moving on Calais?' He jabbed a thumb towards the coast.

'The English? I've been tracking them all the way.'

Marant spat. 'We cleared out our last safe house there a

week ago. First Guernsey and now this. Your King Edward seems unusually ill-disposed towards the noble profession of piracy. He's fucking things up for us.'

The Captain shrugged. He held Marant's gaze. 'Or maybe not.'

A grin spread across the pirate's face. 'God bless you,' he said. 'Always walking towards trouble.' He glanced at the Captain's stick and stump and held up his hands. 'No offence meant.'

'I hear worse.'

'I can imagine. Want to tell me why you're here?'

'There's a supply convoy coming to restock the English army. I assume you know that. I assume you're planning to rob it. I want to help. Then I want to make you a proposal.'

Jean Marant broke into a laugh. 'A proposal? Of what sort?'

The Captain shook his head. The sailors at the table were listening to every word he said. 'Not now.'

'Aye. Well, come inside and get yourself fed and warm and you can tell me later.' He turned and beckoned the Captain to follow him into the smoky tavern. 'God's flesh, it's been a few years. You're lucky I was here. The men won't usually let a cripple cross the threshold. They consider it unlucky. Did Dogwater here mention that?'

The Captain laughed as he walked around the motionless body of the small sailor. 'Dogwater said something about it.

'But I think I've changed his mind.'

An hour later, once the Captain had eaten and dried his damp clothes by the fire, he and Marant set out for the shore, where a few lopsided houses cut through by a single track of sandy mud were what passed for a village. Marant sent his men – a band that had swelled to several dozen – on ahead, so he could follow at the Captain's pace. Slow. The Captain noticed that Marant seemed unbothered by the time. Now and then he glanced at the sun's position, watching it slowly lower towards the horizon behind the blanket drizzling of cloud above them. 'Not quite yet,' he murmured to himself, over and over. 'Not quite yet.'

And when they arrived at the beach – a thin sliver of pebble and sand, bordered by sharp rocks at either end to form a cove – the Captain saw that he was right. There was not a single vessel to be seen in the water that stretched out for miles ahead of them.

'I heard the convoy was coming in at high tide,' he said.

Marant shook his head dismissively. He picked up a piece of cuttlefish that lay on the sand by his boot. 'You never were a sailor. Tide won't come into it. They'll try to break through at sunset, with the light low behind them. Blind the defenders.' He flung the cuttle back into the sea.

At one end of the cove, his men were dragging their boats down the sands, towards the breaking surf. Marant watched them work with a critical eye.

'Philippe has galleys coming up from Dieppe. Genoese. Under one of the Grimaldi boys, if you remember those swarthy, stuck-up bastards. Last job before they fuck off for the winter. They'll do the intercepting. We just have to be ready to take the plunder.' He scanned the sea. 'And you can wager we won't be alone. You know how pirates are. Like sharks. Come sundown, every other salty bastard from here to Portugal will have smelled blood in the water, and they'll all be here, sniffing around the carcass.'

As Marant spoke, the Captain remembered names and faces. 'Who's still working?'

Marant squinted. 'Who was around when you were running your crew? Jean Balaart? The younger Jean, I mean. High-Tide Johnny? The Pach brothers – they had that fine ship, the *Sturgeon*. Any of those mean anything?'

'Aye.' The Captain pictured them. Thieves and throat-slitters all. 'It could be a busy evening.'

'It will be,' said Marant. He shouted to one of his men. 'Gombert, get a fucking move on!' Then he turned back to the Captain. 'Don't worry. When they get here, we'll be ready.'

The Captain had known Jean Marant for nearly as long as he could remember. They had always been in similar lines of work, although in different realms. They broke bones and stole things. Sometimes it was in the name of kings. At other times, it was in defiance of their laws. When he was a young man in the last days of the murdered king, the Captain had built his crew – the Essex Dogs, men called them – in London and the lawless port towns of England's south coast. At the same time, Marant had been building his crew in the ports on the opposite side of the sea. They had a vicious reputation. For taking no captives. For slitting throats and throwing men into the sea.

But they had never crossed the Dogs.

And now, after life had pulled them apart for a time, he and Marant found themselves back together. The Captain sat on the sand beside the lank-haired pirate and watched his gang ready a fleet of boats to rob a royal supply convoy. He felt a sense of peace.

'So,' said Marant, without looking directly at him. 'Are you going to tell me why you've come here? Where your leg went? Who swapped your handsome face for a gargoyle's? Or just what you want?'

The Captain shrugged. 'I'll tell you whatever you like, Jean. But as you know, I prefer to use a few words rather than too many.'

He paused. 'I left my crew.'

Marant laughed. 'I can see that.'

'They were good men. At least, some of them were. But they were content to do the work they always had done. Robbing, fighting. Risking their lives for pennies-a-day contracts. I thought there was something more. I went to work for myself. This war…'

'War is war,' said Marant.

The Captain shrugged. 'I thought this one would be different. I still do.'

'Last I heard, you were in Ghent.'

'I was.'

'Working for the London merchant. The one who ran the government that year. What was his name?'

'John Pulteney. Yes. And for others too. Some I knew. Some I didn't.'

'You were there when the Brewer of Ghent was killed? Van Artevelde?'

'I didn't kill him.'

'Who said you did? You just happened to be there when he died.'

'So did many others. Van Artevelde had the best protection of any lord I've ever known. A private army. The White Hoods.'

'If it were me, I'd have joined them and betrayed him from the inside.'

The Captain nodded. 'That would have been a good way to do it.'

'And if I had been the one *paying* someone to do that, I would have killed him straight away afterwards. Or tried to. Probably when I paid him.'

The Captain nodded. He saw the blackness of the night above the Pont au Change in Paris. The stars and the single lantern twisting as he plunged towards the river. 'That's about right, too.'

'Who did it?'

'*Them*. You know how it is. Who is in charge of anything, Jean? Pulteney's man was one of them. But he was working for someone else that night. A woman. I don't know who. It doesn't matter any more.'

'You didn't see them coming for you.'

'I was too impressed with my own work. I thought the hard part was done. Pride, Jean. It's a sin.'

'Don't you want revenge?'

'What does that even mean?' said the Captain. 'This isn't a fable. Some tale of heroes and dragons. It's God's world. The one you and I know—'

Marant broke off briefly, stood up and shouted more commands at his men as they rigged the boats on the sand. On the biggest, the men were fitting a sharp ram to the prow. He sat back down. 'Where did you hear about the convoy?'

'Merchants. They gossip. I listen. The traders know more about the war than anyone. They knew about the English invasion before anyone. When it happened, I came to see it for myself. I watched the battle. And now I've come to see what happens next.'

'Why?'

'Because the life of a cripple in Paris was beginning to bore me. And because this is where the money is.'

Marant laughed. One of his men brought over a pair of crossbows. Marant offered one to the Captain. He took the other, cocked it with no bolt loaded, squinted and pulled the trigger. The tough waxed string twanged. Marant lowered it, looking satisfied. 'Go on.'

The Captain turned his own crossbow over. It was a fine weapon, well maintained. 'And because this is what the war is really about. Not battles. Not knights and feats of arms. It's about ports and towns and ships and trade. And money. And merchants.'

'And pirates?'

'And pirates.'

'You haven't made me your proposal,' said Marant.

'I think you need someone in Calais. I think you'll be willing to share your profit with them.'

Marant flashed him his golden smile. 'Aye,' he said. 'I do. I would. But I haven't found anyone who'd want to be inside a siege city when they could be outside one. Have you lost your mind along with your leg?'

The Captain didn't answer. For a moment they sat in silence, listening to the gulls and watching Marant's men rig the boats. The thick grey cloud above them had broken up, and the late-afternoon light was sending the long shadows of jagged rocks across the beach.

'You know,' said the Captain, but before he could say any more, Marant suddenly stood, grabbed him by the arm and hauled him upright, thrusting him his crossbow and his stick.

'It'll have to wait,' said the pirate. He pointed his dirty finger out to sea. The first ships of the English convoy had appeared on the horizon. Marant led the Captain across the sand and helped him into the largest of the boats. He clambered aboard the same one and took up position at the stern, with one hand on the steerboard, as his men dragged the vessel beyond the breakers then jumped in and began to haul the oars.

Soon they were cruising into open water. As the long stretch of the coastline came into view, the Captain saw that Marant was right – from every cove and inlet, dozens of boats just like theirs were setting out in the direction of the convoy.

Up ahead, a fleet of large English cogs was moving steadily towards Calais. All flew the King of England's arms: leopards quartered with fleurs-de-lis. Several also bore the symbols of merchants. As the convoy came closer, the Captain saw that it was being pursued by a similar number of sleek, low-riding Italian galleys. The galleys were closing rapidly.

The little boat hit a wave and the Captain bounced in his seat. He gripped the rough plank of the bench he shared with two oarsmen.

When he looked to the stern, he saw Marant was staring intently at him. Keeping one hand on the steerboard, the pirate leaned forward and picked up his crossbow. He pointed it towards the largest of the English cogs and mimed pulling the trigger.

The Captain patted his own crossbow.

Ahead, the Genoese galleys had begun engaging the merchant ships, ramming them at speed and trying to burst holes in their fat, round hulls. From one, the Captain saw a pair of English sailors jump overboard.

Marant gestured to them. He drew a thumb slowly across his neck.

The Captain nodded. Marant took no prisoners.

He slit throats and threw men in the sea.

On the shore, spectators were assembling. A huge crowd. They stood on a rise outside the city and lined the beaches below. Knights and ordinary soldiers helplessly watching the carnage on the water. He assumed King Edward was among them.

Marant raised his fist and howled like a wild animal.

The Captain caught Marant's eye one last time. He pointed to himself, then to the city itself. Surrounded by an army on its three landward sides. Its harbour sheltered by a sandbank untaken by the English.

He knew Marant understood what he meant.

Take me there. Smuggle me in by moonlight. Let's make gold while the city slowly starves. Let's be there to make more gold when it falls.

Marant caught the thought. He shrugged. He tapped his head.

You're a madman. Just like me.

The Captain knew that he had a deal. He re-gripped the bench as the little boat pitched and swayed on the choppy sea.

He whistled a song he used to know.

I am the wolf...

He listened to the pirate howling as the English ships went down.

9

The King of England swore that he would not leave [France] until he had taken the town of Calais. He called the place where he and his host had set up their defences 'Villeneuve la Hardie' [The Bold New Town]...

Les Grandes Chroniques de France

Loveday and Scotsman picked a path among the thousands of tents in the English siege camp that had sprung up on the marshland stretching inland from the walls of Calais. They were heading for the centre of the camp, where the king's and lords' dwellings lay. It was slow, wet going. The soft ground, watered by tiny streams that criss-crossed the boggy fields, oozed under their feet. In places, the mire was knee-deep. The site was quiet – most of the men were taking cover from the drizzle or just sleeping under their timber-and-skin shelters. The stale odour of rotting rubbish and human waste already hung in the air.

'Mary Magdalene feeding the fucking donkey, this place stinks,' muttered the Scot. 'Hold on, Loveday.' The big man stopped, put his hands on his knees and breathed slowly, trying to calm his churning stomach. As usual, he was hungover. Loveday patted him gently on the back, as sympathetically as he could. The previous night, Jakke, Nicclaes and Heyman had announced that they were leaving and going home to Flanders. King Edward had issued an edict ordering Flemish troops to quit the English army, for the good of general order. There had been one too many brawls of the sort Scotsman had fought with Hircent in Wissant harbour. The lords wished for peace to be restored.

So the Dogs had seen the Flemish men off, sitting up with them by the campfire, sharing ale and a couple of wineskins. Scotsman and Hircent had been the last to sleep by many hours. Loveday had heard them chuntering away even as dawn was breaking. Hircent was not leaving. She seemed to regard the king's edict as a challenge, not a command.

'He wants me out, he can come and move me himself,' she said, fondling Heartbreaker.

Loveday, Millstone and the archers felt uneasy about her continued presence. But the Scot seemed to admire her defiance. The two of them carried on as usual by night, when the ale flowed. Drinking toasts as they told each other stories of old bar brawls they had known. Planning drinking sessions in other realms in the future. Rehearsing conversations they had already had half a dozen times before.

Having swallowed down the bile in his belly, Scotsman straightened up.

'Sorry, mate,' he said to Loveday. 'We can carry on now.'

Loveday patted him on the back again. 'Maybe go a little easier this week,' he said, as gently as he could. 'We could be fighting again any day.'

The Scot blinked blearily around the campsite, which stretched for miles, as far as the forests to the south. 'Fuck that,' he said. 'It looks like we could be settling in for a long fucking wait. Anyway, if there's trouble, we can just leg it, eh?'

He dug Loveday in the ribs. But the joke stung. Loveday reddened, and started to protest. 'I wasn't running away. I'm telling you, I saw him—'

'I know, I know.' The Scot backed down, too hungover to argue. 'I was only pissing around.' He changed the subject. 'Are you sure you know where we're heading?'

'Humph,' said Loveday, still needled. He pointed in the direction of Calais itself, the rectangular, high-walled, deep-moated city beyond the northern end of the campsite. 'Hastings said to meet him where the engineers are building the market hall, and he would make us an offer. Listen—'

He paused and the two men cocked their ears. From somewhere closer to Calais' towering walls came the sound of hammering and sawing. 'All we have to do is follow that.'

The Scot grunted agreement. But after a minute he started up again. 'You're sure this is worth it? This Hastings cunt strikes me as slippery,' said Scotsman. 'And as for that silly fucking rug he wears on his head...'

Loveday sighed. 'God knows I hear you. But do you know anyone else who's buying prisoners? Millstone and I have had no luck trying to sell him to anyone else. Northampton won't see me, because one of those wretched squires told him Sir Denis followed us into the woods, which got him killed... who knows when he'll ever pay us – if he even does. And you're running low on rings.'

The Scot looked at his fingers, where his collection was dwindling. Every few days he traded one of the rings he had plundered from Crécy's dead for another skin of wine or barrel of ale. He now had just eight left. 'I suppose you're right. How much do you think we'll get for him? I've never heard of this Artle... Arble...'

'Arnoul,' said Loveday patiently. 'Sir Arnoul d'Audrehem. I haven't either. Then again, how many knights are there? You'd need to be a herald to keep track of them all. Or to know one, anywise. In any case, we've got him and we need to sell him. Fast. We can't even afford to keep him fed.'

The Scot said nothing. They both knew there was nothing to say. Once he and Millstone had taken Sir Arnoul prisoner in the woods outside Thérouanne, they had brought him to the Earl of Warwick's doctors, who had managed to remove the crossbow bolts from his leg and hand. Then, having no place of their own to imprison him, they had lodged him with Warwick's guards, in the pool of other prisoners taken after the battle outside the city.

Yet to keep a prisoner was expensive, and Loveday was beginning to realise why the Dogs had never involved themselves in that sort of work before. 'If we strike a deal with Hastings today, we don't have to worry about him. We'll see what he can give us. You never know, it might cover everything we were supposed to have had by now.'

The Scot just shrugged. And the two men squelched on through the marsh together, dodging tent ropes and wooden stakes, and trying to close their noses to the smell of countless thousands of men, all too long in the field, inured to living among piss and shit and vegetable skins and the bones of the animals they devoured. All caught between their hope of an end and acceptance of their fate, which was simply to wait and try not to die until the ships came to take them home.

They walked until eventually the tents came to an end. And they found themselves in a new place: a vast building site, where a whole town of wood and thatch was being erected, faster and on a grander scale than Loveday had ever seen.

'This is it,' Loveday said, gazing around in admiration at what seemed to be an entire city under construction on the marsh outside Calais.

'And that's him,' muttered the Scot, pointing to where a restless-looking Hugh Hastings stood before the swarm of builders, engineers and labourers, occasionally spitting on the ground and fiddling with his ginger wig, awaiting the Dogs' arrival.

Hastings was alone, and spoke without courtly polish. He recognised Loveday straight away.

'Took your time, by God,' he said. 'Any later and you'd have found me gone.'

Loveday gave an awkward bow in apology. 'It took us some time to cross the camp on the marshes, sir.'

Hastings waved an irritable hand, batting Loveday's apology away. 'Well, you're here now.' He breathed hard through his misshapen nose. Behind him, an engineer working on the market hall dropped a hammer and cursed. Hastings put his hands on his hips. 'So. Shall we make a deal?'

Loveday opened his mouth to speak, but before he could, Hastings cut him off. 'Here's the thing. You've got a decent prisoner. How you pair laid hands on him, I don't know.'

'As it happens, sir, it was me and another of our men—'

Hastings looked incredulous at Loveday's interruption. Then he seemed to recognise Scotsman from the cathedral in Thérouanne. 'You,' he said. 'Now I remember. Spreading muck and filth all over the Lord's house is more your style, isn't it?'

'Hey,' began Scotsman, his red face flushing even brighter

than usual. But Hastings cut him off. 'Shut up and listen. I'm busy.'

'As I said, you have a good prisoner. But your timing is terrible. For one thing, you're late. Two weeks ago, the market was buzzing. The king's men were buying anyone you brought them. You could have stuck a coat of arms on a scarecrow and they'd have paid you a hundred pounds for it. The Flemish were paying. The London syndicates were over here paying, shipping them back to the Tower like cattle.'

He paused. 'But that was two weeks ago. And now the word is that the Tower is heaving. They're sticking prisoners in every castle in southern England. They've got them in Newgate, with the debtors and the perverts. And guess what?'

Loveday and Scotsman shook their heads.

'No,' said Hastings, 'I didn't think you were on top of this game. I'll tell you. None of them are making their money back. If I buy Sir Pierre Pintletugger from you, I'm doing it so that I can sell him back to Lady Pintletugger and her five little baby Pintletuggers for twice what I paid you, plus the expenses I've incurred keeping Sir Pierre alive.

'The trouble is, we've done *too* well. Not only have we captured Sir Pierre, but we've got half of his cousins and brothers too. Meanwhile, the other half had their faces hacked off at Crécy, and all their heirs are taking each other to court to scrap over their estates. Which means...?'

He looked expectantly from Loveday to Scotsman, then sighed.

'It means they're all broke. They can't afford to ransom Sir Pierre back. So the hundred pounds I paid for him is now merely an investment in Sir Pierre's favourite activity. By the time he gets out of jail and goes home, he'll be nothing but a skeleton with an extremely thin and shiny pintle, and I'll be in a cell next to him in Newgate doing time for the debts I've run up looking after him.'

Not for the first time, Loveday felt a little overwhelmed. 'Will the king—' he began. Sir Hugh snorted. 'No, "the king" will not. That's the other half of the problem. Look around you. What do you see?'

'A building site,' growled Scotsman. 'A big one.'

'Aye,' said Sir Hugh. 'Maybe you Scotch savages aren't as stupid as you are ugly. A very, very big building site.' He gestured around him so vigorously that his wig slipped off his head. He caught it and jammed it back in place. 'Opinions vary on what in Christ's name we're doing outside this wretched city, best known for harbouring pirates beyond the reach of any God-given law or authority. Be that as it may. We're here for a while.'

Loveday looked around him and once more took in the scale of the works that were underway. Beside the market hall there was what appeared to be a parade of shops, the first storeys of spacious lords' houses and municipal buildings. A street plan had been marked out with ropes strung between wooden stakes hammered into the soft marshland.

'Take it in,' said Hastings. 'And try to imagine what it's costing. His Grace King Edward has been calling it Villeneuve-la-Hardie – which means Bold New Town. A better name might be "Bankrupt-the-Country New Town". We've not yet paid for the campaign you lot have been on. I've been handing out royal money like there's no tomorrow to our Flemish friends. As I'm sure you saw, we just lost a whole supply convoy to the Italians, ably abetted by every pirate crew along the coast. All of which means our Lord by the grace of the Almighty King

Edward does not want to underwrite the ransoms of any more Sir Pierres.

'Or to put it another way, you boys are extremely lucky to have found me. Because I am going to buy Sir Pierre from you. Or as he likes to be known, Sir Arnoul d'Audrehem. And since I'm a generous man, I'm going to give you fifty pounds for him.'

Loveday's heart leapt. This was more money by far than the Dogs had been promised for their whole campaign. 'Sir, that's a very generous offer. My men will be—'

But Scotsman interrupted him. 'Fuck that.'

Hastings glared. 'Fuck what?'

'Fuck fifty,' said the Scot. 'We want five hundred. I've heard about lords being sold for ten thousand and more. You said it yourself, this is a top man. Give us five hundred.'

Hastings burst out laughing, then stopped as abruptly as he began. 'Have you seen the rocks above Calais harbour?'

Scotsman jutted his rank-bearded chin forward. 'No.'

'Well, go take a look at them, and once you're there, take a long high leap into the sea. I said fifty, by Christ, for all the very good reasons I've been at pains to describe to you.'

Scotsman's eyes flashed in a way Loveday knew all too well.

'Sir Hugh, we'd be glad to accept,' Loveday said.

'No we fucking wouldn't,' said the Scot.

Hastings rolled his eyes. 'Which of you two is in charge?' he asked.

'I am, sir,' said Loveday.

'And which of you two did I see abetting a grotesquely fat woman relieving her bowels on the altar of a consecrated cathedral?'

Scotsman fumed.

'Right,' said Hastings. 'Fifty it is. You can go and let Sir Arnoul Pintletugger know he's under my command, and tell the king's men at the guardhouse to send the bill for all his expenses to me. Or rather, to my lady.'

'Your lady?' Loveday asked, confused.

'My lady Queen Philippa of England,' said Hastings. 'Of whose household I was lord steward until duty diverted me. She'll be here soon enough. You'll like her a lot.' He drummed his fingers impatiently on the backs of his arms. 'Do we have a deal?'

'We do,' said Loveday, and this time the Scot said nothing.

'Thank Christ and all the saints,' said Hastings.

Then a thought crossed his face.

'Until then, since you've proven such accommodating business partners, I'm going to put one more condition on my offer. How do you fancy moving into one of these places next week?' He gestured at a row of half-built shop-front buildings on one side of the market hall. 'It'll beat catching foot-rot and roasting rats in a tent two miles yonder across the bog.'

Loveday and Scotsman glanced at each other. 'That sounds most agreeable, sir,' said Loveday. 'But what's the—'

'The snag? The thing you're going to mope about? The snag, by God, is that this row of buildings is marked out as a special, very necessary area of the camp. In it, you and your men will be overseeing one of the least reputable establishments that will do business here in Villeneuve, which will be owned in part by me.

'You'll get to meet some interesting people and some pretty girls. But the work may be rough, and you in particular—' – he jabbed Loveday in the chest – '—seem likely to endure a measure of misplaced heartache at the plight of the employees.

'Are you catching my meaning?'

Loveday had not the first clue what Hastings meant. Yet a beam was spreading across the Scot's face. For the first time since Loveday had shaken his huge friend awake that morning, he seemed genuinely happy.

'Unless I've got something arse about neb, Sir Hugh here is asking us to help him run a fucking brothel,' said the Scot, still grinning.

'Bravo,' exclaimed Hastings, clapping his hands together.

'Scotsman, no,' said Loveday.

'We fucking accept,' said Scotsman.

Hastings grabbed his wig with both hands and rotated it a full turn on his head. 'One victory apiece!' he said. 'I call that a successful morning.'

He clapped his hands again. 'We'll meet again very soon. Don't forget to pass on the good news to Sir Arnoul. Feel free to knock a tooth or two loose if he objects to the mention of my name. It won't affect his value too much.

'Now, if you'll excuse me, His Grace the Prince of Wales has requested my presence at Mass.'

Hastings nodded brusquely at the two Dogs. Then he strode off towards the campsite, where the grandest tents of vermillion and blue and green and white and gold cloth stood on the driest part of the marsh, and the arms of the English king, Edward, third of his name, were billowing in the salt breeze.

10

The King of England... made many attacks on [Calais], with stone-throwers, cannon, and other missile-throwing devices...

St Omer Chronicle

Ten days later, Romford stretched on his pallet and listened to matins bells toll across the strange wooden town. He rolled on to his back and rubbed his eyes. The bells had woken him from dreams. But he did not mind waking. The attic space in the eaves above the brothel was dimly lit, but it was warm. It smelled rich and woody. Tiny shafts of the new day's light were creeping through the hole where a ladder led down to the rooms below. The golden beams caught dust and curls of smoke. Scotsman and Millstone had been on duty overnight. Romford guessed they had kept the oven burning.

For a moment, Romford lay and enjoyed the comfortable gloom. Along with the distant bells, he could hear the steady breathing of the other men who slept in the attic with him: Tebbe, Thorp and Loveday. From further away came the snores and murmurs of the other men and women sleeping on the ground floor of the building. Invisible above his head, Romford heard the scratch of a rat burrowing around in the thatch packed on to the roof beams above him. Making a nest for winter.

When he had lain like that for a short while, the bells stopped tolling and Romford knew that if they did not rise now, they would be late. So he sat up, folded his night-blanket, stretched the stiffness from his fingers and shoulders, and felt around for his flask. The leather pouch was still a quarter full, though not with tincture. After what happened at the cathedral, he had tipped the last of it away. It was too powerful for him to control. And for all that it soothed his anxiety, he was sick of its rank taste. Of the visions that wrenched him between bliss and terror. And most of all, of Father. Shuddering at the thought of the old, dead priest who haunted him, Romford pulled the flask-stopper with his teeth, then swilled his mouth with herbed ale. Then he crawled across the attic floor and gently shook Tebbe and Thorp awake.

'It's time to work,' he said.

Tebbe had not been long in bed. He groaned. 'Already?'

'Sorry,' said Romford.

The thin archer coughed and dragged himself up to lean on an elbow. He sniffed his fingers. 'That was some night. What day is it?'

Beside him, Thorp yawned. 'Christ and all the archangels, Tebbe, it's Michaelmas. It's all you could talk about last night. You don't remember?'

Tebbe looked groggy. 'I do love Michaelmas,' he said.

'So we heard.' Thorp chuckled. 'I tell you, it's a good job that girl Margie doesn't speak much English. You kept telling her: "It's Michaelmas on the morrow, by God. Fucking Michaelmas! If our luck stays in, someone will bring us a goose."'

Tebbe considered this, trying to recall it. 'That does sound like something I'd say.' He rested on his side and let out a long, rolling fart.

'Happy Michaelmas to us all,' he said, and hauled himself out of bed.

Having roused themselves, the three archers slung their bows on their backs, pulled on their green-and-white caps, crept down the ladder and eased out of the front door of the brothel. When they left, Millstone and Scotsman were dozing with their backs against the oven's warm stone walls. Romford also spied Hircent, behind the curtain-door to one of the cells. She was lying face down on a sack mattress, with a girl under each of her meaty arms.

Out in the street it was a fine autumn morning. The lingering bank of grey cloud that had hung over them most days since the battle had now scattered above the sea and the low, bright sun that emerged made Calais' high walls and Villeneuve-la-Hardie's freshly cut timbers gleam. The sunlight glinted off the new paint on the sign Hircent had hung over the brothel's entrance. It was daubed with a picture of an animal grinning slyly, and emblazoned with words in Flemish and English:

Het Wolvenhuis. The House of the Wolf.

The siege town now seemed to Romford to be bigger than Calais itself. Almost as big as London. Every day, new wooden buildings arose on the islands of hard land in the marsh, built at astonishing speed by the king's engineers and the willing hands of the stalled army. As Villeneuve expanded across the marsh, it developed suburbs, connected by new roads and causeways, where the acres of tents were replaced by thousands of shacks and hovels. Some of the men had fashioned pigpens and chicken yards behind their new dwellings. Here and there were dotted churches, marked with brightly painted wooden crosses on their roofs. Romford found it was difficult to retain a sense of direction in its ever-growing warren of streets. But his daily work helped. He, Tebbe and Thorp had been posted by Hastings to the prince's ever-expanding retinue of archers. They were joined by dozens of other bowmen who were veterans of the great battle. But each day there also arrived a few more, recruited from the prince's lands in England. These newcomers spoke a broad mixture of dialects: some from Cornwall, some from Cheshire and others from the borders of Wales. What they had in common was that they could all shoot.

Fortunately for Romford, although they were called the prince's company, and all the men were dressed in the prince's green-and-white livery, the prince himself very rarely appeared with them. And the tasks given to the company were mundane. Most days they reported in shifts to guard the town's perimeter and gates, or headed out in groups of eight or ten along the coast road to make sure wagon trains bringing supplies from Flemish merchants passed along unmolested. It was quiet work. The king's scouts had reported that there was no new French army in the field, and brought back rumours that Philippe remained so mad with rage and grief that he was not minded to raise one. So for weeks the men had not loosed an arrow in anger. They organised tests of skill and bowmanship. More often than not, Romford would win these, unless he tried his hardest not to do so, for fear of making the other men in the company envious. Nevertheless, his reputation for pinpoint accuracy spread. So he did not mind the days they worked.

Tebbe and Thorp, however, often complained. This morning was no different.

'It's a fine life for those fuckers,' said Thorp, glancing back at the *Wolvenhuis* as they left it. 'Sitting around playing cross-and-pile with the girls all day.'

'Cross-and-pile?' snorted Tebbe. 'Cradle-my-pintle, more like. And Millstone with the missus and whelps at home.' Tebbe seemed momentarily to have forgotten that he had spoken often of the family awaiting his own return.

They carried on in this vein for some time. But before long, the sun warming their faces and the thought of the Michaelmas celebrations to come that evening seemed to drive the tiredness and bad temper out of them. They were soon joking with one another and comparing the talents and specialities of the Flemish girls Hircent had so far recruited, as they made their way to the usual assembly spot on the far side of Villeneuve.

The archers' mood lightened even further when they passed a gaggle of thin and dirty footsoldiers being marched across the town square by two burly knights. Each man carried a long-handled shovel. Their clothes, feet and faces were caked in dried mud. Romford recognised none of them, but he noticed that one of the knights in charge was the Earl of Northampton's attendant, Sir Adrian, who had been good friends with the late Sir Denis, whose murder in the woods near Thérouanne had shocked them all.

The other knight, whom Romford had never seen before, had smooth olive skin and a neatly trimmed beard that covered only his top lip and chin. He was elegantly dressed, fit, lean and strong, and he wore a thick gold chain around his neck. He was calling out to the men in a confident, rapid patter. 'Another fine day for digging, gentlemen. A fine day to bend your back and praise the Lord and soak up the flavour of swamp juice and stagnant water!' The filthy soldiers looked aggrieved, but no one answered him back. Once the group had passed, Thorp gave Romford and Tebbe an excited nudge.

'That was Toussaint,' he said.

Tebbe raised his eyebrows, impressed, but Romford looked blank. The name meant nothing to him.

'The tournament champion,' Thorp explained. 'They say he can somersault backwards in full armour.'

'Doesn't look like he's somersaulting anywhere today,' said Tebbe, with a grin. 'Looks like he's watching those poor, shitty-arsed bastards dig the ditch.'

The thought of digging made them wince. The ditch – a shallow moat that provided a line of defence around the camp – was the only part of Villeneuve that was not emerging at speed. A spell with the diggers was handed down as a punishment to runaways caught trying to desert the army, and to any other ordinary man who displeased the lords. It was a job to be avoided at all costs.

'Could be worse for us, by St Michael's brass bollocks,' said Thorp. 'If things had gone another way at Thérouanne, with Loveday...'

'Too right it could,' said Tebbe, catching Thorp's meaning and frowning. Then he lightened. 'Speaking of St Michael, I wonder if we'll have a goose...'

Thorp rolled his eyes.

The three Dogs were still laughing as they reached the gathering company of around two dozen archers dressed in identical green-and-white short-coats and caps, assembling near the start of the road that led towards the beach at Sangatte. Those who had been there a while looked excited, and were chattering among themselves. But before the Dogs could find out what was animating them, a deep, authoritative voice called the company to order.

It belonged to Sir John Chandos, the prince's steward, a composed man in the prime of his life, with a tightly curled beard that covered his enormously wide and square jaw. Romford knew Chandos a little, for during his time as one of the prince's squires he had reported to him. All that seemed a lifetime ago now, though. Romford was no longer a squire. He was an ordinary archer once more. He stood with the other archers and listened to Chandos speak.

'Welcome, men,' Chandos called to the group. 'And may the blessings of the archangel Michael be upon us all on this Michaelmas morning.'

His eyes flickered over the group. Then he said: 'Can any of you men tell me what St Michael looks like?'

Answers in various accents rang out.

'Wings, sir! And he carries them... whatch 'ou call...? Weighing scales!'

'Old Michael gives the devil a good hiding, sir! Sends the fiend packing back to hell!'

Tebbe called out too, his eyes gleaming. 'St Michael has a fiery sword, Sir John.'

At this, Chandos beamed. 'Quite right, whoever said that. A fiery sword. Have any of you seen a fiery sword in this earthly life?'

He paused for effect, like the narrator of some village mystery play.

'Nobody? Well, men, then I've a treat for you today. Another company will take our duties guarding the gates. We're going to go and have some fun where the siege machines are. Follow me.'

One of the prince's pages was holding a horse nearby, which Chandos now smoothly mounted. The archers followed him on foot for a half-mile or so, towards a place Romford had not yet seen: an area of the marsh outside Villeneuve's sprawl, where the ground was firm underfoot, and the archers had an unobstructed view of the soaring stone walls of the city, surrounded by their two deep moats. As they neared the land, Romford could see that the king's engineers had siege towers and large stone-throwing catapults there in various stages of construction, and in range of the walls. Most of these were of a similar design: tall, triangular frames fitted with ropes, winches and ladders, supporting a long hurling-arm. Others were outlandishly large crossbows strapped to wooden tables, which could be aimed towards the top of the city's walls.

Among all this was a set of smaller devices, each of which featured some sort of metal tube. Some of these contraptions were long and thin, the length of spears or knights' lances, which looked light enough for the engineers to pick up and handle. Others were squat and fat, and were mounted on carts. These looked extremely heavy, their tubes shaped like pears or vases: bulging fatly at one end and tapering to a narrow neck at the other. From around the tubes drifted a strange stink and puffs of sickly yellow smoke.

It was a stink Romford recognised. Just one sniff took him back in time. To the battle.

His memories of Crécy were in no better order now than before. A lot of them were fading completely. But there were certain things he recalled very vividly. One was the stink. As men had slashed and swayed and kicked and trampled one another, a new weapon none of them had seen before roared and flashed and gave off clouds of this same grim-smelling vapour, panicking the enemy lines and making the French horses rear in terror. Romford remembered the smoke enveloping the battlefield like fog. Coughing and wiping his stinging eyes. He remembered shooting an arrow blindly through it.

Romford shuddered. He glanced at Tebbe and Thorp, wondering if they felt the same. They looked intrigued, but not alarmed. Like the rest of the small company, they simply seemed excited by the sight of these weapons and eager to know what Chandos wished to show them. So Romford tried to put away his bad thoughts of the battle.

The men were now standing beside the strange metal tubes. The engineers who had been working on them had stood back, and Romford could view them more closely. They appeared to be improvised and even unfinished – as though they were being built to a design that was changing. Some were loaded with oversized arrows or bolts. Around others were lumps of stone and iron balls the size of a fist.

Chandos was preparing to address the archers again. 'Men,' the smooth-talking steward began. 'What you see here is a weapon that will change war forever.'

There were a few doubtful murmurs around the group. Chandos nodded indulgently. 'You think not?'

He held up an arrow and gestured with it towards a round tower built into Calais' walls. 'We have spoken of St Michael and his fiery sword. Would any of you care to shoot a fiery arrow into the city over there?' Laughter rippled around. 'Quite so. No archer in history would ever choose to shoot a burning arrow. Because?'

'You'd burn your bowstring,' called out one of the northerners. 'Or your bollocks.'

Chandos nodded. 'Inelegant but accurately put. Imagine, though, if we could control fire like St Michael, and use it to shoot missiles far greater than arrows, but with the same deadly accuracy. What then?'

As Chandos spoke, Romford felt a tickling in his stomach. Suddenly, the stink he had smelled at Crécy bothered him less than what the steward had suggested. He considered the possibilities.

'Would you like to see what I am talking about?' asked Chandos politely.

The archers cheered. 'I thought so,' said the steward. He clicked his fingers and an engineer handed him a lit taper. 'Take a few paces back, all of you,' said Chandos. 'Cover your ears and open your mouths.'

Then he lit a short piece of oil-soaked wool that plugged a tiny hole at one end of the fat, pear-shaped tubes, and moved sharply away from it.

Nothing happened.

With his palms flat on the sides of his head and his mouth open, Romford stared at the tiny glow of the wool plug and wondered if Chandos was jesting them, or if his trick had not worked. The rest of the archers did the same.

'It's fucked,' muttered one of the northerners.

Thorp elbowed Tebbe. 'Might as well have put a candle up the arse of your Michaelmas goo—'

He did not finish his sentence.

The fat tube erupted with a bang and a flash. It roared louder than thunder. Like all the demons of hell on the day of judgement.

As it roared, Romford felt as though he had been blown from his feet.

He felt the boom in his gut. In his bladder. He felt as though he were going to piss and shit. The roar made a lump in his throat. It made his ears chime as if angels were singing. He understood why Chandos had ordered them to open their mouths: if he had not, he was sure his skull would have burst.

As the roar's echo subsided, leaving only the ringing sound, Romford realised he had closed his eyes. When he opened them, everything seemed to be moving soundlessly and very slowly, shrouded in the stinking smoke. Then, as the world's sounds came back, Romford heard the whole group of archers coughing and spluttering.

At that moment, Romford realised that he was laughing. And not just laughing. His belly was heaving with mirth, contorting so hard he felt as though he might never stop. Most of the other archers were standing open-mouthed and vacant, unable to comprehend what they had seen and heard. Tebbe and Thorp were looking at each other in confusion.

But Romford understood. There was no sign of the arrow or stone the tube had hurled towards Calais' walls. But that made sense. The angle at which the engineers had set the thing on its cart was much too low, assuming they wanted to shoot at the top of Calais' towering walls. Whatever missile it had spat would have clattered harmlessly into the masonry, and would probably now be sinking in one of the city's two moats.

That could be fixed.

Romford could not take the smile off his face. Nor could he stop his exhilarated heart pounding.

He felt as though in one thunderclap he had glimpsed a new world. What had Chandos called these devices?

A weapon that will change war forever.

He said the words out loud. And when his eyes had cleared of his laughter's tears, Romford saw Chandos was looking right at him.

'Young man,' said Chandos thoughtfully. 'I hoped you in particular would like that.

'The prince has asked me to let some of his best archers test their sights and hands on this new device, which we call an iron pot, or a cannon. Any man in this group may have a turn. But perhaps you would like to be the first?'

Romford nodded dumbly.

Chandos brought him forward and began to explain exactly how this metal beast, too hot for any of them yet to touch, could spit its monstrous flame.

Romford hung on every word. Everything apart from the operation of this thing Chandos called a 'cannon' faded from his awareness.

He was thinking of nothing but angles, projectiles, concoctions of saltpetre, sulphur and coal and wool plugs.

He felt the same way as he had all those years ago when his brother first put a bow in his hands and showed him how to aim at tree trunks.

The same way as the first time he put powder on his gums.

Over the hours that followed, around half the prince's archer company took a turn at firing one of the cannons. They enjoyed the noise and the shock of the blasts, but after a while most had begun to drift away from the demonstration to find their friends and begin the Michaelmas celebrations.

Romford did not drift away. He stayed as long as Chandos and the engineers would allow him, waiting patiently so that he might try lighting each one of the iron pots in turn. As he did so, he studied the difference between each device, tried to figure out the best methods for aiming, taking into account the power of the cannon and the direction of the brisk sea breeze. He watched closely when the engineers packed the saltpetre concoction into the mouth of the cannon. He tried to imagine the effect an army might have if a row of competent iron-pot-men could detonate their weapons in such a sequence that they kept up a constant roar and volley of shots towards a target.

These thoughts delighted him. The ringing in his ears thrilled him. Although around his feet the marsh grass was dying back with winter's approach, the sulphur stink on his fingers was suddenly as pleasing to him as fresh-cut flowers in spring.

As Romford blasted away, up on the ramparts of Calais' walls a few curious townsfolk gathered, popping their heads over the battlements swiftly and cautiously to try and catch a glimpse of what was happening.

Once or twice, archers loosed off arrows in their direction, hitting no one.

But with his last shot of the day, Romford managed to aim one of the cannons so well that it spat a lump of iron against the stone wall exactly where the townsfolk were taking cover.

He timed it so that the missile hit the wall just as one of the citizens popped up his head. Broken masonry sprayed up and tore the gawper's face.

Although Romford was a hundred paces away from the wall and almost the same distance below, as he strained to see through the smoke cloud he saw the man clutch his bloody cheeks. Heard him shriek in shock and pain.

Romford nodded with interest. He reckoned he had blinded the man in at least one of his eyes.

By this time, Chandos, Tebbe and Thorp were the only

remaining members of the archers' company. They watched Romford work with fascination and amusement.

They cheered as the blinded man screeched.

'Happy fucking Michaelmas!' yelled Tebbe.

Fragments of masonry were still dropping from the place where the iron ball had hit the wall.

Tebbe tired of goading the wounded citizen and grinned at Thorp and Romford. 'Shall we get back to the whorehouse? A goose in my guts and a girl on my lap would finish this day off nicely.'

Romford smiled shyly. He was sorry to leave the cannon. But his fingertips were scorched and smudged with soot and his hair and body stank of the smoke. He bent over and wiped greasy black filth from his fingers on the dying marsh grass.

Chandos patted his back. 'We'll have you back here,' he said. 'Go and have some fun with your mates.'

'Thank you,' said Romford. And he ran off to catch up with Tebbe and Thorp, who had already set out for the brothel.

II

The English camp was furnished with sufficient provision of meat, drink, apparel, munition, and all other things necessary...

Chronicle of Raphael Holinshed

In the *Wolvenhuis*, Loveday stretched in his chair and enjoyed the appetising aroma of goose fat sizzling in the oven at the back of the room. Hastings had brought the geese around earlier that day when he came to collect his third-part of the brothel's profits. They were two big birds, not yet plump with winter's fat, but strong and meaty all the same, their throats slashed and breasts plucked to reveal the creamy yellow skin, naked and puckered and dimpled.

'For later,' Hastings had smirked. 'I hear there's a big night planned.'

Scotsman gutted the geese and readied them to bake in the oven, rather than turning them on the spit over the fire. The big man was the Dogs' best cook, and after weeks of preparing nothing but salt pork and beans he now delighted in having good food at his fingertips. He put the goose hearts, necks and gizzards in a pot with water, leeks and a handful of wild herbs to make broth for a sauce. He set their kidneys and livers aside to braise and spread on bread. Then he left Loveday instructions for minding them and went back to bed in the loft, where he and Millstone were sleeping the afternoon away, having shared the last night's watch.

With the two men slumbering, it was quiet in the brothel. Tebbe, Thorp and Romford were still out on duty with the prince's archers, and would not return before the nones bells marked the mid-afternoon. Hircent was out too. Loveday guessed she had gone to fetch the ale and wine for which she charged a penny a cup. Only two of the five Flemish girls she had summoned from Ghent were at work; the others would return when dusk approached. But no men had passed through since they had opened their doors at midday. So the girls loitered, bored, in one of the curtained cells that branched off from the main room where Loveday sat. They spoke softly and occasionally to one another in Flemish. Loveday had no idea what they were saying and could not see them, but he could tell their conversation was stilted, coming in starts, as though they did not know each other well.

As he sat and listened, Loveday's mind wandered. He pictured the girls behind the curtain, and tried to remember their names. There was the younger one with the shy smile, whom Tebbe liked: pretty but for a lazy eye, she wore her light brown hair uncovered and in a thick braid, which she rolled and pinned at the back of her head. She called herself Margie – though the fact that she could hardly pronounce the name suggested to Loveday that it was not her own. She was probably little older than twenty summers. The girl with her now was half as old again. Taller and bony-limbed, she kept her hairline plucked high and severe, and covered the scarred skin on her cheeks with pale brown paste. Though older, she seemed less certain of herself and deferred to Margie. He could not remember her name. Something with an A. Aggie, perhaps? Or Annie?

The names brought to his mind his wife. Alys. He tried to think of her as little as possible. But she still surprised him from time to time. And now, warm and comfortable, Loveday closed his eyes and found Alys's face dancing across his vision. He remembered her looking around as he opened the door to their tiny house, wiping flour from her face with the back of her hand. Happy to see him. Careful not to ask what he had done to earn the handfuls of coin he tossed into her skirts when they sat together by the fire. He traced every tiny detail of her smile. Felt the softness of her skin, her hair, as it yielded to his hard, cracked hands.

A draught blew through the room. And he no longer saw Alys dancing before him, awaiting his return from another adventure, but rather as she was. Dead beneath the wet earth, where he had buried her all those years ago. Her bones flensed by worms. Her blind skull yawning in a sickly grin. Dead, like Pismire. Dead, like Father. Dead, like all the rest of them. Her soul dragged around by demons in Purgatory, kept there another day longer every time he forgot his prayers.

Loveday sat up and shivered violently, all his ease gone. The draught was coming from the brothel's open door, beyond which a pair of well-dressed men stood peering in. Loveday wondered why they had not crossed the threshold. Then he saw the room had grown gloomy around him, lit only by a single lantern and the oven's fire, which flickered and occasionally flared as a bubble of goose fat burst. He called to the men to enter. Then he hauled himself out of his chair, knees and hips clicking, and hurried around lighting the rest of the candles and lanterns.

By the brighter light, he knew one of the men: Sir Thomas Holand, a handsome, broad-shouldered knight who wore a leather patch over a blind eye. Loveday had fought alongside Holand at Caen, where the knight had taken valuable prisoners and – so it was said – been magnificently rewarded by the king. The other man was darker, plainly but expensively dressed, with a gold chain around his neck.

Holand nodded a greeting to Loveday. He looked around the brothel, taking its measure. Then he seemed to realise who Loveday was.

'FitzTalbot? By God, I'd heard you were in the ransom trade. Don't tell me you're a pimp now? Where's the madam of the house?'

Hircent was still nowhere to be seen. 'The madam is on her way, gentlemen,' said Loveday. 'She's…'

'… run away, too, has she?' Holand winked with his one good eye and laughed as Loveday's face crimsoned. 'I'm jesting, FitzTalbot. Are there at least some girls here? Or will we have to make do with you?'

Holand nudged his companion, who did not seem to find the joke as funny as he did.

'Forgive me,' Holand continued. 'Loveday FitzTalbot, this is Toussaint.' He raised both his eyebrows.

Toussaint frowned, impatient to find he was not known by reputation. Holand shrugged. 'I see my friend FitzTalbot here is not a follower of tournaments.' A nasty smile flitted briefly across Holand's face. 'But no matter. FitzTalbot, we have heard good things about the women here. Are they clean? Pretty? Do they have at least a head of hair and some of their own teeth?'

Loveday squirmed. 'Aye, sir. But perhaps if you can wait

until the, ah, until… I'm here to ensure there's no trouble, you see. Not to transact the business.'

Holand put his hands on Loveday's shoulders and braced him affectionately. 'We'll be no trouble at all,' he said. 'Toussaint here has had a hard day shouting at diggers in the ditch. He just wants his weary muscles rubbed. And I said I would join him. Of course, if anything else should be rubbed, that is in God's hands.' He laughed. 'Or perhaps not God's! Now, how many girls do you have, and where shall we find them?'

From behind Loveday, a voice interrupted. Scotsman was standing at the foot of the ladder from the loft, rubbing sleep from his eyes. 'Rooms on your left,' he yawned. 'There's two in at the moment. Margie and Annett. Take your pick.' The Scot whistled and the two girls appeared, faking coy blushes and fluttering their eyelashes. Scotsman turned back to the two knights. 'I know I don't have to tell you lads,' he said. 'But treat them like fucking ladies.'

He looked at Holand. '*You* don't want another eye missing. And *you*—' He just nodded at Toussaint, sizing him up. '— well, I don't want to end up digging your fucking ditch.'

The two knights bowed courteously, and went off with the girls. 'Loveday will see that you pay before you leave,' the Scot shouted after them. There was no reply. Soon Loveday heard the girls feigning giggles, and the sounds of heavy leather clothes being shed.

The Scot peered in the oven and called to the crackling birds, 'How are my wee goosies doing?' He took a deep breath in through his nose and savoured the sweet scent of roasting flesh. 'Praise be to St fucking Michael,' he said. 'Cunt's looked after us this year.'

He stood up and stretched. 'I'll put the kidneys in a bit later.

Watch those smooth bastards, Loveday. Any problems you shout for me. I'm going back to bed.'

Through living and working in the *Wolvenhuis*, Loveday picked up plenty of information about the state of the English and French armies and the course the siege was likely to take. That afternoon proved no different. The brothel's location at the heart of Villeneuve, along with the fact that Hastings was known to be its patron, meant there was a steady flow of customers from almost all ranks of the army below the greatest lords. Typically, these men liked to talk. Some talked to the girls, some to the Dogs, and some to each other. Almost all of them seemed to regard the *Wolvenhuis* as a place where things could be spoken in confidence. They let their tongues wag.

Naturally, not everything said in the brothel was true or trustworthy. Much of the talk was boastful, garbled nonsense, or the baseless chatter of bored soldiers imagining events unfolding in the way that best suited their own hopes. But enough was credible and true, and by keeping his ears open, Loveday had begun to piece together a reasonably accurate picture of the way things stood. Above all, he had concluded that as they camped in their new town outside Calais, the army occupied a peculiar and delicate position.

After the English triumph at Crécy – now many weeks ago – King Philippe of France had disbanded almost his entire army, believing that the English would bolt for home to celebrate their victory. Almost immediately, however, he had changed his mind, and a new French army had been summoned to drive the English away from Calais – though hardly anyone believed it could be raised before Christmas at the earliest.

The French position was thus thought to be very weak. The English were dug in on the islands of the marsh, and once Northampton's ditch was complete, it would be extremely hard to assault them from any direction. After the sack of Thérouanne, every walled city within two days' ride of Calais had shut its gates and hastened to reinforce its garrison. But these were defensive measures, and the only danger they posed to the English was likely to be through raiding the wagon trains that were currently bringing food to Villeneuve from the king's allies in the cities of Flanders.

The English, therefore, believed their position to be promising. Like Hircent's followers, Jakke, Nicclaes and Heyman, almost all the Flemings had departed the army to go home ahead of the winter. But Flemish merchants were continuing to supply the English camp from the cities of the north, despite persistent reports of thieves and murderers targeting them on the roads into Villeneuve. Meanwhile, King Edward had sent orders for a huge surge of food, weapons and military reinforcements to be shipped over from England. When the first supply convoys had been destroyed by French-allied Genoese gallies and broken up by pirates, morale had briefly sunk very low. But it was now widely said that the Genoese had fallen out with the French king over unpaid contracts, had taken their galleys home and were not certain to return, even in the spring. The English could therefore expect to be fed and provisioned until the siege reached a conclusion.

The biggest debate Loveday heard among the clients of the brothel was what that conclusion would be. And now, as he sat and listened to Sir Thomas Holand and Toussaint gossip while Margie and Annett rubbed oil into their backs and thighs, he heard the subject discussed again. It arose as Sir Thomas

Holand was complaining to Toussaint about a legal difficulty he was having, proving the validity of his marriage to a young cousin of the prince, whom he called Joanie.

Loveday settled back into his chair and tried to follow their conversation.

'They call her the fair maid of Kent for a reason, but I swear to Christ, the woman is going to bankrupt me before I have the chance to get inside her,' Holand was saying. 'Everyone knows I married her before that shit Montagu did. Why the king won't just tell him to release her I don't know. The amount she's cost me in legal fees... if I see her at court at Christmas I ought to just bend her over and—' He broke off and grunted as Margie's fingers dug into some tender part of his flesh.

Toussaint snorted. 'Christmas? Tommy, I wager you anything you care to stake that we'll still be here for Christmas. And the only thing bending over will be the half of our army who are shitting bloody water from marsh fever and the flux. The only way you're seeing your fair maid Joanie for Christmas is if you stow away on one of the supply ships and go and abduct her... and if you do that, you'll have even bigger problems with the king's law than you do already. By the way, have you heard what they're doing to deserters?'

Holand sighed impatiently. 'Of course I heard. I speak to the Earl of Warwick as often as you see Northampton.' The one-eyed knight slipped into an uncanny impression of the booming-voiced marshal, Warwick. '*Guard the ports and snatch them off the boats, by God's nails! Flog the poor, fine the rich and put them all in the Tower of London until they're begging to come back here and dig the ditch!*'

Holand returned to his own voice. 'But that's no concern

of mine, because I'm telling you, we'll be home by Christmas. Isn't that right, Margie?'

Margie, hearing her name but having no idea what was being said to her, just giggled.

Toussaint, meanwhile, would not let the subject go. His smooth, self-assured voice drifted in from Annett's cell.

'I'm telling you, Tommy,' he said, 'you're wrong. This isn't one of your frozen forest hunts for pagans in Prussia. In case you're blind in both your eyes now, Calais has two moats fed by filthy seawater, and walls as big as Paris. And...'

Holand finished Toussaint's sentence for him, now mimicking the knight's voice: '...and you can't put a siege tower on the marsh because it'll sink, and you can't dig tunnels because they'll collapse and we won't have enough ships to blockade Calais until the spring, and, and, and...'

He sighed. 'We all know what's really going on. You hear it and I hear it every day. Warwick and your good lord Northampton want to put the siege towers up and attack. The king won't commit. And every merchant in England is writing to His Grace daily to congratulate him on his caution. Why? Because the longer the siege, the more supplies we burn through. The more supplies we burn through, the more the king borrows from them. And the more he borrows, the more they bleed him for in repayments.

'Meanwhile, they stall his requests for ships until the spring, because they know that if we don't get a proper fleet over here, we can't blockade Calais and starve the fuckers out. You know who's running the supplies into the city for the defenders?'

Holand broke off and let out a moan. Across Villeneuve, the afternoon bells had started ringing, announcing nones. In the cell, Margie giggled her fake giggle. Loveday guessed her hands were wandering away from Holand's back towards his beltline. But then the knight stopped her. 'Hold on... whatever your name is, let me tell him this.

'You know who's running it?'

Toussaint mumbled, now only half-interested. Annett was evidently following Margie's lead. But Holand pushed on.

'I'll tell you who. Jean Marant, for the love of Barabbas up before Pilate. Throat-cutter Marant, by God. The guy who used to run the – Christ, girl...'

With some effort, he finished his sentence. '...used to run... the pirate gang on Guernsey. He helped take down our supply convoy. He's working out of a tavern called the Tin Jar up on the bluff near Sangatte. And he's got men inside Calais. Led by some cripple, if you can imagine that. Chucked off a bridge in Paris. Or something...'

By now, Toussaint had stopped paying any attention whatever, and was breathing deep and fast as Annett worked her hands over him. But Loveday was listening as intently as he had to anything in his life. He sat upright in his chair.

Marant.

He remembered the pirate from before. They had crossed paths over the years. In Rye and London. Somewhere else he could not recall. He had a crew about twice the size of the Dogs'.

Toussaint and Holand were both groaning, like cows overdue their milking.

A cripple.

Loveday felt a prickling running up and down the back of his legs and his spine. He saw the Captain's face, as clearly as he had at Thérouanne. He stood up and started towards the cells where the girls were relieving the two knights. He wanted to grab Holand by the throat. Shake out of him what he meant.

Loveday knew a madness was taking him over. He didn't care.

But just as he reached the entrance to Margie's cell, the front door of the brothel flew open and in burst Tebbe and Thorp, each with an arm around Romford. The boy had black grime all over his hands and face, and a dazed look in his eyes.

He smelled rank: of eggs and piss and burning bread. And his own dried sweat, which had stained brown circles all over his filthy green-and-white tunic.

For a moment Loveday stood still in shock, thinking the boy was burned. But then he saw his cheeks were flushed. His eyes sparkled, even as he gazed around in a half-daze.

He seemed speechless. But Tebbe and Thorp were speaking loudly, talking over the top of one another so enthusiastically that Loveday could not make out what either of them was saying. It had something to do with a noise, and the walls of Calais.

A shout came from one of the knights' cells. 'God's tongue and tonsils! What's this? You've put me off my—' Holand burst into the room, shoving his shirt into his belt. He glared at the excited archers. Margie followed, looking apologetic and babbling Flemish.

She tried to pull Holand back into the cell. But he shoved her off roughly, threw a coin in her direction and stormed out of the brothel's door. Toussaint sauntered out soon after, looking a good deal more relaxed. He grabbed one last handful of Annett's arse before he paid her.

Loveday's head was spinning as he turned to the archers.

'Christ, boys, what are you doing? Do you know what those knights were just talking about?'

Thorp dismissed him with a wave. 'Never mind fucking knights, Loveday. You won't believe what we've been doing. By God, that goose smells good.' He slapped Romford hard on the back. 'Tell him, boy – about the guy's face.' He mimed a man holding his head in agony.

Romford looked at Tebbe and Thorp and opened his mouth to try and find the words to explain. Nothing came. He just stuttered, as though he had forgotten how to speak English.

Eventually, Tebbe and Thorp filled in the gaps for him. Each of them seemed to have enjoyed their day more than any other since they left England.

In the oven, the Michaelmas geese spat fat. Not long after, Margie was sitting on Tebbe's lap, and Scotsman was cooking gizzards for gravy. Loveday wondered, just briefly, if everything they had suffered had been to earn them this moment of happiness.

It was not until late that night, when he lay half-drunk in his bed with his stomach full and said a prayer of thanks to St Michael, that he suddenly returned to thinking about what Sir Thomas Holand and Toussaint had said.

A pirate called Marant. A cripple in Calais. A war that was far from over.

The thoughts writhed inside his head like snakes. It took him a long time to fall asleep.

12

Many an encounter and many an assault was made, by the low-born and the high...

Life of the Black Prince by Chandos Herald

For weeks, Squelette moved and watched the roads that led out of Flanders towards the English camp outside Calais.

She moved about the country, changing her watching place each day. Some spots she visited often: a collapsed windmill, a burned-out cottage, an abandoned forge. Others – the hollow of an ancient yew tree carpeted with spiky needles and home to fat, black-shelled beetles who crawled across her face in the night – she used only once.

She stayed away from towns, where she knew her ragged, bone-thin appearance frightened people. She lived simply, but well, off the land. She drank cold fresh water from the streams. She ate berries from brambles and elder trees and filled her pack with nuts from a hazel. She stripped and sharpened young hazel branches and used them to spear fish she caught in stick-traps baited with maggots from rotting toadstools. When the fish did not come, she ate the maggots herself.

And all the while she watched the roads.

She learned which days the butchers came, and which days the cheese merchants. She tracked the cloth-sellers and the armourers. She knew which day pigs were driven along the roads to the market in Villeneuve, and which day the alewives brought their barrels.

She discovered which towns put guards by their gates, and how far they ventured. She established how far outside Villeneuve English patrols would come, and how they were ordered to march to defend themselves.

She learned the routes of the roads and the rhythms of their traffic, so that eventually they grew as familiar to her as her own breath. Until they almost bored her.

She planned her kills and carried them out precisely.

When her home in Valognes was first sacked by the English, she had thought it would be the English on whom she would take her revenge. And one Englishman in particular.

What she had seen since then had changed her mind. She would have her own revenge. But there was so much more to do first.

The English king and his knights brought terror and misery to the people of France. The French king and his knights had let him do it.

The merchants of Flanders and England grew richer every day, feeding the war monster. The French did nothing to drive them away.

It was not a war between peoples. It was a war against the people.

So before she avenged herself, she fought for the people. As though she were the people. She fought not only for the people she loved who were dead, but those whom she had never known, who had also been beaten and robbed and burned and raped and killed.

She picked her targets carefully, and fell upon them like a wraith.

She cut knights' throats when they strayed into the woods to piss.

She shot a grain merchant through the eye with her crossbow while he changed a broken cart-wheel.

She made traps in the road for horses so they fell on their riders and broke their ribs and spines.

After each strike, she made a nick on her thin arm with the fat kind man's knife. A tally to tell the story of her war. She picked the scabs to be sure that the lines scarred. She counted them daily like rosary beads, saying a prayer as she ran her fingers over the raised purple scar tissue. Asking God to watch her do His work. Asked for enough time to fill her whole arm with lines.

Certain things made her especially vengeful.

The charcoal burners' workshop in the forest clearing, where dark blood trails led to the shallow graves of a family of seven.

The village church with all its windows smashed and the dead priest hung up by one ankle from the roof beams and left to die. The flies buzzing around his face, gross and black with his whole body's blood.

And a kidnapping. One autumn morning, a mile at most from the siege town, she watched a group of young women with a few thin, bare-footed boys and girls clinging to their skirts, hurrying away from Calais. She guessed they had either escaped or been ejected from the besieged city.

Refugees.

She had been one, once.

As they hurried along the road to the south, they were caught up and surrounded by a party of riders from the direction of the siege camp.

She was too far back from the road to hear what was said. But she saw pleading. Heard the shrieks when two of the women were pulled away from the group and roughly bundled across the backs of the riders' horses.

Felt the air pierced by their wails as they held out their hands to their children.

She wanted to help. She knew she could not. The road was busy with archers and men-at-arms. They would kill her. Or worse.

So she fixed in her mind the image of the leader of the riders. Memorised the outline of the body. The face with its thin patchy bristles and its black eyes. The huge, round shoulders and torso.

The Flemish-style goedendag. Meaty arms. A booming laugh.

A woman.

13

Write to the King's cousin, Margaret, countess of Kent, stating that... the King desired that she should send John, her son... to the King's assistance...

Calendar of the French Roll, 20 Edward III

One morning in late October, Romford crouched on his haunches in the sandy soil beside his favourite cannon, took a gulp of ale from his flask and wafted his hand to clear the smoke around him. Autumn had arrived. Above him, a band of cloud was scudding in from the sea, and a few fat spots of rain were falling. The drops hissed when they landed on the hot belly of the gun. Romford sensed more rain coming. He shifted his powder bucket under the little canvas tent the engineers had made for him to keep his kit dry. He pulled his thick green-and-white cloak around his shoulders for warmth. Then he peered through the thinning smoke and considered Calais' huge walls, one hundred or so paces in the distance.

The walls were a mess. Romford could trace his marks all over the masonry. His firing spot was on the edge of an island in the marsh that men called the 'sablon', where a company of bowmen, a battery of trebuchets and several other cannon took aim at Calais, protected on their flanks with palisades. The island was directly opposite a round corner tower joining

Calais' south wall to its west. The curved stonework of that tower was a mass of dents and pockmarks and abrasions. At its top, several pieces of crenellation were missing, and at one point, around halfway up the tower, a whole chunk of stone had fallen out; it now lay, broken in three pieces, on the thin strip of ground between the tower's base and the outer of the city's two sea-fed moats. The garrison inside Calais had hung sacks of straw over the sides of the walls, to try to soften the impact of trebuchet shot and the cannons' barrage of heavy metal balls and bolts. Romford didn't mind. He enjoyed destroying the sacks. His last shot had hit one directly, making the straw burst in a puff of dust and dried stalks and dazed insects, already weak and half-dead from the cold.

Romford had now been manning King Edward's guns for twenty days without a break. He had worked so hard that the lines of his palms and fingers were stained black. His arms ached from the effort of adjusting the heavy iron gun's aim and his fingertips were burned hard at the pads. He had set fire more than once to his hair, so that clumps of it were missing and its colour was no longer blond but a grimy brown, thick and stiff with soot. His ears roared and whined constantly, even when he slept.

Yet for all that, Romford felt a thrill each morning as he left the *Wolvenhuis* to go to his station. It was troubling him more and more to be in the brothel. Almost every week, Sir Hugh Hastings or one of his men-at-arms would arrive with a new woman for Hircent to assign a cell and compel to work. They varied greatly in age, appearance and the tongues they spoke. Some were Flemish, experienced whores who had sought out the English army at Villeneuve to find work. Others, though, were scared and miserable prisoners captured during raids on the towns around Villeneuve. Hircent treated these women with great cruelty and contempt. Besides her wicked *goedendag*, she had cut herself a thin birch, with which she would beat the backs of their legs for the smallest misdeeds.

Their cries kept Romford awake at night.

So each time he touched flame to the firing hole of the cannon, setting it to bellow and flash, it seemed to him that for once it was good to be here, and not in his current, uneasy home.

Since the cannon was now cool and the heavy rain had not yet arrived, Romford started loading another shot. He paid special attention to the task of scraping out residue and burned powder from the gun's throat. This was the dirtiest, smelliest part of the job, and it left his hands filthy and oily. But it was also vital. Just after Michaelmas, Romford had seen a gunner lose a hand and half the flesh of his cheek when a dirty hand-cannon blew up as it fired. The man's injuries were so terrible that Romford was not sure if he was lucky or unlucky to have lived. But seeing the accident had sharpened his own focus on keeping his weapons clean. Now, as he prepared the gun to fire, he found himself lost completely in the task, so that he stood up with a start when a hand tapped him on the shoulder and a voice said: 'Why are you doing that?'

Romford wiped his face and looked at the boy who was standing beside him. He had never seen him before, but he could tell that he was of noble blood. He looked about the same age as Romford – somewhere between his fifteenth and seventeenth summer. But he was straight-backed and clean, and he wore neatly tailored clothes and soft calfskin boots, with a gleaming sword at his side, which looked as though it had seldom been used. He had a long, rather thin face, with high cheekbones and a tapering nose, and wore his hair swept back from his face. His eyes were the palest blue. He had no hint of a beard, and his skin seemed impossibly smooth.

Conscious of how filthy and rank he was from his work, Romford now wiped his palms on the arse of his breeches and attempted a bow. The boy smiled and said something Romford could not make out.

'I'm sorry, sir,' Romford said, pointing to his ears. 'The gun. I—'

'Not at all,' said the boy, a little louder. 'I surprised you. I'm sorry. I only wanted to ask what you were doing. It looks...' He gazed intently at the weapon, as though trying to understand it. 'It looks fascinating.'

Romford nodded. 'It's called a cannon, my lord. It's like a longbow, or a crossbow, in a way. Or a—'

'Jacky,' said the boy. Romford was confused, and his face must have showed it, because the boy laughed in a friendly manner. 'My name. It's John, but people call me Jacky.'

Romford nodded. He decided he could not call the boy Jacky. So he continued to tell him about the gun. 'It doesn't shoot as true as a longbow. Not at all. Nor as far, nor as fast. But it makes a roar and a stink, which scares people, and the arrows it shoots – well, they're not arrows. They're more like...' He tried to think of something this young noble would understand. 'Like a juggler's balls, but of iron. They're very dangerous if they hit you.'

He looked at Jacky to see if he understood. The boy was just staring at him, his light blue eyes as calm as a pool. For a moment Romford did not know what else to say, so they both stood there with their arms by their sides.

'Would you like to see me shoot it?' said Romford, after a few moments. 'I could try and knock another bit off that tower.'

Jacky nodded. 'That sounds fine, Master...' He cocked his head enquiringly.

'...Romford,' said Romford, turning away as he felt his face flush beneath the dirt. He looked around for his powder bucket. 'So the first thing we do is...'

But he got no further, because at that moment another voice rang out from the direction of the trebuchets.

'Joseph of Arimathea with his Grail full of bird piss, boys, are we besieging this city or fucking flirting with it? Get your thumbs out of your arseholes and start fucking it up or by God I'll have you all digging the bastard ditch, so help me Jesus.'

Jacky squeezed Romford on the arm. 'I expect you know of Lord Northampton.'

'I do.'

'He can be quite fierce, but he's not bad once you really know him,' said Jacky. 'He and my cousin Eddie are showing me around the camp. I've just arrived. You can probably tell.'

He laughed his easy, friendly laugh once again. 'I'd better go, before I get you in trouble. Maybe I'll see you again some time, Master Romford.'

And with that he sauntered off along the *sablon*, smiling around him as though he found everything amusing, waving as he went, without looking round. Romford watched him catch up with Northampton, who looked as distracted and irritable as he had since the day they arrived at Villeneuve. He watched him pat his cousin Eddie affectionately on the back.

Eddie was the prince.

Jacky said something to him, apparently about Romford and the cannon. Though he tried not to stare, he felt the prince's eyes light upon him and linger.

Although the prince's attention was the thing he had craved for so long, now he had it, Romford felt more miserable than ever. He dared not return the gaze. He did not know if the prince recognised him, or was merely curious about what Jacky had told him. He knew he could never ask. He turned back to his cannon, feeling sick. The rain had finally come in from the sea and the breeze was swirling. But he managed one more shot at Calais' corner tower. He read the wind direction perfectly, and the ball cracked another of its crenellations, knocking it inwards towards the tower's roof.

As it fell, he thought he heard someone yell in pain. But with the ringing in his ears, it was becoming very hard to be sure.

After their meeting on the cannon island, Romford did not expect to see Jacky again. But he was wrong. Just two days later he was drying out his mud-caked boots by the oven at the back of the brothel when he heard a commotion from the front of the room, where Hircent sat to welcome guests to the premises, her chair placed carefully beside the doorway near a corner where her sharp-tipped *goedendag* Heartbreaker stood propped.

At first he thought it must be a client making trouble with one of the girls, or with Millstone and Scotsman, who were guarding the entrance that night. He thought he might have to bolt up the ladder and rouse Tebbe, Thorp and Loveday, who were already sleeping in the loft. But when he looked, he saw there was no trouble. Rather, Hircent had drawn herself up to her full height and was making a fuss of three young men, who had evidently surprised her with their visit.

One was Jacky. One was another young nobleman of around the same age. And the third was the prince.

The three lords were in boisterous mood. Their voices were loud and they bumped into one another and the furniture. Romford guessed they had been drinking for some hours, and were now rolling around the dark streets of Villeneuve looking for more entertainment.

Their arrival sent Hircent into something of a frenzy. The big woman rose from her chair and was bustling around arranging seats for her honoured guests to sit on. Romford realised why she was nervous. Although she now had a large number of women working under her, at that moment all of them were engaged, bar one: a squat, short-sighted young woman called Flora, whom Hircent mostly used as a maid. Hircent bellowed for Flora once the young lords were seated. The girl bumbled over with mugs of spiced wine. The prince snatched one, drank it in one draught. 'More,' he demanded. There was a hard edge to his voice. Hircent shooed Flora off to fetch a jug.

As she went, Jacky spotted Romford. He stood up and strode across the room to the back of the brothel. Romford pretended to concentrate on his boots. But Jacky grabbed his shoulder and gave him a friendly shake. He began talking loudly and enthusiastically. He was certainly drunk, but seemed as blithe and happy as he had when they first met.

'Romford! It is Romford, isn't it? The boy with the gun! Are you waiting too? Eddie's friend Sir Hugh Hastings owns this house, I hear. Have you seen the madam?' He nudged Romford playfully. 'I shouldn't want to tangle with her... inside or outside the bedroom!'

Romford squirmed. 'I – er – no, my lord. I... I live here. At the moment. When I'm not...'

Jacky laughed his tinkling laugh and his eyes widened. 'Here? Why, that must be heaven! Tell me then, who's the best of them?' Without waiting for an answer, he called across the brothel to the prince. 'Eddie! Eddie! Come and meet my friend Romford. This young man lives here in the whorehouse! Have you ever heard of such a thing? Come and meet him!'

The prince walked over, wobbling slightly. He looked at Romford as though he had never seen him before. Romford stood in his bare feet, holding a wet boot in each hand. His heart was pounding. He bowed. As he did, he remembered the smell of the prince's neck when they had lain together in his bed the night before the battle at Crécy. He wondered if he really looked so different now. When he straightened up, the prince was no longer looking at him.

Jacky seemed not to notice Romford's discomfort. He swilled wine around his mouth and looked about the brothel. 'You know, Eddie,' he said, now also ignoring Romford, 'when I am Earl of Kent in my own right, I shall live in a whorehouse too.' He giggled.

The prince looked lazily at him. 'Growing up with your sister Joanie around, I thought we'd had that pleasure already. How many men is she married to at the moment? Willy Montagu? One-eyed Tommy Holand? I have seen her naked so many times, I suppose I ought to marry her too.'

For the first time since Romford had met him, Jacky looked a little wounded. He peered around the room again, and spotted the other nobleman, sulking near the door. 'Hey! Louis! *Kom hier, klootzak!*'

Now the young Fleming joined them too. 'Louis, this is Romford,' said Jacky. 'Romford, this is Louis.' He grinned and raised his eyebrows. '*He's very grand.* When I'm the Earl of Kent, he's going to be the Count of Flanders.' Then he whispered theatrically, 'And he's going to marry Eddie's sister Izzy! What do you think of that?'

Both Louis and the prince looked annoyed by this remark. 'We shall see about that,' said the prince. 'I think dear Louis here would rather marry his horse.'

Louis' eyes flashed angrily. 'I shall not marry your sister, Edward, because your fucking father killed mine on the battlefield, in case you had forgotten,' he spat.

The prince sneered. 'My *fucking father* had Jacky's father's head cut off, in case *you* had forgotten. I don't see him sulking about it. Stop being such a baby.'

Now Jacky pouted too. The prince tossed his hair. For a few moments, the young men stood in a dour silence. Romford realised he was still holding his boots. He put them back on top of the oven. His guts were twisting.

Then, for the first time, the prince turned to Romford as though he knew him. 'Do you have any powder, boy?'

Romford felt both crushed and elated at once. His legs were shaking. The prince looked irritably at him, awaiting an answer. Romford shook his head. The silence returned, more agonising than ever.

Then, mercifully, there came squeals and peals of coquettish laughter as a pair of girls called May and Morgan skipped out of their cells. They were two of Hircent's Flemish recruits. As they came into the brothel's main room, May wiped her mouth with her skirts. Morgan waddled out to the yard, where the wash buckets stood. Romford saw Hircent throw two incredulous and half-dressed archers out of the front door, aiming a boot at their backsides as they went.

Hircent marched over to the young men, her face a picture of exaggerated bonhomie. She put an arm around May and Morgan as they now returned. She seemed oblivious to the uncomfortable mood that hung over the group.

'These two young ladies will make you very welcome,' she said. 'And I have two more coming to you very soon.

'Who would like…?' She left the question hanging.

'Jacky and I will be first,' said Louis. 'I think Eddie will…' He broke into Flemish and spoke rapidly to Hircent. She looked puzzled at first, then nodded as though she understood. She looked at Romford.

The prince looked away. Louis smiled slyly.

'As my lords please,' said Hircent. May took Jacky's hand. Morgan made a playful grab for Louis' crotch. The four skipped off towards the girls' cells.

This left Romford and the prince. Hircent beamed at them, her expression sickly and false. 'Romford, perhaps you would sit with my lord for a time?' She motioned to a pair of chairs that Flora had put together before the oven.

Hircent drew close to him. 'Get rid of those fucking boots,' she hissed. 'And give him whatever he wants, or I'll break your dirty little fingers.'

It slowly dawned on Romford what she meant. His heart thudded. Everything seemed slow and strange, as though he were trapped in a terrible dream. Numbly, he took his boots from the oven-top, handed them to Flora and sat down. Behind a curtain, he heard Jacky slap Morgan on her bony arse.

The prince sat beside him and fixed him with his dull, drunken eyes.

Romford cleared his throat. It was the first time he had been alone with the prince since the night before the battle at Crécy. But this was like being with a stranger. He remembered a little bird fluttering in the prince's tent. He wanted to ask if the prince remembered it too. But he could not find the words. 'Would my lord like more wine?' he asked, instead. His voice was tight and small.

The prince kept staring at him. 'No.'

'Oh,' said Romford.

The prince reached out a hand and gripped Romford's leg hard, halfway up the thigh. Sweat beaded on Romford's forehead. He had spent so long wanting nothing more than this touch. Now he felt only terror. He prayed Millstone would come in from outside, or that Tebbe or Thorp would come down the ladder from the loft.

From her seat at the front of the brothel, Hircent glared at him. She moved her hand momentarily to Heartbreaker.

The prince's grip tightened on his leg. His hard fingers were making bruises. Romford noticed that he did not smell like he had done before. There was meat on his breath.

The prince nodded in the direction of one of the wooden cells. Romford shook his head slowly.

'Yes,' said the prince.

'Please, my lord,' said Romford. 'I have to be at the *sablon* at first light tomorrow. The cannon... no one else fires it so well...' He was jabbering. 'Why don't we try and find some powder?' he said in desperation. 'There may be somewhere in the camp...'

The prince shrugged. Romford realised that they both knew the truth: if there had been any powder to find in the camp, Romford would already have found it.

Across the room, Hircent gestured angrily with her head towards the cell. The prince released Romford's leg and motioned for him to get up.

He stood up.

He walked across the room with the prince prodding him between his shoulder blades. The ringing in his ears from all the cannon roars grew very loud.

He hoped one last time that Millstone or Tebbe or Thorp or Scotsman or Loveday would come and save him.

But nobody came.

Romford pushed the greasy curtain aside and went into the little cell. The prince stood in front of him. His eyes bored into Romford's. Romford held his gaze for as long as he could. 'Do you…' he said. His voice stopped in his throat.

The prince shook his head.

Somewhere, in another cell, Romford could hear one of the girls choking.

He closed his eyes.

The prince hit him in the mouth. A heavy gold ring tore his lip. He hit the floor, gasping.

The prince kicked him and broke his nose.

The prince rolled him over, sat on top of him and banged his face into the floor.

Romford managed to catch half a breath. He held it. He tried to find the silent place inside him where he had retreated when ugly, horrible things had happened to him before. In London, before the war began. In Caen. At Crécy.

He tried to focus on the ringing in his ears when the prince started pulling off his filthy, soot-stained green-and-white shirt.

Later, when the three lords left the brothel, he stayed all night in the tiny cell like one of the girls, wondering whether the bleeding or his tears would dry up first. When he eventually slept, it was curled in a ball on a rough, scratchy straw sack.

The room was freezing cold.

His face and body ached.

The sack looked just like the ones he had blown to pieces with his cannon as they hung from the scarred walls of Calais.

14

In this way, the siege tightened its grip...

Chronicle of Geoffrey le Baker

'What in the name of Christ were you thinking?'

Despite the wide difference in size between them, Loveday was squared up to Hircent, so angry that his spittle flecked the big woman's face. Romford was above them in the loft. Loveday had found him that morning at dawn. Millstone had carried him up the ladder on his shoulder.

The square-shouldered Fleming was unbothered. She looked down her nose at the Dogs' leader. 'They were lords,' she said. 'A count. An earl. A prince. You don't say no to these people.'

She screwed up her face as if she smelled shit. 'Your boy is weak. But pretty, under the dirt. I see them like him before. We need more girls. And boys who are like girls. He can make us money.'

Loveday looked at Hircent in disbelief, and took a couple of steps backwards. 'Make us money? He's an archer. Or he was. He fires those fucking cannon things now. He's not a... a...' He couldn't bring himself to say it. 'And as for lords? I don't care if it was King Edward himself who came in here wanting to stick his pintle in something. These are my men! And weak or not, the lad is one of ours. We look out for each other. We don't sell each other to fucking perverts…'

He was so furious and disgusted that the words dried up. He looked around at the rest of the Dogs for support. Millstone, beside him, was granite-faced, pale and as angry as Loveday, with his jaw set square and his strong hands flexing. Tebbe and Thorp looked appalled. Scotsman sat a little distance off from the rest of the group, his face buried in his palms.

Hircent did not break eye contact with Loveday. Her cold gaze seemed to slash through him. 'One of yours?' she said. 'Maybe. But I am not. I am Hircent. Here you work with me. For me.

'Why are you here? To fight? I think not. You ran away from the fight at Thérouanne.'

Loveday's angry face reddened even more. 'I didn't,' he said quietly. 'I saw someone—'

Hircent ignored him, as though the facts were completely beyond question. 'So you're here to meet old friends? Please. You are here to make money, the same as all of us.'

Loveday gritted his teeth. 'Not like this,' he said. 'By Christ and all the saints, not like this.'

'If you say,' said Hircent. 'So you wait for your ransom from the knight. Your fifty pounds. Then you go home. If you can. Maybe your men will follow you. Maybe they will stay with me. Then they will not be Dogs. They will be with Hircent. They will be Wolves.

'Maybe they already are.'

Thorp now stepped forward, his eyes blazing. 'Stay with you? Mother of Christ and all the rest of them, we're not staying with you another fucking night.'

Hircent snorted through her nose at Thorp. 'Oh yes? So I

am leaving and taking all the girls with me? Or you are leaving and going… where? To a nice little hovel in the marsh, where you can catch a fever in your arsehole and die? Or you are going to swim the sea back to your England?'

As she spoke, the door of the brothel swung open. Sir Hugh Hastings sauntered in, holding his wig in place against the strong, blustery wind that was whipping around Villeneuve. When he looked around the unhappy group, his face fell and he narrowed his eyes.

'Who's leaving? Who's going home?'

No one answered him.

'That's right,' he said. 'Because this place is working nicely. And if anything happens to disrupt that, I can tell you now that all ransom money from that prick of a knight you sold me will be gone, and you'll be digging the ditch for the rest of the time we're here.

'So what's happening here? Somebody, speak.'

There was a short silence, before Millstone spoke. 'Nothing we can't fix between ourselves, Sir Hugh.'

'That sounds right.' Hastings studied Loveday, then nodded at Millstone. 'You should put him in charge.

'Now, listen, all of you, because I've got a few important things to tell you. First of all, the good news. Her Grace Queen Philippa is arriving any day now, and she's going to be bringing her whole household, so you can expect to have a queue of randy courtiers snaking out of the door of this place every night for a long time to come.

'Which means you need more whores. And that's where I have even better news: we've heard from spies inside Calais that the garrison is preparing to kick out a big group of civilians. You all know supply runs are still getting into the city, thanks to Jean Marant and those fiends he sails with. Even so, they still have too many women and children in there, and they need to cut the number of useless mouths before winter really bites.

'But what they call a useless mouth, I call a profitable mouth – and every other hole besides. Does everyone here understand what I mean? They'll be out soon. Don't waste any time. Grab the pretty ones and put them to work. If they piss you around, beat them until they learn not to. It's a war. Let's remember what we're here for.'

Without waiting for a response, Hastings turned on his heel and walked out. 'Remember what I said,' he called, as the door swung behind him. 'Fuck this up, and you'll wish you hadn't.'

Loveday felt sick. Hircent grinned. 'Well. Maybe I won't need your boy after all,' she said. 'Do what you like with him.'

Then she sat down in her chair by the door, put Heartbreaker across her lap and closed her eyes.

Loveday looked at her with hatred boiling in his heart like pitch. He stormed to the back of the room and fetched his short sword. As he came back, Tebbe grabbed him by the shoulder. 'What are you doing?'

'I'm going to do what we should have done a long time ago,' Loveday said.

'Millstone, stay here and watch the boy. Make sure she doesn't lay a finger on him.

'Scotsman—'

The burly Scot pulled his face from his hand for the first time that morning. His eyes looked hollow, the skin baggy and raw around the sockets. 'Aye?'

'Get your axe and put a shirt on. We're going to see an old friend of ours.'

Loveday led Scotsman along the perimeter track, which ran around the edge of Villeneuve, to the inside of the ditch being dug by Northampton's men. The path was wet and in places waterlogged, and often they had to hop and jump through it to avoid sinking to their shins in freezing muddy water.

A lot of the ditch beside them was yet to be dug to its finished depth, but they passed several long sections that were now more or less complete. It consisted of a steep sheer drop twice a man's height on their side, and then a sloping bank up to the outer edge. Stagnant water lay at the bottom. Sharpened wooden stakes were driven into the wet soil at an angle, to impale anyone who fell or rode in. A palisade ran beside the track, to provide cover for archers and crossbowmen who might be sent to defend the boundary. Every fifty paces or so they passed bored lookouts, standing alone or in pairs beside the palisade, peering over it into the grey distance, watching for a French army that never came.

'Wouldn't fancy any cunt's chances of getting in here quickly,' said the Scot, his voice tight, trying to break the silence they had kept since leaving the *Wolvenhuis*.

'Aye,' said Loveday.

Scotsman cleared his throat. He tried again. 'Loveday, I'm sorry. I—'

Loveday cut him off. 'It's done. We can't fix it. We just have to do the right thing now.'

Scotsman fell quiet. They kept walking. They passed huts built on wetland, half-sunk into the mud. Saw areas of the marsh that had seemed solid a month ago, which were now large pools with patches of marsh weed growing out of them. They saw rats by the hundred, and stray dogs with their paws, legs and bellies black with filth. Licking the briny marsh water and barking at its ugly taste.

In the distance they saw the *sablon*, where the main battery of trebuchets and cannon were keeping up their noisy attack on Calais' south and western walls. Loveday could make out Sir John Chandos directing operations, and large numbers of green-and-white liveried archers milling around. Tebbe, Thorp and Romford ought to have been there. Nothing seemed different without them. The bombardment just went on. Dull crashes of stone and irregular gunpowder booms.

They passed simple guard towers being built.

They passed a pair of friars in brown habits tied with ropes, walking in the filth in bare feet.

They passed a pit of dead horses.

Eventually, the perimeter track joined a causeway through the marsh, a raised track two carts' width set on a base of tight-packed stones and wooden pillars. They turned left. After a few hundred paces, it took them to the main gate on Villeneuve's west side. The gate was open. A wagon bearing a load of stripped tree trunks felled in the forests beyond the marsh was coming in. Loveday and Scotsman slipped out in the opposite direction.

The gatekeeper, a tall, listless archer with a nasal voice, called to them.

'Oi, lads, where are you going?'

Loveday turned back to him. 'The ditch. We're on digging duty.'

The guard looked dubiously at Scotsman's axe. Loveday followed his gaze. 'Tree roots,' he said. 'Bastards to get through.'

The guard waved them on. 'They're down towards the seafront today, I think. Careful out there, boys. There's no

French for leagues around, but it's bandit country. Pirates everywhere.'

'Pirates, eh?' Loveday raised his short sword. 'Bring them on.'

The guard shrugged. He dragged the gate shut. 'On your heads be it. Get back safe. God save King Edward!'

'God save my arse and bollocks,' muttered Scotsman.

But when they were out of the guard's earshot, he turned to Loveday and growled, 'Now, are you going to tell me what the fuck we're doing?'

The more Loveday told Scotsman of his idea, the more incredulous the big man looked.

'You want to do what?'

'Just what I said. Jean Marant is running his crew out of a tavern called the Tin Jar. From what I heard the lords say the other night, it's no more than a few miles from here. If we can find him, he might agree to run Romford back to England. The boy... we have to get him out of here.'

Scotsman shook his head in despair. 'If we can find him? What makes you think he'll want to be found? Or that we'll get anywhere near him? Jesus Christ nailed to a fucking maypole, Loveday, there's got to be a bounty the size of a king's ransom on the cunt's head. And the havoc he's causing, he must be running some sort of army.'

'Why?'

'Why what?'

'Why must he be running an army? When did Marant ever do that? I'll bet he's working the same size crew as ever. The smaller you are, the easier it is to hide.'

'But still...'

'Still what? Loveday stopped in his tracks. 'Why would he help us? Christ, Scotsman, I don't know. But I can't sit in that brothel, or in this camp, or in this fucking country any longer and not try to do something.'

They were following a track up a steep slope towards a headland where cliffs dropped to a jagged, rocky stretch of the coast. Loveday slowed to catch his breath and pulled Scotsman's arm to keep him alongside him. 'Tell me honestly,' he said. 'Do you think I should still be the leader?'

Scotsman avoided his eye. 'The leader of what?'

'You know what. Us. The Dogs.'

'Aye. Sure. Who else is going to do it?'

'That isn't quite the answer I was looking for.'

Scotsman sighed. 'Christ's whiskers,' he said. 'What does it matter who's in charge? There's barely any "us" now anyway.'

Loveday nodded. Scotsman went on.

'I mean, how many of us are left? And how long is it since we've had any decision to make about what we do? Where we go? What we fucking eat? All we do is follow orders. And it's a different cunt giving them every week.' He kicked at the muddy track, exasperated. 'I know I've lost my way since the battle. It's just...'

Loveday put a hand on his friend's shoulder. 'I know. I do. It's been hard on us. I've come to thinking it's all my fault. Pismire... Father... and now Romford, half killed while we were either sleeping or looking the other way.'

Scotsman spat. 'Ach. It's not all down to you. That's what I mean. What else could you have done? We're in a fucking war. And a shite war at that. We've got a king who no one sees any more. Bairns like that wee shite the prince, running around thinking they're in charge of the army. Fuckwits in suits of armour who care more about playing catch-me-kiss-me and selling each other like cattle than about what happens to the likes of us. What would anyone else have done different?'

Loveday nodded. 'He saw it before we did.'

'Huh? Who?'

'The Captain.'

'Fuck's sake, Loveday, not him again.'

'Don't you ever wonder what happened to him?'

'No.'

'I think about him every day.'

'Aye, and you're wasting your fucking time.'

Loveday frowned. 'I don't think I am. He left us because he was frustrated. He thought we hadn't seen what war was becoming. That the bigger the armies became, the less our lives mattered. He thought we were fools for taking the forty. That there were bigger prizes on offer. He thought he was smarter than us.'

'He always was a superior cunt. You think bad things didn't happen in fucking wars before?'

'No. But I think he was right all the same. And I think he would know what to do now. That's why I want to see him again. That's why... at Thérouanne...' He stopped again. 'I don't know any more if I saw him or not. But I do know I wasn't running away. Scotsman. You believe that, don't you? All of you, I mean.'

Scotsman just grunted. They carried on walking for a way in silence. Every few paces Loveday glanced quickly at his friend. He had only realised as the words came out that in truth he did not know if he had really seen the Captain at Thérouanne. Yet Scotsman seemed not to care either way. For the first time since he had taken charge of the Dogs, Loveday wondered if he was losing his crew's belief. Their interest. Their trust.

After a while they saw it. Around a mile ahead, a small shack with collapsing thatch was half hidden in a dip in the land. Scotsman pointed with his axe.

'Reckon that's the place? It looks shite enough.'

Loveday squinted. 'Could be.' He stopped again and took a few deep breaths. The salt air cooled his burning lungs. The walk from Calais, no more than a few miles over rolling terrain, had left him winded.

'You feeling alright?' Scotsman looked at him in concern. 'You look fucking awful.'

'Getting old, I think.' Loveday stood up and straightened his back. 'Let's go and see if that's the Tin Jar.'

'Tin Jar. What a fucking name,' said the Scot. 'You know I fucking hate pirates.'

'I know you do,' said Loveday. 'That's why I brought you.'

15

No provisions could be brought into [Calais] except by stealth, and by the means of two mariners, who were guides to such as adventured. One was named [Jean] Marant...

Chronicles of Jean Froissart

A band of pirates cut them off half a mile before the Tin Jar. They came on foot from several directions, rising out of the landscape like mist. They surrounded Loveday and the Scot, blocking the narrow path in both directions. They were tough men with dirty faces. They carried staves and daggers.

One of them wore a filthy bandage wrapped several times around his head. His left eye was completely bloodshot. Someone had hit him hard.

The bandaged man addressed the two Dogs in rapid guttural French. '*Qu'est-ce que vous voulez putain?*' He covered a nostril and blew a clump of snot. '*Dégagez, enculés.*'

Loveday's French was poor. But experience had taught him the curses. He kept his sword in his belt and raised his hands in what he hoped would be a gesture of peace. Scotsman raised his left hand, his calloused palm open. He kept his right hand on his axe handle.

The bandaged man pointed his stave at Scotsman's axe and chattered angrily.

The Scot bridled. 'You want another bandage on your head? We've come to see your master, whatever the fuck he's called. But by the Holy Virgin's nightgown, I'm happy to burst your fucking—'

'Hold your tongue,' hissed Loveday. He still had his hands up, and was trying to keep his eye on each of the men around them, anticipating any one of them springing at him. 'Does anyone speak English?' he said, as slowly and clearly as he could, trying to keep his voice steady. '*Anglais?* We've come in peace. We want no trouble.'

Loveday's heart skipped as one of the men behind him replied in perfect English, with a London accent.

'Turn around,' he said. 'Slowly.'

Loveday turned around. His neck felt clammy. He looked at the speaker. The face was familiar.

'I thought I knew you,' said the man. He had a full black bushy beard and hair tied with twine at the back of his head. He saw Loveday's blank face. 'It's Gombert,' he said. 'You sold me a wagon full of shit you'd stolen this summer. In Caen.'

Loveday's whole body seemed to flood with relief. 'Of course,' he said. 'Gombert! Thank Christ. I mean – how – I mean—'

Gombert smiled. He spoke quickly in fluent French to the rest of the group. The bandaged man scowled. He seemed displeased at having his authority in the group usurped.

'Why are you here?' said Gombert.

'We need to see Marant.'

Gombert translated for the group, adding something of his own. He laughed. 'The men here think you've come to kill him. I've told them the King of England can find better killers than you two.'

'Fuck off,' said Scotsman. 'If we wanted him dead, we'd march over there and do it.'

Loveday shook his head. 'Ignore my friend,' he said.

'Aye,' said Gombert. 'I think that's best. What do you want with Marant?'

'A favour.'

'And why would he help you?'

'Because we plan to ask very fucking nicely,' said Scotsman.

Gombert said nothing.

'And because we've walked out here for fucking miles getting wet feet and risking having our bollocks hung around our ears.'

Gombert chuckled, but again kept quiet.

Scotsman sighed and looked up at the grey sky above them. 'Fine,' he said. When he looked back down, he avoided meeting Loveday's eye. He puffed out his cheeks.

'And because if he helps us,' he said, 'we'll pay him fifty pounds.'

Marant sat at a small table in the corner of the Tin Jar, perched on a three-legged stool. The tavern was cold and musty. The ceiling was almost entirely hidden by thick funnels of spiders' webs, which looked as though they had been undisturbed for years. Scotsman had to stoop almost double to avoid catching the gossamer in his hair or bumping his head against the trophies that hung everywhere from the walls and beams: carved female figures hewn from the prows of ships; saints' pictures stolen from churches and, nailed above the bar, two dried and blackened pieces of leather Loveday reckoned to be a pair of human ears.

Marant looked up as Loveday and Scotsman were led in. He gave no sign that he recognised them. 'Hang up your cloaks and leave your weapons by the door,' he said, in English. 'Unless you want The Hat here to bar you.' He gestured to a sharp-eyed man with huge grey whiskers and an ancient wide-brimmed oilskin hat, who stood behind the bar, beside the ale barrels. The Hat asked them something in French. Marant translated.

'He asked if he knows you from Fat Margot's. The worst tavern in Paris. I told him I highly doubt it. You two might make it in there. You wouldn't make it out.

'Sit down.'

The Dogs sat. For a time, Marant just studied them. Loveday wondered if he was going to say anything at all. He fancied he could hear the spiders spinning their webs among the ceiling beams.

When he could bear the silence no longer, he said: 'It's us, Jean. Do you remember us?'

The pirate nodded. He moved his jaw like he was chewing something. He jabbed his finger at Scotsman. 'I remember him. You could hardly forget a man like that. What was your name again?'

Scotsman told him.

'That's right,' said Marant. 'I wouldn't forget a name like that either.

'Why have you come here?'

Loveday swallowed. 'Two things.'

'Two?' Marant looked amused. His gold teeth flashed. The scars on his face seemed to tangle and untangle when he smiled.

Loveday took a deep breath. 'I don't quite know how to explain,' he said.

Marant drummed his fingers. 'Bring the boys something to drink,' he said to The Hat. 'See if it loosens their tongues. And have a glass yourself.'

The Hat moved to fill tankards. He muttered. Loveday was not sure what he said made sense in any language.

Marant turned back to the table. 'The Hat knows every lousy drinking den in France. Now, you'd better think of a way to explain what you're after. I've some robbing to do. You know how it is.'

Loveday looked down at the backs of his hands. Scotsman spoke for him. 'We've got a fucking problem,' he said. 'Silly cunt on our crew can't stop finding trouble. It's starting to rub off.'

Marant made a face. 'A hazard of our life. What sort of trouble?'

'You fucking name it,' said Scotsman. 'If he's not out of his mind on something, he's trying to drown himself in a fucking river. Last night a rich boy tried to beat his head in and he did absolutely fuck all to fight back. We brought him on campaign because we wanted a bit of fresh blood in the crew. He's a fine archer, and he's got the knack with those fucking stinking new weapons you hear booming all fucking day. But all he's brought *us* is headaches. We need to get him home, or he'll have us all killed.'

'He sounds unlucky,' said Marant. 'My men are superstitious. Why don't you just slit his throat in his sleep? You know what they say: "no man, no problem".'

'That's not the way we work, Jean,' said Loveday.

'So instead you want him taken to England? That's a long journey for just one man. Why don't you all leave?'

'The king's men are harshly punishing deserters. We can lose one man. All of us... it's harder. And—' Loveday scratched his forearm and stared at the table as he spoke. '—we came here to fight. We've lost good friends along the way. We can't just...' The words caught in his throat and felt small when they came out. '...run away.'

'Honour,' said the pirate, amused. 'If I were you, I'd leave that to the lords. Men like us, it's a fool's route to the grave.' He tapped a finger on his glass. 'What you're asking me is a lot. I'm in the habit of running supplies to Calais, not lost boys to England.'

'We'll pay you bloody well for it,' snapped Scotsman. Loveday could hear the impatience in his voice. 'If you're not going to take him, just say so, and we'll fuck off. If you are, let's hear it. I'll bet we're not the first who've asked you. I'll wager you could fill a fucking boat tomorrow.'

Marant tossed back his drink and put the mug down firmly on the table in front of him. 'Maybe so. Maybe not.' He swirled ale dregs. 'I'll think about it. I can't say more than that. The price you mentioned to my men is a good one. I won't ask where you're laying hands on that kind of coin. But whatever the price, I can't do anything like this for a few weeks.

'Where will my men find you?'

'There's a whorehouse in the wooden town,' said Scotsman. 'Same street with the others. It's the one under the sign of the wolf. How long will it take?'

'As long as it takes,' said Marant. 'Now, do you want to show me some of this money?'

Loveday shifted in his seat. 'We haven't got it yet. It's coming soon. The deal is... complicated.'

Marant closed one eye and looked at Loveday through the

other, as though he were sighting a crossbow. 'Hm. That will make it *complicated* for me to help you. Convince me you're serious.'

Scotsman gave a weary sigh and began pulling rings from his fingers. Only half a dozen of his death haul at Crécy still remained. He spread them on the table in front of him. 'Take your pick. It's all we have left.'

Marant picked up one of the rings, turned it over and inspected it. It was dirty, battered gold, engraved with an image of St Christopher carrying the Christ Child. He pushed it towards Scotsman, then pulled the rest of the rings towards himself and started slipping them on his thumbs. 'Very good. As I said, word will find you when the moment is right. If it's not right, you'll have these back. On my *honour*.'

Scotsman sighed. But he was suddenly too tired to argue. He slipped the Christopher ring back on his hand.

Marant stood up, put his mug on the bar and made for the door. Halfway across the room, he stopped. 'You said there were two things. What was the other?'

Scotsman groaned. Loveday ignored him. 'The Captain. You remember him? He used to be our leader. He disappeared two winters ago. We thought he was dead, but we've heard – I've heard – he may not be. That he's been seen around here. Have you—'

Marant shook his head. 'I can't help you.'

'You haven't seen him? He could be injured now in some way. Some accident...'

'God help him if he is,' said Marant. 'A war is no place for a cripple.' He turned his back and paid close attention to a half-burned candle of grey blubber, spreading its fat over one of the tavern tables.

Loveday tried one more time. 'So you don't have a crippled man inside Calais? It's just that I had been told…'

Marant turned round sharply. 'Whatever you've been told, here's what I'm telling you. Perhaps I can help you with the boy. The rest I know nothing about.' He gave Scotsman and Loveday a curt nod each, and left the Tin Jar. The door banged behind him.

At the bar, The Hat was moving tankards around noisily. He asked them another question. Loveday heard the name of a tavern he did not know. He and Scotsman pushed back their stools. 'Come on,' said Scotsman. 'Let's go and tell the little fucker the good news. And everyone else the bad.'

They stepped outside. The air had grown even colder in the short time they had been with Marant. Like it was laced with frost.

'Good and bad?' said Loveday.

'Aye. The good news is our unlucky charm is off home,' said the Scot gruffly. 'The bad news is the rest of us are fucking broke.'

16

The valiant queen [Philippa] longed to see her lord the king, and she prepared ships and boats and put to sea despite the grave risk of being captured... and reached the army outside Calais...

True Chronicles of Jean le Bel

Romford was sighting the cannon at Calais' walls one freezing morning before All Saints' Day when a magnificent fleet of ships appeared in the choppy waters to the north. They were just tiny spots of colour at first, glinting as they disappeared and reappeared from the cloud that hung over the horizon. But as the moments passed, the spots gained shapes, and even in the pale light of the low, feeble sun, they gained brightness and intensity. Romford stopped his firing to watch them come.

In truth, Romford was glad to have a reason to pause his work. He still found the cannon fascinating. But since the prince had attacked him in the *Wolvenhuis*, he had not enjoyed operating it so much. He had not enjoyed anything. It was not just the violence he had suffered, the shame he felt and the confusion at how the prince could have treated him so cruelly, when he knew who he was. Romford also now woke most days with a fierce, crushing pain in his head, as though his brain were a woodsman's wedge forced into the split trunk of a felled tree. Sometimes the pressing and the hurt would ease as his waking hours went by, but when it was cold – and it was now bitterly cold most days – the pain would linger, making him sick and dizzy from matins until vespers. There were moments when his sight blurred or doubled, and his aim, though still good, was no longer quite as true as it had been. The violent clamour of the gunfire, which had always made his ears ring, now also made him wince, as it shook his poor head until he felt as though something sharp was bouncing around the inside of his skull.

Romford had not seen Louis again since that awful night. He had heard it said that the boy had been sent back to the cities of Flanders to await his marriage to King Edward's daughter. He had seen nothing of Jacky or the prince either. They had not revisited the brothel or the *sablon*. Meanwhile, in the *Wolvenhuis* itself, Romford noticed he was never on his own.

The brothel was busy every day now, and almost every cell was occupied. Hircent ruled the girls tyrannically and forced them to work almost all their waking hours. There was little peace, no privacy and no quiet. Yet this was not the only reason Romford was never alone. Without saying as much, the five older Dogs had organised a watch over him. He was never without one of them and he was not sure how he liked this. He was surprised and moved to see how much they cared for his life, in a way that no one had ever done before them. Yet at the same time it felt as though a rift had opened between them and him. He was different to them. Because of *it*. Because of him. He was not sure he was even one of them any more.

Despite these misgivings, when he spotted the ships on the horizon he called to Tebbe and Thorp from where they stood with the other bowmen. As soon as they heard his voice, the two men hurried to his side.

'What is it?' Thorp looked concerned. He seemed relieved when Romford told him.

The three of them stood and watched as the fleet crept closer towards the sands half a mile along the coast from Calais, where smaller supply ships from England usually anchored to unload their wares under guard. This was not an uncommon sight: despite the roughness of the winter seas, vessels still came and went almost daily from the beaches near the camp. Yet as these bright, fat cogs with their square sails of gold, blue and red came nearer, rolling and lurching on the foam-flecked waves, Tebbe began shaking his head. 'Too big to come ashore here,' he said.

'What do you mean?' asked Romford.

'I'm no sailor, lad,' said Tebbe, 'and you're not either. But if they try and bring those ships too close, sure as shit is shit-coloured, they'll strike a sandbank and get stuck. And in this weather they'll go over. Which means...'

Thorp finished his sentence for him. '...there'll be another feast for the pirates. Everything robbed and everyone who can't swim killed.'

As if to prove Thorp's point, a couple of smaller vessels appeared from further along the shore, staying well out of range of arrow shot from the cogs and their escort ships. 'There you go,' said Tebbe. 'Fucking pirates, always sniffing for their supper.' Romford felt alarmed at the mention of pirates. But he continued to watch the sea with them. So did a gathering crowd of others. Before long, the bombardment of Calais' walls had stopped almost entirely and archers and gunners were speculating about who and what the ships were bringing.

The matter was settled when Sir John Chandos and a half-dozen men-at-arms rushed up to the *sablon*, pushing archers out of their way and snapping angrily at anyone who did not move aside fast enough.

They watched with the rest of the men as the small pirate boats circled and feinted around the bright-sailed fleet. From the decks and masts of the cogs, volleys of arrows and crossbow bolts started to fly. Romford's ears were buzzing from his work, as usual, but he thought he heard Chandos say more than once to the men-at-arms: 'Which one is Her Grace on?'

Tebbe and Thorp looked at each other, then Tebbe said: 'It's the fucking queen.'

Romford could see that he was right – he could now make out golden flags stitched with some sort of fierce beasts flying from each of the largest ships. He felt a lump in his throat, and for reasons he did not understand he wanted to cry.

The feeling stayed with him, even when the crowd watched the large ships changing course. 'Heading up the coast to Flanders,' said Thorp. 'They'll put in at a friendly port up there and travel down here by the supply road. I'd say we'll see her arrive tomorrow.'

'If,' said Tebbe. 'God knows why a fine lady like that would want to come and freeze her tits off in this dump.' He wrapped his wiry arms around himself and shivered. 'Cold again today, and it's going to get worse from now until Lent unless Christ sends a miracle or the stubborn bastards in that city decide to give up. Queen or no queen, we've got a shit time ahead of us.

'Those of us who are staying, anyhow.' He glanced knowingly at Thorp, who seemed to flash back a sharp look of admonition. Romford caught what passed between them. But he had no idea what it meant.

He was also still feeling the strange sadness that had gripped him at the thought of the queen. He did not know what had caused it, but he knew that a single phrase was echoing around his mind and sending stabs down to his heart. Stabs like envy.

The prince has a mother, the voice was saying.

The prince has a mother.

Talk for the rest of the afternoon among the archers and gunners on the *sablon* was about the queen. It continued when Romford, Tebbe and Thorp returned to the *Wolvenhuis* at sundown and found Hastings there, sprawling on a pile of stained and poorly embroidered cushions Hircent had bought from a Flemish hawker. The knight had his arm draped around Margie's shoulder. Romford could see straight away that the girl looked uncomfortable. He felt Tebbe stir with anger.

Hircent was in one of the cells. Another new girl had arrived. Hircent was speaking angrily to her. Romford heard the birch swish and strike the straw bed-sack. The girl whimpered. Loveday and Millstone looked vexed. There was an uncomfortable air in the room.

'You told us we would have fifty when Her Grace arrived,' Millstone was saying.

'That's still what I'm telling you. She's arrived, praise Jesus. And you'll have it. Just not all at once.'

Scotsman snorted. 'You seem to have Sir fucking Arnoul all at fucking once.'

'And you seem to have a tongue on you that I should have pulled out with pincers in the market square,' said Hastings.

'Have you ever seen a man have his tongue pulled out? They never get the whole thing, and it tends to rip rather than come out neatly. That's when the knife goes in. More often than not, they drown in their own blood.'

Margie cringed. Hastings tightened his grip on her, so that he had her almost in a headlock. Millstone put a hand on Scotsman's arm to quiet him. The new girl in the cell was sobbing softly.

'My point, which I suggest you accept,' Hastings continued, 'is that my lady the Queen is an astute businesswoman and a truly liberal-handed patron, whose generosity is well known and therefore much in demand. I tell you this at first hand, since I spent a very put-upon year earlier in this war serving as her steward. I guarantee you that the moment she appears in this camp, everyone from the earls to the peasants who dig the shitting-trenches each day will be around her with their eyelashes fluttering and their hands out. Naturally, her payment for the custody of Sir Arnoul will be one of the items I request from Her Grace. But I'm telling you: she will take some time to pay me, and I will therefore take some time to pay you.'

'Then get us started from the profits of this place.' Millstone spoke quietly, but firmly.

Hircent was back in the room, swishing her birch. She made a peculiar sound, somewhere between a laugh and a screech.

'You really don't understand anything, do you?' said Hastings. He sighed. 'I and some of my less chivalrous but very wealthy acquaintances put up the money to get this place running. You peasants and that monster in the corner—' He hooked a thumb at Hircent, who had eased back into her chair and swapped the birch for Heartbreaker. '—keep it going and help us to pay off the debt...'

Hastings tailed off, as if sensing his words were quite wasted on the Dogs. His manner eased somewhat. 'Listen. I take your point. Why you want the money so urgently when you're already living a life of ease and debauchery here defeats me. But as the king likes to say, it is as it is. Trade here is good. We're recruiting new girls on the roads each day. Some of them will be good workers when they're broken in. Meanwhile, I hear dear old Maggie is performing heroics.'

'Margie,' said Tebbe. 'Her name is Margie.'

'Of course,' said Hastings. 'My wife's name too.' He suddenly looked repelled by Margie and released her from his arm. 'Go on, fuck off.' Margie stood up angrily and stormed away to her cell, pulling her shirt up to cover her breasts. Hastings ignored her.

'Like I said, trade is fine and it will remain good if you leave it to those of us who understand it. But since you seem to think I am deceiving you, let me suggest this. The queen will arrive tomorrow. She will make her formal entry to the camp and there will be a good deal of loyal cheering, followed by a reception in the king's hall. Two of you may attend, as my guests, and you will see exactly what I mean about this woman's generosity.'

He stood up from the cushion pile, stretching and rubbing his shoulders in discomfort. 'Christ's spleen,' he said, rolling his neck and making the bones crunch. 'Don't get old.' He repositioned his wig, then squinted at Loveday. 'Well, for some of you it's too late for that.'

When he was gone, Romford scuttled away to the loft room at the top of the brothel to hide from Hircent, as he always now did. Moments later, Millstone clambered quietly up the ladder behind him. Plainly, it was his turn to keep watch. The stonemason said little, and although Romford felt reassured by his presence, he could not shake from his mind the feeling that something was wrong. That there was something the Dogs knew that he did not.

He lay and drifted in his thoughts, trying to understand what it was they were holding back from him. But his brain hurt and his ears rang and the answers would not come. He eventually fell asleep to the sound of Millstone idly drumming his fingers on the shaft of his heavy war hammer, which the stonemason had used to protect Romford in the past, and which he now always made sure to keep by his side when he turned in for bed.

17

The king... announced that at All Saints he would hold a
great, open court in the Queen's honour...

True Chronicles of Jean le Bel

The king's hall stood only a few hundred paces away from
the *Wolvenhuis*. But it was as if it belonged to some other
world. The long building, its walls made from huge thick
timbers driven into the driest part of the marsh and its roof
thickly thatched, was by some distance the largest building in
Villeneuve.

When Loveday and Scotsman arrived there at sundown,
ushered past the sentries on the outer fence by a brusque and
irritable Sir Hugh Hastings, the hall blazed with torchlight and
the room was already crammed with hundreds of people. They
stood around chattering excitedly in small groups on a wooden
floor strewn with rushes and dried herbs, which gave off a
delicious fragrance as they were crushed underfoot. The Scot's
nose twitched. 'That's bay and rosemary,' he said, shaking his
head in astonishment. 'On the fucking floor!' Loveday had
never smelled anything like it. Nor, though, had he ever been
among a crowd such as was assembled before the large wooden
dais at the end of the fragrant, flickering hall.

It seemed to Loveday that the hall contained every knight

and man-at-arms in the English army. There were hundreds upon hundreds of them, and more came cramming into the room with every passing moment, picking their way around the edges before trying to squeeze into the throng as they spotted faces they knew. A few, Loveday recognised: the one-eyed knight Thomas Holand and the prince's steward, Sir John Chandos; a fat young herald employed by the Earl of Warwick, and Warwick himself, joking and laughing among a group including the Earl of Northampton. There were also several knights whose names he did not know, but who had become regular visitors to the *Wolvenhuis*. Yet most of the crowd was unknown to Loveday – and many of them seemed entirely new to the camp. Perhaps to any war camp.

There were not only fighting men, but also preening clerics trussed in fine long gowns stitched with gold thread. Pompous merchants in expensive clothes that would be ruined within a week on the salty, muddy Calais marsh. There was also a large number of ladies: the married and widowed wearing veils or elaborate hats; the younger maidens with their long hair arranged in rolls and plaits that seemed to float at the sides of their heads.

The women's presence charged the air in the room. It certainly animated the Scot. He and Loveday were standing in the back corner of the hall, attempting to draw as little attention as they could to themselves. Loveday knew they looked poor and smelled awful, despite both having bathed in the yard behind the brothel, using the girls' wash buckets. He expected that at any moment a man-at-arms would march them out.

Scotsman, however, seemed unbothered. When a servant walked past carrying a tray of elegant wine mugs, stamped with King Edward's symbols of leopards and fleurs-de-lis, he shot out two hairy hands and grabbed a pair. He passed one to Loveday. 'Whatever it is that bald cunt wants to prove to us by dragging us here, so be it,' he said. 'But let's enjoy ourselves while we're at it.' He nudged Loveday and pointed through the crowd to a young woman about fifteen years old, as tall as many of the men in the room, high cheekboned, with rosy cheeks, full lips and blonde hair so shiny with grooming that it seemed to glow like cloth of gold. 'Christ have mercy, we don't see the likes of her in the fucking whorehouse,' he breathed.

'No,' whispered Loveday. 'That we don't.' But before he could say more, a trumpet blasted from beyond a curtain at the back of the dais. A herald cried for silence. A bevy of priests crossed themselves. And the whole room fell to their knees, as on to the wooden platform walked King Edward, his son the prince, and between them, Queen Philippa.

She was captivating. Not beautiful, Loveday thought, as he stole glances at her from beneath his brows while he kneeled with the crowd in the royal hall. She had a face somehow both long and round, with chubby cheeks and a chin that jutted out, a small roll of flesh hanging behind it. The flush in her face suggested she had recently borne a child, and perhaps was with child again. Her eyes were black, her eyebrows were thick and dark like a man's and her mouth was pinched, with a top lip far bigger than the lower. She wore her hair in great packages tied up in expensive fabric around her ears, secured with jewelled pins and gold. Her red dress and golden cloak did not cling to her, as did those of the maidens Scotsman was drooling over. Yet Loveday found her fascinating. In his years with the king's army – and especially the weeks they had been in France – Loveday had developed an instinctive mistrust of wealthy and noble men. But as he looked at Queen Philippa, he told himself that she was different to all the men of her world. Someone who had brought calm and cleanliness and goodness into this awful place.

A hush had fallen over the room. King Edward filled it. His voice, though soft, was clear, and he projected it so that it rang over the whole hall. He commanded the audience to rise. Then he and the queen sat on high-backed thrones beside one another. The prince stood on his father's right. He tried to look interested. Loveday could see he was bored.

'My very beloved wife and queen,' Edward said. He smiled at her, and she back at him. For a moment, they seemed lost in one another's eyes.

The prince stifled a yawn.

'My queen,' said Edward, addressing the court once more, 'has something to tell you all.'

She looked at him questioningly. He nodded. 'God's mercy, my love. It is your story to recount.'

The room went silent. Scotsman kicked Loveday on the ankle and looked at him questioningly. Loveday had no idea what to expect. He stared at the dazzling woman on the dais and waited for her to speak.

Philippa gazed serenely around the assembled group. She took a breath. Then she began to speak in light and rapid French.

'*Mon peuple bien-aimé, cela m'apporte le plus grand bonheur de m'asseoir ici avec vous…*'

Scotsman kneed Loveday in the thigh. 'What the fuck?' he growled.

'...*les forces obscures se dressent contre nous...*'

Loveday cursed under his breath. In camp, almost everyone spoke English, since this was the language the knightly classes and archers shared. French, however, clearly remained the language of court and courtiers.

'Loveday,' hissed the Scot. 'What's she saying?'

Loveday shook his head.

...*mais notre Dieu et sauveur est avec nous, et tout autour de nous, et son amour s'étend à notre cause au-dessus de toutes les autres...*

'Something about God,' he whispered. 'Er... us above other people...? I think?'

'God,' muttered the Scot. 'Always fucking God.'

Soon, Loveday lost any sense of what the queen was saying and he had to rely on picking out odd words and watching the reactions of the other guests, as well as the king and prince on the dais.

Yet even doing this, he understood that the queen was relaying something they all considered to be of enormous consequence.

As her story went on, murmurs, shocked gasps and little cries of astonishment began to go around the room. A few girls swooned, glancing slyly as they did so to be sure their friends saw them perform. At one point, the Earl of Warwick clambered on to the side of the dais and bade the crowd be quiet with his hands. The king nodded at him in thanks, and the queen continued.

Then, as excitement gathered once more, she stopped, and smiled deliberately to each corner of the hall. She had slowed her tale to a crawl, teasing the audience. Making them hungry.

'...*et donc Davide, le roi des Écossais...*'

'She's saying something about King David,' whispered Loveday to Scotsman.

'The one in the Bible? Lad that fought the giant?'

'No, by Christ,' Loveday hissed. 'The ruler of your lot.'

'You fucking what? Wee Davie the Bruce?' Scotsman reddened and stuck his chest out. 'What about him?'

'Keep your voice down.'

The queen paused once more. '*le roi des Écossais est dans la tour de Londres – notre prisonnier!*'

'Loveday, tell me what the fuck she's saying.'

Loveday's mouth fell open. 'Scotsman, I—'

He understood. But he couldn't get the words out.

The servant with the wine cups passed by. He caught the Scot's accent. He noted his puce face. He jeered. 'Best place for you lot, banged up in the Tower.'

Bystanders were hugging each other and cheering, delirious. A line of courtiers eager to fawn over the queen had already formed. Loveday saw Sir Hugh Hastings far towards the back of it.

Scotsman grabbed the servant by his tunic. He lifted him off his feet. Fabric tore. The servant dropped his tray. He went pale and babbled. The big man grabbed one of his hands and squeezed, crushing his fingers.

'Tell me in words I fucking understand what's going on or you'll never hold your pintle to piss again.'

The servant dripped sweat and kept babbling. 'I didn't mean – I didn't—'

Loveday urged the man to do as he was told.

'King David,' squeaked the servant. 'He's been captured. The queen. There was a battle... somewhere she called Neville's Cross... he's a prisoner in London. They say his ransom will—'

Scotsman released his hand and dropped the man. He landed on his own tray. Shards of broken cup lodged in his shoulder blades. He howled again and leapt up, writhing and staggering as he tried to pull them loose from his back.

Guests were starting to stare. Loveday's guts snarled.

He recalled someone once telling him that violence in the king's hall was treason and they'd chop off your hands for it. He decided this was not the time to find out if it were true.

'Fuck, Scotsman, we need to go,' he said.

But the big man was no longer beside him.

His huge dark frame was already outside the hall, heading out into the night.

'Scotsman!' Loveday yelled. And he ran out after him.

Loveday caught the Scot up in the market square. He grabbed his arm and managed to spin the big man around. His heart was hammering and his breath fogged in the night air as he panted from running. Moonlight hung in the steam.

'Scotsman...'

'Aye,' said the Scot, 'that's right. I fucking am.'

'Come on. We've been at war with them for years.'

'Who's we? I fucking haven't. Where did you and I first cross paths?'

Loveday remembered it vividly. The bracing wind that whipped their faces as they fought in the bloody combat on the beach at Kinghorn, in King Edward's first years. They had been on opposing sides, but had not known it until they met, years afterwards. 'I recall it well. But that's—'

'What? In the past? Fuck it all, Loveday, I fought for the real Bruce when I was a young man. Old Rabbie. Believed in the cunt, too. The old guys used to tell me stories about Bannockburn. I was at Dupplin Moor. I was—'

'Aye, and now you're a Dog. And have been how long? In case you hadn't noticed, we're with the English army.'

'Fuck that. God's bollocks, Loveday. I'm with you and the men. But that's where it ends. As far as I know, we've been fighting the French. Fuck 'em. I don't give two fucks on a Friday about the French. But I don't care about your King Edward either, or his cunt of a son, or his weird-looking queen with her chubby cheeks and that stupid lip on her, like a fucking beak.'

Despite himself, Loveday felt a twinge of defensiveness about the queen. The Scot's argument infuriated him. Yet deep down he could understand it.

'Loveday.' Scotsman's voice softened. 'If there's one thing we've learned since we've been in this shitehole of a country, it's that no one leading this army cares about us. They use us for what they want. They promise us things they don't have or won't give up. They lie to us. They screw us, or they let us be screwed. We owe them fuck all.'

'So all lords are the same? If that's the case, then why do you care...'

'Because even though all that shite is true, sometimes it's different,' said the Scot. 'You think that queen is really going to give us fifty pounds for some prisoner that sly cunt Hastings is holding? You think that for one moment? Deep down? Really?'

Loveday swallowed hard. 'Aye. No. I don't know. I don't know anything any more.'

'I'll go with no. And I'm right. But I still saw the way you looked at her in that hall. She meant something to you. She did something to you. It was like being in love. Wasn't it? Be honest, by Christ.'

'Aye.'

'Exactly. Aye. And it's a fucking curse. It doesn't matter how much they hurt you. You know you're still going to love them.'

Loveday nodded. He was suddenly very cold.

Scotsman sighed. 'That little bastard Davie Bruce is king of my fucking countrymen. I know he's a useless cunt. I knew the stupid fucker was bound to get himself captured one day. And I know if he's let out, he'll do something even stupider.

'But he's still my fucking king. Or the king of my people. If there's a difference. And Christ will come back to Earth wearing a pretty fucking dress and driving a haycart before I sit around celebrating him being in the Tower of fucking London.'

'What do you mean?'

'I mean I'm fucking going.'

'Where?'

'Home.'

Loveday laughed, despite the cold and the desperation of the evening. His laugh formed a white cloud and floated away. 'Home? Where even is home?'

'Not fucking here, that's where. I don't know. Where we were before. London. Essex. Portsmouth. Fucking Scotland, if I must.'

'You're drunk.'

'You're wrong. For once. Or, I mean, you're wrong a lot of the time, but I'm not drunk now. I'm going. And I'll tell you how. I'm taking that pirate his fifty pounds and he's taking me somewhere. Anywhere. Any of you cunts want to join me, you'll be very welcome. I'll take the lad, of course. Not that he'll improve my chances of staying alive. But I'm telling you, Loveday. This is it.'

Loveday shook his head, confused. 'Scotsman, we don't

have fifty pounds. We don't have anything. That's the whole point. We've been waiting for the queen.'

'Haven't got fifty pounds my bollocks. I've been thinking about this ever since we were in that piss-poor excuse for a tavern with the pirate. Marant is a businessman, isn't he?'

Loveday shrugged. 'Pirate, businessman. Aye. There's not much between the two.'

'Well then. The cunt should be happy to take payment in kind.'

'Payment in what?'

'Payment in fucking kind, Loveday. Look around you. Who do you see?'

Loveday looked. The square was deserted. The streets were empty. All the noise in Villeneuve was coming from the king's hall.

'See?' said Scotsman. 'Fucking nobody. And I'll bet there's no prick worth talking of guarding our fifty-pound fucking hero. I'm going to break him out and take him to Marant. And you can help me, Loveday, or you can go to hell, and I'll meet you there shortly.'

He turned on his heel and strode off towards the prisoners' pen.

Loveday scrambled to keep up.

There was a single guard on the door to the compound. A spotty-faced squire little more than Romford's age. Shivering at his post.

Scotsman let him choose between a broken neck and his keys. He slapped him senseless as a thank-you.

They found Sir Arnoul d'Audrehem's cage. The knight was at his prayers by candlelight. His leg seemed better. His hand had almost healed. He looked well fed and strong.

Sir Arnoul stood up in alarm when the two Dogs burst in. He crossed himself and backed into the cell's furthest corner. He kept whispering his prayers.

'Come with us, you daft cunt,' said Scotsman. 'And you can stop praying, too.

'It looks like God's been listening.'

18

Receipt for compensation paid to Jean Baudet for a ship, the Saint Peter of Marolio, laden with building supplies, which was taken for the relief of the town of Calais in November 1346.

Entry in the Treasury Journal of Philippe VI 'Le Bel'

When they came for him, he thought he must be dreaming. Lately, Romford's dreams had been as vivid as anything he had experienced when he had eaten the Host. He blamed the ache in his head. The ringing in his ears. The sounds of the *Wolvenhuis* that still found their way into his brain at all hours of the day and night. Foxlike screams of men fucking women. The leering banter and clatter of coin. The swish of Hircent's birch.

So he assumed he was dreaming when, in the black of the night, strong hands touched his shoulders and shook him.

When a voice like Loveday's whispered urgently in his ear.

You're leaving.

You're going home.

Romford actually laughed out loud. The idea of escaping the hell in which he lived was so impossible that even to hear it suggested seemed hilarious.

But there was Loveday's voice again, the strong hand on the

shoulder once more. And hope, floating to him through the dark.

You're going home, lad. It's over for you. Get up. Go with Scotsman. Do as he tells you. I'll see you again one day. I... I'm sorry. It wasn't meant...

A gruff clearing of the throat.

I'm sorry.

Romford shook his head. He sat up. Loveday moved away. Romford heard him a little further off, talking with the Scot.

You're sure? Really sure?

Aye.

So this is goo—

Christ, Loveday. Don't you fucking goodbye me.

As Romford felt around for his pack, he heard the sound of the two men embracing. There was barely anything to it. A few quick slaps on the back. Cleared throats. Then silence.

The pirate with gold-studded teeth and a scarred face who greeted them in the tumbledown tavern on the hillside outside Villeneuve did not seem pleased to see them. 'Jonah in the whale's guts,' he said. 'Are you trying to get us all killed?'

His voice was salt-scoured by the sea. Romford avoided his gaze and took stock of where they were. 'The Tin Jar,' Scotsman had said, when they arrived. 'Shittest inn in Christendom.' Romford saw cobwebs. A feeble fire smoking. An uneven tavern bar, presided over by an ancient fellow in a stained and greasy hat. Stuffed fish on the wall and a dead man's ears.

He was sitting by the fire, trying to get some warmth back into his bones. On the other side of the room, apparently aloof to all around him, sat another man. Scotsman had dragged him there behind himself and Romford. This man was a knight, with long blond hair that fell forward over his face. His hands were bound and he sat with difficulty, one of his legs being much weaker than the other. Romford understood him to be the knight Loveday and Millstone had captured in the woods near Thérouanne.

Scotsman was arguing about the knight with the gold-toothed man. 'Well, I can't fucking take him back to Villeneuve.'

The salty voice: 'And I can't take him forward.'

'Sell him to Philippe—'

'Philippe? King Philippe? What's he got to do with this? We're fucking pirates. The admiral of the French fleet has let it be known that for now we're free to harass merchant convoys in the narrow sea and escape a hanging. From time to time, he pays me handsomely to risk my crew's necks taking wine and crossbow bolts into Calais harbour.

'What he doesn't do is come knocking on the door asking if Jean Marant has any lame knights he wants to sell to the king.'

Scotsman puffed, exasperated. 'So what the fuck do you expect me to do?'

'Expect…? I didn't *expect* you to come here at all. I *expected* you to do as we agreed. To cash in your captive, then wait for me to tell you when the sailing to England would be, at which I'd take custody of that black-fingered waif you've just dumped by my fireplace. You know why I *expected* that? Because it's what we agreed. But of course, I should have remembered I was dealing with the Essex Dogs. You had a good captain once. But I gather he tired of leading around a bunch of fuck-ups, and at last I understand why.'

Romford now understood that the salty-voiced man was the pirate Jean Marant. He had heard the Dogs and many other men speak of him. Marant covered his face with his hands. Scotsman folded his thick arms.

Marant put his hands down and took a deep breath. 'Do you know who he is?' He meant the bound knight. 'Anything about him?'

'He's called Sir Arsehole Arsebollocks, or something like that. Loveday and Millstone picked him up in a wood near Thérouanne. Saved his life.'

'And?'

'And nothing. That's it. What do I look like, his fucking squire?'

'His serf, maybe.'

'Aye, well. Knights all look the same to me. Talk a lot of shit, suck their horses' cocks and won't have a fight unless they're wearing a hundredweight of tin.'

Marant pinched the bridge of his nose. Romford kept still.

'Who were you meant to be selling him to?'

'Sir Hugh Hastings. Cunt. He was going to get the money from the queen. He took too long.'

'The queen?'

'Aye, the queen. Of England. Philippa. Imagine a duck with tits. Now stick a crown on it. You've got the idea.'

'So you're stealing from the Queen of England. Do you have any idea how dead you are?'

'Ah, fuck off. We're not stealing from anyone. She never paid us.' Scotsman spat on the tavern floor. The man in the hat muttered darkly.

'Now you've angered The Hat, too.'

Marant and Scotsman glared at each other. Then another voice chimed.

'Take me to Calais.'

It was the knight.

'If you untie me first, I will be happier, of course. But you help me go to Calais. If you do this, I pay you to take this young man onwards, to where he needs to go. He is sick, I think.'

'The fuck—'

'Shut up.' Marant pulled his black hair into a bundle behind his head. He spoke to the knight for a short time in French.

Scotsman banged the table. 'What are you saying? That's my prisoner, for fuck's sake. If you want to talk to him, talk to me.'

Marant laughed. 'He says he's not your prisoner.'

'Is that so? I'd love to know who tied his fucking hands.'

'He says he surrendered himself to your comrades. Formally. These things matter to a knight. He says if they were here, he would consider himself duty-bound to obey them. But since they are *not* here, he considers himself free to choose the terms of his imprisonment until they reclaim him.'

Romford had never seen a man's face turn the colour that Scotsman's went. The big man was momentarily speechless. The knight looked impassive. He was inspecting his bindings with interest.

Marant grinned. 'The rules of war are strange, are they not? But Sir Arnoul is very experienced in them. What's more, he claims to be an honourable man. He says he feels duty-bound to defend Calais. He now says he will pay *me* to take him there. But since he feels grateful for *your* help in freeing him, *he* will pay *me* to take the boy home.'

Romford could see the Scot growing very confused. 'I need a fucking drink.'

'Then you had better apologise to The Hat. He detests spitting. He has a peculiar theory that it spreads plagues.'

Scotsman apologised. The Hat poured him ale. The pirate and the knight spoke to one another some more, in French. Romford squirmed closer to the small fire. Everyone ignored him.

Eventually, Marant addressed the two Dogs. 'So. We have a deal. A ship runs supplies in to Calais today, captained by a friend of mine. We call him *Le Baudet*. The Donkey.' Marant put his hands to his head like long ears, stuck out his gold teeth and brayed. He laughed. 'He's slow, stubborn, but he gets the job done. I will send some men to escort Sir Arnoul. After that, they will take care of your boy.'

Scotsman nodded. 'And what about me?'

Marant looked puzzled. 'You?'

'Aye. What in the name of Christ do you think I'm here for? I want to get home as well.'

Marant rubbed the bridge of his nose once more. Then he shrugged. 'Fine. We'll take care of you too. But you must help get Sir Arnoul into Calais.' The pirate came over to the fire and threw on a few pieces of green wood.

Scotsman was quiet.

Marant put his hands on his hips. 'Well. Do you have any objections?'

'Aye, I've got a lot of fucking objections.'

'And do you have any other choice?'

'Ah, fuck off.'

Romford and Scotsman stayed in the Tin Jar all morning. Sir Arnoul, his hands unbound, dozed a little, prayed, and ate the blackened pieces of fish The Hat slapped down before the men when they grew hungry. Marant did not eat, but kept a brooding watch from the door. Around midday, one of his men came and whispered something to him.

'It's time,' he said. That was all the farewell he had.

Gombert and a pirate called Dogwater, who wore a dirty bandage on his head, led Romford, Scotsman and Sir Arnoul down a narrow path to a cove. A rowing boat was ready when they got there. Two crossbows and a few bags of bolts lay beneath the oarsman's bench. A few had spilled loose.

A ship of moderate size lay at anchor in the deep waters off the shore. Gombert and Dogwater took an oar each and rowed them towards it.

Scotsman and Sir Arnoul squeezed together in the stern of the boat, facing forward. Romford sat in the bow.

They were barely halfway to the larger ship when the choppy seas started to make him feel very sick. He wished he had some Host to help settle his stomach. Instead, he picked up a crossbow bolt and tried to concentrate on cleaning the dirt from under his nails with its jagged, dull-grey barb.

Before long, Gombert and Dogwater brought the tiny boat alongside the ship, which sat low in the water, as though it carried a heavy load. 'Here you go,' said Gombert. '*Saint-Pierre de Marolio*. Full of rocks, by the look of it. Ballast for repairing the walls.' The sailors tossed down a rope and Dogwater secured the boat, so it could be towed along behind.

Next, a rope ladder came down. Romford watched it unfurl. As it did, he started to believe for the first time in what was happening. He really was going home. As the belief gathered in him, he stopped feeling sick and started to enjoy himself. He smiled at Scotsman as the big man puffed and struggled to clamber up the ladder. He studied Sir Arnoul's ascent, lopsided as he used his stronger leg to carry his injured one. He watched

Gombert spring up the ladder so easily it seemed he were floating, even as he held a crossbow in one hand. By the time it was Romford's turn, he had seen enough to understand how to climb the ladder with the least effort. He skipped up, taking note of everything: the roughness of the rope on his fingers and palms. The chafe of the wood. The sway of the ship's side as he scaled it.

Dogwater came last. He had his crossbow slung on his back. Looking at it, Romford realised that he still had a bolt in his own hands. Its flights were stiff with salt. Its tip was grimy with the soot he had picked from under his nails.

The *Saint-Pierre de Marolio*'s crew unfurled the sail and they cruised a short way up the coast. A patchy mist now hung over the sea, and the shore came in and out of view. Romford stood beside Scotsman and they stared over the side. Scotsman tugged his beard and looked anxiously at the land.

'I won't fucking miss it,' said the Scot.

The mist cleared and for a fleeting moment Calais came into view. Romford was fascinated to view it from an angle he had never seen before. Out at sea, he understood its geography a little better. The city's walls formed a sharp rectangle, with a castle built into the walls on the corner nearest him. Protecting all this from the sea side was a long spit of land that ran parallel to the beach in front of the seaward walls. It was barricaded and defended at its tip and the narrow point where it joined the mainland. Romford thought it must be the place he had heard men on the *sablon* describe as the Risbank.

They had spoken of it as though it were the key to the defence of the city, and now he understood why, for behind it lay a sheltered harbour, accessed only by a small causeway between the Risbank's tip and Calais' beach. That was, Romford guessed, where they were heading to drop Sir Arnoul, before he and Scotsman were taken home to England. A shaft of weak winter sunlight caught the walls of the city for a moment, and they seemed to glow gold.

As he stared at the gold, a seemingly unconnected thought danced across Romford's mind.

Why would this large ship go all the way to England just for him and Scotsman?

But he had no time to contemplate an answer, for there was a bustle among the sailors. The sail was furled and the anchor dropped again. Scotsman looked around in surprise. Romford kept looking out to sea. The golden light that shone from Calais' walls had entranced him. He felt as though his body were connected to it. The mist had closed again, but he thought he could feel the light glowing somewhere within.

Gombert and Dogwater came over, bringing Sir Arnoul with them. Gombert grinned at them.

'What's happening?' demanded the Scot. Romford felt his nervousness.

Gombert smiled even more broadly. 'Mist,' he said. 'Can't get this big bastard in there safely until it clears. We're going to row the small boat in. Marant said you were going to help us.'

Scotsman looked doubtful. 'We only just got out of that fucking thing. Take Sir Arsehole over, and we'll wait for you here.'

Dogwater spoke irritably in French to Gombert, and pointed to the rope ladder, slung once more over the side of the *Saint-Pierre*. Sir Arnoul frowned slightly as he listened, but Gombert stepped in and seemed to reassure the knight.

'If you please,' he said to Scotsman and Romford. 'We will need four of us as we come into the harbour.' He tapped his crossbow. 'Cover. We may have to defend ourselves as we come in. We've got our orders.'

Scotsman grunted. 'Nothing's ever fucking easy, is it?' he said.

Gombert shrugged. Behind him, Dogwater shinned down the rope ladder, and one of the crew of the *Saint-Pierre* guided the little rowing boat back around so he could leap into it. He kept it steady as Sir Arnoul and Scotsman climbed in.

They took up their same positions in the boat. Gombert and Dogwater pulled the oars. The ship disappeared. Romford watched it shrink. Something felt very wrong.

Gombert and Dogwater were pulling against the current, and after they had been rowing for some time, the little boat seemed to have stopped making any progress towards Calais at all. Scotsman and Sir Arnoul began to grow restless.

'You two cunts need to put your backs into it,' said the Scot. 'You're not even sweating.'

The pirates laid their oars on their laps. 'It's your turn anyway,' Gombert said. His smile had disappeared. He tapped his crossbow again. 'We'll watch for trouble as we get closer.'

Scotsman looked disgusted. 'Some fucking service this is.' But his impatience got the better of him. He elbowed Sir Arnoul sitting beside him. 'Come on. You look strong enough to work this out.' The two big men took the pirates' places on the bench and started to pull the oars. The pirates knelt behind them, facing outwards, aiming their crossbows at the sea.

Romford watched them. He followed where they were

pointing their crossbows, studying the paths their bolts would take if the triggers were pulled.

They arced nowhere.

Romford found that odd. It was as if the pirates were not aiming their crossbows at all. That it was some dance. Some piece of theatre.

With Scotsman and Sir Arnoul pulling in a rhythm, the boat now picked up speed. But as it did, Romford's sense of something amiss began to grow. He became acutely aware of the smallest movements around him. He felt almost as if he had eaten Host.

His hands moved slowly. His thoughts moved slowly. Everyone else moved slowly too.

At this pace, Romford watched Scotsman and Sir Arnoul pull the oars. And he saw Gombert and Dogwater pass a signal. The signal was so slight and so fleeting, it was only just visible. But Romford saw it, and he understood in a flash what was happening.

The pirates were not going to take them to Calais at all. They must have decided to betray both Sir Arnoul and Scotsman. And him.

That meant—

Romford saw the two pirates turn together and raise their crossbows. Gombert lifted his, clublike, and prepare to slam the heavy wooden butt of it down on the back of Sir Arnoul's head. Dogwater turned his directly on the base of Scotsman's skull. The line of the bolt's path went straight towards the point where the Scot's head met his neck.

Romford's heart roared like a cannon blast. Something terrible was happening. He knew he ought to feel fear. Yet he also knew there was no time for fear. There was only action.

For some reason, he remembered Father's voice at Thérouanne. 'Toad. Can't even shoot straight.'

Romford shook his head. 'No. That's not true.'

Since he re-entered the boat, Romford had been sitting on his heels in a squat, to keep his arse dry. That meant his knees were bent and his feet flat on the little craft's unsteady floor. Which was good. It meant the force he would have to use to launch himself towards the two pirates was very little at all. He charged his legs. They tingled.

But he still had to make a decision. Did he push himself at Gombert or at the bandage-headed Dogwater?

That was easy. His right hand was planted on his right knee. His left was by his side. And the left held something.

The crossbow bolt.

He had been picking his nails with it now for so long that the whites were almost see-through. Like expensive glass. He was gripping it in his fist, the point poking out between his forefinger and curled thumb. That was awkward. It would be better if he had it the other way around. But he could not risk turning it around, or it might be dropped or lost. Then, what he aimed to do would be a far less certain business.

He had to work with what he had.

But what he had was certainty. And belief. And love.

Romford drove his weight through his heels.

Scotsman and Sir Arnoul heaved the oars. Gombert and Dogwater nodded to one another. Gombert slammed the butt of his crossbow into Sir Arnoul's skull with a sickening crunch.

Dogwater, however, was a heartbeat behind him. And as he steadied himself to pull the crossbow's trigger and put a bolt in the back of Scotsman's head, Romford was flying towards him.

He was almost fast enough.

Romford slid, as he had planned to, on to the floor of the boat just behind Dogwater's leg. He wrapped his right arm around Dogwater's ankles, to pull him off balance, knowing that this would drag the aim of his crossbow high.

Dogwater pulled the trigger and Scotsman slumped forward.

But as he did so, Romford's left arm was cocked back. He held the crossbow bolt by his ribs. Then he drove it upwards with every scrap of his strength.

The barbed tip of the bolt sunk into Dogwater's calf. Once it was in as far as it would go, Romford pulled as hard as he had pulled anything before. He used the strength he would have exerted on the toughest longbow string he had ever drawn.

The bolt slid out. It pulled a chunk of something purple and alive with it. Romford did not look at it. He twisted his body so he fell on his right side, and thrust the bolt upwards again. It passed his face so closely he smelled the live flesh stuck to the barb.

Then it disappeared once more into the soft flesh of Dogwater's right groin, where the blood pumped through to the whole leg.

The bolt disappeared again. And now he did not pull, but twisted and drew it, so that he opened a hole in Dogwater's thigh big enough to fit most of his fingers into.

Romford felt it start raining. The rain was warm. He opened his mouth and let the rain fall into it. It tasted of metal and meat. It got in his eyes and made everything pink.

But he did not stop to think about it. Because now he was lying on his back, and looking at Gombert's face, a man's height above him.

Gombert was pointing his crossbow at Romford's face.

Romford looked at it as long as he dared. Long enough for Gombert's finger to tighten on the trigger. Then he rolled.

The bolt shot out. It grazed the side of Romford's face and disappeared through the hull of the boat.

Gombert suddenly looked scared.

Romford grabbed the pirate's legs. Everything was warm and slippery, but he managed to hold on. He squeezed with every ounce of strength he had. The slippery metal rain made it hard to grip. But it helped him too. Gombert lost his footing in it. He fell.

As Gombert fell, Romford scrambled, slipping, until he was on top of the pirate.

He grasped Gombert's hair with both his slick wet warm hands. He thought back to how the prince had smashed his head into the floor of Hircent's brothel. He tried to use exactly the same technique. He did it more times than the prince had. Harder with each blow.

After ten or eleven blows, the hull of the boat cracked. Three or four blows later, Gombert's skull did. Still Romford did not stop. He kept beating head and boat together until he opened a hole in the back of Gombert's skull and something grey plopped out.

Only then did he let go. Only then did he stand up and look at what he had done.

Everything was red. Everyone was red. Water was coming into the boat and making some of it less red.

All four other men in the boat were lying down in the red.

Gombert was dead. Dogwater was nearly dead. Sir Arnoul was moaning, and seemed as though he would not awake for many hours.

Scotsman was bleeding from a deep cut that ran the length of the top of his scalp. He was curled up in a ball.

The two oars of the boat were making crazy circles as the water threw them around.

Romford sat down on the bench and took an oar in each hand. He was not used to rowing, but he had watched it done for long enough to understand what he had to do.

Looking over his shoulder, he pointed the small boat towards Calais' harbour.

It was hard to move the boat with the tide, but he did it. He avoided the rocks in front of the Risbank. He swung into the harbour out of the range of arrow shot until he felt sure anyone from Calais would see that he was not a threat.

He rowed into the harbour as the sun was setting. He was exhausted. He was trembling. His skin felt tight and itchy and sticky.

When the waters stilled, he stood in the boat and raised both his hands. He was dimly aware of a crowd of people on the harbourside. He could barely raise his eyes to look at them. He hung his head and looked down.

He caught his reflection in the water of the harbour.

There was none of him that was not covered in blood.

Gasps and shouts arose among the crowd. Someone threw a stone at him. It splashed into the water a few yards from the boat.

Romford sank to his haunches. It was all he could do to lift his face and look again at the crowd.

A one-legged man leaned on a crutch among them. Even from a distance, and through his weakness, Romford could see that his skin had been burned, or eaten by some pestilence. His straggling hair was grey and swept back, revealing patches of his livid scalp beneath.

Yet there was something cool in his eyes and a hard beauty to the lines of his face that even the hideous scarring could not obscure.

The boat was floating on the harbour's incoming tide towards the dockside. The shocked voices of the crowd grew louder.

As he drifted towards them, Romford's mind travelled back to the night after the Battle of Crécy. When he had lain by the campfire and eaten the Host for the first time.

He heard Millstone's voice.

He was always a handsome bastard.

The boat bumped gently against the harbourside. Hands grabbed it and pulled it in.

The man with the wooden leg and the crutch looked into the boat and spoke to Romford in English.

'I see Dogwater upset you,' said the Captain. 'I know the feeling well.'

19

When the men of Calais realised King Edward wasn't going to leave that winter... they sent five hundred people out of the city through the English lines...

True Chronicles of Jean le Bel

*I*t was nearly Christmas when her chance came. By then, Squelette was ready.

She certainly looked ready. She was painfully thin. Her cheeks were sunk and her knees and ankles wider than the leg bones between. Her breasts were gone. Her hipbones stuck out like little shelves. Her hair was falling out and her teeth and fingernails were loose.

She was always hungry and always cold.

Living off the land had become much harder as autumn turned to winter. The nights were freezing, and the bushes and ground were bare of food to forage. She had abandoned her crossbow when she ran out of bolts. She could not stand in the streams to fish without shivering so hard she scared the fish away.

She chewed bark and roots on the days when she found nothing else to eat. She took clothes and blankets from the homes of the dead.

By day and by night she had started coming closer and

closer to the English camp. Several times she had come right up to its perimeter fence, to catch a glimpse of campfires blazing on the marsh.

But she had so little strength that she could not contemplate adding to the scars on her arm. A knight or archer – even a merchant – would have overpowered her with ease.

She thought more and more about killing for food.

Then, one day, it happened.

The roads away from Villeneuve started filling with women. Not only women. Children and older people too. But mostly women. They spoke hard northern French and carried pathetic bundles of possessions and little parcels of food. They were thin and weak. Not as thin and weak as she was, but not far from it.

They could only have been from Calais.

Squelette did not have to think about it for long. The city, like her, must be starving. The garrison had ordered those who could not fight to leave. Had sent them out to meet their fate.

Squelette guessed correctly what that fate would be.

The refugees were escorted by groups of English archers and men-at-arms to a point where painted warning signs and piles of stones by the roadside marked a mile from the siege town's perimeter. Then they were told to be on their way.

Some, delirious at being freed from the besieged city, made off along the road at a run. They jangled handfuls of coins and whooped as they ran.

But more of them shrank back, refusing to go any further. Unwilling to leave the escort. Some of them sat down, cross-legged, on the road, even when the archers in the escort pushed and kicked them, swearing and spitting.

Squelette knew what they feared. She had seen it happen already. She had seen who roamed the road beyond.

And she knew what she wanted to do.

She waited until several groups of refugees were escorted along at once, then she slipped into the road among them. No one paid her any notice.

The refugees came to the mile point and began arguing among themselves. Squelette left them and trudged on, as though resigned to her fate.

She went further than she thought she would need to. But not much further.

A pair of Flemings overtook her on horseback. They went a little way beyond her, then turned their horses to block the road. One of them dismounted. He spoke to her in broken French.

He asked her where she was going. She told him she did not know. He asked her where her husband was. She told him he was dead.

The Fleming was a flabby man, with a bald round head and eyes too close together. He spoke slowly and stupidly. He blinked a lot. He told her she must come and work for him. She told him she did not want to. She refused twice more. He became angry, and he hit her.

She fell. She was so weak it required no pretence. She hoped he was too stupid to search her.

He was.

The man bundled her over the back of his horse, tied her so she would not fall, and remounted. His partner threw a blanket over her so she could not be seen, or identified easily as a person.

They took her into the siege town called Villeneuve, talking *in Flemish as they rode. They thought she was unconscious, or they did not think she understood Flemish, or they did not care.*

Their names were Nicclaes and Jakke. They spoke about how they had recently returned to the English camp, summoned to help run a brothel. They discussed her potential as a new slave of that place.

They concluded she would probably not last long in the job before a man killed her or she starved or caught a disease or she fell pregnant and died from the potion they used to kill the child.

They spoke about where they would bury her when she did die, and agreed that if the ground grew any harder, they would just throw her body in a ditch.

Then they stopped riding and untied her, and the man who had hit her picked her up and took her into a warm building and threw her on a sack in a tiny room that smelled of sweat and seed and sorrow. They tossed her some stale bread and a cup of ale.

She heard their master berating them for choosing her – a dirty scrawny bitch with no tits and hair like a boy. But she was not thrown out. And no one came to touch her or beat her that night.

So she ate and drank in silence and slept until she was kicked awake the next morning by the master, and told she was now a whore and if she tried to run she would be caught and beaten, and if she tried to run again she would be murdered.

She said she understood. She pretended to cry. She pretended to be afraid of the master's birch, and cowered in the corner so the master would feel powerful.

It was all exactly as she thought it would be.

It was better than she thought it would be.

The master's wiry chin hair and round shoulders and meaty arms were just as she remembered.

It was the giant woman from the road.

The woman told her to go and wash in the yard. She said she would find her new clothes. She said she would feed her for several days before she was fit to work. She said she would deduct the cost from the money men would pay to use her. Squelette made her eyes wide and tried to look frightened and she kept her tears going until the woman went away.

Then she felt around the room until she found a crack between the boards of the floor. She unbound the knife from her thigh and hid it. She went and washed as she had been commanded.

She came back and put on the dress the woman had left her and ate the food that she had left her. Then she sat on the sack and strained her ears and listened to everything she could hear.

She learned that the woman's name was Hircent. That she ran the brothel with the Flemings Jakke and Nicclaes.

She learned that in three days it would be Christmas, and the King and Queen of England would be holding a Christmas court, and that this would be a very busy time in the brothel. She imagined that this was the time she would be set to work.

On Christmas Day.

She remembered the last Christmas she had spent in Valognes. With her family. In their home. Before the war came and took everything away.

Now Christmas was coming again.

PART 3

BURGHERS

FEBRUARY–AUGUST 1347

20

Gift to Peter Fulk of Winchelsea, in compensation for a ship
of his, which the king for certain causes lately caused to be
sunk in the port of Calais...

Calendar of Patent Rolls, 1345–8

Calais castle was freezing. The Captain paused on the tight
spiral staircase that led up to the war room. His heavy breath
misted. He leaned on the stone wall beside the wide edge of
the triangular steps and adjusted the leather straps on his leg.
A gust of salt air blew through an arrow slit and stung the
tight, raw skin on his face. He blinked hard and peered out at
the sea.

Three or four deserted ships listed at anchor in the harbour.
Fog hung over the Risbank. He saw nothing beyond.

A few turns below him, the city's governor, Jean de Vienne,
was also labouring up the stairs. 'Cannon are quiet today,
Jean,' the Captain called down. 'Perhaps the king's giving up
for Lent.'

The older man was breathing too hard to respond. The cold
and damp in the castle irritated his gout. The Captain could
tell he was in pain. 'Keep going,' Vienne barked.

The Captain shrugged. He gripped his stick and carried on
hobbling up the stairs. At the top, he mopped his forehead

with his sleeve and brought his breathing under control once more. Then he knocked briefly on the thick iron-studded oak door. He let himself into the room where the council was waiting.

About a dozen of them were already there. The group split evenly between military men and merchants. On one side of the table, to the right of Vienne's place at the head, sat the castle's commander, Jean du Fosseux, a dour, efficient soldier.

With him was a loud-mouthed, rather stupid knight born and raised in Calais, named Enguerrand de Beaulo. Sir Arnoul d'Audrehem was with them too, his face thin and drawn, and a large chunk of hair still missing where he had been hit by the pirate on the little boat that had floated into the harbour nearly three months ago.

The Captain raised a hand to greet them all. Then he took a seat at the other end of the long table, alongside the men with whom he and Marant did most of their business.

Calais' burghers: the traders and moneymen who wielded the real power in the city.

At the centre of this group of merchants sat Eustache de Saint-Pierre: ancient and still acute, despite being stoop-shouldered, part-deaf and short of sight, with a weak arm and mouth slack from an apoplexy. Several places away was Jean d'Aire, almost as elderly and almost as rich as Eustache, the papery skin of his hands covered in liver spots and large tufts of hair protruding from his nose.

Two middle-aged cousins – Jacques and Pierre de Wissant – separated the old men. A few lesser merchants made up their number. Saint-Pierre acknowledged the Captain as he swung himself into a chair and propped his stick up against the table beside him. The rest ignored him. He knew that his scarred face was hard for people to look at. He also knew that merchants resented pirates.

They remind them too much of themselves.

The talk around the table quietened as Vienne shuffled into the room, sat down in his high-backed wooden chair, removed his shoes gingerly and put his feet on a cushioned stool. He nodded around each face at the table, taking stock of who was there. He pushed away a sheaf of parchment sheets that had been placed in front of him for his inspection and turned to Fosseux and de Beaulo.

With a single, terse word – 'defences?' – he invited them to begin.

Fosseux gave an efficient description of circumstances that had not changed for many weeks. Despite the length of the bombardment, the English trebuchets and cannon had done no more than superficial damage to the walls and towers, and there was no shortage of stone still available for repairs. The gates remained secure and in good condition. The moats remained deep and full of water. The channel at the mouth of the Risbank could still be navigated by supply ships – here he glanced at the Captain – if they chose their moment well. There was an ample supply of bows and crossbows, while the large fixed catapults and springalds above each of the gatehouses were in good working order. There was saltpetre and coal for making gunpowder in the castle cellars, and it was possible that the city blacksmiths, tasked with casting cannon for the defenders to use, would soon have a model that worked.

The problem was manpower. The dysentery that had spread among the men of the garrison seemed now to be under control, but there had been serious losses. Also, dozens of men had lost fingers or toes to the cold lately, and more than one had died from the shock of amputation. 'By God's grace we have enough men to defend ourselves against ordinary bombardment, assuming Philippe comes to relieve us by Easter,' he concluded. 'But should we need to defend any more serious attack, or if Philippe does not—'

But before he could offer his thoughts on the likelihood of the French king arriving at such a date, de Beaulo interjected and began his customary speech about the natural bravery of the men of Calais, and their worth being twice that of ordinary Frenchmen.

Vienne cut him off and turned to the merchants.

The ancient Eustache de Saint-Pierre nominated one of the Wissant cousins to speak for them. Pierre de Wissant began. He itemised salt pork, bacon and cheese supplies, the dwindling numbers of live chickens, cattle and sheep, and the ratio of preserved mackerel to salmon. He forecast grain prices for the spring. He referred to familiar debates about the need to balance further reduction of the city's hungry population with the need to retain skilled craftsmen and churchmen to attend the daily needs of the garrison. His subtext throughout was mild reproof to the military leadership, who did not seem to realise that it was the merchants who were keeping the city in a state to defend itself.

The Captain had now heard all of this many times on many other days, and knew there was little he could contribute.

His role was simple: he represented Marant's gang inside Calais' walls.

The pirates' importance to the city's survival gave the Captain a seat at the council table. But the negotiation and deal-making he undertook on Marant's behalf was all done elsewhere. In squalid taverns. At the docks. In the private

apartments of men like Eustache de Saint-Pierre. He appeared
in this high castle room only as a reminder to the war council
of the real nature of the fight they affected to direct.

The war room was one of the few in the castle allowed
sufficient firewood rations to warm it. As the merchant spoke,
the Captain began to feel comfortable, and then a little drowsy.
His mind wandered. He began thinking about the peculiar boy
in the cells who had arrived in Calais covered in blood, with
two of Marant's pirates dead at his feet. And the Scot who had
once been one of his crew. Who had only been on that boat,
and not in the sea with his throat slit, because of what the boy
had done. Who was almost recovered now from the serious
injury he had suffered and was becoming increasingly irate
about his imprisonment.

Marant had ruled that he and the boy were safe from
retribution. The pirate was unsentimental about his men.
Dogwater and Gombert had failed in their job, and in the
pirate's view, they deserved to die. But Vienne's men, who now
guarded the Scot in the castle dungeons, were frightened of
him. They did not even like to take him his meals, since he was
given to raging and breaking things when he saw them. They
were too afraid even to let him out of his cell to exercise in one
of the castle's damp enclosed yards.

It was a shame. The Scot had been one of his best men, once.
He could use him again now. The boy, though, had something
about him too. He looked harmless. But how harmless was a
young man who had killed two pirates single-handedly?

The Captain's attention drifted back to the war room. The
other Wissant cousin was talking about the regulation of silver
circulation within the city and the need to avoid a crisis of
coin. All at the table looked bored.

Wissant petered out.

Vienne looked around. 'Thank you all,' he said. 'May God continue to protect us, at least until the king realises that it is his job. Does anyone have anything to raise before we go about our business?'

The Captain raised his hand. 'I should like to address the matter of two men in the cells. The men who arrived on the small boat—'

Vienne cut him off. 'No.'

'No?'

'I know what you want. The answer is no. Spies, most likely. They stay in the cells. After what they did to your master's men, I can't see why I should do anything else, save hanging them.'

The Captain ignored the word 'master', though he noticed that it irked him. He looked around the room to see if Vienne's was the general feeling. Most of the men at the table avoided his eye. Either because they did not wish to take a side in an argument in which they had no stake, or because they simply did not care.

'So be it,' he said. 'It's just...' He tailed off deliberately. 'I suppose honour and virtue are suspended in these extreme times.'

The Captain did not direct this remark to Sir Arnoul. But he counted down in his head the moments until the knight took his bait. Sir Arnoul's own recovery from his injuries had been slower than Scotsman's, and he still stumbled and slurred a little when he spoke. But the Captain knew there were instincts inside him that he would be unable to contain.

'If I may, good Sir Jean.' Sir Arnoul spoke to the governor in a courtly French, hoping to flatter Vienne with his elevated diction. 'The boy saved my life. He acted with great perspicacity and no little disregard for the safety of his own person. His fellow, meanwhile, had earlier rescued me from my own imprisonment. It seems a cruel fate for his reward in this to be the ignominy of his own cell. Upon my honour, as a knight, I cannot...'

Jean de Vienne endured this speech with more patience than he had shown de Beaulo. He flexed his gouty feet on their cushioned stool and chose his words carefully.

'With respect to your dignity and your honour, Sir Arnoul, I thank you for your words,' he said. 'But for the sake of public order if nothing else, I cannot have men loose in this city who speak no word of French, who appeared here from the English camp in scandalous circumstances and who have already killed two men in cold blood.'

The Captain interjected. 'Hardly cold blood. Those men were rogue elements within our friend Marant's crew. Marant has disavowed them. He condemns their actions. And I can teach him French.'

'Rogue elements? Marant's crew is nothing but rogue elements.'

The Captain raised his palms and said no more. But Sir Arnoul tried again. 'The boy, at least. I would be willing to stake my own honour...'

Vienne sighed, impatient. 'The boy, then. Since we need every pair of hands. But not the Scot. I have heard he is a danger to himself and everyone around. Indeed, we ought...'

But before he could say more, somewhere outside the war room came a boom, followed by an awful wrenching sound like the felling of a tree.

Around the table, men leapt up.

'God's liver—'

The dull-eyed de Beaulo was closest to the door. He scrambled out of it, half tripping on his own feet and hurrying down the stairwell.

Moments later, he rushed back in. His eyes were wide. His jowls wobbled a little. Words seemed to stick in his mouth as he tried to relay what he had seen.

'Speak, damn you,' said Vienne, hobbling towards him.

'The sea,' de Beaulo exclaimed. 'It's on fire!'

They hurried as best they could from the castle out to the city walls, making their way up to the walkway at the top of the ramparts. Ugly clouds of black smoke blew. The men coughed and spluttered through it. They made their way to the walls above the Lantern Gate, which stood nearest the mouth of the city's harbour. As the smoke began to clear, the Captain realised what de Beaulo had meant.

A fierce, dry heat was blowing off the sea as though it were a breeze from the Indies. It came from the direction of a large merchant ship in the water below them, burning as it sank. The ship was on its side, the mast pointed towards Calais in accusation. It groaned like a speared whale. Flames licked from those parts of the hull that still sat above the waterline. But most of the smoke was coming from a slick of oil or pitch that had spilled out all around it, and was being carried slowly towards the harbour's pier by the tide. The vessel had not been in the harbour earlier that morning. But the Captain could guess what had happened to it.

Jean d'Aire's eyes were clouded by milky discs, pale blue

like blackbird eggs. The elderly merchant tugged the Captain's sleeve. 'What's happening?'

'The English have sunk a ship,' said the Captain. He sniffed the air. It reeked. 'That's why there has been no cannon fire today. They've packed all their cannon powder in that ship, lit it and left God and the wind to do the rest.'

D'Aire snorted. 'Or the skipper was pissed as a porpoise. I know the English. Can't drink, but won't do anything else. In any case, there's one less ship out there to bother your friend Marant on his supply runs.'

Eustache de Saint-Pierre, standing close by, laughed bitterly. 'Or one to bother them every day from now on.'

The Captain nodded. Saint-Pierre was right. Whoever had sunk the ship had done a fine job. They had steered it into position in the channel, broken open the pitch barrels, lit a fuse to the powder that blew a hole in the hull and got off the ship before it all started to burn. Presumably they swam to the Risbank, in strong tides and seas cold enough to kill a weak man of shock.

The danger they had endured was impressive. And their mission had succeeded. The wrecked ship would lie just below the water surface at the centre of the harbour channel, making it impassable to all but the very best sailors.

Marant's job had just become harder. Which meant that the Captain's job had become harder too. But harder was not necessarily bad.

Harder just means costlier.

The ramparts were growing busy. The noise and smoke had brought people hurrying up the walls.

The Captain had seen enough. Marant would find out about

the harbour blockage before long and make his decisions accordingly. He would let the Captain know.

The Captain moved off against the flow of men and women, went back into the chilly, dingy castle and down the spiral stairs once more. He went all the way to the bottom of the central tower. To the dungeons.

The jailer on post at the entrance was bored and irritable at being stuck at his post. 'What's going on up there?' he said. 'It fucking stinks.'

The Captain ignored his question. 'It smells no better down here,' he said. 'I've come to see the boy. Let me in.'

The jailer grumbled as he fitted the large key to the door. The Captain palmed him a silver denier. As usual, this shut him up.

The cells were humid and gloomy, set in a cramped corner of the castle's underbelly, lit only by small grilled holes in the wall that allowed the air to move in and out.

Scotsman and the boy were kept in the two at the furthest end of the row. The Captain tapped his stick deliberately as he walked along the cells, to announce his arrival.

'Fuck off,' came Scotsman's voice.

'That's nice.' The Captain carried on walking at his deliberate pace. *Tap, tap, tap.*

'You deaf?'

'It's funny,' said the Captain as he came to a halt in front of the small barred door. 'That's how a lot of people seem to greet me these days.'

Scotsman stood up. He had been face down on the floor. Since recovering from his head injury, he had spent his days fighting invisible enemies in his cell to regain his natural strength. For hours on end he leapt and jumped, squatting down and pushing himself up off the floor, sweating and straining to increase his stamina and the strength of his body.

This, combined with the meagre rations fed to the prisoners, had given him a truly extraordinary physique. He was thinner than the Captain had ever known him. But it now looked as though his skin had melted over his muscles. His hair and beard were vastly long, so unkempt that his face was barely visible. But his eyes glimmered from the small gap between the two.

'You'd fetch a hundred bezants in a Saracen slave market, you know.'

'Fuck off,' the Scot replied.

'You already said that. And you know, it doesn't matter how strong you get, you'll never pull the walls down,' said the Captain.

'Aye, but when I get out of here, I'll pull a few cunts' arms off,' said the Scot. 'Or legs.'

The Captain smiled. 'Sadly for you, today is not that day,' he said. 'Nor is tomorrow. Or the next day. You seem to have frightened our friends up in the castle.'

Scotsman turned his back on the Captain. He began squatting again, throwing himself to the floor, then leaping back in the air.

The Captain watched him. 'Your friend, on the other hand…'

Just for a moment, the Scot froze. Then he checked himself and carried on his exercises. 'What about him?' he grunted as he worked.

'Governor de Vienne has graciously allowed him his

freedom, to come and work for me. On condition he does not kill any more of my colleagues.'

Scotsman carried on leaping and pressing up and down. Steam rose from him and sweat coursed down his back. His hair stuck to his skin. He said nothing.

The Captain watched him carefully. 'I can bring him by to say farewell to you, if you like.'

'Fuck that,' panted the Scot. 'Every time I think I've got rid of that little prick, he always finds me again.'

The Captain smiled. Somehow, even with his back turned, Scotsman sensed it.

'Grin all you fucking like, you faithless, turncoat bastard,' he said. 'Even you won't handle that one.'

'I think I will,' said the Captain. 'I handled you for a time.'

'Aye. And then where did you go?'

'Here and there,' said the Captain. 'And now, here.' He tried once more. 'Try to calm yourself. I can get you out. Out of here. You can help me a while. Then I'll get you home.'

'Home,' said the Scot, 'is all any cunt in this war talks about. The lot of them are fucking dreaming.'

'Maybe you're coming around to my way of thinking about the world.'

'Fuck off.'

'So be it,' said the Captain. He tipped the jailer another silver denier as he walked out of the dungeons.

21

The English and the Flemings dug ditches and trenches
around their army and across the dunes to the sea...

Chronique Normande

'God's arse and bollocks!'

Tebbe flung the snapped shovel down in a rage. The
blade had hit a rock. The impact shattered the wooden shaft
and jarred his hand. Tebbe danced in pain, while the useless
handle lay in the ditch bed, the broken ends facing each other
like jagged teeth. 'Jesus shitting silver fucking nails,' Tebbe
cursed.

Up on the bank, Toussaint heard him and marched over.
'Blaspheming in my ditch? You use that filthy mouth to give
your fellow Christians the kiss of peace?'

Tebbe picked up the broken shovel blade and waved it at
the knight in accusation. 'Spade's fucked.' He spat pink-flecked
phlegm. He had been coughing it up since Christmas.

Toussaint shrugged. 'It looks fine to me. Keep digging, or
when the bell rings we all stay and work another hour.'

Tebbe looked incredulous. 'Looks fine? How do you make
that out?' He knelt down and scraped the earth with the spade
end, like a mole. 'You want me to scratch around like this for
the rest of the fucking day?'

Toussaint nodded. 'Just like that,' he said. 'Or argue with me and see where it gets you.' He brushed a speck of dirt from the sleeve of his warm padded jacket, trimmed in soft fur. 'Your decision.'

Tebbe fumed. But he bent down and started scraping with the remains of his shovel. Over the many weeks they had been in the ditch, the Dogs had learned better than to argue with Toussaint. It only made things worse.

When the knight had marched over to another point on the ditch-side to berate a different gang, Loveday moved next to Tebbe. He knelt down and handed him his own shovel. 'Use this for a bit,' he said. 'We'll take it in turns with the broken one.'

Tebbe briefly tried to refuse. But his desperation trumped his pride. 'That's good of you,' he said, standing up. He coughed again, his eyes streaming as his chest heaved. When he had regained his breath, he said: 'I don't know how much more of this I can take.'

Tebbe thought he had spoken quietly, but somehow Toussaint, who had astonishingly good hearing and a strong dislike of his men complaining, came striding back over.

'Don't like the ditch? Don't love my glorious ditch?'

Tebbe's shoulders slumped. He shook his head, mute and meek, expecting a barrage of rebuke. But it did not come. 'Well then,' said Toussaint, 'let me tell you something that'll please you. Tomorrow you get to leave it alone for a while.'

The Dogs looked at one another in confusion. 'Where? Why?' said Thorp, leaning on his own shovel and wiping his brow, smearing freezing mud in a streak across his already filthy forehead. 'We're going home?'

Toussaint smiled, and Loveday saw menace in his eyes. 'Not

quite. We're visiting another ditch,' he said. 'You'll find out where in the morning.

'All I'll say for now is that this other ditch doesn't need digging.

'It needs filling in.'

The four Dogs had been labouring in the ditch for many weeks. Furious at Scotsman's abduction of Sir Arnoul and Romford, Sir Hugh Hastings had thrown the rest of the Dogs out of the brothel and sent them to the digging crew. There, under Toussaint's relentless gaze, they dug from sunrise until an hour before darkness, day after day. Most of their colleagues were archers and footsoldiers like themselves. Almost all were there for attempting to abscond from the army. Or, thought Loveday, for having had the ill luck to be caught. Loveday had wondered at first whether Scotsman and Romford would soon be returned in disgrace to join them there. But as the days and then weeks passed, he was not sure how to feel about the fact that they had not returned.

Either they were home and free. Or they were dead.

Meanwhile, for the four Dogs who remained, their sentence was apparently unlimited. They were more like prisoners than soldiers, and the work Toussaint put them to was dismal, uncomfortable and often pointless. When sections of the ditch fell in, they cleared them. When dead animals or men were dumped in it by night, they dragged them out and buried them in shallow graves a few feet below the frozen marsh. And when there was nothing else to do, they just dug: making the ditch wider or deeper, though it was already wide and deep enough by far.

They were all in poor health. The winter was hard on them. It was freezing every day, and firewood was strictly rationed across the whole camp, with timber mostly reserved for the king's ever more elaborate fortifications near the walls of Calais itself. So even though the Dogs occasionally warmed up around a small nightly fire, their ever-damp clothes reeked and mouldered on their backs.

Tebbe coughed relentlessly. Thorp complained of pain that shot up and down his right leg and kept him awake every night. Millstone had lost weight and his hair was thinning. All their knees and backs ached. Their toes were black, and they had lost nails from the wet and cold. But they had no choice. Each morning, the Dogs were marched from the miserable huts where they were now billeted to the place they were to dig that day. At the end of the day, they were marched back like serfs. Bound to the land like beasts.

Their only consolation was that they had not been in the brothel at Christmas when Hircent had been murdered there.

Her throat had been slit expertly at the voice box. So that she could not scream when her breasts and eyes were removed and piled neatly beside her. When her belly was opened and her guts hung around the cell like mistletoe.

Her murder had sent fear and rumours around Villeneuve. Men looked over their shoulders constantly, and guards on the perimeter of the siege camp had been doubled. The grisly details of Hircent's death were spoken of in quiet, sober tones. Some said it was an outrage that such a foul crime had been committed within Villeneuve; others that it was God's judgement on the whole army for their loose living.

Loveday felt differently about it from day to day. He had been so angry with Hircent for what she had allowed Romford to suffer. Yet he could not find it in himself to celebrate the awful tortures she had herself endured in her last moments.

So what he mostly felt was relief.

Relief that Hircent's murder was one thing the Dogs could not be blamed for.

When the four Dogs reported for work at dawn the next day, they found Toussaint in high spirits. 'Praise God,' he kept saying, partly to himself and partly to anyone who came close to him. 'Praise God for choosing us to do this job.' But he still did not tell them where they were going. He and a few of the Earl of Northampton's men-at-arms simply marched the crew across the frozen ground of the marsh, between the sinking hovels of Villeneuve's outer quarters and through the wooden town itself.

Eventually, they came to a place on the very far side of the town, close to the easternmost point of Calais' rectangular walls. And at last Loveday understood what was happening. A crowd of several hundred men were already hard at work. They were taking rubble from carts and wheelbarrows and dumping it into the outer of Calais' two moats, forming a wide dam-bridge across to the bank of the inner moat. Behind them, the king's engineers had just finished work on a movable shelter, which resembled a long, open-sided shed with a thick roof covered in a patchwork of leather and raw animal skins.

Behind this was something even more extraordinary. Set back at a safe distance of around a hundred paces, a large viewing gallery had been erected facing Calais' walls. Servants were scampering up and down two dozen banked stands of benches, sweeping and inspecting the seating.

'Fuck is that?' said Thorp.

Loveday was about to answer when Toussaint interrupted. The knight ignored the viewing gallery completely and pointed to the covered movable shed near the moat. 'Ever seen one of those before?'

Millstone replied. 'Aye. Plenty of times. It's a cat. A sow. Some men call it a weasel.'

Through a coughing fit, Tebbe said, 'What do you want us to do?'

The knight eyed him disdainfully. 'You should see an apothecary about that cough. Or a barber. Get yourself bled.' He looked back to the weasel. 'That wonderful device is to protect you.'

Tebbe nodded slowly, wiping pinkish froth away from the corners of his mouth. 'From what? The rain?'

At that moment, from the top of Calais' walls, a lump of rough-hewn stone was heaved over the ramparts from some unseen defenders above. Behind it came a diatribe of abuse in coarse French. The Dogs watched the stone plummet downwards. It missed the ditches, the diggers and the engineers completely, and landed at the foot of the wall, where it shattered in a sharp spray of dust and grit.

'From that,' said Toussaint. He addressed the whole group. 'Today we're finishing that dam-bridge.

'This evening, God willing, we're going up those walls.'

'Up the fucking walls?' said Thorp. He looked at the vast defences in front of them. They soared as high as cliffs.

'Yes, up the fucking walls.' But this time it was not Toussaint who replied.

It was the Earl of Northampton.

'Unless you think we're going to take this city by sitting

around growing our beards and getting frostbite on our balls for another five months, we're hauling our arses up those walls,' Northampton continued. 'The king's running out of patience with these stubborn bastards, and by God so am I.'

He swept a hand through his grey hair, now so long that it skirted his shoulders. 'So get under that weasel and start filling the fucking ditch in, or I'll have the court surgeon come over and turn you into a new choir of eunuchs for the queen's chamber.'

The engineers finished moving the weasel into place and Toussaint directed his digging gang towards the carts full of rubble. As the Dogs moved off to join them, Loveday felt a hand on his shoulder.

He turned around. Northampton was still there. 'Christ, FitzTalbot, you look worse than my horse,' he said. 'And my horse is fucking dead. How many weeks have you been in that godforsaken ditch?'

Loveday shuffled his feet awkwardly. The earl had not spoken to him in months, since Sir Denis's death in the forest and the Dogs' subsequent recruitment by Hastings to run the brothel. But now he seemed to have reconciled himself to those things. He was looking at Loveday with something between affection and pity.

'I don't know, my lord. Several,' Loveday replied. He really had lost count. 'It was not quite Christmas when Sir Hugh... and now it's nearly Lent.'

Northampton grimaced at the mention of Hastings' name. 'Aye, well. It sounds like you've done your fucking penance.'

Loveday took a deep breath. 'We've only ever tried to do our best,' he said. 'But the war has been hard on us.' He felt his voice crack. 'And if I may, my lord, I'm sorry. About Sir Denis. He was good to us. I swear we didn't see what happened to him, but he deserved…'

Northampton placed his hands on Loveday's shoulders to quieten him. Even through his thick leather gloves, Loveday was reminded how heavy and strong the earl's hands were. His grey eyes were the hardest Loveday had ever seen. 'He's with God now. He'll be fine. He's probably charmed his way into heaven already and has a pair of pretty saint-girls kneeling beside him with their heads in his lap. Smooth bastard that he was.'

He puffed his cheeks. 'Listen, FitzTalbot. War's hard on all of us. It's fucking war. We all have to find a reason to stay here and keep doing what we do. The people I'm forced to spend my time with do that by telling each other it's a noble enterprise. Virtue, glory, chivalry – all that shit. The tragedy is, a lot of them fucking believe it. Then they get their throats cut while they're draining their cocks.'

The earl looked around the crowd of men clattering tools and shouting to one another around the weasel and the ditch. 'Where's the big ginger one?'

'Gone, my lord.'

'Gone as in dead? Or gone as in fucked off until he gets caught, whipped, fined and sent back?'

'I'm not sure. I've been trying to think which would be worse.'

Northampton almost laughed. 'Well, God bless the big bastard either way. I told him at the start of this thing to try and have some fucking fun. Did he take my advice? Did any of you?'

Loveday thought of Romford staggering in to the *Wolvenhuis* with gunpowder residue all over his face. Of Tebbe eating his Michaelmas goose, with Margie on his knee.

He heard Tebbe coughing under the weasel.

'We did our best.'

'And you fucked that up as well?'

'It seems so.'

'Can I ask you something, FitzTalbot?'

Loveday nodded.

'Why haven't you tried to run away too? Every day I get a list of men just like you who've fucked off. Granted, most of them have probably drowned in the sea or will be back here within a month to help you in that ditch. But at least they tried. What's the fucking matter with you?'

'I brought my men. And I'm responsible for them. It's the honourable thing to do.'

'Fucking honour? You sound like Sir Denis now. Tell me the real reason.'

Something in the earl's grey eyes made Loveday want to tell the truth. 'Everyone thinks I ran away from the fight at Thérouanne. I expect you do too. But I'm no coward. I may be old and nearing the end. But I don't run. Not from that. And not from this. In any case...' He took a deep breath. 'I've nothing to go home to, my lord. My men do. But I don't. I have nothing left but my men and my job.' He paused. 'And I keep thinking I'm going to find someone. Someone I've heard is in there.'

'In there?' Northampton pointed to Calais.

'Aye.'

'What kind of someone?'

'An old friend. Or someone I thought was a friend. I still think he could be.'

Northampton closed his eyes briefly and shook his head. 'FitzTalbot, you're a good man. But Christ knows you're a daft cunt. Would you like my advice?'

Loveday nodded.

'Forget about hunting for the past. It's gone. Think about the world that's coming in.'

Loveday nodded. The earl sounded like the Captain. But before he could tell him so, Northampton pointed to the viewing stands behind them, where people were beginning to take their seats, as if to watch a staged joust or mystery play. 'Put on a good show for that lot, and you'll see your fortunes turn. Do you understand?'

Loveday shook his head. 'Not really, my lord.'

Northampton nodded thoughtfully. 'Aye,' he said. 'Fair enough. In that case, just put on a good show and I'll get you out of the ditch.'

Loveday nodded. 'I think we can do that.'

Northampton looked a little rueful as he clapped Loveday on the back one more time.

'I've heard that before,' he said.

It did not take long for the large crew working behind and beneath the weasel to finish the rubble bridge across the moat. The Dogs joined one of the lines of men that snaked between the carts and the weasel, the men passing stones from hand to hand then dropping them into the murky green saltwater.

The work, although hard, was at least a change from digging. Yet as the Dogs heaved and hurled rocks, they became aware that the work was only the prelude to something much bigger, which they could not yet see in its entirety.

Behind them, more engineers had appeared. So too had a huge crowd of archers and men-at-arms: tough, weather-beaten men holding pikes and others bearing axes, knives and short swords.

Further back again, the wooden stands that were built at a safe distance from the walls had begun to fill with well-dressed noblewomen and courtiers.

The Dogs crouched on their haunches, drinking ale from their flasks as steam rose from their sweaty faces into the chilly late-winter air. 'What in the name of Jesus are they doing?' said Tebbe, pointing to the spectator stands.

Toussaint appeared and heard him. 'Watching,' he said. 'So we need to give them something to watch.' He showed them a wagon where a burly royal armourer in a greasy leather apron was handing out weapons to those who lacked them. 'Go and take what you need,' he said. 'Pick something light that you can use one-handed. Unless you can climb a ladder with your teeth.'

Tebbe and Thorp glanced at one another. 'You know we're handiest with our bows?' Thorp said. 'And Millstone has a hammer—'

'We've got archers,' said Toussaint brusquely. 'And we don't need hammers. We just need brave men with weapons they can carry. So get over there and choose from whatever's left. And hurry up. Here come the barges.'

The ladder-barges were some of the most unusual war engines Loveday could remember seeing. There were around a dozen of them, which had been winched into Calais' inner moat somewhere on the other side of the city perimeter. Flat-bottomed, long and wide, they took up almost the entire width of the moat. At the back and front of each was a stoutly defended wooden booth from which men with bargepoles guided the boats along the brackish moat-water. Between the booths were long open spaces with wooden fixtures on them. Otherwise, they were empty – just floating platforms with fixtures to hold the base of ladders.

'Christ,' said Tebbe. 'They don't exactly look steady.' He was turning over the small axe he had taken from the armourer, which had a dull and partly rusted blade on one side of its head and a spike, slightly bent, on the other. He looked disgusted with it. He had a battered iron cap on his head, the buckle missing from its strap. The other Dogs were similarly poorly armoured: Loveday with a short sword much inferior to his own, Millstone with a small, spiked mace whose loose head he was trying to fasten properly to the shaft, and Thorp with a pair of daggers whose leather-wrapped handles badly needed repairing. 'Do we not even have crossbows?' asked Thorp.

Toussaint ignored him. The barges were already being eased into position. From somewhere within Villeneuve jogged men-at-arms, metal armour covering their shoulders and torsos, carrying long wooden ladders in sections, each wide enough to take two or even three climbers abreast. They laid them down on the bank of the moat, near the entrance to the weasel and the rubble bridge, and began screwing them together.

A cheer went up from the spectator stands. Loveday squinted in their direction. The weak winter sun was starting to slink away to their left, dipping fast towards the high ground at Sangatte. But he could make out the figure sitting in the centre of the stands, with the densest crowd of young women and men around her. 'That's the queen,' he said.

The Earl of Northampton now clambered on to the platform the carpenters had made for him. He was shouting something, but over the hubbub of the men, Loveday could not hear what. All he knew was that the crowd liked it. Raucous cheers went up in the stands, and the archers and men-at-arms by the moatside started shifting eagerly.

At the top of the section of Calais' wall, defenders were showing their faces. A few waved swords and clubs defiantly.

Thorp was jiggling his leg. 'Hardly a fucking surprise attack, is it?'

Millstone set his jaw. 'It's a performance.'

The men-at-arms who had put together the huge ladders now picked them up and prepared to run them across the dambridge and on to the barges waiting for them in the inner moat. For the time that it took to position them on the barges, so that they were leaning against the walls, they were going to be terribly exposed to attack from above. They would rely on cover from two ranks of longbowmen, who stood on either side of the main body of men, taking aim at the top of Calais' walls.

One of these wings was all bowmen dressed in the prince's green-and-white livery. 'Should have been us over there,' said Thorp. 'If Scotsman hadn't fucked everything up.'

Millstone grunted. 'Should have been you and Tebbe,' he said. 'Loveday and I would have been standing here regardless.'

As he spoke, the archers nocked their bows and sent up their first swarm of arrows towards the top of the walls. Then the first of the men-at-arms sprinted forward with their ladder, stepped on to one of the waiting line of barges, and heaved the ladder upright, securing it to the fixtures in the base of the barge. It came to a couple of feet below the top of the wall.

The archers kept up their volleys of arrows. Some bounced

off the walls and clattered down on to the barges themselves. Others flew over the walls entirely. And a few found their target. Screams came from defenders invisible behind the crenellations. Sporadic crossbow shot was returned from arrow slits along the walls and tower. Loveday saw an archer hit in the shoulder. The impact of the crossbow bolt spun him around. He cursed in what sounded like Welsh.

The crowd in the stands cheered.

With the exchange of arrows and bolts going on above them, men-at-arms with ladders scampered forward on to the next barge. They ran low and kept their faces turned away from the tops of the walls.

Defenders heaved rocks over the sides.

More and more men were pushing on to the bankside, and the Dogs were now crammed tightly together with Toussaint and the rest of their crew. Loveday could smell a light wax on Toussaint's well-made shoulder plates, and the mail vest they covered.

Thorp, pressed on the other side of Toussaint, turned his head as best he could. 'How many times have you stormed a wall with ladders, sir?' he shouted to the knight.

Loveday noticed a bead of sweat slide down Toussaint's temple. His jaw was tense – a knot of muscle bulged and pulsed below his ear.

'A dozen or more,' he said. Then he added: 'In tournaments.'

Ahead of them, the last of the ladders was sliding into place at the wall. The spectators in the stands were drumming their feet. Then, on the stage where Northampton stood, drums began beating and trumpeters gave a long blast.

The signal was like a trigger pulled on a crossbow. The energy and the crush of the crowd was suddenly released, and

Loveday was swept forward with them as men raced towards the weasel and the dam-bridge over the first moat.

Whoops and screams swirled. Men elbowed each other to be first towards the point of the attack. Somewhere, something was on fire. Loveday lost sight of the other Dogs as the powerful tide of the crowd drove them in different directions. Only a hacking cough told him Tebbe was close.

He was already drenched in sweat when the crowd shoved him into the mouth of the weasel. Then he was across the uneven dam-bridge and on the land between the moats.

All around on the thin strip of solid ground, men jostled to get on to the moored barges. The men-at-arms who had raised the ladders on their decks were shouting at them to stay back, for fear of sinking the barges or tearing them from their moorings. Others were trying to stop any more men from coming through the weasel. All the while, the deadly whispers of arrows and bolts continued overhead, joined by the thuds of rocks being catapulted over the walls.

Loveday was sprayed with water as one of the men waiting to board a barge lost his footing and fell in the moat with a splash.

He looked around frantically for the Dogs, to try and take a head count. Sweat stung his eyes and he swept it away with his forearm.

Then someone leapt at him.

He saw the shadow from the corner of his eye. But the man was on him before he could turn.

He hit Loveday hard in the ribs, knocking all the air out of him. Shoving him so hard that he lost his footing and hit the ground with a thud. His short sword flew out of his hand.

His head smacked the hard ground.

The huge man smothered him, pinning him to the ground, as heavy as a house.

Loveday couldn't breathe. He could not even yell.

All he knew for certain was that he was about to die.

22

There was an absence of firm ground on which [the English] could set up siege engines...

Chronicle of Geoffrey le Baker

Loveday writhed beneath his attacker, gasping to fill his lungs with air as he scrabbled for his blade with his hand. It was out of reach. Panicking and straining to breathe, he somehow found the energy to punch the man in his ribs and arms.

The man on top of him was yelling in his ear, but Loveday had no idea what he was saying. Only when he had unleashed half a dozen blows did he realise the man he was battering was Millstone.

'Calm down, for Christ's sake,' the burly stonemason was shouting. 'Calm down! It's me.'

Loveday dropped his arms. He croaked like a toad, still struggling for breath. 'What in Christ's name are you doing?' he managed to say. Then, as Millstone rolled away, Loveday saw what lay where he had been standing.

A huge, rotten pig carcass, hurled from the walls above, lay burst open on the ground.

White ribs glistened where they had ripped through the skin. A neat row of little yellow teeth grinned from a flesh-stripped skull. It was as large as a man. It stank.

Despite himself, Loveday laughed. 'That would have been some way to go.'

'Aye,' said Millstone. 'Now get up. There's plenty more ways to die yet.'

Loveday found his sword and stepped over the rank splatter of the pig, crouching as he moved, with his left arm curled over his head as though this would shield him. Millstone followed.

Someone yelled their names.

Millstone pointed – on the nearest barge, Tebbe was hunkered down, beckoning them urgently to join him in the bargeman's shelter at the back of the craft. One man-at-arms was controlling the numbers of men trying to get on the barge. Another was sending climbers up the ladder in pairs. At the top of the wall, two young men were alternately hacking at defenders and ducking down beyond the range of the blows that were returned.

Tebbe was still shouting at Loveday and Millstone. 'Get over here!'

Loveday pointed to the man-at-arms blocking anyone else from getting on the barge.

Tebbe coughed hard into the crook of his elbow. He shook his head. 'Fuck him!' he shouted. 'Fucking get on!'

Loveday grimaced. Jumping on to the barge looked dangerous. But before he could argue further, Millstone had set off at a jog. The man-at-arms closest to Tebbe was arguing with a middle-aged, red-faced archer with a Cornish accent. Taking advantage of his distraction, Millstone leapt, surprisingly deftly, on to the back of the barge, and slid into the shelter beside Tebbe.

Smoke stung Loveday's nose. Something somewhere was burning. It smelled awful.

From far away, on another side of the city, he heard the boom of cannon.

Then he stood at the edge of the barge, bent his creaking knees and jumped. When he landed, the barge wobbled. The man-at-arms holding the bottom of the ladder rounded angrily on him. But before he could berate the Dogs he was called back to the ladder, to help down the two attackers returning from their exertions at the top. Both had blood leaking from their heads. One of them was clutching his arm, which hung limply by his side, and moaning.

The man-at-arms bundled the youths off the barge. He returned his attention to the Dogs. 'Two of you get your arses over here, if you're so fucking keen.'

Anxiety flooded Loveday like poison.

Millstone seemed to smell it. 'Come on,' he said to Tebbe. 'Us first.'

But through the anxiety, something else surged in Loveday. Something familiar. A fierce sort of stubbornness. A strange concoction of desperation and pride. And an almost uncontrollable need to see what was inside Calais.

And who.

'No,' he said to Millstone, as firmly as he had ever spoken to any of the men. 'You've saved me once today.'

And before the stonemason could answer, Loveday grabbed Tebbe and pulled him towards the ladder, where the impatient man-at-arms was holding his hand out to drag them into place.

The cacophony of the battle on the walls was so loud by now that the man-at-arms had to yank Tebbe and Loveday's faces inches from his own and scream his instructions to them.

Broken arrows and fragments of stone were raining down on them.

'Get up fast,' the man-at-arms was yelling. 'Keep your head out of the way. Strike upwards. Do as much damage as you can. If you can get over, one of you wave like fuck and I'll send the whole of fucking England up behind you. If you can't and you feel like you're fucked, get down so I can send some other cunt up. Remember – watch your fucking heads. Are you going up together?'

The Dogs nodded.

'We'll cover you,' screamed the man-at-arms. He waved frantically to one of his colleagues, directing archers on the bank. Pointed to the Dogs and mimed climbing.

The archers started shooting, aiming either side of the ladder. Tebbe smacked Loveday on the back. He shouted something Loveday couldn't hear.

They both tucked their weapons under their left arms. Put their right feet on the bottom rung of the ladder. Loveday felt the boat rock underneath him. He had to make a conscious effort not to piss in his trousers.

Then he started climbing.

When Loveday was first a man, a little younger than his twentieth name day, a year or two after he had married Alys, builders had come to the village to repair the crumbling stone tower of the church. It had taken them the whole summer, and on the days when the Captain had let the Dogs idle between jobs, Loveday had liked nothing better than to lie in the meadow beyond the churchyard and watch the men working high on the scaffold they had put up.

He had admired their nonchalance as they climbed and swung from level to level, scampering up and down the wooden struts and crossbars like the fat little auburn squirrels that lived in the woods. Strong and nimble, they could swing and leap around the sides and top of the tall church tower with tools in their hands, buckets of lime or sand slung over their arms, hooking and unhooking pulleys even as they hung in the air with just the strength of one shoulder. These leathery-skinned men, who worked stripped to the waist in all weathers, their bodies marked with inked scratches in the shapes of crude crucifixes and the initials of saints, made it look so easy that Loveday had begun to dream that he too would one day be like them.

Then, on a night near the end of the harvest, when the village was dancing and singing into the long, warm evening, Loveday had been able to resist no longer. He had slipped away from the revellers, wandered through the deserted churchyard and clambered up the scaffold himself.

It had felt like magic to begin with, as he pulled himself slowly from one level to the next. At first, he had been higher than the thatch of the village houses dotted along the rough tracks that led out into the fields beyond. Then higher than the roof of the manor. Then higher than most of the trees.

Loveday had climbed and climbed. He had felt the rough warmth of the stone, slowly releasing the trapped heat of the summer's day. He had pressed his fingers into the scratches on the tower's stone, unseen by anyone since the masons who had hewn them generations ago.

He had seen birds below him circle and dive.

And on that evening, he had seen some part of life on Earth that the ordinary human eye could not see. He had chanced upon a space allowed only to a very few. Between the realm of man and God.

He had looked at the sky fading from blue to a midsummer's bruised mauve and cried out with happiness.

But then he had looked at the ground. At the tiny gravestones, the size of pebbles below him. At the stirring of the summer breeze among the treetops.

At things he had no right to see and no business being above.

He had become paralysed with fear. So scared that he had sobered up. Tightened up. And lost all his confidence.

He had tried to climb down from the church scaffold. Yet his legs had cramped with doubt. His hands shook. His limbs had refused every move he tried to make to climb down.

Darkness fell. It had taken him almost until dawn to lower himself back down to the ground.

Just that feeling now gripped Loveday as he scaled the ladder beside Tebbe. The ladder swayed, but was not as unstable as he had imagined it would be; the barge was roped tightly to the bolts driven into the bankside.

Nor was there any barrage of missiles aimed at them from above.

What scared him, as they clambered upwards together, was the quiet.

Before they were halfway up the ladder, the roar of the men below had quietened and levelled out to little more than a hum.

The clatter of drums and blare of horns and trumpets was like a band playing in the next village.

What filled Loveday's ears instead was the sound of his own laboured breathing. The thud of his heart. The screech of seabirds over the top of the city. The creak of the wide ladder he was clinging to. And Tebbe's scratchy cough.

They said nothing to one another. They just climbed.

The higher they got, the more Loveday could smell the burning he had noticed below. It mingled with the salt on the air.

Cannon powder?

They kept climbing.

They passed arrow slits, bracing themselves for the appearance of a nocked arrow.

A couple of dozen yards away to their right, another pair of Englishmen were hacking upwards, trying to land blows on a man-at-arms who swiped at them alternately with a long, sharp halberd.

They looked up with every step, waiting for the tumble of a stone or another stinking animal carcass.

When they were five rungs from the top, they stopped. Loveday pulled his short sword from his armpit, where it was still clamped, and motioned to Tebbe to do likewise.

His blood was screaming in his ears.

Tebbe pulled out the little axe with its blade and spike. He whispered loudly to Loveday. 'Together?'

The archer had sweat pouring down his forehead. He looked pale and sick. But he had the same intensity in his eyes that Loveday had always seen when they had gone into battle together.

'Aye,' said Loveday. He took a deep breath. Wondered if he would ever take another. He had hooked his left arm around the ladder rung nearest his face. 'Together,' he said. 'Like we always have been.'

Tebbe grinned. He coughed once more. Struggled for breath. But then he said Loveday's war cry for him. '*Desperta ferr—*'

Before he had even finished, Tebbe set off.

Together, thought Loveday.

He heaved with his crooked left arm and pushed with his feet. He drew his short sword back, trying to catch up with Tebbe as he prepared to swing at whoever might be lurking, waiting for them behind the wall-top. But he was not fast enough.

His slowness saved his life.

Loveday was looking straight up as the lip of the cauldron appeared at the edge of the wall, between two crenels.

Placed perfectly to see leather-gloved hands tip it forward.

He was close enough to the edge of the ladder to swing instinctively so that he was hanging off it, his elbow still crooked around its rung but his feet dangling in thin air, with only the moat below.

He was in the perfect position to see the whole cauldron of scalding pitch and sand gush out, straight into Tebbe's chest.

Thick black sludge with flames licking off it engulfed the archer.

Tebbe's hair caught fire. His long ponytail flared like a candlewick and disappeared.

The pitch covered his face and seared the flesh. It filled his mouth and destroyed his throat. Melted his lungs before they could even blow out a last breath.

Tebbe never even screamed.

The leather strap of his shoddy helmet burned through and the hat tumbled away, falling silently down to the barge.

Then his hands slipped from the ladder and he too dropped straight downwards. All around him, tiny droplets of fire and searing sand-tar fell like hellish snow.

The smell of the pitch was awful. The stench of Tebbe's burned hair was worse.

Loveday turned his face away. The heat singed his eyebrows and beard. Some of the pitch caught on his shirt and sleeve and he felt it blister the skin beneath. He ignored the pain. He kicked his legs uselessly in thin air, holding all his bodyweight in his left arm, still clamped tight around the ladder.

He could barely believe what he had just seen. But he knew it was coming for him next.

He tucked his chin into his chest and, for one heartbeat more, just dangled, waiting for the agonising burn of a second pitch bucket to hit him.

It never came.

Loveday felt his arm start to slip. He kept kicking his legs until he managed to wrap one of them back around the ladder. He realised he had to get down again. Get away from the danger on the top of the wall as quickly as he could.

Yet his legs were frozen, clamped immobile to the side of the ladder. Which had started moving sideways.

Below, Loveday now heard frantic yells. He did not dare to look. Could not bear to see what had become of Tebbe.

He could also smell a new sort of burning.

The ladder was on fire.

'Down! Get down, for Christ's sake!' Millstone's voice floated up to him, clear as a chorister's.

'I can't,' Loveday shouted, or thought he did. His jaw was clamped shut. 'I can't!'

But he could not stay on the burning ladder either. So Loveday closed his eyes tight one last time. Then opened them wide and took the only option he had left.

He forced his mouth to open. Clamped his teeth around his short sword's blade.

And started climbing up.

★ ★ ★

Five rungs lay between Loveday's place on the ladder and the top of the wall. He scrambled up them. His sword blade covered his tongue in rust crumbs. Its rough, chipped edge scraped the corners of his mouth bloody. He didn't care.

Anger was building inside him. He let it take over. He flew up the rungs. He clamped his hands on the top of the parapet, grabbing on to the crenel and heaving as though he wanted to tear it clean off the wall.

He threw his right leg up, then rolled his belly on to the top of the wall. Landed on the path that ran behind the parapet.

He pulled the rusty sword out of his mouth. Wiped blood across his face with the back of his hand, and gave one last war cry before they cut him down.

All he saw was a lad in leather gloves running away towards a fierce fight going on around the top of another ladder, thirty or more paces away along the wall path.

In the other direction, there was no one between him and a great square tower that jutted out from the wall.

So for a moment he just stood there – his legs trembling and his mouth leaking blood into the bristles on his chin.

He looked down from the parapet into the city of Calais. It was far bigger than it had seemed for all the months they had been outside in Villeneuve. Below him lay a mass of rooftops, some thatched and some tiled and others still flat and populated with wood stores or washing lines. A tight grid of streets cut between the buildings, and here and there, at the heart of what he supposed were parishes, stood small churches. Their bells were tolling in alarm, as though there was a great fire spreading.

The Captain was in there somewhere.

He had to be.

Madly, Loveday thought of finding a way down into the streets alone. Then he recalled what he had been told by the English knight at the bottom of the ladder.

'*Wave like fuck and I'll send the whole of England after you.*'

He turned back and leaned over the point of the wall over which he had launched himself. 'I'm here!' he yelled. 'Get up here!' He brandished his rusty sword above his head.

A cheer erupted from the spectator stand. Loveday saw women and young men on their feet, roaring in excitement.

But a heartbeat later, a volley of arrows and crossbow bolts fizzed around his ears. He threw himself back down behind the wall, cursing himself. The crowd understood what had happened. The archers below did not. They thought he was a Frenchman.

He knew why. They had not seen him clamber over the wall. They had seen Tebbe fall and the ladder collapse. They assumed he had fallen too.

Loveday shuffled sideways and stole a glance between the crenels to the moat below. It was as he had thought.

The ladder had burned through and broken in half. It was sinking in the moat. The barge was being unmoored and dragged away.

The nearest ladder to him was now twenty paces away towards the tower. If he didn't get to it, he was trapped.

Loveday took a deep breath. He puffed out the recklessness that had swept over him in the moment he had scaled the parapet. It would not keep him alive now. He dried the sweat off his palms on the gritty surface of the parapet path where he sat. Told himself what he had to do.

Get to the next ladder. Get back over the wall. Get out of here and never come back.

He slapped himself in the face. It hurt. He hauled himself into a crouch and prepared to scamper to where he thought he had seen the next ladder positioned.

Two men-at-arms came out of a door in the tower beyond.

Loveday's heart skipped. He had been spotted. And the men-at-arms were much closer to the point of the next ladder than he was. They were only lightly armoured. But they carried long swords. And they were heading straight for him.

Loveday looked down. Now there was no doubt about it. He was scared. He did not want to be, but he was. To leap from the parapet into the city was certain death. To go over the other side meant the same, even if he managed to land in the moat. To run from the men-at-arms would only bring him headlong into the melee where the lad who had killed Tebbe had gone.

And the one thing he could never do again was run.

He had to stand his ground.

Loveday felt like he was going to vomit. He swallowed hard. His spit tasted of blood and rust.

Then he put both hands on the hilt of his blunt sword and planted his feet, ready to fight. His knees shook. He cursed them. He tried to override the fear. To anticipate which of the men would strike at him first. He tried to think what their training would tell them to do.

He forced himself to imagine all the knights he had known over the years. To remember how they had fought. He pictured Sir Denis. Sir Adrian.

Sir Arnoul.

The French knight had said something when he and Millstone had found him in the forest. What was it?

Make me your prison.

Then he heard Northampton's words to him when the earl had clamped his hands on his shoulders that very afternoon.

Virtue, glory, chivalry – all that shit. The tragedy is, a lot of them fucking believe it.

He had an idea. His mind was racing so frantically he could not tell if it was fear or bravery that put it in his head.

Or stupidity.

He did it anyway.

Loveday bent down. He placed his short sword on the ground in front of him. Then he stood with his hands raised, palms facing forward. The men-at-arms stopped, confused, and shouted something in French.

Loveday called back. 'I surrender! I surrender! *Make me your prison!*'

His voice sounded ridiculous to him. But he stepped past the sword and walked slowly towards them anyway. '*Make me your prison*,' he said, trying to sound as reasonable as he could. He realised he was affecting a French accent. He kept saying it.

The men-at-arms shook their heads. The taller of the two hawked and spat. He raised his sword to eye level. He pointed the blade directly at Loveday.

At his heart.

Loveday kept walking. He was five paces away. Then three. Then no more than a sword's length.

Close enough to see everything.

The dents on the men-at-arms' breastplates. The bags under their eyes. The whorehouse pox spreading around the short one's mouth. The scuff on the flat of his sword's blade where it had been sharpened on a whetstone.

And Thorp's face, as it appeared above the parapet.

The crossbow in his hand.

Thorp put one hand on the parapet to steady himself and tucked the crossbow butt under his chin so he could shoot it with the other. He shook his head at Loveday like an exasperated schoolmaster.

The man-at-arms nearest him looked down in surprise.

Thorp shot him in the thigh.

The man howled and Thorp ducked back down. In his place, Millstone appeared, and vaulted over the wall. The man who had been shot was rolling on the path, writhing in agony. The other was rooted to the spot in shock, still pointing his sword at Loveday's chest. In one pace, Millstone was behind him. He grabbed him in a chokehold, left elbow fastened around his neck.

Realising what was happening, the man-at-arms thrashed and bucked and kicked. Millstone tightened his grip. The man's face turned purple. He opened his mouth. His tongue began to swell up.

Millstone kept holding as he curled his right arm around the man's forehead. The man's eyes bulged. They flashed from side to side in terror, like a horse in a storm.

The man was still trying to kick. He tried to grab behind him with his hands. Millstone kneed him in the back of the thighs to stop him struggling and tightened his left arm again. The man tried to say something. A squeak was all he could muster before he passed out.

His body went limp. Millstone inhaled sharply. Then he jerked his arms hard away from one another and the man's neck snapped like a chicken bone.

Thorp reappeared and he now climbed over the wall too. The man he had shot was trying to crawl away, dragging his wounded leg along and leaving a smear of blood behind him like a snail. Thorp followed him and kicked him in the guts, rolling him on to his back.

'Thorp,' said Loveday. His voice quailed. He wondered, absurdly, where Thorp had found the crossbow. 'No. We can leave him.'

Thorp glanced at Loveday like he did not know who he was. He reloaded the crossbow and stood over the man-at-arms. The man was whimpering. Tears were rolling out of his eyes and down his temples. He looked in terror at the jerking body of his companion.

Thorp put a foot on his chest. A bead of sweat dripped off the end of his nose.

The man-at-arms started shaking his head. He copied Loveday. '*Make me your prison*,' he said.

Thorp shook his head. He had the crossbow in two hands now. The butt tight against his shoulder. He held it steady.

'We don't take prisoners any more,' Thorp said.

He shot the man in the face.

Suddenly Loveday found he was crying too. His whole body shook. He sank to his knees so that he did not fall from the walkway's edge. He put his hands on the ground and wept. 'I'm sorry,' he whispered, though he did not know who to.

Thorp picked him up roughly by his collar. 'We need to go,' he said. 'Now.'

Millstone was dusting his hands, as though he had just finished changing a cart-wheel. He used a thumb to massage the muscles in his left arm. Further down the wall defenders were breaking away from the melee and running towards them. 'Thorp's right,' Millstone said.

They scrambled on to the ladder, Loveday first, followed by Millstone and Thorp. Now the archers below had worked out who they were, thick covering volleys of longbow shot flew over them at the parapet, stopping their pursuers in their tracks.

They stepped on to the barge and then on to the bank. Loveday turned to Millstone. 'Tebbe,' he said. 'I...'

He was still crying. Millstone just patted him on the shoulder as though he were an elderly man, or a fool.

A familiar hand clapped Loveday on the shoulder.

'Well,' said Northampton. 'I definitely can't send you back to the ditch now.'

The earl had brought a herald with him. The young man had a round, hairless face, with several rolls of fat beneath his chin. His tabard was clean. Its colours were impossibly bright.

He loitered beside Northampton and the Dogs. Northampton glared.

'Christ thrice buggered and put back to bed, get on with it,' said Northampton to the herald. 'I'm supposed to be in charge of a fucking battle.'

'Dogs of Essex,' said the herald, 'Her Grace the Queen salutes and commends your bravery, and sends you this token of her admiration. To... you, ah, all.'

He held out a small strip of ribbon. It looked like a woman's garter.

Loveday tried to speak. He retched. He spat a pool of yellow liquid at the herald's feet. He started crying again and put his hands on his knees.

The herald was still proffering the little ribbon.

'Fuck me,' said Northampton. He snatched the garter. 'Fucking women,' he said. 'What kind of soft cunt wants a garter in a war?' He grabbed the back of Loveday's filthy shirt and hauled him upright. 'Where have your mates gone?'

Loveday wiped his mouth and looked numbly around. Thorp and Millstone were searching the moat.

'Looking for...' Loveday couldn't say Tebbe's name. 'Will the queen send us home?'

'I highly fucking doubt it,' said Northampton. From the far side of the battle at the walls, a huge cannon boom sounded, followed by screams of agony.

'That's a fucking cannon blown,' the earl said. He passed Loveday the garter. 'Well, God alone knows how, but you've impressed the queen,' he said. 'You never know, you might end up with my job.'

Then he strode off back to his platform.

23

Around Easter there came a fleet of thirty ships which...
scandalously brought supplies into the port of Calais...

Chronicle of Henry Knighton

The first ship of the relief convoy came into Calais shortly after dawn. It had been weeks since any skipper had dared bring a large vessel on the delicate passage past the sunken wreck in the harbour, so the Captain and Romford were waiting to see it in. They had already been awake for hours; the Captain had insisted on being at the heavily guarded Water Gate as soon as the morning guards, in their clanking breastplates and armour, had replaced the thickly woollen-clad nightwatchmen. And when these armoured sentries had winched the chains that raised the two portcullises and lowered the double drawbridge, the Captain and Romford had been the first to cross on to the harbour island, where a clutch of storehouses was arranged at the end of a long pier, jutting out into the calm waters protected from the sea beyond by the sandy spit of the Risbank.

It had been so bitterly cold before the sun rose that even under the rough woollen cloak and tunic the Captain had given him, Romford's skin rose in goose bumps. It did not get much warmer afterwards. But the Captain seemed not to notice the cold, and he distracted Romford from his discomfort by showing him the layout of the city. He pointed out the Lantern Gate at the far end of the harbour, where a huge beacon burned every night, guiding ships into the harbour. He urged Romford to appreciate the shape of the city walls – huge and high and oblong behind the deep moats that ran around even on the seaward side. He showed him how the castle that was built partly into those walls at the north-eastern corner protected the angle of the city most vulnerable to attack from the coast, while blocking access outside the city to the harbour island. He pointed out the wrecked spars of the dead ship in the Risbank mouth, and described the perils it now posed to anyone bringing ships in.

Romford listened intently to every word this raw-faced, one-legged man told him. Some of it he had already learned during his days as a gunner on another side of the city, on the *sablon*. But much of it was new, and by the time the Captain was finished, Romford had almost forgotten the cold. They had also been joined at the harbour by a growing crowd of citizens and city officials, who all began to murmur in earnest as the first ship of the convoy was spotted looming at the harbour mouth, ink black against the blue and yellow of the pre-dawn sky.

The Captain had explained to Romford that the ship expected that morning was part of a supply fleet of several dozen that would be coming to Calais from a place called Dieppe. Romford did not know where Dieppe was, but the Captain said it was where the finest sailors plied their trade.

All the time he had been in France, Romford had been used to hearing of people like this described as the enemy. But that was when he was with the Dogs in the world outside Calais' walls. Now he lived among the enemy, so he tried not to think of things in these terms any more.

Instead, he accepted where he was, and marvelled at the size of the ship when it finally cruised slowly up to the harbour's long, wide pier, waves forming at its crusty bows and rippling outwards to slap against the green, weedy stone of the dock. He admired the deftness with which it was manoeuvred – as lightly as if it were a rowing boat – by whoever was at the steerboard.

For days, there had been constant speculation in Calais as to whether a vessel of any useful size would be able to make it past the wreck and into the harbour. Now, here was the answer.

This ship was bigger even than the great cog *Saintmarie* on which Romford and the Dogs had first travelled to France. A proud, wood-carved statue of an angel with its wings open and throat pressed heavenwards sat on the prow. The mast soared like a church spire. High up it, just above the grey billow of its square sail, a man with a horn and a booming voice stood in a tiny booth resembling a barrel. He shouted down instructions to the crew, and to the dock workers waiting to tether the ship to posts at the water's edge.

Here and there, arrows poked out of the ship's hull where it had been shot at on its journey. But it bore no serious damage. It was like a fortress and a warehouse that cut through the water. Romford found it mesmerising.

Moments later, he found it even more intriguing. As soon as the ship was docked and a couple of thin, serious priests had blessed it, dipping their bony fingers into silver bowls of holy water and flicking it on the ship's flanks, the crew started jumping down.

Romford was surprised to see that they were almost all women.

The Captain, standing beside him, tapped his stick hard on the ground in approval at the sight of the women leaping on to the hard ground of the harbour island. 'Ever seen anything like it?' he asked.

Romford shook his head.

A limber young woman with a filthy face and a mischievous glint in her eye, who had just sprung down from the ship, overheard the Captain's words.

'Harder getting out of port than in,' she grinned. 'Pulled the fucking thing out of the dock at the other end, so we did. Waist deep in the sea, by God's blistered bollocks.' The woman wore a man's shapeless shirt much too big for her, and she pulled the neck of it open to show her shoulder, where the skin was rubbed livid red with rope burn. 'Harbour was silted up, of course. As fucking usual. We had to get down and haul the bastard through the shallows by hand. Three hundred of us slipping about in the fucking slime.'

She looked Romford up and down and gave him a saucy wink. 'Where'd they find you?' she asked. She did not wait for an answer. 'Well, boys, see you on the next run.'

'God bless you all,' said the Captain as she departed. He turned to Romford once more. 'They breed them strong in Dieppe. Men and women both.'

The Captain spoke all these words to Romford in French. From the day he had taken Romford out of the cell beneath the castle, he had insisted that this was the only language they spoke to one another. 'It may be the difference between living and dying,' he had said.

At first, the new words had caught in Romford's throat and

he felt like his tongue was the wrong size for his mouth. But the Captain was a firm and surprisingly patient teacher. Romford had been surprised how quickly he had become accustomed to speaking the new language, once he had no other choice. He felt one day he might think in French. Dream in it. Pray in it.

Gangplanks and steps were now being run over from the dockside to where the ship was moored, and the whole harbour had become a flurry of activity. Calais' citizens had until this moment struck Romford as intense, serious and tired. Most had become ground down by the constant bombardment and the boredom of being stuck in the city for six months, with no hint of when help might come. But today, for the first time since Romford's arrival, there was a buzz of excitement in the air.

The Captain caught the mood. He clapped Romford on the back. 'Get hold of the cart,' he ordered. Romford jumped into action. He lifted the wooden handles of the heavy two-wheeled porter's wagon they had brought with them. It was heavy. Yet Romford liked using his muscles again after so many weeks lying in the damp gloom of the castle's dungeon.

'Remember,' said the Captain, as Romford followed him to the ship's side, 'we only want boxes marked with the sign.'

'Only with the sign,' Romford repeated. He pictured the symbol the Captain had scratched for him with the end of his stick in the dirt of Calais' main square: a cross with short lines extending from each of its arms.

Romford parked the cart at the bottom of one of the gangplanks leading on to the ship's deck and ran up to hunt out crates and cases marked with the peculiar sign. As he did, he noticed the Captain deep in conversation with an old man he had seen before. The man was obviously wealthy: a soft moleskin cloak trimmed with fur hung on his spare, rounded shoulders, while around his neck was a bright gold chain. He was also truly ancient. As Romford ran about the great ship looking for boxes, he thought the man reminded him of Noah.

Hadn't Noah lived for more than nine hundred years, thanks to his adventures aboard a great ship like this one?

Soon Romford came to a place near the stern of the ship where almost every box and crate bore the peculiar tailed-cross mark. There were scores of them, many so heavy that Romford had to ask passing crew members for help loading them on to his trolley. At first, he felt shy asking. Yet soon he realised his French was good enough to make himself understood. And the women were mostly willing to help him, some even teasing him by squeezing his arm or slapping him on the arse as they did.

Their rough humour was infectious. And for once, Romford found he was not wary or afraid of approaching strangers. Not fearful of being hit or kicked or shouted at or scorned.

It was a pleasant feeling.

But it was more than that, too. Since he had killed Gombert and Dogwater in the little boat, Romford had more or less stopped being afraid of anyone.

So it was more than pleasant. It felt like power.

The Captain kept Romford working for days, for there was plenty of work to be done. No sooner had the first ship from Dieppe been stripped of its supplies, and the women jumped back on board to return it to its home port, than another came in – then another, and another. Not all were as large as the first, giant cog that arrived, but during the course of the week, at least four vessels came in to be unloaded every day.

Romford learned that they had all been supplied at either Dieppe or another port, called Saint-Valery. They had been given safe escort to the mouth of the Risbank by fighting vessels commanded by the pirate Jean Marant, whom he had met in the tavern full of cobwebs where Scotsman had carried him that night before Christmas.

When Romford first learned this, he had been concerned that Marant would be angry if he discovered him helping the Captain. But the Captain had told him to pay this no mind. He used words Romford had heard the other Dogs echo in the past: 'You're looking at war the wrong way.' Then, at the end of each day, he had given Romford coins he said he had earned by his work.

Romford had never owned many coins before. This was the first time anyone had given him any for his work since he had first set foot on the beach the previous year. The Captain and he lodged each night near the city's great cathedral, in a tavern under the sign of the Beehive, where the Captain paid for Romford's board and keep. Romford liked to lie on his pallet and straw sacks by candlelight at the day's end, pull the coins out of his pack and spread them on his thin blanket. He traced his fingers over the silver discs, with their stamped patterns and edges chipped rough through years of changing hands. His fingertips felt flared crusader crosses and fleurs-de-lis, and rubbed the lines of simple icons of the church where Christ's tomb lay, and sequences of letters he could not read. He was not sure what he would do with the coins, or how much they were really worth. All he knew was that the Captain told him if he saved enough, he could change them all for one or two fine gold pieces, which, the Captain said, were easier to hide, transport and exchange. The Captain even showed him one: a gleaming gold English piece that showed King Edward himself aboard a great ship, wielding a sword in one hand and a shield in the other.

'Gold, boy,' the Captain said. 'That's what war's about.'

Despite this, however, the Captain never quite explained to Romford what he was really doing to merit the growing pile of coins he stashed in his pack, alongside his blanket, a couple of bowstrings and his aleskin. In one sense, Romford did know. He and a handful of other workers hired by the Captain were running up and down ship gangplanks, hauling marked boxes on to porters' carts or occasionally a wagon hitched to a thin donkey, and then taking them to various dwellings, inns and warehouses, usually in Calais' darker corners: the basement of a tumbledown and apparently abandoned merchant's mansion at the end of a street near the house of the Carmelites; a hard-to-find shed behind filthy pigpens in the run-down corner of the city near the defensive structure called the Snail Tower.

But why he was doing this, and what design lay behind his scurrying errands through the city's warren of streets, was never revealed to him. He only knew that it had something to do with the rich old men the Captain spent much of his time consulting with, at the Beehive inn and other taverns like it. These men included the half-blind one with milky blue eyes and the more youthful cousins from Wissant, where the Dogs had once stayed in the bakery. All of them seemed to know something he did not.

Romford resisted the urge to peek inside the crates and sacks and boxes he delivered for them, knowing that the Captain would be angry if he did. But sometimes he could not help catching a glimpse through a broken fastening or between loose wooden slats. He saw bales of dyed cloth and sacks of raw wool. He smelled strange spices and peppers, which tickled his nose and made him recall with a shudder Father riding his back in the marketplace at Thérouanne. Once or twice he wheeled barrels so heavy they could only have been full of some metal, rather than ale or wine.

His work seemed different from that of the other porters and citizens who crowded on to the supply ships. They unloaded goods more obviously suited to the needs of a city under siege: sacks of grain and milled flour, cheese and meat, salt, ale and wine, wrinkled apples and papery onions. Some ships were crammed with livestock, arriving in from Dieppe or Saint-Valery stacked with wooden cages of hens, the whole vessel noisy with clucking and reeking of chicken shit; or with whole herds of cows and sheep ready to be driven, wobbly-legged and confused, off large ramps and on to land, to be herded away to the city's butchers. Others brought sheaves of arrows, or timber and stone for repairing defences and building new fortifications. None of these containers carried the mark of the tailed cross. So Romford left them alone. But he could not help wondering why he did one sort of work, and all the others did something else.

By the time Easter approached, the last big boats of the supply convoy had been unloaded and departed. For Romford, however, there was still work to be done. Often the Captain sent him out at night, or in the very early morning, to creep into the harbour and meet smaller vessels. These were evidently not part of the official convoy, and were piloted by men who looked to Romford very much like pirates. They would drop cargo into Calais that was exclusively marked with the tailed cross, and Romford would move it into the city by stages – often in collaboration with the nightwatchmen who let him out of the Water Gate or Lantern Gate when both were supposed to be closed until dawn. Many times, Romford and the Captain were the only people at the harbourside to meet these deliveries, and once the goods were inside Calais, the Captain would insist on Romford moving them covertly and quickly, so that as few of Calais' citizens as possible would see them transported through the streets.

At other times, when the boats did not come, Romford was kept busy simply moving stock and supplies between their various storage places. Then there were days when the Captain only wanted him to follow him on his own errands, waiting outside whichever inn or house the Captain happened to be in, and running messages scrawled on scraps of parchment between an increasingly familiar network of merchants.

The work was hard, but Romford did not find it physically taxing. He asked the Captain one day if he might have a bow to keep his arm strong at the town's archery butts, which stood against the walls in a scrubby, dirty square in the corner nearest the castle. But the Captain refused. 'Too many folk in this town have seen what you can do with a weapon in your hand,' he said. 'We'll leave that for another day.'

So Romford stuck to doing what he was told. He was sometimes bored, and occasionally alarmed by the crashes and booms that thundered against the city walls. More often, though, he was simply curious about what he was doing, why he was doing it, and what would happen to him if the city fell to the English. He considered different ways by which he might find an answer.

Only one seemed at all plausible. So during Easter week, as Calais' citizens made their preparations for what in normal times would be a great holiday of mourning and celebration, Romford summoned the courage to ask the Captain if he might take an afternoon to himself.

He needed to go and see Scotsman.

'Why?' said the Captain, when Romford asked him if he might do it.

'Because we were friends once,' said Romford. 'And I wonder if we still are.'

'Aye,' said the Captain. 'Well, you can ask him the same question from me. Hold out your hand.'

Romford held his hand out, and the Captain filled it with a pile of mixed silver coins.

'You'll need to buy your way in there,' he said. 'Use these. Remember, there will be a number of men whose palms you must fill. Don't give it all away to the first of them.'

Romford nodded earnestly. 'It'll be a good...'

'...lesson for you.' The Captain finished his sentence for him, and smiled.

Romford bribed the man on the door of the castle and the jailer at the foot of the dungeon. He bribed the guard who controlled access to the cells, and then bribed him again to leave him alone with the prisoner.

But when he sat outside Scotsman's cell and looked into the gloom beyond it, he could see only the shadowy hulk of the great man who sat on his haunches in the corner of his cell.

Though Romford had spent many weeks locked in the same conditions as the Scot, in the few weeks he had spent above the ground he had already forgotten how terrible the gloom was. How it found its way into your bones.

'Scotsman,' he said quietly. 'It's me. I've come to see you.'

His tongue felt strange speaking in English. He felt stupid for telling the Scot what he surely already knew.

The Scot just grunted. Romford tried again. 'How are you faring?'

Scotsman blew air out of his cheeks. 'Fuck off back up there,' he said. His voice was harsh and rasping. 'Don't fucking come back unless you're taking me with you. Christ.'

He shifted position on his haunches. A thin shaft of light from the high grille caught his face. It was all hair. Not a single feature was visible.

'Scotsman – I'm—'

'Save it,' said the Scot. 'It wasn't you.'

'I want to ask you something.'

'You want to ask me what the fuck that bastard is doing up there?'

Romford nodded silently in the dark.

'You're the one who's up there,' said Scotsman. 'Can't you work it out for yourself?'

'I've been trying,' said Romford. 'But it makes no sense to me. We don't fight on the walls. We don't try to escape. When ships come in with supplies, we seem to hide more of it than we give out to the people of the city.'

Scotsman listened in silence.

'It's as though...' Romford paused as the thought formed in his own mind. 'As though he wants the siege to continue.'

'Mm.'

'He isn't on the English side. But he isn't on the French either. He's on the side of... of the war.'

'You want my advice?' asked Scotsman.

'That's why I came to see you,' said Romford.

'Listen to him. That cunt thinks about things more than anyone I ever met. Learn from him. He'll teach you plenty that one day you'll use. Get as much out of him as you can. God knows, he was always the one who got us paid in the past. Which is more than that silly fucker Loveday has managed for us since.

'But there's one thing you can't do.'

'What is it?' asked Romford.

'Don't trust the cunt,' said Scotsman. 'Not even for a heartbeat.'

24

The young count of Flanders... declared he would never marry the daughter of the man who had killed his father... so he was placed under house arrest... twenty men followed him constantly, wherever he went, watching him so closely he could hardly go for a piss...

True Chronicles of Jean le Bel

After she opened the belly of the brothel-master, slashed her chest to ribbons and pulled her eyes out, Squelette left the siege camp.

It would have been easy to stay near and strike again. As long as there were English, there would be targets. Temptations. But she knew eventually she would be caught. She had now avenged many others. The time was coming to take revenge for herself.

The revenge she had in mind was too dangerous – and too difficult – to take in the English camp. So Squelette went away. Further than she had been from the English since they had come to her home in Valognes and taken everything she cared about. She went away, and she waited.

She followed the roads around Villeneuve. She drifted between towns. St Omer. Artois. Ghent. It was very cold everywhere and everything in the countryside was dead or asleep. So she begged and stole and found places to sleep at night where she would not freeze to death.

One day, she stole an old fur from a merchant's house. It was grey, with a long white stripe running lengthways along it. It was large enough to wrap around her body, down to her knees.

She kept it rolled in her pack during the short winter days. But at night she wrapped it around her shoulders and imagined she was the animal that had once worn it. She went out into the bare, silent countryside and draped it about her then dropped to her hands and feet and howled. She howled so her breath made a cloud about her face and her voice carried into the blackness of the sky.

She howled and wished that the man she wanted would hear her. The man she had most reason to hate of all the English. Who had attacked her and hurt her the worst. The man she would kill last.

The prince.

She picked up his trail in Ghent just as the days had begun growing longer. For a time she did not see him, but she knew that he was near. She learned it from the chatter of the people.

'The English king's son is coming. His sister will marry Louis, the Count of Flanders. Against the young count's will. The prince is here to see that it happens.'

She sniffed for him by day. By night, she howled at the moon. She told him she was coming for him. And eventually, as spring was arriving, she found him.

He was in a small town by the sea called Bergues.

She saw straight away that it would not be easy. The prince

and his entourage moved houses often. He had at least a dozen men in his bodyguard, and often twice that number.

The guard was heavy because the prince was doing a difficult job of his own. He and an English lord they called Jacky were watching Louis, the Count of Flanders: the one who was to be married. Where the count went, the prince and Jacky went. In the guise of chaperones, but with the eyes of jailers.

As the wedding approached, the young lords went to the taverns and brothels much less. Most days, they went out to hunt the birds and beasts of the forest. They often bickered and squabbled, and the prince taunted the count about his marriage. Yet the prince also did his job well. He and his men made sure the count could go nowhere unseen. If the count even wandered from the hunt to piss among the trees, two guards stood no more than a yard from him, their backs turned but their eyes scanning, alert to any movement.

They made it hard for Squelette. There were so many of them, and only one of her. But the more she watched, the more she thought it could be done.

By watching the young count, she saw that, from time to time, the guards took their eyes from the prince.

It happened once or twice on every hunt.

So it could be done.

It had to be done.

It would be done.

Since the time to strike was when the lords went out to hunt, Squelette decided the way to strike was like a beast. A beast of the forest, who could creep unseen, at one with the trees.

That was easy. She was already living like an animal. After

the winter, she was so thin she had almost disappeared. She stank like a beast. She found shadows and corners by second nature and she knew how to move through a forest unseen, as if she had been raised in one.

At night when she wrapped the grey fur robe around her, now full of fleas and with patches of the fur falling out, she felt like she was putting on her real skin.

She was transforming. She was preparing. She sharpened her knife. She carved her fingernails to points like claws.

Then her chance came.

A week before the wedding, the count and prince rode out to a chase beside a river to hunt. They wore thick gloves on their hands. Servants carried hawks. Fine birds with leather caps that covered their heads and eyes like executioners.

Squelette went with them.

She tracked them as they rode in their usual languid manner through the forest trails. Watched them laugh and swig wine, then argue and speak harshly to each other. She stayed in the forest when they emerged through it to a riverbank where there were ducks and doves and other good things for hawks to kill.

She stayed behind the tree line where it grew close by the river, moving to a point where the path was tight between the greenery and the water. She kept her eyes on the prince. Noticed the pursed lips and fine curls of hair on the crescent of his jaw and chin. Remembered what he had done to her.

She fastened the fur around her shoulders. She traced the inside of her arm with her sharpened claws. Decided she would use them first, before the knife.

She watched the lords stand around, letting the hawks soar and drop on weaker birds, pulling them out of the sky with their talons and ripping them to pieces with their beaks.

She waited for her moment, and was ready when it arrived.

The hawk the young count was flying spied some tasty prey of its own fancy a long way off upriver. It stretched its wings and disappeared until it was a dot in the sky. Among the men on the ground, this caused a commotion. Part laughter, part anger. The group spread out and tried to spot where the bird had gone.

Squelette shrank back into the bushes and let them go past her. The count, Louis, was at their head, his servant with his horse beside him and his guards following in single file along the path. They came so close to Squelette she could smell the leather of their boots.

Jacky went in the middle of the group. The prince loitered at the very back. He seemed bored. He called instructions ahead for his men to keep Louis in their sight.

When the prince passed her, Squelette growled. Then she retreated, rustling the undergrowth as she went.

The prince took the bait. He peered into the thick greenery. He caught a glimpse of her fur. He drew his sword and went in after her. 'Jacky,' he called. 'There's something in here.'

Squelette retreated again. The prince followed. She led him fifty paces through the forest, changing her direction and growling to make him follow. She saw him peering after her. She smelled his excitement and watched the way he held his sword, so she would know exactly how to pounce.

She drew up behind a thick tangle of bramble and led him on his final steps towards her with her voice.

She coiled herself, ready to leap. She bit her cheek in her excitement and her mouth watered at the taste of blood it released.

The prince's boots crunched in the undergrowth. He was close enough for her to touch.

She stood up and snarled and leapt at him with her claws and teeth out.

From behind her, Jacky thrust his sword straight through her side.

Squelette gasped. She collapsed forward. Blood bubbled from her mouth.

She could not see. But she heard a voice say: 'What in Christ's name?'

Another say: 'Some peasant girl. Dressed as a fucking wolf.'

Disbelieving laughter.

Then shouts from the direction of the river. 'My lords,' they said. 'Come quickly! The count has escaped!'

Cursing and blaspheming. Angry yells. Men pushing and shoving one another in frustration.

The men's voices receded. She was left alone in the clearing. She was bleeding so fast. The hole in her side was scalding hot. Everywhere else, she was colder than she had been even in the dead of winter.

She heard the screeching of the hawks and wondered if they would come down and feast on her.

She tried to say a prayer, but her lips were blue and still before the words formed.

25

King Edward began to consider how to overcome the French... so he ordered the building of a lofty castle of thick, heavy timber on the sea shore and filled it with bombards, springalds and other machines and artillery...

True Chronicles of Jean le Bel

The underdeck of the cog was stuffy and damp. It was little more than a crawl space below the deck on which the sailors and most of the cargo stood. Romford was alone in it, fetching the last of the marked crates the ship had brought in. He crept around slowly, bent almost double. The torch in his left hand belched smoke that tickled his throat. But the crackle of the small flame kept him company, and its smell masked the reek of the bilge water that slopped around his ankles. The dark, cramped space reminded him of Calais' castle's cells.

At least, he thought, he was almost done. The cog had appeared unannounced in Calais' harbour, after more than a week in which nothing had come in. It had brought only a small quantity of food; the bulk of its load was boxes for the Captain and his merchant friends. The sailors who had scrambled down from its sides when the ship had moored alongside the harbour had been tired and harassed. 'Fucking swarming out there,' one had said. 'The scum are everywhere.

Four English ships to every one of ours now. And more coming every day.'

Romford found the last of the crates he was looking for at the very back of the underdeck. It had been tucked in front of a pile of rubble, which he supposed was the ballast that kept the ship from rolling over in the waves of the open sea. It was a middling-sized container, clearly marked with the tailed cross. Romford wedged his torch handle-first between two rocks in the rubble pile, took hold of the crate's sides and started to drag it towards the pool of daylight in the centre of the crawl space, where the hatch opened up to the deck above.

As soon as he put his arms around it, he knew it was rotten. The crate had been sitting in the bilge for long enough that the wood was in places as soft as packed hay. Romford gripped it with as little pressure as he could and dragged it backwards. It was an awkward job. His feet slipped in the foul water. He bumped the back of his head on the deck above. The edges of the crate kept catching on the ship's thick ribs, which held together the overlapping clinkered planks of the hull.

When he was halfway to the hatch the crate gave way, the wood finally coming to pieces in his hands. Romford fell backwards, bouncing on his arse and ending up lying in the salty bilge holding a section of rotten timber. The mire soaked his shirt. It splashed and went in his mouth.

'God's... bastard... shit!' Romford said out loud. His voice echoed around the cramped space. He was surprised to hear himself curse. 'Sorry,' he whispered. He scrambled back to his feet, spat, wiped down his hands and tried to assess the damage he had done.

Some of the crate's contents had spilled out. Stranded between his guttering torch and the pool of daylight by the hatch, Romford could not see what they were. He sighed, and started edging around the box to fetch the torch and work out how to fix the mess.

But just as he reached the ballast pile, something rocked the ship. The torch dislodged from the crack between the rocks and fell into the water. It went out with a hiss, and the underdeck grew darker than ever.

For a moment, Romford crouched in exasperation, his hands on his knees. He spat again. The Captain was waiting on the harbourside for him. He would be annoyed to see him return without this final box. But there was nothing else to be done. He would have to fetch a new torch.

Romford started back towards the open hatch, feeling his way so he did not fall over again. But as he did so, the ship lurched again.

At the same time, the foot-stomps above him became quicker and heavier than they had been all morning. Shouts floated down through the hatch. People were running about on the deck.

Romford froze. Something was wrong.

From the front of the ship came a loud bang. It shook the cog so hard that Romford was knocked off his feet once more, back into the slime. This time, he landed on top of the contents of the crate. Through his wet shirt, he could now feel what had spilled out when the box broke.

He felt the rough scratch of sackcloth. And inside it, hard metal shapes. He was lying on a pile of coins. Hundreds, maybe thousands of them, parcelled in small bags.

Instinctively, Romford grabbed four of the bags, two in each hand. Then he crept towards the hatch. When he was nearly under it, he stood still for as long as he dared and listened.

The footsteps above his head had stopped. He could still hear men yelling at one another. But now they sounded far away. So far as he could tell, he was alone on the ship.

Something slammed the cog again. Romford gripped the coin bags tightly as he staggered. This time, he kept his footing. But the underdeck suddenly seemed a lot brighter.

A hole had been punched in the hull of the cog. The ship was being rammed.

He had to get off.

There were only a few steps leading up to the deck. And Romford was almost certain that there was no one left above him. He took a deep breath, and as stealthily as he could, he clambered out on to the deck.

Fresh sea air blasted his lungs. The deck was a mess of ropes and netting, and a few food crates and barrels that had been left where they stood as the crew abandoned ship.

Romford could hear shouts and curses coming from both the harbourside and the sea. Beneath his feet, the ship was starting to list.

It was sinking.

At the back of the deck lay a dead man, with a small bow by his side and an arrow sticking through his throat. He had fallen from the tall aft-castle at the back of the ship. His body lay awkwardly, as though many bones were broken.

Romford wrinkled his nose at the sight. But he did not panic. He knew what to do. It was as though he heard the Captain's voice in his ear. Guiding him. Teaching him, as he had taught him how to speak French, and how to count coins, and where to hide marked boxes in dirty warehouses in a besieged city.

Take the bow. Get off the ship. And for God's sake, lad, don't lose the coins.

Romford ran to the dead man. He placed his coin bags down beside him and unpeeled the corpse's fingers from the bow. He slung the bow over his back, untied the dead man's arrow bag and cinched it around his own waist. There were only four arrows in it.

There was plenty of room for his coin bags. He stuffed them down inside.

The dead man was wearing an archer's ring on his right thumb, of the sort that Tebbe and Thorp wore to protect their hand's webbing from the bowstring's scrape. It was carved from creamy whalebone.

Romford had never had such a ring. He worked it off the dead man's hand. He slipped it on his own thumb. It fitted perfectly.

For a moment, Romford crouched with his back to the side of the ship where the dead man lay. He looked at his face. Saw thick black eyebrows that contrasted strangely with the man's smooth, pinkish skin. His eyes were closed. He reminded Romford of a butchered sheep.

Romford reached down and flattened the dead man's hair, combing it smooth and neat with his fingers.

Something crashed into the cog. The ship shook again and listed even more.

He did not have much time.

He checked he had everything: bow, arrows, coin bags. He looked to the side of the ship closest to the harbour. He could see a rope ladder slung over the side.

He was about to run for it when a guilty thought struck him.

The ring.

It wasn't his. It wasn't right to take it.

The ship was now going down fast. Romford worked quickly. He rummaged in his arrow bag. He used an arrowhead to slit open one of the coin sacks. He took out the first one his fingers gripped. Gold caught daylight and glinted.

Romford slotted the coin into the dead archer's mouth.

He remembered a priest saying something about there being no coins in heaven. Or no rich men. But he didn't know whether that was really true.

He closed the man's mouth around the coin. Then he ran to the rope ladder and scrambled off the sinking ship. He jumped the last two rungs, landing in a crouch. He was back on Calais harbour.

No one was left on the pier. The Captain was gone. So was everyone else.

But while the land was deserted, the harbour was swarming with boats. None was remotely the size of the great cog, which was now groaning as it tipped on its end and sank.

Yet there were so many of them. Scores of little vessels were darting about in the water, full of men with weapons, chasing each other around the harbour.

Most of the boats and men were English.

The few defenders were falling back towards the harbourside. They were being massacred as they went.

Romford saw two English boats close on a little fishing boat carrying five or six Calais men. The English sailors had long swords, helmets and thick, leather-covered padding on their torsos. The Calais men had poles and staffs. They flailed left and right with their sticks. The English hacked and stabbed and cut them to shreds.

Romford did not wait to see more. He ran for the Water Gate. But before he got there, he knew he was too late. The Water Gate's portcullises had been slammed shut. Its drawbridges were raised.

Romford stood helplessly in front of it. He looked at the tiny arrow slits in the barbican. He knew defenders would be watching him from inside. Feebly, he waved his arms. 'Hey!' he shouted. But his voice sounded pathetic.

'Hey!' he shouted again. He realised he might as well be yelling at the stone wall. He turned around and frantically scanned the harbour and the carnage happening on the water.

He understood finally what was happening.

Behind the English raiding boats that had forced their way into the harbour, the Risbank was alive with movement. Carts, horses, men, materials. Archers, engineers, knights, noblemen.

For months, the English had declined to extend their siege town along the Risbank, believing they did not have the military strength to hold it against French attacks from the sea. Something had changed their minds. What was it the crew of the sinking cog had said?

The scum are everywhere.

The English must believe that they could control the sea.

No, not believe.

They *could* control the sea. They *had* control of it. Now they were moving up the Risbank, to fortify the strip of land that formed one whole side of Calais' harbour.

From inside Calais, Romford heard church bells tolling an alarm.

For a few more moments, he stood staring at the closed Water Gate. Then he realised that if he stood any longer, he was sure to die.

There was only one more way into the city: the Lantern Gate. It was three hundred yards away.

Romford set off running. The coins in his arrow bag banged against his leg as he went. He unslung the bow from around his back without breaking a stride. Pulled an arrow from his arrow bag, just in case.

He felt something disturb the air above him. Then it happened again. Then something thudded into the ground just behind his heels.

Crossbow bolts.

His chest burned. He kept running.

Ahead of him, the harbour turned into a strip of muddy beach for fifty yards or so. He jumped down on to it and kept moving. His feet, already soaked from the cog's bilge, sank into grit and grey-black shingle as he ran.

At the end of the strip of dirty sand, a little rowing boat was being carried in on the surf. It bounced up on the waves and three men-at-arms leapt out. One of the men grabbed the boat's bows and started heaving it out of the water.

The other two spotted Romford and smiled. They drew their swords.

Romford did not stop. He started shouting. 'St George!' he cried in English. 'King Edward! God protect England!'

The men-at-arms paused at the sound of their own language for just long enough. Romford kept running and tried to keep his head completely still.

He thought of a picture he had once seen daubed on a tavern sign. Of a Saracen on horseback, shooting an arrow as his horse thundered along beneath him. He did not have a horse. But the idea was the same.

Without breaking stride, Romford nocked the arrow and

drew the bow. He drew it a long way short of its full tension.
He had not shot for weeks. But he knew he needed accuracy,
not power.

He let the arrow go.

It hit the first man in the eye.

Still Romford kept running, now moving in a semicircle, as
though the imaginary horse he was on was prancing sideways.
It meant he kept his distance from the second man-at-arms
for long enough that he could pull the second arrow from his
arrow bag.

Nock. Draw. Release.

The man-at arms turned his head to track Romford. He
presented a tiny patch of skin above the line of his mail shirt.
Romford hit it. The arrow opened the man's throat.

The third man dragging the boat realised too late what was
happening. 'Holy Christ—' he said. Romford stopped running.
He planted his feet and drew his third arrow as far back as
he could. He shot the man-at-arms in the groin. As Romford
released the arrow, he felt himself rising up on his tiptoes. As
though he were standing in the saddle.

The man spun and slumped sideways against the boat, lying
on his side, facing Romford. He had not fastened his leather
shirt properly. Romford took his last arrow out of the bag. He
took his time, then shot him in the gut. The arrow buried itself
right up to the fletchings.

Romford had used all his arrows. He looked behind him.
More English boats were coming towards the beach. For a
fleeting second it occurred to him that he had killed men from
the land of his own birth.

He found it interesting. Nothing more.

The man he had shot twice was writhing in agony. His

face and body were covered in sludge and sand, glued to him with blood. He was tugging at the arrow in his stomach. He screamed every time it moved.

'Excuse me,' Romford said, in English.

The man-at-arms lay still for a second, holding the arrow shaft in disbelief. Blood was leaking between his fingers. He looked at Romford. He opened his mouth but no words came out.

'You need a surgeon. If you pull the arrow like that, it will take you a long time to die, and it will be very painful,' said Romford.

Then he ran off.

He clambered off the beach on to the section of the harbour beside the Lantern Gate. The drawbridge was still down. But the portcullis was closed. Behind it stood the Captain. He had been watching everything.

'Are you going to let me in?' called Romford. He put his face to the grille of the portcullis.

'Are you going to pay me?' asked the Captain, with a smile.

Romford looked behind him. More Englishmen were now running up the beach. 'You're joking,' he said.

'Maybe,' said the Captain. 'But maybe not. You don't have long to decide.'

Romford stared at the Captain. He pulled one of the coin sacks out of his arrow bag and held it through the grille. The Captain clicked his fingers and the portcullis was winched up enough for Romford to crawl underneath it. Then it was released, and the drawbridge started creeping up.

Romford slumped on the uneven cobbles of the barbican floor, leaning against the cold stone of the wall. He was suddenly exhausted, and his hands were trembling.

Beyond the drawbridge, Englishmen shouted taunts across the moat.

'There are Calais men still out there,' said Romford.

'But none of them came to me with any sacks of coin,' said the Captain. 'So who cares?' He held out his hand for Romford to pass him the bags.

'Good lad,' he said.

'Don't you care if they die?' asked Romford.

The Captain studied him for a while. From beyond the Lantern Gate's closed drawbridge came more yells and splashes, along with the distant boom of cannon on the Risbank firing. He shook his head.

'No more than they care if I do.' He stood over Romford, and prodded him in the side with his stick. 'Shall I tell you what you think? You think when war goes well, it's about brotherhood and loyalty and friends looking after one other. And duty to the king. That sort of thing.'

'Am I right?'

Romford nodded slowly.

'And let me guess who filled your head with those thoughts,' said the Captain. 'A fat man called Loveday? A stonemason called Millstone? Our hairy friend down in the dungeons?'

He did not wait for Romford to reply.

'They're fools who should have listened to me when they had the chance,' said the Captain. He jiggled the coin bags. 'How many of these do you think sank with the cog?'

Romford shrugged. 'There were a lot more,' he said. 'The box was rotten. I—'

The Captain nodded. 'Well,' he said, after a few moments. 'It was good of you to rescue what you did. But now you stink like a sewer rat, and it's starting to make my eyes water.

'Let's get you back to the tavern and clean you up. Then I'll tell you the story of war as it really is.'

'Two years ago, some powerful men sent me to Ghent to kill a man called Jacob van Artevelde,' said the Captain.

He and Romford were sitting by a table at their lodging inn beneath the sign of the Beehive. Romford's filthy clothes had been rinsed and squeezed and hung to dry on a line of twine in a yard behind the tavern. His shirt danced in the breeze as though it were alive.

'Who sent you?' asked Romford. It was chilly inside the inn. He pulled his blanket around his shoulders. 'Why? Who? What happened?'

'One thing at a time, lad. The men who sent me were the same who control this war. Who rule realms.'

Romford nodded. 'Lord Northampton? Lord Warwick? The king?'

The Captain smiled. 'Not those men, no. Kings and lords raise their flags above armies. They strut around in their armour and wave their flags and listen to heralds tell them their families' legends. They believe they rule everywhere and everyone. But there are other men behind them, who make it possible for them to play their games.'

The Captain picked up one of the coin sacks from the sunk cog. It was sewn shut. He tugged a loose thread and pulled out a coin. It was thin, beautiful, pure gold, its edges worn but its markings clean and bright. A lion prowled across the bottom of one side. Above it was stamped writing: some strange symbols Romford had never seen before, which curled and danced like wisps of grass.

The Captain turned it over in his fingers. 'This is Saracen gold. Best in the world. Mined in Africa, beyond the great desert, in a land where every man lives like a king, and gold lies on the ground like pebbles. Brought to the Saracens' lands by camel train and struck into coins and sent out into the world.'

Romford said nothing.

The Captain put the coin on the table and span it. It blurred, then slowed and rattled as it settled.

'The man in Ghent, Artevelde, was a rich man. And a powerful one too. People called him the Brewer of Ghent. He made this stuff.' He tapped his mug. 'Ale. So he made money. And he came to understand money. He knew how to earn it, and how to use it to make himself more powerful. He used his money to bring all the people in Ghent and the other cities in Flanders to his side.

'He had them chase out their lord, the count. Had them understand that they were free. And that if they gave him a say in how they made their gold and how they spent it, that they would stay free. And so it was – for a time.'

The light in the tavern was fading. There was no fire in the grate. There was little firewood in the city. Romford shivered. 'What happened?'

'What happened, boy, is this Artevelde made so much money that he forgot himself. He stopped thinking like a man who made money. He grew close to kings. To the English kings. Eventually he started to think like them.

'He let it be known that he could decide who would be the new Count of Flanders. That he was the man to choose. It was said he was going to choose King Edward's son...'

The Captain stopped. He looked sharply at Romford. 'What's wrong? You're pale.'

Romford shook his head dumbly. Thoughts of the prince flooded his head. Thoughts of his companion Louis. Hadn't he said he was going to be the Count of Flanders one day?

The Captain let it pass. 'That was a mistake. He stepped out of the realm of making money. Had he put the prince in power in Ghent, all the men who made money in that part of the world would have seen their profits dry up. Their freedom diminished. Their fortunes hitched too tightly to the king and his son's interests. I knew some men who thought this had to be stopped.'

'Which men?'

'Men whose names you have never heard. And if you were not here today, you never would. Sir John Pulteney of London. William de la Pole of Hull. Merchants. They trade with Flanders. They loan the profits of their trade to the king, so that he can fight his wars. They take their payment in tax revenues, in trading privileges. In times of peace, they earn well. But in times of war they earn even better.

'In Artevelde they saw a man who was about to broker peace. That would not do. So they asked me to help them stop him.'

'Why you?' said Romford. He looked at the Captain's stick. His face. The ruined stump of his leg.

'Because I knew them and I had worked with them before. And I understood that this was a new way of warfare. I wanted to be part of it. I tried to convince my men – the men you have met. But they were afraid to see what was happening. They feared change. From what little I've seen of them since, they still do. So I went my own way.'

'And you did it?'

'Aye. And the job was easy. But I made one mistake. I trusted them to pay me and to use me again. To value me. To regard me with loyalty and brotherly care.

'When I led the Essex Dogs, those were lessons I taught them. I would say "bury your dead, leave no living man behind". Words that sounded wonderful in that world. Words that in fact were dangerous. I didn't unlearn my lessons fast enough. It nearly had me killed.'

'Was that how—?'

'A man betrayed me. He paid me a handsome sum of gold. Then he broke my leg and threw me over a bridge. The leg was no good after that. I had someone take it off. The river-water had some poison in it that got into my skin.

'But I lived. And I learned. And now I am here. Once more working with merchants.'

'The boxes – with the marks...'

'Aye. They're a part of it. But the bigger picture is this: we are in a delicate position. The English will take this city. We cannot stop that from happening. But we can bend the war in such a way that we can make ourselves rich *as* it happens. The longer the siege goes on, the richer the pirates who tried to kill you become. The richer the merchants supplying this city become. The richer the men lending gold to the English become. The richer—'

The more the Captain spoke, the sadder Romford felt. 'Men are dying,' he said. 'Women—'

The Captain nodded. 'And it will soon be worse. The English have just taken the Risbank. As you saw with your own eyes. There will be no more ships in here now. No more food. The city will starve. It will be terrible. You will never have known anything like it. But at the end of it—'

Romford looked at the Captain. 'Don't you care?'

'Whether I care or not is of no consequence. Look at me. I am half a man. Broken. Half-eaten. Condemned to lurch around on this stick. What do you think I want?'

Romford considered this a while. After a few moments he said: 'Revenge.'

'On who?'

'The men who did this to you.'

'Wrong. I don't care for vengeance any more than I care for loyalty. All I want is this.' The Captain took the sack of coins and emptied it carefully on the table. Gold and silver coins of all sizes and styles slid out and formed a loose pile. 'This,' said the Captain. 'And only this. And I think if you stay with me a little longer, you will see I am right.'

He stared at Romford so hard that his eyes seemed to pierce Romford's, like the arrow he had put in the English soldier's face on the beach.

'What do you want from this world?' asked the Captain.

Romford shook his head and pulled his blanket once more around his thin shoulders and his bare chest. The wispy blond hairs on it were standing up with the cold of the room and the intensity of the Captain's words.

'To go home,' he said.

He picked up one of the coins from the pile on the table and twirled it with his fingers. 'But I don't know where that is.'

They both watched the coin in silence until it clattered to a stop.

26

[The English] kept such a close guard upon the harbour and port of Calais that nothing could sail in or out without being battered and wrecked. This was a greater blow to the city's resistance than anything else had been.

True Chronicles of Jean le Bel

The flurry of activity Romford had seen on the Risbank included the building of a huge wooden fortress, its defences made from thick tree trunks hewn in the forests of Boulogne. One late spring morning, Loveday, Millstone and Thorp sat among them. The pillars still gave off a light aroma of sap and bark. It almost masked the sour smell of the men camped inside the perimeter. The three Dogs were loitering in their tent, waiting for the Earl of Northampton to arrive.

'Another day of watching the fucking sea and pulling catapults around,' moaned Thorp. 'Why do we bother?'

'We bother,' said Millstone, 'because the alternative is going back to the ditch.'

On the other side of the fort, cannons boomed. Despite himself, Loveday jumped. Thorp narrowed his eyes. 'You still not used to it?'

'I suppose not,' said Loveday, although they all knew the truth. Since the battle on the walls of Calais, they had all changed. Millstone had become harder and more closed off than ever. Thorp swung between silence and ill temper; Loveday knew he was nursing the loss of Tebbe, though Thorp could barely bring himself to mention his friend's name.

Loveday himself had grown jumpy and anxious. The burns down the side of his arm and body from the pitch that had killed Tebbe had healed well, the yellow pus-blisters receding and scabs falling off to leave dull purple spots. But his hands trembled all the time. He spilled his ale and missed his mouth with his food. And he had lost almost all his physical strength. When the Dogs were pressed into dragging fort timbers along the Risbank, he was barely able even to lift a log. At night, he woke up sweating so much it was as if he had been hauled up from the seabed. His thoughts rotated constantly between a cast of the lost and dead. Pismire, Father, Tebbe. Scotsman, Romford. And of course, the Captain.

His decline had changed things among them. Now that the Dogs were only three, there was little need for any of them to act as leader. Even so, Loveday had ceased to fill the position. Millstone now took decisions that concerned them all. Thorp acted as his deputy. They treated Loveday with respect and they shared everything among themselves, as they had always done. But it was clear that they saw him as he was starting to see himself. As an invalid. A casualty of war.

The fort the English were building on the Risbank was huge. In design, it reminded Loveday of camps he had known in the wild borderlands of Scotland during the wars with the Bruce. The tree trunks of its wall were shorn of their bark and planed smooth, then driven deep into the soft, damp ground. Every twenty paces along the walls rose three-storey guard towers. On the side facing the mainland, a gatehouse three times the size of a regular guard tower was patrolled by men-at-arms. On the other side, a smaller gatehouse led out to a platform at the tip of the Risbank, where cannons and catapults faced out to sea.

Inside the fort lived several hundred men. Many were new to the siege. Since Easter, ships of all sizes had been arriving almost every day, bringing fresh troops recruited all over England and Wales. Loveday thought they were different to the men of the army the Dogs had come over with the previous summer. They were harder, rougher, surlier and coarser. Millstone said he had heard they were being recruited in a new fashion. Their pay would not be made in coin but in pardons for all crimes they had committed against the king's peace.

'Bunch of murderers and rapists come over to escape their past,' said Thorp, when they spoke of these new arrivals.

'Same as it ever was,' Millstone replied. 'Now it's just being said out loud.'

When the three Dogs were eventually briefed on their day's duty, it was not Northampton who came to speak to them but Sir Hugh Hastings. The Norfolk knight looked terrible: his eyes were bloodshot and sweat stood out on his forehead, though the spring morning was still unseasonably chilly. His wig was tangled and unkempt and he could not speak more than a dozen words without coughing, often very violently.

He had kept the Dogs waiting – out of spite, thought Loveday. Hastings had still not forgiven them for what happened to his brothel in Villeneuve. For Romford and Scotsman's escape. For Hircent's murder.

'There you are,' he said, as he shuffled over. 'Been looking for you.'

'This is where we always are,' said Millstone.

Hastings coughed. He did not bother to cover his mouth. 'Expecting Constable Willikin, were you? Your saviour from Northamptonshire. If I had my way you'd still be in the ditch.'

Loveday felt Thorp bridle with anger. 'We're here because the queen—' Thorp began.

Hastings fixed him with his pink watery eyes. 'What do any of you know about the queen?' he asked.

Millstone placed a firm hand on Thorp's arm. 'The queen requested we be posted here. That's all we know. That's all anyone knows.'

'The queen has another little princeling in her belly. Did you know that?' said Hastings. 'We all know what that does to a woman's brain.'

Millstone nodded calmly. 'It's a blessing.'

'For you. For now.' Hastings coughed again. He spat. 'Well. I can't waste the day. You're out on the boats today.'

'The blockade ships?' said Millstone. 'With respect, Sir Hugh—'

'*We're not sailors.*' Hastings used a sing-song, childish voice. 'I know that. And I wouldn't risk sinking another ship in the harbour by putting you three on one. I said boats. Our lookouts here and on the mainland have spotted enemy spies trying to leave Calais. Pretending to be refugees. They starve themselves a little, stop eating the horsemeat or whatever they're down to in that godforsaken place. So they look the part. But they're not. Your job is to intercept them. See that they get a nice long drink of the saltwater. Think you can manage that?'

The Dogs looked at one another uncertainly. 'Spies?' said Loveday.

'Oh, the fat man speaks,' said Hastings. 'Spies, yes. And try not to capsize the boat while you're at work. You don't want to lose your pretty garter.'

Loveday let this pass, though Hastings' barb about the garter stung. He had the token from the queen tied around his wrist.

Millstone finished the conversation before it could take any more unpleasant turn. 'As you wish, Sir Hugh. Where will we report for this duty?'

Hastings pointed to the fort gatehouse at the tip of the Risbank. 'There. One of my Norfolk men is organising the boats.' He coughed so hard that his shoulders shook. 'A man who can actually get something done,' he said, once he could speak again.

'You can't miss him.'

They brought their weapons down to the gate at the Risbank's tip: Millstone his hammer, Loveday his short sword and Thorp the crossbow he had picked up during the battle on the walls. He now preferred it to the longbow he had used all his life. 'Better for close encounters,' he said.

Outside the fort's gate, the Risbank was a flurry of activity. Catapults and cannon platforms were manned by fresh troops, who strode around with an energy that told the Dogs none of them had suffered a cruel winter in Villeneuve.

Loveday cast his eye around for anyone who looked like he might be Hastings' man. He spotted a figure in the shingle at the Risbank's edge, bent down beside a line of small, oared boats. 'That must be him,' he said.

Millstone nodded. They made their way between the stone-throwers and guns to the boats.

As they arrived, the figure stood up. And when he turned around, Loveday's blood ran cold. He looked older than Loveday remembered. He had fresh scars on his face, and his beard and hair were much longer than they had been. But there was no mistaking who it was.

Beneath the shaggy mop of hair, the Dogs could see that both his ears had been removed.

The man squinted at them. Then grinned. The few teeth he had left were brown and black.

'Essex Dogs,' said the no-eared East Anglian. 'There aren't many of you left now, are there?'

Loveday opened his mouth to answer. He could only croak.

The no-eared man had been one of the East Anglian crew the Dogs had clashed with on the march to Crécy.

They had almost come to blows on the beach when the whole army landed. Again when they had been sent to burn ships at Barfleur.

Then, during the sack of Saint-Lô, Father, Romford and Millstone had fought with their captain, a vile, scrawny man called Shaw.

Millstone levelled his steady gaze on the no-eared man. 'I see you have even fewer of your crew.'

The no-eared man narrowed his eyes nastily. Millstone had smashed Shaw's head to pieces with his hammer and burned his body inside an apothecary shop. The no-eared man had been there to see it. 'Some gone. Some dead,' he said. 'But I'm here. And I will be longer than any of you Essex pricks.'

Millstone nodded. 'We never learned your name.'

'Faine,' said the no-eared man. 'Feel better for knowing?'

'Not really,' said Millstone. 'But I shall if you show us which boat is ours, and cause us no more trouble.' He twirled his hammer.

Faine regarded Millstone with mild amusement. 'You touch me, and Hastings will have you strung up from one of those trebuchets,' he said.

'Maybe so,' said Millstone. 'But you won't be there to watch it.'

Faine grunted. He pointed to the shabbiest boat in the row.

'What's that?' snapped Thorp.

'What you get for being pricks,' said Faine. 'It's watertight, unfortunately. Don't fucking whine.'

The Dogs went over to the dilapidated little boat. Faine did nothing to help them. He just smirked as they dragged it down to the water.

'Enjoy your day's fishing,' he called, as Millstone pulled the oars and they moved off. 'I'll be watching, and I'll let Sir Hugh know exactly how you get along.'

Loveday could see none but English patrol boats on the harbour water. Calais' two sea-facing gates were closed and their drawbridges raised. For more than an hour the Dogs rowed aimlessly around in front of the Risbank, taking turns to pull the oars. They were joined by other crews as Faine sent out more men to join them. But there was nothing to see and no one to intercept.

For a while, Loveday felt anxious. But after a time, he and the other two Dogs relaxed a little. 'Can't conjure up spies who aren't here,' said Thorp. It was also the first spring day that had felt genuinely warm. The sun came out and they all stripped down to their shirts, and then their bare skin. They enjoyed the sensation of the sun burning them after so long in the dark and cold. Loveday stared down into the harbour water, watching how it changed its depth. Sometimes he could see sand and rock at the bottom, with weed swaying lazily in the current. From time to time, a shoal of brown or silver fish would glide beneath the boat. He trailed his hand in the water and thought of Romford and Scotsman.

Thorp was watching him 'What's on your mind?' asked the archer.

'I was wondering about the others,' Loveday said. 'Where they are now.'

Thorp tightened and looked off into the distance. Loveday realised he thought he meant Tebbe. Thorp had still not spoken a word about what had happened on the ladder.

'Not... them,' said Loveday, then cringed inwardly. Now he had added thoughts of Pismire and Father to the conversation.

Millstone came to his rescue. 'He means Scotsman and the lad.'

Thorp nodded, and still said nothing.

Loveday filled the silence, but he found himself gabbling as usual. 'I was just... just wondering how long it took them to get back. Home, I mean. Or where they went. If they stuck together. Whether we'll ever...'

Thorp seemed to understand what he meant. He considered it.

'The lad, I doubt it,' he said. 'He doesn't know our places. Where the work is. As for...' Strangely, Thorp used Scotsman's given name. It made the hairs on Loveday's back stand up. As though they were speaking of a dead man.

'That fucker,' continued Thorp, 'if he's alive, we'll see him alright. You can hardly miss the bastard.' He pooled his hands in the cool water of the harbour and splashed it on his face and hair.

'Bollocks,' said Millstone.

Thorp looked at him sharply. 'What's that? You think you'd mistake that ginger fucking lunk for—'

'Not him,' said Millstone. He rested one oar on his lap and pointed to the far side of the harbour, near where Calais' castle marked the north-west corner of the city's defences.

Loveday and Thorp sat up and shaded their eyes against the sun's glare. It took them a moment to see what Millstone meant. When they did, their hearts sank.

Six or seven fishing boats had appeared from the city and were heading towards them. Even from far away, the Dogs could see they were all overloaded with people. In each of the boats someone was waving a flag, although from the distance they were at, Loveday could not make out what was displayed on it.

'Christ's ribs, what are they doing?' said Thorp. 'Fuckers must see that we're out here waiting for them. Worst spies since God made Adam.'

Millstone pulled the oars hard so the boat turned towards the little fleet. 'They're not spies,' he said. 'They're just hungry. How long's it been since Easter?'

Thorp and Loveday looked at each other. They had stopped counting days a long time ago. 'Weeks at least,' said Loveday. 'A month, perhaps.'

'Food must be nearly gone, then,' said Millstone. He was breathing heavily as he spoke, and sweat was beading in the thick curled hairs of his chest. Loveday wondered why he was suddenly rowing so intensely.

Then he looked behind them and realised that every other English boat in the harbour was doing the same.

Thorp was slower to catch on. 'What's the hurry?' he asked.

'We need to talk to them,' Millstone panted. 'Tell them... Before...'

Thorp understood. Loveday understood. Millstone wanted to warn the people on the boats what was happening. In case they couldn't see for themselves.

The English were closing in for a kill.

It was hopeless.

Though Millstone rowed hard and fast, many of the other men in the boats were fresh recruits: their muscles not wasted by the winter and their appetite for blood stronger than their instinct for mercy. The Dogs were overtaken by three other English craft, with more closing hard behind them.

What was more, the fishing boats coming out of Calais could make no distinction between the dozen English patrol vessels packed with jeering murderers and rapists and the one rowed by a semi-naked, sunburned Millstone, in which Thorp and Loveday stood shouting and flapping their arms.

First, the refugees tried to row away from the English. Then they tried to plead. They waved their flags, made from scaffold poles mounted with rough sheets, blankets or just sackcloth and daubed with the sign of the Cross.

They chanted hymns and prayers. Some held thin hands

skyward. Others rolled their eyes and clasped their hands towards the English, even as they tried to escape them.

Loveday watched in horror.

Most of the men and women aboard were old. But even those who were young looked as though they had lived a thousand years. Their ragged clothes hung loose from their shoulders. Their eye sockets were dark and sunken. Their cheekbones pressed against sallow skin as though their skulls were trying to escape from their faces.

'Shit,' said Thorp. 'Do we look that fucking rough?'

But before Millstone or Loveday could answer, the first crossbow bolt thudded into the side of one of the fishing boats.

Loveday looked to see where it had come from. The English boats had now formed a line across the harbour, daring the French to come any further. A barrel-chested Englishman with a bald head roasted pink by sun was pumping a crossbow gleefully in the air.

For a moment, there were no more shots. The two lines of boats floated opposite one another – the English shouting taunts and the starving refugees calling out prayers and pleas.

Then the first of the fishing boats tried to make a break.

Although the fishing boats were larger than the English patrol craft, they were heavier and slower, and they were rowed by thin, drained, elderly and weak people. The English swarmed at them, coming up alongside and lashing out with clubs and sticks at the frightened people who were closest to the sides of the boats.

Some of the English boats were trying to drive the French back towards the harbour and prevent them from getting towards the open sea. But others were actively trying to sink them. Aboard one of the English craft, a lad Loveday reckoned to be about Romford's age, wearing a mail vest much too large for him, was thrusting a spear at the side of one of the fishing boats, trying to punch a hole in its hull. His mates beside him cheered him on, as though he were doing nothing more than baiting a bull at a fair.

On the bows of another of the French boats, an elderly man was ranting and waving his fist at his tormentors. An English boat manoeuvred alongside. One of the sailors aboard picked up a spare oar and hit the man on the side of the head with it. He collapsed, bleeding. A woman holding a child no more than two summers old was crying hysterically.

Loveday shuddered. The man holding the oar seemed to feel that he was being watched. He turned and stared directly at Loveday.

He leered. He mouthed: 'Spies.'

It was Faine.

As the fishing boats were chased down, the harbour filled with terrified screams.

'No more,' said Millstone. He turned the Dogs' boat and started rowing towards the Risbank. Thorp and Loveday sat blankly in the stern, not knowing where to look.

One of the fishing boats was sinking. People were leaping overboard.

In front of them, on the far side of the Risbank, smoke was rising after another volley of gunfire and trebuchet shot rained on to the open sea.

Thorp stared at his feet. 'Even if they get out of the harbour...' he said. He didn't finish his sentence.

As they neared the shingle of the Risbank's beach once more, Loveday spotted a splashing in the water in the middle of the harbour, a long way from where the boats were circling. At first he thought it was a seal, but after a few moments he realised it was two or three people swimming.

He pointed it out to Millstone and Thorp. 'Should we go and help?'

The two Dogs said nothing and would not meet Loveday's gaze. He felt his eyes sting. Then their boat hit sand and they clambered over the edge and hauled it up the beach. After that, the Dogs stood, dejected, wondering what to do next.

As if to answer the question, Sir Hugh Hastings walked down the beach towards them, coughing as he came.

'Back early?' he spat. He looked out across the harbour, then nodded with cruel satisfaction.

'A job so well done that not even you could ruin it,' he said. 'Perhaps I'll put you on this task every day from now on.'

Millstone stepped up to the knight, moving so close that their chests they were no more than a handspan apart.

'You send us back out there,' he said to Hastings, 'and by my faith I'll put you in the ground. And they can hang me from whatever tree they like.'

His eyes bored hard into Hastings. 'I think you know I'm serious.'

For the briefest instant, a look flitted across Hastings' face that Loveday had never seen him wear before.

Fear.

But Hastings recovered himself quickly. He took half a step back and stifled a cough. 'You touch me,' he croaked, 'or ever speak to me like that again, you'll wish they'd hanged you.'

He put the flat of his palm on Millstone's chest.

Millstone yielded and stepped back. But he never let his eyes leave the knight's. And eventually it was Hastings who turned on his heel and staggered back towards the entrance to the fort.

Loveday's lungs felt tight. He realised he had been holding his breath.

He exhaled hard and put his hands to his waist. But he could not think of anything to say, and neither Thorp nor Millstone looked as if they wanted to speak of what they had just seen.

So the three Dogs made their way back to the fort too, trying not to hear the last of the howls that echoed across the harbour whenever there was a lull in cannon fire from the other side.

For the rest of the afternoon and long into the evening, Loveday found his thoughts kept returning to the people he had seen swimming in the harbour.

Were they trying to get to the Risbank? Into the open sea? Did they really think they could swim to another city?

The thought plagued Loveday. So did another.

What was happening inside Calais, if throwing yourself from a fishing boat into the cold, deadly sea seemed better than staying put?

27

The King of England... had shut off and enclosed the town of Calais with such a great siege, both by land and by sea, so that supplies were in no way able to be taken to those who were in the said town... For which they lived in great despair and misery...

Les Grandes Chroniques de France

After the English built the fort on the Risbank, a silence fell over Calais. Romford noticed the sound dying before he realised the food had all but disappeared.

Although the harbour was now closed even to fishing boats, and the Lantern Gate and Water Gate were permanently barred, he and the Captain still made their rounds of houses and hiding places every day, Romford shifting stock around and the older man continuing his whispered meetings and negotiations with the city's burghers. Day by day, Romford felt the energy of the citizens in the streets drift away. As though something was evaporating under the sun.

In the spring the days had followed a rhythm, with people queuing in the early morning to collect their rations of grain, fish, ale and meat, guards rotating their positions on the walls and towers with the tolling of the church bells, and all hands hurrying to the docks when a new ship came in. Yet as Whitsun approached, and the days grew hot and sticky, the city fell into a sullen torpor.

Every week, rations were cut. Strict measures were put in place by Calais' governor, the stern, gout-lame Jean de Vienne, to control prices. Floggings and hand-loppings were threatened for profiteering, though Romford doubted whether the governor would really be willing to ruin any limb that might one day be needed to defend the city's walls.

All the same, though prices stayed stable, every week there was less to buy. First, the fish vanished: a fate Romford thought strange and cruel whenever he listened to the distant waves beat the shores outside Calais' walls. Then the stored vegetables ran out. Finally, even bread became scarce.

One of the merchants the Captain knew, an elderly man called Jean d'Aire with milk-blue, half-blind eyes, had a cold cellar beneath a house just off the market square, where, in the winter, he had kept barrels of the autumn's fruit. The last few of these still held a few shrivelled, sour apples covered in coarse sawdust. Whenever Romford was sent down to Jean d'Aire's house to move other crates around, the Captain told him to bring up a handful, and insisted that they both eat as much as they could bear. The foul taste made Romford gag. But the Captain would not let him refuse. 'You ignore me, lad, then your gums will turn to mush and your teeth will drop,' he said.

He was right. Soon Romford started to see people in the streets with symptoms of the mouth-rot the Captain had described. They dragged themselves listlessly, their lips curled away from their gums, teeth blackening in livid, puffy beds of flesh, and rashes of angry purple spots covering their arms. So Romford kept choking down the nasty brown pungent balls of tree-flesh whenever he was told to, swallowing them, pips and stalk and skin.

As time went by, he understood that he was lucky to have anything at all.

In the afternoon of a hot day in the late spring, the Captain sent Romford to fetch water from the well sunk in the corner of the empty marketplace. Romford's belly gnawed. Besides rotten apples, all he had eaten for many days was hard strips of cured and salted meat, and even these were becoming hard to find. Tough strands of flesh stuck in his teeth, and the salt that cured them dried his mouth, making his head ache and turning his piss brown. He had not shit for a week.

The heat trapped in the marketplace was stifling and Romford felt dizzy. The silent crowd waiting their turn around the well squinted and shuffled in the sun. Everyone was suffering in much the same way.

After he had waited almost an hour for his turn at the well, the Captain came to wait with him. The older man was thin and drawn and his skin rawer than ever, but he seemed unbothered by the discomfort. His eyes flashed around the crowd, as though he were reading in them the state of the whole city. He nodded greeting to Romford. 'Feeling the pinch?' he asked.

When Romford nodded, the Captain leaned on his stick and surveyed the hot, dusty square.

'You'll get used to the hunger soon enough,' he said. He scratched the symbol of the tailed cross in the dirt at their feet. 'You might even come to like it.'

'How long do you think we'll last?' Romford asked.

The Captain shaded his eyes and looked towards the sun,

sinking in a sky streaked with pink and orange. Then at the castle turrets, whose shadows were creeping long over the city.

Somewhere far away, a cannon roared.

'Our friend Governor Vienne is stubborn,' he said. 'My guess is he'll throw more people out before he even begins to contemplate giving up. He truly believes King Philippe is coming to save us. It'll take a good deal of proof to assure him that he's not.'

'Will he throw us out?' Romford's stomach cramped as he spoke.

'*Us?*' The Captain laughed. 'It would be a great failure on my part if he did.'

Romford made no reply. He looked towards the front of the line at the well, which had stopped moving.

Raised voices were coming from ahead. A woman with a puckered mouth and greying hair pulled back on top of her head was accusing a man in front of her of taking water before his turn. The man was shrilly denying her charge. She pushed him, and he pushed her back. Her pail of water spilled, and she flew into a rage.

Around them, others began shouting. A stocky sunburned man pushed the quarrelling pair aside so he could take a turn at the well, and he was in turn yanked and dragged by others.

The Captain watched this with an expression somewhere between boredom and amusement. Then he left Romford and walked forward, taking slow measured paces marked out with his stick.

'Hold your peace,' he shouted to the tussling townsfolk.

'Mind your own affairs, cripple.'

The Captain spun on his left leg and spotted the middle-aged man who had called out to him from the crowd.

'My affairs?' said the Captain, in a quiet voice.

Romford felt uneasy.

'Yeah, your own—'

The Captain flipped his stick and swung it, handle end first, at the man's ankle. He stopped it a hair's breadth from the knobbly bone.

The man looked down in surprise, shocked by the speed of the Captain's movement. As he did, the Captain whipped the stick up and tapped him sharply on the chin. It was not a hard blow, but the surprise of it made the man sit down on his arse in the dirt.

Everyone around the well stopped shoving and stood, watching, in silence.

'My affairs are the same as yours,' said the Captain. 'We are all working to keep this city from falling.' He looked about the whole crowd. 'We are fighting the English. Not each other. Stay calm. Endure the dearth as Christ did in the desert. And when this is over, we will be rewarded.'

He nodded. 'Come on,' he said to Romford. 'We'll draw water elsewhere.'

He moved off calmly towards the road leading out of the hot square, back towards the Beehive inn. Romford followed him. The brooding hostility of the starving townsfolk hung in the air. But no one followed them, nor called after them.

'How will they be rewarded?' whispered Romford, when he was sure they were out of earshot.

'They won't,' said the Captain. 'But it does no good to tell them that.'

His face was set hard. Romford's belly cramped again. By the time he drew water from the city's other main well, the deep hole by the Snail Tower, the sun had fully set.

* * *

Although the Captain said no more that day of what had happened at the well, or what was happening to the city as it slipped into starvation, the memory bothered Romford. And when he fell asleep that night on his hot, scratchy mattress, alive with bugs, he dreamed of men turning another man above a fire. Impaled on a spit thrust through his mouth and arsehole.

As the man roasted, those around the fire sliced strips off his thighs and buttocks with their knives and dropped the hot slivers of meat into their mouths.

Then the faces of the men warped and changed until they were all familiar. They were the Essex Dogs. Almost all the comrades he had arrived on that beach in Normandy with so long ago were there. Loveday and Millstone. Tebbe, Thorp, Darys and Lyntyn. Scotsman and Pismire. The Captain, his leg grown back and his face handsome and tanned, was turning the spit.

The man they were roasting was the fat, piggy-eyed Sir Robert le Straunge.

Romford shrank to the back of the group, not wanting to eat Sir Robert's meat, though he was so terribly hungry that his whole body was wracked with pain. Seeing him retreat, each of the men called to him in turn, speaking with their mouths full, spraying out half-chewed morsels of flesh and a mist of grease.

Then they were joined by other faces Romford knew: the Earls of Northampton and Warwick. Sir John Chandos and Sir Hugh Hastings. Hircent, Margie and Flora. Louis, Jacky and the prince.

'Eat,' they all said.

'I'm not hungry,' pleaded Romford.

Pismire had cracked open Sir Robert's skull and was scooping warm globs of brain on to bread.

'Eat, you prick,' he said. 'Or did I die for fucking nothing?' Pismire rolled his eyes and nudged Scotsman. 'Every time you think this cunt has livened up, he lets you down,' he said.

Romford felt a flash of anger so strong it woke him up. He was panting in the dark, his whole body drenched in sweat.

He slicked his wet hair back and wiped the sweat off his damp body, feeling his ribs pressing hard against his shrunken skin. He shifted in bed and tried to shake the last of the dream away.

Something caught his eye.

Father was sitting at the end of his mattress, trying to reattach a part of his rotten, broken jaw.

'He's right,' said Father, clicking the bone finally into place.

His hand snapped down to the floor and he grabbed something. Romford heard a loud screech. Father lifted up a thin rat by its pink tail. The rat thrashed about, trying to scratch and bite Father. Father hit it hard against the floor, stunned it, then bit its head off.

He crunched bone and spat out fur. His left arm came out of its shoulder socket and he pushed it back in.

He tossed the rest of the rat to Romford.

'There you go,' he said. 'That'll keep you going.'

Romford scrambled back on his straw mattress, terrified at Father's appearance. He knew he had eaten no Host. Father drummed his splintered fingers impatiently.

'Leave me alone,' said Romford. 'I'd rather starve.'

'No you fucking wouldn't,' said Father. 'Being dead is no fun, I can tell you.'

He cackled. Romford gave the rat back to him. Father

shrugged and took another bite. Romford closed his eyes tight and waited for Father to go away, as he had when the Host had summoned him.

But when he awoke and sat up in his bed at dawn, Father was still there. He was rocking back and forth and muttering to himself. There was rat blood smeared all round both of their mouths.

28

Fifty of the lesser townsfolk were expelled from Calais...
The king ordered them back into the town, but those within
refused to admit them...

Chronicle of Henry Knighton

Midsummer came, and its thick heat hung like a rug over
the fort on the Risbank. The reek of the place was worse
than anything Loveday had ever known. The foul trenches
that served the campsite overflowed every day, usually by mid-
morning. The sea at the Risbank's shore lapped with yellow-
brown scum, poisoned fish and floating turds. Inside the fort,
the men took less and less care of the state in which they
camped. They lived among drifts of rubbish: animal bones and
broken pots, collapsed straw bales, scraps of vegetable skins,
fragments of blackened firewood, twisted arrowheads and
abandoned shoes.

The waste piled up where the perimeter fence formed corners,
and in places between the men's tents it was ankle deep. The
putrid vapours spread sickness. All the Dogs suffered the gut-
rot that went around the camp, causing such hard cramps that
some of the ordinary men and archers had cut holes at the arse
of their breeches to save themselves the trouble of pulling them
down fifteen times a day to shit. On the other side of Calais,

the siege town and camp at Villeneuve was now thronging with tens of thousands of villains shipped over from England to serve away their sins, as well as troops arriving from fighting in other parts of France Loveday had never heard of. It was said that among the new recruits the gripe was so severe, men were shitting themselves to death.

Yet the Dogs knew that things inside the besieged city were worse. Each night, the citizens lit the great fire-signal above the Lantern Gate. Faine, with his usual smug spite, told them what it meant. The no-eared East Anglian said he had his information directly from Sir Hugh Hastings. The knight was known to be very sick with a fever of some other sort from the common camp illness, and now seldom emerged from his pavilion, outside which flew his yellow and red banner. But he evidently spoke from his bed with his favourites.

'The French king is finally raising another army,' Faine sneered. 'Took the snivelling cunt long enough but he's at it. We'll be seeing them soon enough.' Faine said the citizens of Calais were keeping the lamp lit so that French spies – and eventually the king himself – might know there was still hope alive within the walls. 'So he knows there's something in there worth saving,' said Faine, in his broad Norfolk accent. 'Which there fucking won't be once we get in.' He waggled his tongue.

Faine was tiresome. Yet they could not escape him, for every day he brought them make-work ordered by Hastings: scraping weed and barnacles off the hulls of the patrol boats or hauling around ballast and shot for the trebuchets that overlooked the harbour. When they came back to their humid tent at night, and sat outside it eating camp-slop and gazing wearily at the Lantern Gate fire and the stars, Thorp complained bitterly about Faine, Hastings and all the others he blamed for their miserable lot, a list of rogues stretching back from Toussaint all the way to Sir Robert le Straunge.

Thorp's nightly complaining lowered the mood of their little group. Loveday listened to him, knowing that it stemmed from his grief for Tebbe. But Millstone tired of hearing it. One sticky evening, as they sat in the squalor of the camp without a hint of breeze to lift the stink or dry the sweat that beaded on their heads and necks, the stonemason interrupted Thorp.

'We all chose to come here,' he said, in his quiet, firm voice.

'We did,' said Thorp, 'but—'

'And soon enough it'll be over,' continued Millstone. 'One way or another.'

Thorp was silent for a moment.

'Tell me this, Thorp,' Millstone continued. 'Once this is over, and we're home, and there's another war, and another offer of forty days' pay, what will you say?'

'I'll tell the fuckers to poke it up their holes until it's somewhere darker than Satan's own dungeon,' said Thorp. But his voice seemed to waver.

'Will you?' said Millstone, nodding, and staring at the dirty yellow grass between his feet.

Thorp did not reply.

Then Millstone repeated his own words, and they all knew it was not a question at all.

'Will you.'

Early the next morning, just as the sun was casting its first light over the grey sea beyond the Risbank, Sir Hugh Hastings appeared in the camp for the first time in nearly ten days. Loveday was awake before Millstone and Thorp, and was returning through the campsite, having drained his watery bowels in the foul trench before it overflowed.

He barely recognised the Norfolk knight. Hastings had lost a huge amount of weight, and was carried on a litter by two servants, propping himself up on his elbows, squinting his bloodshot eyes against even the day's gentle first light. Despite the summer warmth trapped in the sandy soil, he was wrapped in furs. His forearms were lined with barber's scars from many rounds of bleeding.

Most shocking of all, Hastings was not wearing his wig. A few long, thin strands of grey hair, which Loveday guessed might once have been a red-blond, were plastered with sweat to his head. Beneath them the skin was peeling away in flakes.

Loveday tried to keep out of the litter's way, but the knight saw him, and with some effort crooked a finger to beckon him over. Loveday looked around to see if Hastings could possibly mean anyone else. Save for a few archers pissing against the perimeter fence, there was no one anywhere near them.

'Sir Hugh,' said Loveday, trying to disguise his revulsion.

'Up early,' said Hastings. Even those two words seemed to cause him immense effort. 'Matins, is it?'

Loveday cleared his throat and shuffled awkwardly. 'We've not prayed much of late,' he said.

Hastings coughed, and winced in pain. The servants holding the litter flexed their shoulders and rolled their necks impatiently. 'Set me down,' the knight croaked. They obeyed, and he lay back for a moment in the litter, his eyes closed, trying to regain his breath.

Loveday tried to think of something sympathetic to say. 'I'm sorry for your illness, Sir Hugh. I trust God...'

'God has made his mind up,' said Hastings, his eyes still closed. Then with some effort he clambered back on to his elbows and looked at Loveday. 'But I've come for one last bit of fun. They're letting out...' He lay back again and seemed to go to sleep.

Loveday looked at the servant at the front of the litter. He was a flat-nosed man of about Loveday's own age, with short-cropped grey hair. He seemed unimpressed with Hastings' plight. 'Marsh ague,' he said quietly to Loveday. He had an Essex accent.

'Where are you taking him?'

'Beach,' said the servant. 'He reckons they're kicking a few more out of the city today. King's orders are to leave them there.'

Loveday shook his head in confusion. 'Leave them there?'

'Aye. Make a spectacle. Let 'em starve. Any who ain't *useful*, anyway.'

In the litter, Hastings was breathing heavily and irregularly. Sweat beaded on his forehead.

'Useful?'

'Come on. You know what he's into, don't you? He's got three places over there now.' The servant nodded towards Villeneuve.

From the other end of the litter the other servant, a younger man with a similar accent, piped up, 'Best slags this side of the narrow sea.'

The flat-nosed Essexman rolled his eyes. 'Anyway. Apparently he's allowed to take his pick of anyone he wants from the harbour island, and the rest can fucking sit there and die of thirst.' He shielded his eyes in the direction of the rising sun. 'Hot as it's been, it won't take more than a day or two.'

Loveday realised his right hand was trembling. The servant saw it too. 'Been here too long, have you, mate?'

'We've been here a month,' chimed the other servant. 'Don't seem that bad.'

On the stretcher, Hastings came around from his brief sleep. He looked around and saw that he was still on the ground. He struggled back to his elbows and opened his mouth to berate Loveday and the servants. Nothing but a gurgle came out.

'Best be off,' said the flat-nosed servant. 'You're a Colchester boy?'

'Aye,' said Loveday. 'FitzTalbot. Men call me Loveday.'

'Don't know you,' said the servant. 'Good fucking luck to you though.'

Then the two men picked up Sir Hugh Hastings and carried him off to the beach.

An hour later, there was a general summons to the harbour-facing shore of the Risbank, announced by blasts of trumpets from the beach.

Loveday had told Thorp and Millstone what to expect. They went there quietly.

The whole of the fort's garrison assembled to watch. Hastings sat at the filthy shore-front, near Faine's fleet of boats. He had been lifted from his litter into a sort of wheeled barrow converted to a chair.

The Earl of Northampton, who now normally spent every day aboard the larger blockade ships out in the open sea, stood on the far end of the beach, as though trying to keep as far away from Hastings as possible. With him were two other noblemen of about his age. Loveday did not recognise either, but he gathered from the conversation around the Dogs that they were the king's cousin Henry Grosmont, Earl of Derby, and a knight called Sir Walter Manny, recently released from a prison in Paris.

The hundreds of men crammed on the stinking sands watched as a ghastly spectacle unfolded on Calais' harbour island.

In the middle of the morning, at the gatehouse below the place where the lantern burned at night, a drawbridge was slowly lowered and a portcullis raised a small way. Out from the darkness of the gatehouse tunnel staggered a few dozen ragged, skeletal figures. From the Risbank it was impossible to guess their ages, though a few were small enough that Loveday assumed they must be children.

At the sight of them, the trumpets blared louder than ever. Unlike the refugees who had tried to escape weeks earlier, these people did not try to resist their fate.

They just sat down on the harbour island.

Behind them, the portcullis at the Lantern Gate dropped. The drawbridge was pulled up.

A few of the townsfolk dragged themselves to their feet and weakly waved their arms towards the Risbank.

Hoots went up from the troops.

'Sit there and die, yer wretches!'

'Devil's waiting for you!'

The Earl of Northampton and the tall, fair, slim Earl of Derby strode through the crowd towards the line of boats where Hastings lay.

Loveday edged through the crowd so he could hear what was said.

Their talk was strained. The flat-nosed Essexman was

standing behind Hastings, pretending he was oblivious to the
argument going on.

'...Christ's weeping wounds, his orders are to leave them
where they are,' Northampton was saying.

Hastings coughed and glared up from his barrow-seat at the
two nobles standing in front of him. 'And *she* says otherwise.'
The effort of speaking caused him another great coughing fit.

The Earl of Derby moved back in disgust as Hastings sprayed
pink-flecked spittle on to the sand. He seemed to Loveday to
be unquestionably the most senior man on the beach.

Northampton's face was set hard, his fists balled at his side.
He looked as though he wanted to kick Hastings' barrow-
chair over. He shouted over to Faine, who was pushing off
the first of the boats into the harbour. 'Hi – you – get over
here, unless you want your nose to go the way of your fucking
ears!'

Faine looked at him, and then at Hastings.

He ignored the earl completely and went back to launching
the boats.

Loveday realised his hands were shaking again. He held his
right wrist with his left hand to try to keep them steady.

Northampton snarled with rage. But Derby put a calming
hand on his arm. He leaned in and put his face so close to
Northampton's that their foreheads touched. He murmured
and Northampton nodded, with his head still pressed against
the other earl's.

Loveday could not be sure what it was, though he fancied
from the movements of the earl's mouth that he said 'it is as
it is'.

Still holding his hand, he slipped back through the crowd to
find Millstone and Thorp, who were loitering, faces downcast,

as around them the trumpets still raised their racket. They watched the scene in the harbour a little while longer.

It was long enough to see Hastings' boats come within a few lengths of the harbour island, and their crews to loiter there, making sure none of the townsfolk could find a way to escape. To see one boat dock at the harbour and armed men leap off and select just four or five of the townsfolk to bring back to the Risbank. To see them return, and to realise that each of the starving, bewildered people they dragged off the boats was a young woman with her hands bound.

One of the boats was rowed by Hircent's former henchmen Jakke and Nicclaes, who each received a weak pat on the thigh from Sir Hugh Hastings as they passed him.

Millstone led the Dogs off the beach before they could see any more. He did not say a word about what had happened for the rest of the afternoon. But when the Dogs retired to their tent that evening, Loveday could feel his friend lying awake, a calm anger rising off him in the darkness.

Loveday did not realise he had fallen asleep until he awoke with a jolt in the dead of the night, troubled by an urgent, liquid cramping in his guts. He knew right away that Millstone was missing.

He held his breath a moment and listened. Thorp was asleep beside him. The archer did not stir when Loveday sat up and crawled to the opening to their tent.

'I'm going to shit,' whispered Loveday. Thorp did not reply.

Outside the tent, the summer night was humid and sticky. There was cloud in the sky and when the moon was covered Loveday had to pick his way by feel among the tents in the compound. He aimed for a spot at the fence where a few rough foul-holes had been dug.

He clenched to keep his guts under control. He also scanned around the dark camp for Millstone. Tried to tell himself that his friend had been troubled by his stomach as well. Yet he had an uneasy feeling that it was not so.

Then the moon came out and he saw him.

At the point in the fence where the shitting holes lay, two wooden posts had fallen over. Through the gap, Loveday could see down to the moonlit beach, where Faine's boats had been dragged up the sands for the night. Millstone was beside one of them. Untying it.

'Saints alive,' muttered Loveday. He sucked in his belly, squeezed through the gap in the fence, and crept down the beach towards where Millstone was crouched. He did not dare to call out to him, for fear of attracting any nightwatchmen in the guard towers.

He thought he could hear gulls screeching over the water. Then he realised that it was the cries of the starving, thirsty people dying on Calais' harbour island. And he realised what Millstone was planning to do.

Had he lost his mind?

A prickling excitement had replaced Loveday's dire need to shit, and he trotted the last few steps to where his friend was pulling loose the rope on the nearest boat.

'Millstone,' he hissed, as loud as he dared. 'God's eyes, man, what are you doing?'

Millstone stood up and turned around.

There was something odd in his bearing. Something new in the shape of his shoulders. His face caught a moonbeam. He opened his mouth.

Gold teeth glinted.

'Coming for a cruise, are you?' said the pirate Jean Marant.

'Taking people *off* the harbour?' said Marant, keeping his voice low as he dragged Faine's boat down to the water. 'You don't learn, do you, Loveday? I take things into Calais. I don't take people out.'

Loveday shuffled alongside him, crouched in a half squat, trying to keep low in case they were spotted. He did not dare to think what Hastings would do to him if he were found with the pirate stealing a boat.

'How did you get here?' he whispered.

Marant stopped for a second and looked at Loveday as if bewildered. 'I prayed hard, and God sent an angel,' he said. 'What do you think? I'm a pirate, man. You can help me if you want,' he said, resuming dragging the boat. 'Otherwise, I'd be obliged if you'd fuck off.'

Cursing silently, Loveday did as Marant asked. 'You know they're going to die on the harbour,' he said.

'I do.'

'And you don't want to help them?'

'I am helping them.'

'How?'

'I'm taking them a fucking message, Loveday. From a certain Philippe VI, King of France, which has been handed down to me by the admiral of the French fleet, who, if you ask most seafarers on this stretch of coast, is less use than a rudder made of fucking butter, but who has been paying me and my men handsomely to undertake tasks no other man dares try. What else can I tell you?'

'What does the message say?'

'It says fuck off asking me about things that are none of your business.'

The boat was at the water. Marant vaulted over the side. Loveday stood in the water and held the stern so it would not move off. Small waves slapped against his knees. He felt his feet sink into the sand and shingle.

'Scotsman and Romford, Jean. Did you…'

'Did I?'

'Did you get them out?'

'I did.'

'Did they get home?'

'They got out. Where they are now, I don't know. Would you release the boat, please?'

Loveday kept his hands on the boat. It was dragging him deeper as the tide pulled it into the harbour's water. In the moonlight, he saw Marant growing impatient. A crossbow and a handful of bolts lay by the pirate's feet.

'Loveday—'

'Is he in there? Are you taking the message to him?'

'Who?'

'Jean, please. The Captain.'

Marant put his hands on Loveday's. For a moment, he held them. Loveday felt the callouses and ridges of his palms, as tough as leather on the back of his own beaten-up hands.

'Tell me this: why do you care?'

The boat tugged again. 'I feel…' Loveday's guts churned and he sweated as he clenched his arse. 'We've suffered here, Jean. God knows we've suffered. I've lost almost every one of the men. I feel like he's the only one who can help me make sense of it. He always knew…'

'For what it matters,' said Marant. 'I think you never knew him at all. And worse than that, you don't know yourself.

'There was a reason you parted. You didn't understand it then and you won't do now. You're wasting what's left of your life hunting something that isn't there.'

Marant unpeeled Loveday's fingers from the side of the boat. Loveday let him do it.

He watched the pirate put the oars in the saltwater and start to row, as fast and silent as a shark, across the harbour, towards the black mass of the city beyond.

Loveday turned back up the beach. Halfway up it, he doubled over as his guts cramped. He squatted where he was and shat so noisily that a nightwatchman came to the hole in the fence and peered out at him.

'Filthy bastard,' he called. 'Get back in here as soon as you're done.'

Loveday waved at him and grunted in pain and relief. He went back in the water to clean himself as best he could, then trudged, dripping, back through the camp to the Dogs' tent.

Millstone was in his bed, sleeping soundly.

In the morning, when Loveday awoke and went once more to the trench, he noticed there was a sombre mood among the men in the compound. He walked past Sir Hugh Hastings' pavilion. A crowd had gathered outside the entrance. Two men-at-arms were standing guard there.

Loveday craned his neck to try and see what was happening inside.

The flat-nosed Colchester man who had carried Hastings on his litter and wheeled him in the barrow was on the edge of the crowd.

'What's going on?' Loveday asked him.

'Dead,' said the servant. 'Terrible thing. Miserable old cunt choked on his own pillow.'

Then he grabbed Loveday by the sleeve, leaned in to his ear and whispered, 'Tell your mate good on him. That's from a lot of us.'

Loveday reeled. He thought of Millstone's empty bed the night before. Of his anger. Of his silence.

He nodded dumbly. The man saw that he understood. He pushed Loveday roughly away, assumed a mournful expression and turned back to the crowd at the pavilion entrance.

Loveday stumbled away feeling numb from his feet up to his face. It was as though he were floating, even as he heard the tramp of his old legs plodding onward.

When he reached the Dogs' tent, he found Thorp busy clearing rubbish from the patch of ground outside the entrance.

Inside the canvas Millstone was still fast asleep.

His chest rose and fell steadily. His dark face was calm and relaxed.

29

The French king… came to the hill of Sangatte, between
Calais and Wissant… they marched armed, with banners
flying, by moonlight, so that it was a beautiful sight…

Chronicles of Jean Froissart

J ean Marant was sitting at a table with the Captain when
Romford came down the ladder into the main room of the
Beehive inn.

'Who's this salty cunt?' said Father.

Romford did not answer. He slipped back into a corner of
the tavern, hoping the pirate would not see him. But without
looking over, Marant called out, 'No need to hide from me,
son. I'm nothing for you to be scared of.'

Romford came out of the corner. He stood by the table. 'I'm
not scared,' he said, as respectfully as he could. 'But I thought
you might be angry about… about your men.'

Marant looked at him with a level gaze. 'I know our friend
here has told you I'm not,' he said. 'But you may as well hear it
from me too. It's a rough world the Lord's made for us. A man
does what he must to live in it.

'I say when you kill a pirate in fair combat, that's how God
wants it. And by our customs, you have the right to take his

possessions and his place on the crew. You kill two pirates...' Marant exchanged glances with the Captain. 'Well. That I don't recall happening before. Do you follow what I mean?'

Romford did not reply to this directly. 'How did you get into the city?' he asked.

Marant cocked his head and narrowed one eye. 'You know, you sound an awful lot like another mate of yours,' he said. 'I got in by rowing a small boat in the dark and keeping my fucking head down. I'm a—'

'—pirate,' said Romford.

Marant smiled. 'You ever want another job, you tell me.'

On Romford's back, Father was growing restless. 'Tell him to fuck off or you'll put his eyes where his bollocks are supposed to be and his bollocks up his arse,' he purred, nibbling Romford's earlobe. 'We've got rats to catch.'

Romford jerked his head back and Father almost lost his grip.

The Captain watched Romford twitching. 'The hunger is tormenting him,' he said to Marant. Then to Romford, he said: 'Sit with us.'

Romford obeyed. The Captain was gnawing something black and wrinkled. It looked like salted meat. He fumbled in a bag by his foot, pulled out a piece and gave it to Romford. 'Leather,' he said. 'It'll fool your belly a while.'

Romford took the leather and chewed it. It tasted like the thing it was. His belly still felt tight and sore.

Marant put his palms on the table and splayed his fingers. He joined his thumb- and forefinger-tips so they formed a triangle, and looked hard at it, as though he were trying to divine some cipher hidden in the grain of the wood.

Still staring, he spoke to the Captain. 'In your best judgement, is the rest of the city's remaining population as close to despair and derangement as this lad?'

The Captain did not answer for a long time. He just chewed. Then he pulled the leather from his mouth. A string of gluey spittle briefly hung from his lip. He wiped it away, and in a quiet voice he said: 'I believe it is.'

'So,' said Marant, still staring at the triangle formed by his fingers and thumbs, 'we go to Governor Vienne.'

'Is Philippe—'

'Two days away,' said Marant. 'Maybe less. He's finally raised an army and burned half of Flanders, for whatever good that has done. Now they're aiming to camp at Sangatte. Near the Tin Jar, which will annoy The Hat. Then again, everything annoys The Hat. We'll see the army from the castle here when they arrive. And they'll see the light at the Lantern Gate. So everything is in place. And it will play out as it must.'

'Just Vienne to convince, then,' said the Captain.

'Aye,' said Marant. 'Just Vienne.'

Romford could not follow what they were talking about. They made no effort to explain. So he just chewed his leather and tried to keep Father from wriggling about on his back.

They took Romford with them through the streets of Calais, hurrying as fast as the Captain's leg would allow through the warren of houses, churches and abandoned shops.

Starving people loitered at every corner. No one even bothered to beg. They just huddled in patches of shade. Romford saw one group standing guard at a pathetic fire made of a broken window shutter, grilling the skinned corpse of a thin cat. Another group stumbled towards the Milk Gate, where they had heard of a dead donkey that was not yet completely rotten.

They came to the gatehouse of the castle. Two hollow-eyed men-at-arms leaned on their long-poled pikes. One recognised the Captain and raised his eyebrows weakly. The other looked at Marant. 'Hey,' he said. 'Aren't you...'

'Yes,' said Marant. 'Let us in.'

The guards looked at one another sleepily. 'They're all in the tower,' said one. 'Vienne. Beaulo. D'Audrehem...' He ran out of energy merely trying to remember names.

'Stay here, lad,' the Captain told Romford. 'We may be a long time, and we may be no time at all. But when you see us, be ready to move.'

The Captain and Marant were in the castle for a long time.

Father was not happy to wait. He squirmed and complained until Romford let him down off his back. Then he went around the square outside the castle gates, sniffing for rats.

Though the dead priest had to haul himself around with his broken limbs, he moved surprisingly fast. When he spotted one he pounced like a cat, and bit the rat's head off with his broken yellow teeth. He shared his kills with Romford. The taste was disgusting. But before long, Romford's extreme hunger overcame his dislike. He screwed up his eyes and ate his share. The rat flesh was strong and sour. The blood tasted like metal.

By and by, Romford had eaten so much that his stomach stopped hurting. Father became quieter. Then his body faded until it seemed almost translucent.

After that, he was gone.

When Marant and the Captain eventually came out of the castle, Marant stared at Romford in alarm. 'Is that blood on your face?'

One of the castle guards called across the square, 'Mad bastard has been talking to himself and leaping around the place catching rats. Eating the fucking things raw. Never seen anything like it.'

Marant reached out and used his thumb to wipe a streak of rat blood from Romford's cheek. 'I could really use a man like you,' he said thoughtfully. Then the Captain nudged the pirate and Marant seemed to remember where he was. He held up a letter, unsealed and rolled up. 'Behold,' he said. 'The end of the siege.'

'What does it say?' asked Romford. He could still smell rat blood. He wiped his nostrils with his forearm, but only worked it deeper into his nose.

Marant passed the letter to the Captain, and the Captain unrolled it. It was written in French, in a hasty but trained hand.

Know, most gentle lord, that your people in Calais have eaten their horses, dogs and the rats. And there is nothing left here which has not been eaten, unless we eat the flesh of men.

The Captain glanced at Romford. He continued reading.

Wherefore, right honourable lord, if we do not have ready succour, the town will be lost. And we are all agreed, if we do not have aid, to go out upon the enemy and die with honour sooner than perish here by default...

'It goes on,' said the Captain, lowering the parchment. 'But you see the point.'

'*Go out upon the enemy and die with honour,*' scoffed Marant. 'That's what happens when you put blockhead knights in charge.

The Captain nodded. 'But it's exactly as we thought it would be,' he said.

Romford looked at them both. 'What have you done?' he asked softly.

The Captain laid both hands on his shoulders and looked him dead in the eye. 'Saved a lot of lives, by God,' he said. 'And made a lot of money. You, my lad, are about to be a partner in the greatest act of warfare seen since the days of the ancients.'

'How?' said Romford.

The Captain rolled up Jean de Vienne's letter. He tapped it against Romford's shoulder.

'By taking this where it needs to go,' he said.

It dawned on Romford what the Captain meant. He pushed his hand off his shoulder and pointed at Marant. 'He's the pirate,' he said. 'Not me.'

'Oh, I think you've proved you're the man for this job,' said Marant. 'And I'm needed here. I'll get you out to the Risbank. After that, you only have to get to Sangatte. It'll be easy. You row like all the demons in hell are after you and take this to the Tin Jar. My men will do the rest.'

'No,' said Romford.

'Yes,' said the Captain.

'Listen,' said Marant. 'Let me tell you a few things about what's about to happen. Once this letter leaves Calais, the end begins. If you leave tonight, then in two days' time, this siege will be over. Once this letter is out in the world, one way or another, it's done. Either Philippe comes and rescues his loyal governor, or, as the Captain and I think more likely, he doesn't, and the loyal governor does as he threatens, and throws open the gates for a glorious sally unto his capture and honourable ransom, and the town's seizure by the English. Do you follow me?'

Romford nodded.

'Good,' said Marant. 'Now, the Captain and I dearly wish you to take this letter out of the city and deliver it.

'We have come to this decision for two reasons. First, you're capable of doing it. Second, the Captain here has developed an affection for you, which I am beginning to understand and even share. In any case, I strongly advise you not to be here when the siege is relieved and either King Philippe or King Edward comes through the gates. Both kings will consider you a traitor and hang you in chains. Unfair as that may be.'

Marant paused and waited for Romford to absorb this.

'I can see you're not quite convinced,' said Marant. 'So let me say this. If you take this fucking letter to my fucking inn, then not only will you be assured of all the great wealth you have amassed during your employment here by the Captain, I'll also personally guarantee you Gombert and Dogwater's share of what my crew has earned during the siege. As I said before, it's your right.' He paused. 'Would you like to know how much that is?'

Romford nodded very slightly. The pirate leaned in and whispered in his ear.

Marant then straightened up and said the same thing in the Captain's.

The Captain's eyes gleamed. For the first time Romford could remember, he laughed.

Just for a moment Father reappeared, clinging to Romford's back. He seemed to have heard the number Marant had whispered. He humped Romford's back violently. 'Say yes, you worm. You can buy me a pair of new legs like that fucker's.'

'Go away,' hissed Romford.

Father vanished.

Romford looked at Marant, and at the Captain. He considered the great edifice of Calais' castle. He thought about what he had been threatened. And what promised. He thought about everything the Captain had said to him about war. He thought about all the time he had spent in Calais, and tried to imagine what he wanted to do with the rest of his life.

He still tasted rat blood.

He looked the pirate hard in the eye. He felt the power he had first known as he drenched himself in Gombert and Dogwater's gore.

He decided to use it.

'I'll do it,' he said. 'But I have one condition.'

The Captain laughed again. 'I told you he'd say that.'

'That you did,' said Marant. He fiddled with a gold ring on his finger. Looked at Romford with his head cocked, as though he were a mystery he could only partially understand. 'That you did.'

'How much fucking coin did you just give that prick?'

'I don't know,' said Romford, as he dragged Scotsman by the arm up the stairs from the dungeon. 'A handful. Some. I have more.' He adjusted his pack on his back. The strap dug into his skin and hurt his shoulder. The bag held all the silver and gold he had collected during his many months of work. 'Come on,' he said. 'We need to hurry.'

Outside, Scotsman clapped a huge hand to his forehead and staggered. 'Jesus fucking Christ in bed with his own twin sisters, it's bright,' he said. Romford realised the Scot had seen little daylight since the winter, and the afternoon sun bouncing off the stone of the castle was making his eyes sting. He slowed for a moment.

The big man was an extraordinary sight. The ropes of his hair now reached the small of his back. His beard touched his navel. Through the shredded rags of his shirt Romford could see his skin was milk-white, but it covered a frame that was as intimidating as it ever had been.

The Scot saw Romford inspecting him. 'Well,' he said. 'I'm still here. But I've eaten some things in that place you wouldn't fucking like to see.'

Romford used his tongue to remove something stuck between his own teeth. 'I can imagine,' he said. 'Would you like to know—'

'—what we're doing?' said Scotsman. 'Aye. But if it's got anything to do with those two cunts over there, I'll tell you now it's a fucking bad idea.'

The Captain and Marant were standing just inside the castle gatehouse. The Captain waved something in greeting.

It was Scotsman's axe.

'I'm sorry,' said Romford. 'But this is the only way to get home.'

'I remember telling you something like that before,' snorted Scotsman. 'And now look where we are.'

He strode over to the Captain and snatched the axe from his hand without a word of greeting.

'Whose head am I planting this in so I can get out of this shithole for good?' he asked.

'Ideally, nobody's,' replied Marant, in English. 'At least, not until you've delivered what's hidden inside it.'

The Scot inspected the weapon. Marant had detached the head from the handle and refitted it with Jean de Vienne's letter to the French king folded tightly and concealed inside the join.

Scotsman swung the axe. He twirled it from hand to hand. Tapped it on the ground. 'Humph,' he said. 'Seems fine. But if this fucker falls apart when I need it, I'll be back to ram whatever's left of it up your arsehole.'

'Let's pray it doesn't come to that,' said the Captain smoothly.

'Fuck off,' said Scotsman.

The Captain rolled his eyes. He told Scotsman and Romford exactly what they had to do.

They chewed leather and made plans until midnight, when the Captain took them back into the castle and led them by torchlight through a series of tight corridors to a small door and a spiral staircase leading to the very bottom of the main tower.

As they crept down the stone steps, the Captain's stick tapping and Scotsman's heavy feet tramping, Romford heard moving water, and felt the air grow damp.

At the bottom of the staircase, another door opened into a crypt-like cellar built into the castle's outer walls. A saltwater channel ran through it. Romford realised where they were.

'That's the moat,' he whispered. 'So it goes under the castle...' His voice bounced off the stone walls. The Captain put his finger to his lips. He led them to the edge of the moat. Two small rowing boats bobbed in the water, tethered to iron rings.

'And it goes out as well,' he whispered. He pointed to a metal grille in the wall. It covered a space just wide and high enough for the little boats to pass through.

'Son of fucking...' said Scotsman. But then he held his tongue. They all looked at one another. Marant hopped off the stone into the first of the rowing boats and checked over the oars. 'Now or never,' he said.

Romford and Scotsman loaded the second boat with everything they needed. It did not amount to much. Romford had his pack of coin. In one of the Captain's warehouses, they broke open a crate of armour and found him a thick black leather cap, which reminded him of the helmet he had worn almost a year before at the battle at Crécy. He chose a snug-fitting leather coat that reached below his waist and felt thick enough to protect him without restricting or roasting him on the hot night. He also took a crossbow, a stiff cloth bag with two dozen bolts loose in it and a knife.

Scotsman had even less. He had changed his clothes for the first time in half a year, squeezing into garb he stripped from a man-at-arms they found dead of hunger outside a house near the Snail Tower. Besides this he only had his axe and two pieces of armour. He loaded the man-at-arms' helmet and mail shirt into the boat rather than wearing them, despite the Captain's advice to the contrary.

'They won't stop an arrow if you're not wearing them,' said the Captain.

'Aye, but if I fall in the fucking water, they won't drown me either,' said the Scot. 'So why don't you—'

The Captain raised his hands and conceded the point.

He stood on the side and leaned on his stick. 'I wish I was coming with you,' he said.

'No you don't,' said Scotsman.

Marant chuckled in the blackness.

The Captain's face flickered in the torchlight. Romford thought of thanking him, or making some grand farewell, but the Captain seemed as calm as though he were sending him off to the well for water.

'God keep you, lad,' said the Captain. 'You've been fine. Now listen to our pirate friend here, and keep that crossbow loaded.' He nodded. He said no goodbye. He just limped off to the little door that opened on to the spiral staircase. 'I'll send your regards to the governor.'

Then the door creaked, and the Captain was gone.

Scotsman sat at the bench in the little boat and manned the oars. 'I'm trusting you,' he said to Romford. 'Keep that fucking crossbow where I can see it.'

The men brought the two tiny boats quietly into the moat and around as far as the Lantern Gate. Marant led the way. The castle loomed vast beside them in the moat. A small channel, only a handspan wider than their boats, then took them out of the moat and into the calm water of the harbour.

The moon was nearly full, and so bright in a clear sky that Romford felt sure they would be seen by the English on the Risbank. But Marant was unbothered. And once they struck out into the harbour, Romford saw why.

In the fire bowl set above the Lantern Gate, a huge blaze was burning. Scotsman looked at it in wonder.

Marant whistled for their attention. He pointed towards the Risbank. 'Fuck is that place?' hissed the Scot.

'That's a fort, they… we… King Edward built,' said Romford. 'It's the reason we've been so hungry.'

But as he spoke, he could see what it was Marant was showing them. Although it was the dead of night, hundreds of English were moving out of the fort, streaming along the Risbank back towards the mainland.

Marant brought his boat alongside Romford and Scotsman's. 'Are they abandoning it?' Romford asked him.

'No,' said Marant. 'They're going to look at something they've waited a long time for.'

Romford looked from the flame to the Risbank, and he understood.

'Fuck is it?' said the Scot impatiently.

'The French army is arriving at Sangatte,' said Marant. 'They're going to defend the perimeter of the siege camp. Or, more likely, to have a good stare. It must be quite a sight in the moonlight.'

Romford felt a flood of relief. Since the Captain and Marant had explained what they wished him to do, he had been trying to picture in his mind the probable layout of trebuchets and cannon on the spit of land outside the Risbank. Trying to assess angles of fire and shot, and what the best line for the boat might be to avoid a direct hit from one of the English siege weapons.

He guessed almost all the operators would now be abandoning their posts to catch a glimpse of the first French army they had seen since Crécy – if they had even been there.

'Pull hard,' he whispered to Scotsman. 'This is our chance.'

The Scot bent his back. As he rowed, he kept glancing down

at his axe, as though it might fall through the hull of the little boat.

Marant kept up with them, stroke for stroke, until they were within clear sight of the Risbank fort, where the trebuchets stood unattended and guard posts were quiet. Then they both slowed their boats. Marant once more brought his boat alongside theirs.

He laid his oars on his lap. 'Hey,' he said to Scotsman. 'I've got something for you.'

Scotsman grunted. Romford could smell in the dark that he was sweating.

'What?' he said.

Marant fiddled with his hands, then passed a few small items to the Scot. 'These are yours,' he said. 'I didn't get you where you wanted to go. And your hostage wasn't worth them.'

Then the pirate pushed his boat off theirs and headed silently back towards Calais.

The Scot opened his hand. Five dead men's rings lay in his palm. He stared, speechless for a moment.

Eventually, he said: 'Fucking pirates.' He slipped two of the rings on to his fingers and threw one into the sea. 'For good luck,' he said. He shrugged. 'You never know when we might need it.'

He handed the remaining two rings to Romford. 'That'll buy you a good drink one day,' he said gruffly. 'Now where are we fucking going?'

For some reason he did not understand, Romford blushed in the dark. He twisted the rings on his fingers, beside the archer's thumb-ring he had taken from the harbour ship months ago.

Then he pointed out the course to take.

As the boat started moving, he remembered the Captain's advice.

Keep that crossbow loaded.

He ratcheted back the string and set a bolt in it. Sighted around the silent Risbank.

The Scot rowed a wide course around the Risbank's trebuchet point, heading as far as he dared into the choppy open water of the harbour mouth before turning back to head parallel with the north shore of the Risbank in the direction of Sangatte. Here he kept them a few hundred paces out from the sands, safe from breaking waves, but closer to the land than the huge hulks of the English blockade ships at anchor in the deeper water. It was hard work. The more he rowed, the more he puffed, until he was so out of breath that speech was beyond him.

All the while, Romford kept sighting around with the crossbow. But he saw nothing, and heard only the distant yells and whoops of English troops more than a mile away in Villeneuve, trying to catch a sight of the French army arriving on the high ground at Sangatte.

They were almost free.

Almost past the Risbank.

Almost on their way to the pirates' coves and inlets Marant had told them lay below Sangatte.

As the Risbank fort receded, Romford's heart was thumping. But he did not stop sighting with his crossbow.

So he was the first to see the English boats following them.

Five of them in total. Silhouetted grey against the dark of the sea and the sky. Each boat much larger than the tiny craft the two Dogs were in.

He spotted them as they turned out of the harbour mouth.

Just before the storm of arrows started.

★★★

For a fleeting moment, Romford thought he would not tell Scotsman they were coming. The first volley of arrows had fallen well short of their boat, and the Scot was labouring so hard at the oars that he could not hear anything above his own breath and the even roll of the waves.

But Romford knew that was madness. So in the calmest voice he had, he said: 'They're coming.'

'Eh?'

But Romford did not need to say more. Another volley of arrows flew towards them. They still fell short, but now the Scot saw the outline of the boats, and heard the splash of the arrows landing in the sea a dozen boat lengths away from them. He pulled even harder. The boat lurched in the water and sprang forward.

He panted as he heaved. 'Fuck... Christ... What...'

'Keep rowing,' said Romford urgently. 'They won't hit us.'

On that at least, he knew he was right. The Englishmen were standing in their boats, trying to shoot with longbows. It seemed to Romford they were very inexperienced at doing those things together.

They were too far away. They had a moving base beneath their feet. And they were poor shots. They were wasting arrows.

But they were gaining on them.

'Shoot back, for fuck's sake,' gasped the Scot.

Romford ignored him. He kept sighting at the boats, as he felt around with his hand to draw the bag of bolts closer to him.

They were gaining.

Even with the Scot pulling as hard as he could, the English were moving two boat lengths for every one the Dogs did.

They were going to be caught.

Romford tried to think fast. He considered if he should row. He could feel the Scot tiring with every heave of the oars. But Romford was not a faster rower. And though he had never seen Scotsman handle a crossbow, he thought there was little chance he would be a good shot.

Romford tried to count the men in the boats. It was hard to be sure in the dark, but he reckoned there were five or more in each.

More men than he had bolts.

But not too many more.

An idea hit him like a wave. For a moment, he turned his head away from the crossbow's sight.

'Scotsman,' he said. 'Stop rowing.'

Even in the dark he felt the Scot's incredulous look. 'Stop? The fu—?'

Another volley of arrows landed short. They were wasting more. That was good.

'Stop rowing,' said Romford. And he heard something in his own voice that almost frightened him.

It shocked the Scot too. He let the oars rest. 'I hope you fucking know what you're doing,' he panted.

Romford did not answer him. He just turned back to his crossbow and let the first boat come into the very edge of his own shooting range.

A volley of arrows flew around them. A few insults were screamed. The English were close enough to hit them. But it was unlikely they would.

Romford held his crossbow steady and exhaled as slowly as

he was able. He felt his heartbeat slow a fraction. His hands steadied. He let the roll of the still boat take him to exactly where he wanted to be.

Then he squeezed the trigger.

The Englishman in his sights screamed. He pirouetted and crashed into the other men in his boat. He went down holding his chest.

'Go!' shouted Romford.

The Scot started rowing again.

As the Scot pulled the oars again, moving them a little further up the shore, Romford heard the Captain's voice drifting in his mind.

Keep that crossbow loaded...

He heard Marant's voice mocking the contents of the letter hidden in Scotsman's axe.

...go out upon the enemy and die with honour...

But most of all he heard the lines of a song.

It was a song men had sung in Wissant many months before.

I am the wolf
High, wild and free
A law unto myself

He let the voices swirl and roll and repeat in his mind like a prayer. And every time he felt the Scot tire at the oars, he called on him to stop, then picked out an Englishman and shot him.

Some he shot in the heart. Some in the neck. One in the eyeball. He killed every Englishman in the first boat and watched their bodies drift out to sea. He killed both oarsmen in the second. He killed the front-most archer in the third.

As the first light before the dawn crept into the sky, the job became easy. He hummed out loud while he worked.

I am the wolf
Without a pack

He loaded. He shot. He killed.

The English were screaming with anger. Romford liked to hear them howl. He knew their rage would make them shoot even worse. Again he told the Scot to stop rowing. He took aim at a man in the third boat. A man whose form struck him as somehow familiar. A man who seemed to be missing his ears.

He remembered him from somewhere.

Saint-Lô. An apothecary. Father. Shaw. Millstone.

For the first time, that memory did not scare Romford. He sighted the crossbow carefully.

'Hurry up,' said Scotsman. 'Christ, lad, be quick. They're almost on us.'

Romford did not rush. He went through his routine. He aimed the bolt right between the no-eared man's eyes. He exhaled. He smiled. He pulled the trigger.

He felt a sharp whip across his face as the crossbow string snapped.

Romford stared at his crossbow in disbelief. For a second he could not understand what had happened. Then pain seared his face where the string had whipped across it. Blood started to ooze from the cut. He felt a flap of skin hanging down.

'Shit,' said Scotsman. He threw the oars down inside the boat and grabbed his axe from the floor. He stood up and roared.

'No,' said Romford. 'We need to...'

But he realised the Scot was right.

The English stopped shooting. They rowed in hard.

Romford pulled the knife from his belt and picked up a crossbow bolt. He remembered where he had hit Gombert and Dogwater.

The first English boat rammed them, and Romford fell over.

The Scot's boots were too small for his feet. Romford saw them as he slipped, tried to stand up, grabbing the big man to try to pull himself upright to fight.

Scotsman pushed him out of the way with his left hand.

Scotsman hauled an Englishman from the boat that had hit them. Smashed his skull open on the bench where he had been sitting to row.

Threw him one-handed in the sea.

Romford managed to get up. He slipped over again on grey-pink jelly. He got up again. An Englishman was on the Scot's back. Romford stabbed him in the spine. The blade jammed in bone and wouldn't come out.

Someone had him, arms clamped around his. Fingers pressing in his eyes.

★ ★ ★

No one had him.

There was blood everywhere. Pooled in the boat. An arm without a body was gripping at nothing.

I am the wolf
Without a pack
Banished so long ago

There were men in their boat. On every side. Lurching.

Spray. Blood. Salt. Romford lashed out and broke someone's nose.

The boat was sinking.

'Fucking take it.'

'No—'

'Fucking take it and go!'

'Scotsman—'

'You can fucking swim. I can't. Go. Fucking live, boy. Live. Go. Get home and fucking live.'

Scotsman was standing up. Shirtless. Axeless. Fighting two men at once. Three men.

Men were leaping at him from all sides. Blades started to find their mark.

The Scot was laughing maniacally as he went down doing the thing he did the best.

★ ★ ★

The water was so cold. The salt dug claws in the open flesh of Romford's face. He tried to swim but the pack on his shoulder was too heavy. The axe in his hand dragged him down even harder.

Romford held his breath till his lungs burned.

He let go of something.

For a second, his head was up above the water and he gasped at air. He caught a throatful of water and went back down.

The sea pulled him upwards.

A wave caught him.

It smashed him into a rock. It rolled him and scraped him. Lifted him and smashed him down again.

He heard Father screaming at him. Not words. Just the raw screams of a madman.

He heard Pismire.

Or did I die for fucking nothing?

He heard Tebbe and Thorp talking about girls in the brothel and blackberries on the Michaelmas goose. He saw the prince and smelled the sweet rich perfume of his hair.

Saltwater was filling his nose. His mouth. His throat. His lungs.

Keep that crossbow loaded, said the Captain.

'I'm so sorry,' Romford tried to say.

Then the waves smashed him into the rocks once more and everything was done.

30

When the besieged people of Calais saw the shameful flight of [King Philippe]... they opened the gates and their captain, John of Vienne... came to the presence of the King of England, sitting on a little nag as he could not go on foot because of the gout, and with a halter tied round his neck...

Chronicle of Geoffrey le Baker

The road out of Villeneuve up to Sangatte was packed with jubilant English troops. Most walked. Some jogged or even sprinted, trying to get ahead of the crowd. The sun beat down. Already, the very first of the English who had made it up to the abandoned French camp were coming back to show off their prizes: swigging wine and waving new weapons. Peasants wore bright knights' helmets crooked on their heads. Archers held the reins of great stamping stallions. A gang of kitchen boys raced carts down the hillside where it dropped away from the road, dragging their vehicles up with cheers, then whooping as they sped pell-mell down the dry grassy bank.

'He came, he saw, he fucked off,' said Thorp. Loveday and Millstone looked blank. 'I don't know,' said Thorp. 'Something I heard once.'

The three men laughed. The absurdity of what had happened

was still settling on them. Two nights ago, the Earls of Derby, Northampton and Warwick had been organising the army for battle: a clash of arms they said might be as deadly as the one fought at Crécy. Rumours swept around that King Philippe had at last joined forces with his son, Prince Jean, and the new Count of Flanders. That their army was as large as any ever raised in France. That every town and city in Flanders was aflame. That a new fleet was coming to smash the English blockade.

When the French had arrived at Sangatte by night, the Dogs had run with the rest of the army to catch a glimpse of them from afar. It had been a terrifying sight. The fury of countless thousands of torches, burning all together below the frigid blaze of the moon. Word spread that the French had already destroyed an English wooden fort as big as that on the Risbank, which guarded the bridge over the main road into Villeneuve from the south.

That, at least, seemed to be true. The Dogs had seen flames leap from the fort. Seen its blackened husk hissing and smoking beside the road.

Yet the reason they had seen it at close quarters was the same reason they were now strolling along the road to Sangatte with twenty thousand other happy Englishmen.

As quickly as the French king had arrived – apparently ready to swoop down and reduce Villeneuve to ashes, bring the English to battle and free Calais from its torment – so he had departed.

'Soft bastard pissed his breeches,' Thorp was saying. 'Took one look at our boys and didn't fancy it. Didn't want to take another hiding.'

Of the three of them, Thorp was the most excited by this

turn of events. And there was something in the tone of his crowing that Loveday recognised.

As if he was talking to Tebbe.

Loveday wiped sweat from his forehead as they neared the place where the French had camped. Millstone whistled as the Dogs took in what vast riches the enemy army had left behind.

Clean, new tents stood proud in neat lines, most of them full of fresh blankets and men's packs. An impromptu breakfast was being served at a grand pavilion, which Loveday reckoned must have been King Philippe's kitchen-tent. The warm air carried the delicious scent of fresh-baked bread and roasted chicken.

The three Dogs sat down at a long table and Millstone went to fetch them a share of the food and drink.

'Fucking miracle, this is,' said Thorp, his mouth full of soft, warm bread. 'No other explanation.'

Loveday and Millstone nodded. But after a while, Millstone spoke. 'I don't know,' he said carefully. 'There must be more to it than that.'

Thorp laughed. 'More than a miracle?'

'Less, then. But there's something else. Something we're not seeing.'

They had just finished their second helping of food and were about to go and find a cart and claim a new tent when the Earl of Northampton strode through the site. He was almost as cheerful as Thorp.

Loveday tried to avoid Northampton's gaze, but the earl spotted him and marched over. 'Essex Dogs!' he cried. 'Still here! Holy Mary riding bareback, the Lord could send the

Rapture and you bastards would still be here at the end of it, pintles in your hairy palms and those same dozy fucking faces on.'

'Good day, my lord,' said Loveday, trying to stand, but only making it partway up, so that his arse was hovering over the bench and his thighs were jammed under the table.

'Sit down. Eating well, I see,' said the earl. He leaned over to Thorp's bowl and picked up a hunk of bread soaked in pig grease. 'Fucking delicious,' he said. 'Say what you like about the French, but the bastards don't fuck around when it comes to vittles.'

He swallowed the bread. 'You had the gut-rot?' he asked.

The three Dogs all nodded.

'Aye, me too. This should sort it out.' The earl now picked up a piece of blood sausage from Loveday's bowl, threw it in the air and caught it in his mouth. 'Save you from going the same way as our friend in the wig.' He looked meaningfully at Millstone. The stonemason held his gaze and gave nothing away.

'Aye,' said Northampton, still chewing. He tried another approach. 'I gather Sir Hugh left a bequest for a most magnificent tomb in his favourite church in Norfolk. Commemorating his heroic service in this and other wars.'

Still none of the Dogs said anything. 'His wife will be most grieved,' Northampton continued. 'But then, she's not the only East Anglian widow this war has made. Corpse washed up on the Risbank this morning. Head smashed to pieces. Missing its ears. But they seemed to have been removed long ago.'

Northampton sucked blood pudding crumbs from his fingers. 'Well. Do with that what you please. Fuck, that's good.' He clicked his fingers at a kitchen boy, who scuttled off and returned with a wooden bowl full of chicken livers and more bread.

As the Dogs sat awkwardly, Loveday could feel his leg jiggling under the table. They were all desperate to discuss what the earl had just told them about Faine, but felt unable to do so until he left them alone.

Northampton, however, did not leave. He squeezed on to the bench beside Loveday and ate his chicken livers. After a while, he said, 'None of you have asked me what happens now.'

'Aye, my lord... we were hoping...' began Loveday.

The earl talked over the top of him. 'I'll tell you. *Now* there's a big fucking scene planned. Down at the city. I can't say any more than that, but by Saint Barnabas's bronzed bollocks, it'll be one to remember. Want to see it?'

Loveday looked at Thorp and Millstone. 'Of course, my lord. But – well. We're not exactly...'

Northampton raised his eyebrows, then understood what Loveday meant. 'You look and smell like shit?' he said. 'This is true. Very true.' He scratched the long grey stubble on his cheek and thought for a moment. 'Fuck it. Get back down to Villeneuve and go and see my steward. He'll lend you some livery.'

He turned to Loveday, hitting him on the leg to stop him jiggling it. 'Have you still got that fucking frilly garter?'

'I have,' said Loveday, frowning at the earl's irreverence.

'Right, well, assuming it's not completely wrecked from you tugging your yard over it, here's what you need to do. When you've cleaned yourselves up, take it down to the smart seats by the city gates, flash the frill around. Act like you own the place and it's your brat she's cooking in her belly. Enjoy the show, then get the fuck out of here.'

'Out of here?' said Loveday, confused.

Northampton grimaced, as though talking to the Dogs caused him physical pain. 'When did you come over?'

'With the ships, my lord... I mean... at the start of all this. We have been here a goodly while now.'

'Fuck me,' said Northampton. 'I suppose you have. By Christ, you're overdue.' He breathed deeply and amended his instructions.

'Get clean. Get dressed. Watch the performance. *Then* go and see the king's treasurer: boring, grey-faced prick called Walter Wetwang, if you can believe that. Tell him how many forties you've done. After that, the ships start leaving tomorrow with the tide. Get yourselves on one.'

'On one, my lord?'

'On one, FitzTalbot. On one. Get on a ship. Go home.'

The Dogs did everything the earl had told them. By the time the fiercest heat of the day was ebbing away, they had washed, their beards and hair were cropped and they wore clean coats and breeches of soft blue cloth, embroidered with gold stars and slashed with strips of white and red linen.

'I can't believe it,' Thorp kept saying. 'Christ on the tree, I can't fucking believe it. Home.'

Millstone was quieter. 'We've heard that before,' he kept telling Thorp. But Loveday could feel his relief. In their minds, he and Thorp were already halfway back to England.

Loveday tried to enter into the same mood as the other men. Yet he found it hard. He pictured his cold hut. Alys's overgrown grave.

Was that even home?

They made their way to the spectator stands that the royal

engineers had erected facing one of the largest gatehouses in Calais' walls.

Just as the earl had told them, the little scrap of fabric Loveday had treasured since the awful day on the ladders was enough to have a royal servant usher them to seats near the edge of the stand. When they sat down, there were few others there. But as the shadows grew long, the benches began filling up. Servants wearing royal livery began walking up and down the aisles between the benches, handing out mugs of good wine, and hot pies fresh from the oven. There was a celebratory mood in the air.

But Loveday still felt confused.

'We still don't know what happened,' he said to Millstone. 'Where was the battle?'

A familiar figure slid into an empty space on the bench in front of the Dogs. He turned around and fiddled with the patch over his eye.

'This was the battle,' said Sir Thomas Holand. 'You've been in it all this time. You just didn't know it.' He patted Loveday on the knee. 'You three have come up in the world. Last I saw you, you were cracking skulls in a whorehouse.'

Loveday shifted in his seat. Holand turned back around for a moment and surveyed the city in front of them. The soaring walls, battered but no less imposing than the day the English army had first arrived.

'You want to know why there was no fight?'

'Aye,' said Loveday.

Holand leaned on his elbows, relishing the chance to show what he knew. He lowered his voice conspiratorially. 'Because someone didn't want there to be one,' he said. He raised the eyebrow above his good eye.

Millstone looked sceptically at Holand. 'Philippe didn't want one. We know that. What we don't know is—'

Holand shook his head. 'You don't know anything about anything,' he said. Outside the city gates, a group of important-looking noblemen had arrived and were inspecting the site. A bridge had been run across the double moat leading up to the gatehouse, evidently without resistance from defenders on the walls above. Between this and the spectator stands, a grand stage with royal flags at each corner of it had been wheeled into place. Two thrones were placed on it, shaded by canopies of brightly dyed silks. One of the noblemen gave orders to adjust the stage position minutely. Loveday recognised him from a distance. It was the king's cousin, Henry Grosmont, Earl of Derby.

Another nobleman was overseeing the arrival of a second raised platform. It was mounted with a gallows and a chopping block.

Holand pointed to the noblemen. 'Derby. You know who he is?'

'We do.'

'Aye, well, he and Manny – that's the madman over there by the headsman's station – they've been leading all this.'

'All what?' asked Loveday. He was growing frustrated. As though Holand had been watching some entirely different siege to him.

Holand sighed, as though he were talking to a particularly slow-witted child. He began again.

'Look. Philippe raised a big army. You know that?'

Thorp was also growing annoyed. 'Fuck off, of course we do. We saw the fucking—'

'Right. Well, he took it around a few towns in Flanders and

burned them. He took down our fort near the bridge that leads up to Sangatte. But once he saw our defences and how many of us are here, he panicked. Taking us out would be a big job. Not impossible, but big. It would need to be worth the trouble. Have you seen the size of the fucking ditch around this place? Toussaint may be a stuck-up prick, but he's done a great job digging it.'

The Dogs glanced at one another. 'Aye, we saw the ditch,' said Millstone. 'Too much of it, if anything.'

'Well. Getting through that would be no small feat. Let alone being sure of beating us if he did. He could try and starve us out, but that would take too long, you understand?'

Satisfied that for once the Dogs were following him, Holand went on. 'Good. Now hear this. Overnight, someone intercepted a letter from the boys in charge inside Calais to Philippe. Well, I say intercepted. It washed up on the fucking beach. Hidden inside an old axe-head, if you can believe that. Not even written in a cipher. It said they were all starving, and ready to give up. Awful negotiating position to start from. It's almost like whoever wrote it actually wanted the English to win, not the French. Because what do we do? Mad bastard Manny sends it straight to Philippe's camp, and they figure the game is up. Cut their losses. Give it up.'

Holand shook his head. 'Every time you think you've seen it all... Anyway, you'll see them soon enough and—'

He was interrupted by a trumpet blast. The spectator stands, now full of expectant men and women, dressed as if for a tournament, hushed. From somewhere behind the stand came the queen, flanked by attendants.

Loveday flushed when he saw her. She was ripe with child,

her belly huge and her breasts full, her eyes bright and her hair glossy and thick.

The queen went up to the dais that faced the gates. Then a signal was given and a team of engineers swarmed forwards, carrying tools and short ladders. They set to work unbarring the gates, shouting to whoever was inside, who was working on the same task.

A chatter began again in the stands, while below, in and around the dais, the great and good of the English camp began to arrive. More trumpet squawks announced the most important, including the Prince of Wales and his cousin, Jacky. Northampton arrived, along with Warwick, a number of bishops, and a pair of red-hatted cardinals, who wore gloomy expressions. Outnumbering all of these, however, were merchants, finely apparelled and surrounded by their own bevies of scurrying servants. Loveday nudged Thomas Holand again. 'Who are they?'

Holand broke off from his conversation with a lanky knight who had settled in front of him and turned back. 'Rich fuckers?' He chuckled. 'They're the special guests.' He pointed out a few, none of whom Loveday had ever seen or heard of before.

'That's John Pulteney, you know, London, Cinque Ports... fingers in everything, beautiful house in Kent, did that year in Newgate but no one mentions it now... and... there's William de la Pole, from Kingston, hard to say whether he stinks more of money or fish...' He continued, reeling off names that meant nothing to the Dogs, some of them English, some Flemish and others Italian.

Seeing the Dogs were nonplussed, Holand laughed. 'You really are pig-chasers, aren't you, boys!' Once more he rolled his eyes at the effort of explaining the world to such an ignorant audience. 'Who do you think has paid for all this?' he said. 'Boats. Troops. Weapons. Food. Timber. Wine. Women... I mean... fucking everything. Who?' Silently, he jabbed his finger in turn at each of the wealthy men he had just named. 'Him. Him. Him. Him. And you know why? Because as soon as this charade is over, they'll be in that city like rats into a brand-new sewer. Carving up the best bits for themselves. This is going to be the richest town in France. Only it won't be in France any more. It'll be a little nugget of London, and the fellows who paid for all this won't just be rich. They'll look after their children, their grandchildren, their great-grandchildren...'

Holand waved at a royal servant walking up and down the stairs of the stands with a wine jug. He bade him fill the Dogs' cups, then his own. He took a long gulp. Angled his face to enjoy the warmth of the afternoon sun.

'Listen, Loveday. You're a good man, but you don't see what's right there in front of your face. Men like you get paid to fight. Men like me *pay* to fight, and we either hope we can impress the king so he covers our losses and keeps us in his favour, or we gamble on capturing our cousins and selling them back to their families and turning a small profit. That's the game. But men like that...' – he pointed out Pulteney and the others – 'they're in charge. They underwrite everything, because they make it back sevenfold. Every penny you earn, every pound I spend, passes through their hands. Same for you. Same for me. Same for the king. Then when God sends good fortune, they're there, with their hands open, ready to claim the lion's share of the rewards.'

For a moment, Holand regarded Pulteney and the rest of the merchants milling around the royal dais with a sort of admiration. 'Knowing them, they'll already have done the

deals with their mates inside Calais to take over their existing
businesses, turn them into partnerships. Money makes money.
And then they'll all underwrite the next campaign, wherever
that might be. I hear Poitiers is looking possible...'

As Loveday struggled to digest this information, another
fanfare announced the arrival of King Edward. The crowd
parted to allow his great black stallion through. The great men
he passed stepped back like parting waters. They bowed and
sank to their knees before him.

In the year the Dogs had been on the campaign, Loveday
had set eyes on the king only a handful of times. Now he
looked more magnificent and dreadful than ever. Tall, strong
and heavily bearded, he rode with a perfectly straight back.
Despite the heat, he wore all black silk, adorned with a few
pieces of ceremonial armour, and a tabard bearing his arms of
English lions and French fleurs-de-lis.

'Sit tight,' said Holand to the Dogs as the king dismounted
his horse smoothly and allowed his servants to escort him to
his throne beside the queen. Holand turned back around to
give his whole attention to the scene before him. But before he
did, he said:

'The play begins.'

It was slow and exquisitely choreographed.

When the king and queen had settled, and been told the
engineers' work was done, the king waved his hand. Thick ropes
had been attached to the gates, and teams of men-at-arms now
wrapped their hands around these and hauled. With a creak that
sounded like the falling of a tree, the gates began to move.

The crowd was silent and still.

At a distance, set far back from the stands, thousands of ordinary troops from Villeneuve had gathered. They were held back by hastily erected fences, guarded by more burly men-at-arms in royal colours. As the gates moved, they let out a stifled cheer, but were either told to quieten or felt the mood for themselves.

Loveday felt his head grow light.

The gates finished their slow opening.

Then from within came a frail man riding a tiny nag. He wore a filthy shift of linen, which had once been white, but was now stained brown and yellow and hopelessly crumpled. Around his neck hung a noose.

'All the saints...' murmured Thorp in a tiny whisper.

The nag plodded forward. It was as hungry and weak as its master.

Behind it walked five other men, dressed identically. All were in similar states of exhaustion and hunger. Two were very old: one with thin, papery skin and another blind, or close to being so. They held one another's arms as they stumbled along. Two others, brothers or cousins, followed. They were younger, but also moved as though they were both one hundred years old.

Loveday was about to tap Sir Thomas Holand on the shoulder and ask him who they were when a herald with an astonishingly loud voice stepped out in front of the stands.

'The burghers of Calais,' he announced.

Although he had his back to the scene behind him, he seemed to know by heart exactly what was happening.

As each of the men stumbled forward to approach the king and queen's dais, the herald called their names, introducing them to the spectators.

'Sir Jean de Vienne, Governor of Calais... the most

worshipful masters Eustache de Saint-Pierre and Jean d'Aire…
my lords Pierre and Jacques de Wissant…'

Then came a figure the three Dogs recognised.

'Hey,' whispered Thorp, as a bony figure walked out, also in
a dirty linen shift and with a noose about his throat, 'isn't that
the knight?'

Millstone nodded. 'Aye, it is. Sir Arnoul d'Audrehem.' He
shook his head. 'All the trouble he caused us.'

Having introduced the six men, the herald now launched
into a rehearsed speech about their responsibility for the long
resistance Calais had put up, their stubborn refusal to open the
gates that had now swung open.

Jean de Vienne remained on his pathetic little horse. Some
condition in his feet meant he could not stand unaided. The
other five burghers stood behind him, all with their faces
downcast.

The herald continued. 'Against God, and against the might
of His Noble Grace King Edward…'

But Loveday was not listening. For behind the burghers,
more people were emerging from the gates. They moved just as
slowly as the six men with nooses around their necks, shuffling
in ranks.

There were at most a few hundred of them: Loveday
supposed these were all that remained alive of Calais' citizens.

They too were dressed simply in knee-length undergarments,
men and the few women among them alike. Each of them was
ragged and thin. Some carried tapers and others crucifixes.
All were chanting and wailing and holding out their hands
theatrically, begging the English king for mercy.

This was everyone who had survived the ordeal behind the
walls. The horrors they had endured meant most of them now

looked identical, their faces stripped back to skin and bone and their hair razored.

Yet despite their similarity in dress and emaciation, in the group were two faces Loveday recognised instantly.

One was salt-whipped and covered with knife scars, gold teeth catching the light.

Jean Marant.

The other was even more disfigured, his skin red-raw as though it had been burned by fire. His hair was grey, with patches missing from the close crop. He limped on a crutch, so that he could only supplicate and beg to the king with one of his hands.

Loveday knew him as well as he had on the day they had parted, more than two years before.

'There he fucking is,' said Thorp.

'Didn't I tell you?' said Millstone.

Loveday felt as though he were tumbling. Like his seat had dropped out from under him. As though he had been cast from the highest tower of some huge building.

Green spots danced in front of his gaze. He heard a buzzing in his ears.

Before the stands, a performance was underway. It followed the strict pattern of a dance. It was narrated portentously by the loud-mouthed herald.

The leading men of Calais, with Jean de Vienne at their fore, offered their lives to King Edward.

The king affected great anger, tearing at his clothes almost hard enough to rip them. He took off his crown and waved it at the burghers. Pointed at the scaffold.

'The king tells the burghers they have caused him great misery and hardship,' boomed the herald.

'The burghers weep for clemency.'

The king shook his head in an exaggerated manner.

'The king refuses. His heart is hard.'

The king pointed to the gallows.

'The six burghers fall to their knees.'

This took some time, for Vienne was obliged to dismount gingerly from his little horse. The older men also found it hard work lowering themselves. But when the scene was set, they continued.

'They offer the keys to the city.'

'The king sends for the executioner and calls on God for his mercy on these condemned men.'

At this there was a playful gasp from the crowd in the stands around the Dogs.

'The queen implores her husband to have mercy.'

Also struggling to get to her knees, Queen Philippa waddled towards the king and, with the prince on one side of her and Jacky on the other, managed to kneel on a cushion provided for the purpose.

'The king is adamant...'

The scene continued, but Loveday had lost all interest. His eyes were fixed on the raw face of the Captain.

Loveday knew what he would be thinking. He was bored by the melodrama. He had already considered everything that might possibly happen. Had foreseen what was most likely. Had anticipated the many ways things could unfold and put himself in the right place to take maximum advantage of them.

Always thinking. Always calculating. Always asking the same question.

What next?

It was always *what next?*

And here was he, Loveday. Who had done none of those things. Thought none of those things.

Who sat here on the winning side, alive despite everything, wearing some lord's clean clothes, with half a dozen or more forties due in his hand tomorrow. A berth on a ship home. A few good men left with him. Many more broken, dead, missing.

Yet, at the end of it all, a spectator.

In everything.

He stared at the Captain. He tried to stamp this image of him on to his mind, so he would never forget it. He told himself that this was how he would now think of this man whom he had followed for so long.

Burned. Starved. Lame. Shorn. Calling out for mercy.

Defeated.

Yet somehow, Loveday assumed, winning.

He had waited for this moment. Had dreamed of seeing the Captain again. But now he knew.

He heard Northampton's words. Said to him long ago, before he climbed the ladder on that awful day Tebbe died.

Forget about hunting for the past. It's gone. Think about the world that's coming in.

Why had he never been able to do that?

In front of him Thomas Holand, who had also stopped watching the scene, was swapping gossip with the lanky knight.

'You think this has been bad, think about Caffa. Tartars giving the Italians hell. Did you hear? Chucking diseased plague bodies over the walls. Every bastard one of them coming up in black lesions. Pissing blood out of their eyes and arseholes. Armpits swelling up like blood puddings. Dead in three days.'

The lanky knight was laughing. 'God spare us that here!'

Tebbe and Millstone were staring at the Captain. Loveday

had not taken his eyes off him from the moment he had come through the gates.

Finally, the Captain felt their gaze.

On the dais, the queen's pleading reached a crescendo and the king was playing to perfection his role of the husband softened by the love of his good wife.

The executioner was sent away. The burghers' pleading turned to tears of thanks and relief.

The Captain kept up his performance too. He did not take his eyes off King Edward and the queen and the merchants. Nor did he let up his own pleading and his prayers.

But for the Dogs' benefit, he let the tiniest smile dance across his lips.

Gave Loveday the very subtlest glimmer of a wink.

EPILOGUE

Grant for life to Queen Philippa of all the houses of Jean
d'Aire in the town of Calais, with all the houses, cottages
and all void places... on condition that... she find certain
men for the defence of the town, as the king and council
have ordained...

Calendar of Patent Rolls, August 1347

Loveday saw Millstone and Thorp on to their ship at Calais
harbour the next morning. Another ship called *Saintmarie*,
although not the same one that had brought them almost a
year earlier. The Dogs now carried packs heavy with silver
coin. They had been paid eight and a half forties a man. More
money than any of them had ever seen.

At the office of the treasurer, Thorp had argued for Tebbe's
pay, to take home to his family. The head of the office, Wetwang,
a humourless man, flatly refused.

Instead, the Dogs pooled their pay and made out a quarter-
share of the total. Thorp carried it. He promised to deliver it
as the first thing he did when they got back, after the good
day's drink they would have to celebrate their safe return to
whichever port the *Saintmarie* made dock in.

'You're sure you won't come with us?' Thorp asked, as they
stood by the gangplank.

Loveday shook his head. 'Not just yet.'

'Christ, Loveday, you saw him. You won't—'

'I'm not looking for him any more.'

'What then?' Thorp spat in the sea. 'They're not paying us to stay now.'

'I don't...' Loveday felt suddenly like he was on the ladder again. Paralysed. Caught between climbing up and going down. 'I won't be long behind you. I feel like there's something I need to see.'

'What?'

'I don't know. I'll only know when I see it.'

The three men embraced awkwardly. Feeling the smallness of their group. Thorp spat into the sea again and kept clearing his throat. He seemed unable to talk.

Millstone finally managed to get a few words out. 'Until Southwark, then. Next spring?' Loveday had never seen Millstone cry. But now the big stonemason would not meet his eye.

A sailor called down to them to hurry up. The *Saintmarie* was ready.

'Aye. The spring.'

None of them quite believed it.

Once they were gone, Loveday walked alone in Calais' warren of streets. He dodged royal servants carting piles of rubbish and bones away to the great fires being lit in Villeneuve, where the siege camp was being torn down. He saw piles of possessions – furniture and kitchen utensils and blankets and curtains – being dragged out of abandoned properties and stacked up for inventory by the city's new governors. He saw the last few pinch-faced citizens stumbling away, empty-handed, from homes that were no longer their own.

He saw the death of a city. And he saw the city coming back to life: shuttered windows being opened and locked doors unbarred. Many shops and business premises seemed already to be open for business, as though there had never been a siege at all, nor any want or dearth or hunger. Stacked outside those that were back in business were piles of crates marked with some symbol Loveday did not recognise. A cross, its arms extended with tails.

Everywhere, the takeover was happening. Loveday overheard negotiations as English owners bartered with royal agents for possession of properties in the streets away from the main squares. The king was already in the castle. Outside it all the best places had been hung with the queen's livery. The next best were being taken over by the merchants Loveday had seen around the dais. But there was plenty more to be claimed, and no shortage of claimants.

For a moment, he stood outside a modest little shack, its roof in need of new thatch and door sagging on its hinges, and wondered if the coin in his pack was enough for him to claim it as a place for himself. Then he shook his head at the absurdity of the thought and moved on.

He did not look for the Captain.

And he did not see him either.

He spent the night in a tavern under the sign of the Beehive.

He drank himself to sleep at a table on his own, and woke up there as dawn was breaking and a girl with her hair shorn was sweeping up shards of broken mugs and the night's filthy straw from around his feet.

A throbbing head, fat tongue, churning stomach and painful

bladder told him he was at best very hungover. Probably still drunk.

He staggered to his feet, knocking his stool over. He cursed, stumbled again, apologised to the girl and thanked her.

She didn't understand, and seemed frightened of him. He grabbed a half-drunk jug of wine from a table, left her a handful of coins scattered in its place and let himself out of the bolted door.

The sun was rising over quiet streets as Loveday weaved his way drunkenly back in what he thought was the direction of the harbour. His legs were wobbly, but the cool air cleared his head a little. He sipped from the jug, pissed in an alley and went out to stare at the sea.

He had no idea what he was looking for. He was just delaying going back to so little.

'You old fool,' he said out loud. 'Go home.'

Against the long pier, a great cog had come in overnight and docked, though it was so early that the deck was silent, the gangplank drawn, and no one was yet waiting to board. He guessed it would be some hours before it went. So he walked on, along the seafront, seeing up close the city walls he had stared at for so long that spring from the Risbank.

Nothing now seemed special about them. The stone knew nothing. Or told nothing.

Which amounts to the same thing.

He kept going.

Where the buildings of the harbour stopped, the stone front gave way to a small beach. He clambered down on to it. At the other end of it, he saw something strange.

He squinted in the low morning light. Something grey was hunched on the shingle.

It looked like an animal. Bigger than a dog, but thinner. Perhaps it *was* a dog, he thought. Some poor cur, which had somehow survived in the city without being eaten.

He started walking towards it. When he was halfway along the beach, the animal sensed him coming. It looked up.

A wolf?

Loveday laughed. He really was drunk. It couldn't be. Wolves didn't live on beaches. Or in cities. And yet, there it was.

He stood still, trying not to make a move that would frighten the wolf, or make it attack him. After a while, very slowly, the wolf got up and moved off down the beach.

Although it was still some way away, the hairs on the back of Loveday's neck stood up as he watched it move. He felt somehow as if he knew the wolf. As though they had seen each other in another place. Another life. Somewhere very long ago.

Loveday was about to turn back for the harbour when he realised the wolf had left something at the far end of the beach.

He went towards it.

At first, he thought it was a fisherman's abandoned net, or a tangle of rags, wrapped around something grey-blue.

Then he thought it might be the remains of a large fish the wolf had been eating. Some rare morsel washed up as a gift of the sea.

But when he got close to it, he saw the bundle was a person. A lad, curled up tight around a heavy pack. He was wet through and unmoving. He was covered in long grey hairs. As though the wolf had been sheltering him.

Loveday crouched down and put his hand on the shoulder closest to him.

The shoulder felt very cold. But the faintest lift and fall of the small body told him the young man was still alive.

A surge of blood ran through Loveday's body. He realised he had to get him warm. He dropped to the sand and hauled him up to sitting and wrapped both his arms tightly around his thin wet shoulders and pressed his whole body to him, his chest against the young man's back.

The young man was limp and weak. He sagged in Loveday's arms like a child's doll. His head lolled. His arms flopped.

Loveday gripped him tighter still, and tried to press even harder against him. As he did, he smelled the stale booze on his own breath and the salt in the young man's matted hair. He was soaking now, too, grit and sand and water all over him.

He didn't care.

Loveday pressed himself close to the boy and tried to give him all the warmth from his own body. He felt as though his whole life depended on saving this one.

'Hey,' he said as he held him. 'Hey, mate. I've got you. Come on. Try and wake up.'

The young man stirred faintly. He coughed. Water drooled from his mouth.

'Mate,' said Loveday again. 'Try and wake up. You'll be alright.'

With some effort, the young man raised his chin from his chest. He opened an eye and out of the corner of it tried to see Loveday.

'There you go,' said Loveday gripping him even tighter. 'There you go, mate. I've got you. You're safe now. Let's get you home.'

Then the young man half turned, and Loveday's own body went cold.

A pale-blue eye. A light beard now. His cheek a torn mess, where something or someone had sliced through it.

But a face Loveday would have known anywhere. He wrenched the young man around in his arms and cradled him like he was a baby.

'Christ,' said Loveday. 'Christ, boy, what the devil are you doing here?'

'Father?' said Romford.

Historical Note

On 26–27 August 1346 at the Battle of Crécy, a tired and hungry army led by King Edward III of England destroyed a larger, fresher one commanded by Philippe VI of France. Even by fourteenth-century standards, the fighting was vicious. At least fifteen hundred French knights died. Many thousands more ordinary soldiers perished. 'Never since the destruction of great Troy had there been such mourning,' wrote one poet. Some of the cream of northern Europe's nobility were among the fallen, including the blind crusading hero King John of Bohemia and Louis I, Count of Flanders.

The battle was a humiliating disaster for the French crown and a triumph for the English. It confirmed Edward III's reputation as a bold commander whose cause was favoured by God. Even to get to Crécy, Edward had led his army on a perilous six-and-a-half-week march from the Cotentin peninsula of Normandy, deep into French territory. His army had sacked the cities of Saint-Lô and Caen, and forced crossings of the rivers Seine and Somme. They had burned villages and destroyed lives. They had suffered their own privations of heat, thirst, worn-out boots and the discomfort of life under canvas. Plenty of the fifteen thousand men who landed in France had not survived the course. Yet the battle had been won, against ridiculous odds. It looked like fortune was smiling on the English.

Despite all this, however, Crécy posed as many questions as it answered. Above all, King Edward had to decide: what next? His troops were exhausted, hungry, injured and diseased. The English parliament and people had been funding wars continuously for nearly a decade, and Edward had run up vast debts to domestic merchants and foreign bankers. The pretext for Edward's war was his claim to be the rightful King of France. But despite the presence of another English army in the field in Gascony, marching on Paris to enforce that claim was out of the question. Philippe was beaten. But he was not broken. The war was not over. Indeed, it had barely even begun.

The day after the Battle of Crécy was one of prayer, plunder and housekeeping. Masses were sung. The dead were tallied, plundered, robbed, then buried or left where they lay. Survivors cut rings from dead men's fingers and stripped bodies of arms and armour, much of which was burned to prevent it falling into enemy hands. Then Edward revealed his next move. He had decided to march his army to the north-east coast of France and take aim at a port city that might be seized and held as tangible reward for the blood spilled and costs incurred during the summer's campaign. The place Edward had chosen was Calais.

Calais had many attractions. As the closest French port to the south-east coast of England, it was already connected to the commercially prosperous Cinque Ports of Kent and Sussex. It was highly defensible for whoever held it: equipped with a huge, complete circuit of stout stone walls, a castle and two deep moats. Beyond these, Calais was protected by the sea on one side and an expanse of marshland cut through with rivers and watercourses on the other. It had long been a haven for the pirates who were a bane of English mercantile shipping in the Channel; they could be cleared out if it were conquered. And it was near the cities of Flanders. Edward had gone to great trouble and expense during the first decade of his reign to convince the independent-minded urban oligarchs of Flanders that he alone could help them resist eventual absorption into the kingdom of France. He had encouraged and financed pro-English politicians in Flanders, such as Jacob van Artevelde, the so-called Brewer of Ghent, who was murdered by a mob in 1345. Taking Calais would be a fine restatement of Edward's commitment to the Flemish cause. So it was to Calais that the English marched, stopping along the way to plunder and then burn cities such as Wissant, the better to keep their hand in.

Calais was, for some of the reasons already explained, a very ambitious target. It was so well defended that modern historians have debated whether Edward was really serious about taking it. On the day he arrived outside Calais, Edward wrote to England explaining that 'our expedition has been very long and continuous. But we do not expect to depart the kingdom of France until we have made an end of our war, with the aid of God.' What did he mean by this? Did 'the end of the war' imply actually seizing Calais? Did it mean a truce? Did it suggest Edward was trying to force Philippe into another battle, which, if won, would oblige the French king to resign his crown to Edward? Perhaps even the English king's most senior advisors – such as the Constable of the Army, William de Bohun, Earl of Northampton – were asking themselves the same thing in the autumn of 1346. But if there was uncertainty or ambiguity about Edward's war aims to begin with, it soon became clear the English were in for the long haul.

From the start of the siege of Calais in early September 1346, there were three main spheres of military operations.

The first was the city and its surrounding marshes. As has been mentioned, Calais was stiffly defended by walls and moats. The walls were almost impossible to scale, even when ladders balanced on barges were brought into the moats. Nor could they be battered down. The marshland around the city was too soft for large trebuchets and heavy siege engines to be very effective. Gunpowder-fired cannon, which had been deployed at Crécy and were also used outside Calais, made a lot of smoke and noise, and were good for maiming men and scaring horses. But fourteenth-century guns were not yet of sufficient quality to destroy stone walls.

A quick siege, then, was out of the question. Edward was obliged to keep a large army indefinitely outside the walls of Calais, or risk being driven away by an attack from Philippe. For tired, battle-drained men, this was not an ideal prospect. To make the experience a little more bearable, the English built a semi-permanent siege town of wooden dwellings, shops and civic buildings on the marsh. They dug a deep ditch around the perimeter. They called it *Villeneuve la Hardie* (Bold New Town) and supplied it with goods shipped in from England via friendly ports in Flanders.

Villeneuve was an extraordinary place. The chronicler Jean Froissart wrote that it comprised 'houses of wood, laid out in streets, and thatched with straw or broom; and in this town... was everything necessary for an army... butcher's meat and all other sorts of merchandise, cloth and bread... might be had there for money, *as well as all comforts*' [my italics]. It was fitted with viewing galleries over Calais' walls, where sporadic skirmishes could be watched by the non-combatant nobility, including Edward's wife, Queen Philippa, who arrived in time for Christmas 1346. Its thousands of inhabitants could be fed, sheltered and occasionally entertained. All the same, the fact remained that their main job was to hunker down and wait for something to happen.

The second sphere of military operation was the towns around Calais. Here, English interests were entwined with those of their Flemish allies. While the Crécy campaign had been underway in summer 1346, a combined Anglo-Flemish army led by the vigorous East Anglian knight Sir Hugh Hastings* had been busy attacking border towns like Béthune. When Edward's main army arrived at Calais, this campaign of piecemeal harassment in the Flemish marches could recommence.

The most famous escapade in this part of the struggle for Calais took place at Thérouanne, where a detachment of English archers and men-at-arms fell upon the city during market day in mid-September 1346. There was a battle around the gates. The English won. They sent the bishop who was commanding the town's resistance running for his life, then plundered the market. They captured a high-ranking French knight called Sir Arnoul d'Audrehem, who had broken his leg. (Sir Arnoul later either paid his ransom or escaped imprisonment and found his way into Calais and helped organise the city's defences.) And according to one chronicle, written in the nearby town of Saint-Omer, some very disgraceful deeds took place in Thérouanne's

---

* Hastings died at the very end of the siege of Calais from disease and/or a heavy blow to the mouth, and was buried wearing what appears to have been a wig made of orange cow-hair; his tomb in Elsing, Norfolk is adorned with a famous funeral brass thematically dedicated to the glory of war.

cathedral: during the battle for the city, an archer shot the head off a statue of the Virgin Mary, and one vile individual desecrated the high altar by using it as a toilet.

Eventually, the English left and went to Villeneuve to join their comrades. For the sake of good order, Flemish troops were kept away from Villeneuve: the assumption was that English and Flemings didn't mix. All the same, the English connection with Flemish affairs continued throughout the siege of Calais. One interesting subplot of the campaign was King Edward's efforts to marry his daughter Isabel to the young Count of Flanders, Louis de Male, who had inherited his title after his father was killed at Crécy. Louis was strongly disinclined to marry Isabel and in the end he never did. In the spring of 1347, he managed to abscond from his pro-English attendants while out hunting with hawks. Louis fled to the French court, where he was safe. He eventually married one of Philippe VI's cousins.

The third and final sphere of military operations at Calais was the sea. In 1340 Edward III had defeated and destroyed a French fleet at the Battle of Sluys. This, in theory, gave him the upper hand in the English Channel for years to come. In practice, however, his naval advantage was slender. Throughout the autumn and winter of 1346–7, the English found they could supply their army by sea, but they lacked the ships to enforce a full blockade of the coast. The French were even shorter on ships and early in the siege lost the use of several dozen hired Genoese galleys, whose crews refused to serve through the winter. However, the French were able to call on the considerable talents of their native pirates, most notably those led by a resourceful and ruthless privateer from Boulogne named Jean Marant.

Marant and his associates among the pirates of the English Channel were larger-than-life characters who frequented a tavern not far from Calais known as the *Pot d'Étain* (the Tin Jar). The line that divided respectable medieval merchants from corsairs was porous, but Marant and his friends were generally to be found on the wrong side of it. Nevertheless, during the siege of Calais they proved invaluable to the French cause. Early in the siege they helped sink and rob English supply convoys. Once winter set in, they switched their focus to keeping Calais fed and provisioned. Marant worked with the Admiral of France, Pierre de Revel (aka 'Floton'), running major relief convoys from the cities of Dieppe and Saint-Valery into Calais. Even when the English began deliberately scuttling ships to block the approach to Calais' harbour, Marant and the pirates managed to get supplies through.

In the winter of 1346–7, it became clear that the pirate convoys, and the Calaisiens' own military resistance, organised under the command of the governor, Jean de Vienne, were the only things likely to keep Calais in French hands. Philippe VI was hamstrung by a lack of troops, money and political direction. Not until March 1347 did he take the sacred French battle flag known as the *Oriflamme* and start assembling a serious field army to try and drive the English off. And even then, he seemed curiously hesitant to deploy it.

All the while, the English were gaining in strength. With the king camped at Calais, his lieutenants in other theatres of the war won a series of stunning victories. In October 1346 English troops in Northumberland smashed a Scottish army at Neville's Cross, capturing King David II. The same month, an army in south-west France sacked the great city of Poitiers.

In June 1347, English troops in Brittany captured Charles of Blois, Duke of Brittany, at the Battle of La Roche Derrien.

At Calais itself, spring 1347 saw a huge surge of English troops and ships. Thousands more men were ferried from England to Villeneuve: some were experienced warriors, but most were simply criminals and roughnecks who served in exchange for immunity from prosecution for crimes they had committed, up to and including murder. Their arrival swelled the population of Villeneuve to more than twenty thousand – making it bigger than most English cities.

Even more useful to the English was the arrival in the waters outside Calais of hundreds of ships: enough, finally, to stop almost all of Marant's pirate supply runs into Calais' harbour. The last significant convoy came in around Easter. After, the seas swarmed with English ships, while the surge of troops meant that Edward could take command of a strip of land called the Risbank, which protected Calais' harbour from the seas beyond. The English built a wooden fort at the tip of the Risbank, past which it was almost impossible for any large enemy ships to sail. From this point on, only two fates were possible for Calais: Philippe VI would come to relieve the citizens, or they would starve.

They starved. At least twice during the siege, Jean de Vienne and his fellow citizens tried to cut down the number of hungry mouths in the city by sending out refugees to find their way through the English lines. (On the first occasion, Edward let them pass; on the second, he left them trapped in no-man's land to die.) But nothing could keep the city going forever. At the height of summer, Philippe finally brought an army close enough to Calais that they could see the English in Villeneuve, and watch the beacons lit by night on Calais' walls by the increasingly desperate citizens. Jean de Vienne tried to smuggle a letter out to the king, advising him that conditions inside the city were bleak: the cats, dogs and horses were being eaten, he said; people would be next. But the message was intercepted by English sailors, who retrieved it after the panic-stricken messenger hurled it into the sea attached to an axe. So the letter never reached Philippe – and even if it had, it is not certain he could have done anything to help. In the last days of July 1347, the French king ordered his army to retreat. Seeing this, the garrison of Calais, now half-mad with hunger, bowed to the inevitable. They sent word to King Edward that they were ready to give up.

A famous sculpture by Auguste Rodin, which stands today in front of the town hall in Calais, brilliantly imagines the best-known historical vignette from the siege of Calais. It shows six 'burghers' (i.e. wealthy citizens) coming out of the city to surrender its keys and their lives to Edward. The six are dressed in their undershirts, and wear nooses around their necks, as Edward had commanded they should. The king made them plead for their own lives, which he had declared should be at his mercy if the rest of the emaciated citizens of Calais were to live. At first Edward insisted that they should die, but according to a number of chroniclers, his heart was softened by the pleas of his heavily pregnant queen. Edward relented and sent the Calaisiens on their way. Most of the merchants of the city were evicted, although an exception was made for one or two who seemed to have cut deals with the Crown to stay. The rest were packed off to Paris, and their homes, premises and commercial privileges in

Calais were parcelled up between English businessmen who had financed Edward's French campaigns, presumably in the hope of just such rich reward.

For the rest of the Middle Ages, Calais was an English possession, in the form of a 'Pale', comprising the city itself and a number of other fortresses dotted around the marshland where Villeneuve once stood. Together, these served as both an English military super-compound on the edge of north-west Europe and an economic 'Staple', which had a monopoly over tax collection and the cloth trade. Calais remained in English hands until it was reconquered for the French in 1558 during the reign of Mary Tudor, following a siege that lasted only a week.

Despite its exciting events and melodramatic conclusion, the 1346–7 siege of Calais is not very well known today to anyone but the most attentive medieval historians. The names of most of the thousands of people who fought or suffered in the siege – on both sides – have long been forgotten. That is a pity. In the summer of 2022, as I was beginning work on this book, I went to Calais and stood for an hour by Rodin's sculpture of the burghers. It struck me that what is so moving about these six figures is that each of them seems to be experiencing proximity to death in his own unique way. This one crippled by grief, this one stoic; this one disbelieving, this one defiant. Rodin's genius was to create a vision of individual humanity shining through the pity of war. That is a fine aim for any artist trying to reimagine an historical event, whatever their medium.

Further Reading

There is no satisfactory, full-length scholarly study of the siege of Calais. But the following selection of secondary books and articles were especially helpful to me as I wrote this novel. They may prove similarly useful to readers wishing to dig deeper into the real history. Needless to say, *Wolves of Winter* remains a work of fiction, whose liberties, inventions and errors I am proud to call my own.

BOOKS

Rémy Ambühl, *Prisoners of War in the Hundred Years War: Ransom Culture in the Late Middle Ages* (Cambridge, 2013)

Jill Eddison, *Medieval Pirates: Pirates, Raiders and Privateers, 1204–1453* (Cheltenham, 2013)

Fernand Lennel, *Histoire de Calais* (2 vols) (Calais, 1908–10)

Michael Livingston, *Crécy: Battle of Five Kings* (London, 2022)

Andrew McCall, *The Medieval Underworld* (London, 1979)

Konstantin Nossov, *Ancient and Medieval Siege Weapons* (Guildford, 2005)

Clifford J. Rogers, *War Cruel and Sharp: English Strategy under Edward III, 1327–1360* (Woodbridge, 2000)

Susan Rose, *Calais: An English Town in France, 1347–1558* (Woodbridge, 2008)

Jonathan Sumption, *The Hundred Years War I: Trial by Battle* (London, 1990)

George Unwin (ed.), *Finance and Trade Under Edward III* (Manchester, 1918)

ARTICLES

Jordan Bruso, 'The Siege of Calais during the Hundred Years War: An English Perspective, 1344–1347', MA Thesis, University of Maine (2022)

Kelly R. DeVries, 'Hunger, Flemish Participation and the Flight of Philip VI: Contemporary Accounts of the Siege Of Calais, 1346–47', *Studies in Medieval and Renaissance History* 12 (1991)

Craig L. Lambert, 'Edward III's siege of Calais: A reappraisal', *Medieval History* 37 (2011)

Charles de La Roncière, 'La Marine au siège De Calais', Bibliothèque de l'École des chartes 58 (1897)

Clifford J. Rogers, 'Frontier Warfare in the St Omer Chronicle', Military Cultures and Martial Enterprises in the Middle Ages: Essays in Honour of Richard P. Abels (Woodbridge, 2020)

Jules Viard, 'Le Siege de Calais: 4 septembre 1346–4 août 1347', *Le Moyen Âge* (1929)

Acknowledgements

Writing books is hard. A few thanks are due to my own Dogs, who dragged me along when I wanted nothing more than to run away.

At Head of Zeus, Anthony and Nicolas Cheetham first trusted me to write the Essex Dogs trilogy. Bethan Jones, Richenda Todd and Laura Palmer have helped me develop it editorially and taught me so much about writing fiction. Peyton Stableford has kept me pointing in the right direction. Dan Groenewald and his sales, publicity and marketing teams have taken the Dogs to a wider audience than I ever imagined possible. Thanks also to Terezia Cicel and her colleagues at Viking in New York for believing that Loveday, Romford and co. could break America.

Ash Fields created incredible character art that has changed the way I think about the Dogs.

Walter Donohue has read every word of everything I've ever written and made all of it better.

Over the years a number of friends have been either open, enthusiastic or just uncomplaining about reading/discussing Essex Dogs works in progress: Shane Batt, Ed Caesar, Honor Cargill-Martin, Leon Carter, Sara Cockerill, Julia Dietz, Daisy Dixon, Rick Edwards, Rob Fellows, Wayne Garvie, Blake Gilbert, Emma Gregory, Elodie Harper, Duff McKagan, Oliver Morgan, David Morton, Jonathan Phillips, Leona Powell,

Kristen Rizzo, Sam Simpson and Paul Wilson, thank you for your service.

Michael Livingston, Kelly DeVries and Clifford Rogers were so generous in sharing their published and unpublished work and helping me navigate the scholarly material around Calais.

I am extremely grateful to Rich Machin and the estate of Mark Lanegan for permitting me with such grace to turn excerpts of the song *I Am The Wolf* into a medieval earworm. Thanks also to Duff and Brian Klein for helping make that connection. I hope Mark would have approved.

Special thanks Georgina Capel and Rachel Conway and all at GCA for everything, always.

And finally, boundless love to Jo, Violet, Ivy and Arthur Jones.

I do this for you.

About the Author

DAN JONES is the *Sunday Times* and *New York Times* bestselling author of many non-fiction books including *The Plantagenets*, *The Templars*, and *Powers and Thrones*. He is a renowned writer, broadcaster and journalist. He has presented dozens of TV shows, including the Netflix series *Secrets of Great British Castles*, and writes and hosts the podcast *This is History*. His acclaimed debut novel, *Essex Dogs*, was the first in a series following the fortunes of ordinary soldiers in the early years of the Hundred Years' War. He is a Fellow of the Royal Historical Society.